Echoes of Evil

ECHOES OF EVIL

~

by
KEN R. ABELL

RESOURCE *Publications* · Eugene, Oregon

ECHOES OF EVIL

Resource Publications
An Imprint of Wipf and Stock Publishers
199 W. 8th Ave., Suite 3
Eugene, OR 97401

Scripture taken from the HOLY BIBLE, KING JAMES VERSION, Public Domain.

www.wipfandstock.com

ISBN 13: 978-1-62564-709-2

Manufactured in the U.S.A.   07/01/2014

For my sisters—Jane Ann, Janice, Jennifer. In a different time and place they often challenged and inspired me. The years and miles get piled higher with each sunrise, but long ago and faraway cannot change all the good memories.

&

For Anita Irene, who more than half a lifetime ago purchased me a clunker of a Remington manual typewriter, and in her own formidable way made it clear that I had to put up or shut up. The fingerprints of her heart are all over every word I've written since that day.

&

For our sons and grandchildren. May the understanding that life is hard always be tempered by the truth that toughness and tenacity up against adversity is the grease that allows grace to prevail and strength of character to develop its muscles.

&

For the men of the Navajo BIC Overcomers Program who I have been privileged to walk alongside. Their stories enrich my life in ways that are beyond measure.

Contents

Acknowledgments

In remembrance of and appreciation for my Dad. Like all of us, he had a full array of flaws and imperfections, but in a short-lived tenure on this side of eternity, he taught me boxing lessons about life that toughened and tested me. The determination and gravel in my gut are there because he told me that only quitters and losers stay down.

A shout out THANK YOU to Kathi Ellicott, whose detail oriented thoroughness lines up with my obsessive compulsive tendencies. When it comes to words and punctuation, her copyediting skills are a hidden talent that richly blesses me. Not to mention that she is the most astute political commentator I've ever known.

In memory of my good friend, Gus, a sensitive and rambunctious Sheltie who spent many early morning hours curled up near my feet waiting for me as I wrote. Gus had a heightened awareness when it came to matters of the heart, and was the inspiration for the tricolored dog you will meet in these pages.

ALSO BY KEN R. ABELL

Nonfiction

An Ordinary Story of Extraordinary Hope

Fiction

Days of Purgatory
Shadows of Revenge

Websites

www.wantedman.org
www.danceswithcorn.com

chapter one

The Storm

"The Lord is slow to anger, and great in power, and will not at all acquit the wicked: the Lord hath his way in the whirlwind and in the storm, and the clouds are the dust of his feet."

~Nahum~

When Deacon Coburn stepped out of the barracks at Fort Union, the mid-February sky was concrete-colored and threatening. He turned up the collar of his sheepskin parka and took a long look at the clouds, which were heavy and ridged with black webs. The dreary gray covering was rolling low and slow. He felt a tightness begin to clutch at the small of his back.

He tugged the brim of his hat down and headed to the livery. He admired the construction of the pine-log buildings. The outpost wasn't a typical military garrison, but rather it had the feel of a quaint frontier town; there were no stockades or breastworks. The straight streets were spacious and laid out orderly, crossing each other at right angles.

He took long strides, a purposeful set to his broad shoulders and a no-nonsense expression gathered in a net of wrinkles around his eyes. The cold was bone-deep. His breath plumed behind him like puffs of downy feathers. Tension cramped across his lower back. He entered the dank and musty stables, and gave a sharp whistle.

"There you are, mister," a voice said from the cavernous backside of the structure. A rusty-haired man led a horse out of the stall and brought it along the corridor. The insignia on his ragged blue jacket had three stripes. "I fed your mount a bait of oats and gave it a rubdown. It's saddled up and ready to go, but you're plum nutty to even think about hitting the trail." He petted and paid attention to the animal. "I don't know much about horse-flesh, but a halfwit graduate of Huckleberry University could see that this buckskin is a premium example of it."

The gelding was one-of-a-kind, tall and thick-chested, with a shiny black mane and animated eyes. Its coat was primarily creamy-gold, but its gene pool had given it distinct markings; its hindquarters were brush strokes of silver-dapple. It gave a huffing snort of a greeting when it was brought alongside its owner.

"It's just a youngster," Deacon replied casually. He took hold of the bridle, which was a unique and intricate piece of work. A series of stones were woven into the horizontal leather straps. "The sire is a muscular steel-dust, the finest stallion I've ever seen."

"I noted the *WT* brand. That's a new one for me."

"It's an up and coming operation in Colorado."

His lips pursed approvingly. "By the way, the name's Fralick. Karl Fralick."

Coburn shook his hand and introduced himself, then took a lingering stroll around the animal. He double-checked all aspects of the gear. "I got a ways to go this morning."

"You'd be wise to wait on the weather, mister."

"I can't wait, Sergeant."

"I'm no Sergeant. I'm not even a soldier."

Coburn scrutinized him. The man was not yet in his thirties, skinny and pale-faced, with a few freckles across his nose. He had a studious and highbrow manner. "Karl, I don't want to be a meddler, but you do know you could be charged for sporting that rank."

Fralick laughed easily. "No chance of that occurring, mister. This shabby coat sags on a nail here in the livery. It belonged to a well-loved scallywag of a Drill Sergeant. We take turns wearing the garment to honor his memory. He was killed a year ago by Smoky Crowe."

"Smoky Crowe," Deacon murmured, eyes squinting. "There's a name I'm not wanting to hear. That scoundrel is more ghost than man. He appears and vanishes at will. Is he Apache or Ute? Was he born in some desolate badlands and cared for by coyotes? He's cut a wide swath of territory for a long time, wreaking havoc among settlers and sojourners."

Fralick agreed. "Some old-timers told me stories that curdled my blood."

"I don't doubt it. His debauchery is legendary." Deacon turned aside and spat a gob of spittle in disgust. "Smoky Crowe is an unholy terror. He dips his arrowheads in a poison concoction he cooks up." The frown deepened around his eyes as the knot in his back grew larger. "We don't know what he looks like because any white man who puts eyes on him dies. As far as I know there's never been a picture sketched of him."

"I have no desire to see Smoky Crowe. Not now or ever."

"Wait a minute." Deacon snappishly held up a hand, almost in protest. "I heard a tale about a Texas Ranger putting that sick renegade out of business several years ago."

"You heard wrong, sir," Karl said sharply. "The Ranger ran him to ground, but no corpse was ever discovered. I suppose Crowe lay low, hidden in a canyon somewhere."

"I reckon. He's wily and ruthless."

Fralick nodded grimly. "He's back in business. He's got some outlaw riding with him now. A gringo, if you can believe it. A while back they tortured and killed a woman in San Antonio. The scuttlebutt says the pair is on the lam here in New Mexico, but who knows?"

"Thanks for the information, Karl."

"Not sure what you can do with it."

"If nothing else, it'll keep me alert and watchful," Deacon answered, giving a halfway shrug. He lifted the right side of his parka and withdrew his Smith & Wesson. He flicked the cylinder open and carefully examined the loads. Satisfied, he returned it to the holster.

Fralick regarded him with barefaced bewilderment. His cheeks reddened as he moved around a bit. He realized there was no scabbard attached to his rig. "You'll need more than a pistol if you have a run-in with Smoky Crowe. Where's your rifle?"

"A rifle ain't going to help much if I cross paths with that sorcerer," Deacon said, rubbing two-week's worth of scruffy whiskers. "Besides I don't carry one. Not since Gettysburg."

"That's reckless behavior, isn't it? Especially riding alone?"

"Reckless or not, it is what it is," Deacon replied matter-of-factly. He held his hands at half-mast and pushed a forceful smile at him. "A man has to be true to his convictions regardless of the shifting sands of circumstance, or he ain't worth doodly-squat."

Fralick was unconvinced. "You'd lose your life to uphold a conviction?"

"*Some trust in chariots, and some in horses: but we will remember the name of the Lord our God*," Deacon said, quoting a portion of a Psalm. "My dying time will come at the Almighty's bidding." He took a few steps toward him. "Tell me something, Karl. If you're not a soldier, what attraction has you living on an army installation?"

"I was in medical school back east, but got the itch to see the west," Karl told him, almost wearily; as though he was bored with his story. "I've been here since '75 doing pick-up jobs and studying doctoring with a civilian surgeon on the post. That's three long years of book learning and practical hands-on work. Old Doc Rimmer has the suffering soul of a drunkard, but he knows more about healing and fixing folks than professors and most physicians."

"That's usually the way of it, isn't it? Well, best of luck to you, Karl."

Fralick jammed his hands into the coat's pockets. "I appreciate the sentiment, sir. It's laborious hours, but Doc Rimmer says I'll be ready to hang my own shingle soon enough."

"It's been swell jawing, but I need to put miles behind me."

"You ought to wait a few days. Let the weather clear."

"I can read the sky too, but can't wait," Deacon said, pulling on a pair of cowhide gloves. "I have to get to the Suncurl Café in Santa Fe. I gave my word to a lady."

"Santa Fe? Are you daft in the head or something?"

Coburn was grinning. "Crazy? You ain't the first to suggest it."

"That's more than a hundred miles. You'll not make it before the snowstorm."

Coburn took hold of the reins and stepped into the saddle. "If that's how this ride goes I'll manage it or be reassigned to glory, one or the other. I gave her my word."

Fralick patted the horse's rump. In response, it swished its tail happily. "I'll tell you this much, sir; if I never see you again, I'll not forget your horse."

"Never is a long time, friend," Deacon countered flatly. He reached around an inside pocket of the parka and came out with a wool scarf, which he arranged over the top of his hat and tied under his chin. He touched a finger to the brim, then leaned forward and dipped his head to speak soothingly to the gelding. "We have hard tracks to make, Gilgal. Let's get to it." He gave the horse a gentle nudge. It trod outside and broke into a loping southward trot.

The frigid air felt like needles on his face. He surveyed the vast expanse of the valley stretched out before him. The day was fresh and he determinedly bore into it. A window cracked in the fast-moving clouds, letting through a shimmering stream of sunlight. He enjoyed it while it lasted, but the breach soon closed. The uneasiness at the base of his spine climbed up his back.

All that was two days ago. Then the storm struck.

$\approx \approx \approx$

Max Dawson had been on horseback for almost six weeks when the skies split open. It was as though the hand of God gutted the clouds; the innards spilled and tumbled in a whoosh that had no immediate end. A white barricade formed. The wind went from stillness to outrageous in a heartbeat. It blew and whipped the wall of snow into a fluctuating maze.

Dawson hunkered over in the saddle. The horse, a soot-gray mustang mare, seemed completely unperturbed by the sudden change; one moment the air was thin and crisp, the next it was dense with snowflakes. The fleet-footed animal had stamina and grit. It plodded along without flinching, staying on a northerly course.

A gusty blast caught the brim of Dawson's black Stetson. The hat flapped crazily for a moment. She yanked it down and tightened the chin-strap, pulling the bead against her jawline.

She was on familiar turf on the outskirts of Santa Fe. She had a destination in mind and no worries of getting to shelter, being fully confident in her ability and the horse's mettle. The storm was a mere delay; nothing was going to stop her from the task burning in her veins.

To say that Max Dawson was willful and hardnosed was being kind; obstinate and pigheaded were more accurate descriptions. Those were qualities inherited from maternal and paternal ancestral lines. Her family tree was populated by tenacious and inflexible people. Her given name was Maxine, but before her sixth birthday she had handed it back to her parents. She much preferred Max—in fact she demanded others comply with her wishes.

She was a good looking woman who knew precisely how to use her beauty. She could be as hard-nails tough as the violent northeaster blowing just now or as tender as a cool springtime breeze. Born and nourished in the rough and wild southwestern border country, she had no qualms about throwing down against any wrongdoer. Neither did she have any hesitation or misgivings in switching on her feminine charm to accomplish her purposes.

When she was going on sixteen her mother had insisted that she attend a proper finishing school to sand-off and refine her tomboy tendencies. Talk of such undertakings began two years earlier after she had taken on a rattlesnake and came out victorious.

Max had resisted the entire idea and avoided all references to the possibility of having to be enrolled in a highfalutin academy, but her opposition was futile and mattered not. She rapidly discovered that she couldn't out-stubborn or bend the lines of authority. Her mother, Lacey Coe Dawson, had been equipped with steel where others only had vertebrae and a spinal cord.

The resolute character of the woman who bore her always made her smile. Max ducked her head against the wind and flexed her knees. As the horse kept a steady pace through the fierce snowfall, she recalled a conversation she had with her mother before being shipped off to the east. The early-summer day had been bright and cheery. A gentle zephyr eased up from the river and they sat in rockers on the porch relishing the breeziness.

"Resign yourself to it, Max," her mother said, hands engaged in needlepoint. "It'll be an adventure in the big city that'll be a wonderful education. You'll return to us richer and wiser."

"Resign myself to it?" Max rejoined hotly. She had an oily rag in hand, energetically cleaning a Sharps rifle. "I'd rather be staked out in the desert or get chased by comancheros." Her tone was biting and sarcastic. "I see no reason to pursue this silliness."

"Mind your tongue, young lady," Lacey replied, calm and stern. "You are free to be upset with this decision, but nowhere is it written that you are allowed to sass back. If you think you're too big in the britches for me to take a switch to you, you'd better think again."

Max used a wooden rod to push the rag down the barrel. Her face was set in the exact guise as her mother's; shatterproof lines creased their eyes and constricted their mouths into feisty puckers. Even so, the rigidity of demeanor, which held firm, couldn't diminish or mar their strawberry-blonde beauty. The women were mirror images separated by twenty-five years.

"Do you understand, Max?"

"Yes, ma'am."

"And?"

"I'm sorry for bucking you, Mom."

Lacey measured the sincerity of the apology and softened. "I don't ever expect you to be prissy or high society, Max. I want you to see another way of living, is all."

"Yes, ma'am."

"You are your father's daughter, to be sure."

"Yes, ma'am."

Lacey frowned, a hint of age surfacing on her brow. "I suspect your wardrobe will always be buckskins or dungarees, but it'd be nice to see a few pretty dresses in your trousseau."

"Yes, ma'am."

"You can turn off the *yes ma'ams* anytime, young lady."

Max gave her a twinkly-eyed smile. "I'm going to miss teasing you, Mom. Likely as much or more than I'll miss the lonesomeness of an early morning ride along the river."

"Three years will pass quick enough."

"Philadelphia. You know I don't like cities."

"Yes, my dear. Your father despises cities and you dislike them . . ."

"I despise them too," Max cut in, resting the rifle on her lap.

"You best change your attitude, girl," her mother said, in a style that made clear it was an order, not an option. "One's success in any endeavor is directly connected to one's attitude."

"Yes, ma'am."

Lacey stared at her and spoke strictly. "Go into this schooling with a positive attitude and you will do well. Your father and I anticipate nothing less than a hundred percent effort."

"You'll get it, Mom. What choice do I have?"

"Not much, Max," Lacey admitted, shrugging.

"It's all I know how to give because I've heard it all my life." She leaned forward and pushed her bottom lip out. With a grin working to get free, she lowered her voice in imitation of her father and said, "*A Dawson never shirks a duty and never quits. Ever.*" The grin got loose and filled her face as she hooted a laugh. "You know Daddy."

"Yes, I do, Max. I know your father all too well."

Just then, a burst of wind crashed so strongly that it knocked the mare off-stride. Max stiffened her hands on the reins as the memory faded away. She shook her head tersely. The span of time at the boarding school had been a grueling change for her. She applied herself and was restored to Texas with her wildcat spirit intact, along with knowledge of social etiquette and manners to be put into practice whenever and wheresoever she pleased.

She even had a half-dozen frilly dresses in her closet. At least the garments were there the last time she'd been home; before the events took place that had her on the trail. Now, there was an obligation requiring the application of her instincts and all the fortitude she could muster. A leather portfolio tucked in an inside breast pocket of her heavy duster contained a wanted poster with the likenesses of two men on it. She intended to hunt both culprits down and kill them.

That is, if the man she was actually tracking didn't administer justice first.

Eliza Weitzel was in the root cellar checking on stock and supplies. The wind was screeching like a panther, vibrating the door and making the timbers groan. She tinkered with the wick of the oil lamp to get a brighter glow. The flame jumped and shimmied as the gusts from outside invaded through gaps and cracks.

She sat on a stool, smiling as she appraised the smallness of the enclosure. Digging it, she had worked side by side with her husband and son, becoming efficient on the shovel. They had spent their first winter in New Mexico housed here. Hans had taken advantage of whatever free time arose by drawing and redrawing plans for their homestead, *Freiheit*. Caleb had passed hour after hour training a redbone hound pup—Rainy learned the lessons well and became an integral member of their family. A tiny laugh slipped out; those had been precious days.

Four years later, after arson destroyed their home and barn, they had spent another winter here. A blackened souvenir, lumber redeemed from the fire, remained sturdy and upright beside the iron and wooden entrance archway that had *Freiheit* emblazoned on it. She treasured the charred memento for it stirred resilience and hope; she appreciated the strength evident in the dugout room for it reflected the will and valor of the people it had harbored.

She stood and picked up a wicker basket with a loop handle. She gathered potatoes and carrots from bins, careful to replace the lids. She added several onions. She had another quick look around, then snuffed the lamplight and waited a few moments for her eyes to adjust to the darkness. Her familiarity with every nook and cranny of the underground bunker served her well. She climbed the rungs and put her shoulder to the door.

She pushed on it. The wind immediately grabbed hold and slammed it back. It bounced idiotically as the hinges squeaked a noisy complaint. She stepped up and was careful to make her way to the back porch. She put the basket down. She folded her arms over her bosom to watch. A smile ripened as the plummeting whiteness entertained and amazed her.

After a while, she returned to the root cellar entrance to close and bar the door. The chore was a wrestling match against swirling squalls, but she stuck to it and prevailed. Hurrying to the house, the bottom of her coat flapped like broken shutters and jostled her off balance.

When she got inside, she stamped her feet on the braided welcome mat and enjoyed the warmth of the house. She placed the vegetables on the table and shed her outerwear. She went to the cast iron cook-stove and loitered beside it, listening to the cracking bullwhips of air against the windows. The logs snapping in the hearth were a counterpoint melody to nature.

She shivered, but not because she was cold. A chilly centipede of a feeling crawled up her spine and made her quivery, which contradicted the heat on her backside. Her brow darkened as she clasped her hands tightly at her waist. She inhaled a sudden breath; it was almost a gasp. She took shaky steps, turned a chair away from the table and sat.

The image of her daughter-in-law pressed against her brain. Her instincts told her there was trouble. The instant evaporated in a fleeting rush, but not before she saw Sally Twosongs clearly; worry or dismay filled her dark eyes. Something was terribly wrong.

Eliza covered her mouth. There was urgency in her, but she subdued it and took charge. She wouldn't be held captive by a bad feeling. She was sensitive to the fluctuating tides of emotion, but adamantly refused to borrow woes from tomorrow. Her response was to accept the possibility of misfortune then stand against it with all the depth of faith available.

Being true to her upbringing and know-how, she got busy preparing beef stew for supper. She organized the venture in a bustle of efficiency. As she peeled vegetables and cut a steak into cubes, she quietly and with much conviction cried out for mercy and protection. She named each of her loved ones and requested that guardian angels would encamp roundabout them.

Her heart was indomitable, her prayers intense.

Avis Lahay was fourteen years old. She had been bullied or browbeaten most of her life, so she could easily become wary and withdrawn. There was neglect and mistreatment in her past that wanted to resurface to continually intimidate her. However, buried underneath the mousey timidity, seeds of courage were beginning to germinate. More and more, she was discovering that the soil within had nutrients conducive for boldness to take root.

Her life had been ordinary drudgery for so long that she was still in awe of the transitions and changes that had come in a tumultuous dash. Until two years ago all she had ever known was hardships and difficulties. Doing laundry, scrubbing floors or some other menial engagements occupied waking hours not spent in a classroom under the tutelage of a foul-breathed school marm who doled out criticism and punishment with an obvious glee.

The meager meals had been eaten in an angry atmosphere where hair-pulling fights were the normal distraction. One day she was living in a crowded dormitory with two dozen other girls of various ages. Then, after a visit from a pair of ramrod-stiff strangers, she was whisked away to go shopping for a new wardrobe. A few short weeks later she was decorating her own bedroom with a businesswoman who made her feel like royalty.

There were no explanations. Neither was there any resistance from her. On the contrary, she embraced the new conditions with a deepening sense of gratitude. Each morning when her feet hit the floor, she sat still for several moments to purposefully be thankful for the turn of events that had recalibrated her future. She was doing just that now.

The how and why of the radical alterations to her life were a hidden mystery. She was certainly curious and had been single-minded in wanting to learn the reasons, but that dogged focus had become blurred by the sheer wonder of her good fortune. She was treated with respect and routinely given responsibility. Her days were spent in productive activities.

Whenever she probed around in search of details or enlightenment, she was thwarted or diverted. In the last few months she had decided to simply be indebted to her lucky stars and take full advantage of all the opportunities her new situation offered. Even so, the not knowing gave rise to doubts and reservations that unsettled her by and by.

The sound of the wind slapping against the outside walls was loud. She stood. The room was chilly. She pulled a fluffy housecoat on over her flannel nightgown. A pair of fur-lined doeskin slippers soon cuddled her bare feet. She crossed the room to a roll-top desk. She was tall for her age and beginning to lose the gawky awkwardness of puberty.

She took a seat in a large wooden swivel chair. She finger-combed a jumble of tangles out of wavy auburn hair, which to her, seemed to be getting darker with each passing year. She yawned, then fumbled around and lit a few candles. She slid open a secret pigeonhole drawer and retrieved a leather bound notebook; it was soft and engraved with a pattern of flowers.

Her mind jumped as she considered matters. She found this practice of meditation and self-examination to be both rewarding and challenging. Every morning when she rose or every evening before retiring, she made the time to chronicle happenings—the habit had started a week after her arrival with much encouragement from her benefactor.

Avis picked up a pen and thumbed the book open to the first blank page. She unscrewed the lid off the ink well. She twirled the pen around her fingers whilst she thought, then dipped the metal nib into the ink, tapped off a drop and began writing.

February 15, 1878

Dear Diary: I haven't even looked outside yet, but I already know the weather is nasty. I am running behind schedule because I tossed and turned and was restless for most of the night. It was very late before I finally fell into a healthful sleep. I don't know what the problem was because I'm not anxious or particularly concerned about anything.

Maybe that's not completely true. It's been quite some time since I asked about how I came to be here and why, but I suppose, way down inside, the queries still float around. I'm not sure what difference, if any, having the specifics would make, but I do wonder if any reason will ever be given me. I wish I could push it all away and forget about it forever, which is what I am trying to do, but it comes up time to time.

I have no complaints. Not only have I learned much about cooking and hosting in the restaurant business, yesterday I began being taught numbers and bookkeeping. Expectations are high and boundaries minimal. I'm never yelled at or told how stupid I am. And I never get my knuckles rapped with a stick or locked in a closet for not jumping fast enough.

My only apprehension is that all this could be gone as swiftly as it came into being. I don't ever want to go back, but since I know nothing about what brought me to this place, I realize there are no guarantees. I appreciate the possibilities that are present for me, but my hopes have been slashed into pieces too many times for me to think it couldn't occur again.

That's enough for I must go. I have to embark on my daily mission.

Avis Lahay let loose a low sigh as she closed the notebook. She plunked it in its special compartment and put all writing materials away. She moved about the room in a deliberate hurry. She went to the washstand, poured water from the pink-patterned pitcher into its matching basin. She scrubbed her face and hands, then brushed her hair until it was shiny. She changed from her nightclothes into layer after layer of warm apparel.

When she was persuaded that she was bundled up as well as she could be against the bitterness slam-banging at the window, she had a passing glance in the mirror. A smile filled her face, which was encircled by a furry hood. She blew out the candles and departed. There was a quick stop that had to be made at the outhouse before she would be on her way to the stables.

Five minutes later, she was scurrying through the blizzard toward her destination.

In southern Colorado, the snow was falling in large fluffy chunks. The wind had become as still as a funeral parlor. Charley Jondreau was taking advantage of the respite. He had the piebald pinto moving along in an easterly direction at a speedy gait. It was diffused and leaden, but there was still plenty of daylight to burn and he had miles to put behind him.

The last settlement he'd skirted was Durango. He fully expected to arrive at the boiling mineral waters of Pagosa Springs before nightfall. Then, after a few hours of shuteye, he would cut to the north and keep making tracks through the snow. His final destination on this journey was the *WT Ranch*, which was in the vicinity of Wagon Wheel Gap.

His back trail had both the admirable and the atrocious. Shame or regret was foreign to him; he humbly accepted the whims and vagaries that came calling and put his shoulder to whatever needed doing. He was an old soul with a good heart and a self-fashioned moral code that could become as unyielding as a bulwark fortress. Those qualities persistently combined to put him in the center of strife of one kind or another.

Upon heading south from Kansas in the summer of '72, Jondreau had walked with Liam Greer until he could walk with him no more. For two full years he faithfully strove to be a good influence, but the young man had crossed one too many lines. Jondreau finally accepted the reality that the odds were stacked against ever getting his feet planted on a straight and narrow pathway—the kid did well in fits, but then, was seduced by age-old wickedness and the promise of power and riches. Jondreau could no longer stomach the irresponsibility.

Since going their separate ways, Greer had cut loose from all restraints. He went on a killing spree and developed a coldblooded reputation that sent tremors across the countryside. He became notorious as Kid Greer, a wanted man with a hefty price on his head. The most recent bulletins crackling like wildfire was that he had partnered up with a marauder who was tutoring him in the ancient arts of revenge while preying on weakness or innocence.

Jondreau knew that to be factual. He had *seen* the diabolical alliance established in a ceremonious blood oath. The circumstance galled him and stuck in his craw; it violated his standards of right and wrong, but for the time being, he had dusted off his hands and moved on. He understood that sooner or later, Kid Greer would be on the lookout and gunning for him, though he wasn't concerned about any such showdown.

He leaned back in the saddle to scan the crags and peaks that could be discerned through the barrage of snowflakes. The San Juan Mountains were half a continent away from the marshes and peat bogs of his birthplace in the Great Lakes region, but he had no uncertainties. There was unflinching courage and wanderlust in him that had to be frequently indulged. He was a nomadic explorer, seeking truth and beauty wherever it could be found.

The Iroquois blood in his veins gave him an almost mystical appreciation for the force and language of nature. He related to it with the same ease as social butterflies circulating to collect prattling gossip in respectable ballrooms. The natural world had much to tell him and he practiced being quick to listen. Just now he knew that on his route the wind had been confined to its storehouses for a few days; he only had to contend with the deepening snow.

His mount was savvy and sure-footed. He trusted the animal and gave it free rein. It instinctively picked its way through the pristine whiteness on a course of least resistance. He flipped up a side of the elk-hide poncho to reach into a pocket of his mackinaw. He got a large sliver of dried beef and held it between his teeth as he repositioned the cold-weather garb.

Suddenly his posture went rigid as though an unseen lance had stabbed into his vitals. His mouth wrenched open. The impromptu meal was lost before a bite had been taken. His eyelids fluttered and pulsated, then became motionless. His eyeballs rolled back and disappeared as an immense twitch surged through his body. His hands clenched and jerked hard.

The horse whinnied and stopped in its tracks. It stood and waited patiently to be released, but its master was entirely unaware of proceedings around him. Jondreau was mesmerized by goings-on elsewhere. An acidy stench saturated his nostrils. What he *saw* inside his head was murky and indistinct. The vision riveted him and he strained to filter through the haziness, but could not. Ashen ribbons of light obscured the image; focus refused to become clear.

He thought he could make out a bronze-skinned woman rocking a newborn baby. Her glossy hair was twined in braids. He grasped that she was alone and crying, but was unable to discern any of her features, which ignited frustration in him. The room she was in started spinning. He reached out in an effort to rake away the streaks that kept her hidden.

Then, just as swiftly as the visitation occurred, the specter of premonition was gone. A gasp of a moan escaped his lips and a shudder convulsed his shoulders. He felt a cussword begin to form but squelched it before it could take hold of his tongue. In recent months the blessing of his sixth sense had become more of a curse because it was consistently elusive and disturbing. The stinking manifestation that accompanied each psychic incident tarried. He pinched the bridge of his nose and blew to jettison the sour residue of the smell of the skunk.

He had a look-see as though reconnecting with the scenery surrounding him. It didn't bring comfort—he was troubled by the extrasensory impression. He had *seen* the captivating maiden many times, but the child was a new revelation; as was the sobbing. He crooked forward to murmur a command to the horse. It gave its body a shake before stepping nimbly.

A scream pierced the wintry tranquility. Jondreau glanced to his left to see a mature hawk perched atop a stark bare aspen, which resembled a skeletal finger amongst a forest of bony digits pointing skyward. He felt peace touch his core because of its primal call to him. The majestic bird could have easily remained secreted on its roost; it was almost indistinguishable for it was camouflaged in a downy cloak of snow.

It spread and waggled its wings. He grinned widely and doffed his droopy-brimmed hat. It craned its neck in response and unfettered another shriek akin to a raspy steam whistle, then leapt off the branch. He laughed aloud, cheerful and content. It flapped mightily, its rust-red tail feathers fanning out as it swooped upwards to a corridor in the sky directly in front of him.

Charley Jondreau whispered orders to the pinto to follow the raptor.

In the high desert, a hundred-odd miles to the south, the whirlwind was horrendous and crosscurrent crazy. Its icy ferocity was conjuring terrible notions in Gray Cloud's overactive imagination. He was downright scared; he was sure he was encircled by a battalion of giant trolls armed with massive slingshots flinging lacerating pellets of snow from every direction.

Above the din of the storm he heard a coyote howling. His fear abruptly increased. The strangeness of the shrill yowl stirred up a serpent's nest of superstitions within. The trickster beast should be burrowed in a den to outlast the tempestuous squalls. Instead it was singing its song. He worried on the meaning of it. His nerve endings were jumpy and inflamed.

The Navajo man, grandson of Gray Eyes, kept prodding his horse to keep it moving. A bugger of dread had him repeatedly looking over his shoulder. He was thoroughly steeped in the oral tradition of storytelling and in his mind just now many eerie accounts about skinwalkers were being fused together with old wives' tales to do vile things to his judgment.

His brain was overloaded by creepy probabilities. Some monstrosity with blood-drenched talons and sharpened teeth could pounce on him at any moment. He only had a mile or so to go on his return from a hunt. It had been successful, but he seriously wondered if he was going to stay alive long enough to butcher the kill. A disemboweled elk was strapped over a pack-mule. He had to constantly tug on the lead-line because the animal was exhausted and dragging.

His mitten-covered hands hurt and tingled. He was bent low over the neck of his mount. His cheeks felt brittle and painful, as though tiny tacks were stabbing the exposed skin. The wind lashed at him. His eyes were squinted almost shut. He held tight and steady, plodding forward. Shelter and warmth were ahead, beckoning him.

He felt a sneeze coming. A tic crinkled his nose. He sat bolt upright. Coldness burned him from the inside out. His eyes widened in alarm. He tilted his head back and sniffed, tentative and testing at first, but then he inhaled hugely. The trepidation in him corkscrewed through his bowels. He choked and swallowed hard. There could be no mistaking the odor; a substantial waft of tobacco smoke was being hurled about on the furious airstream.

He sensed evil closeby. He remembered. The reminiscence horrified him. He goaded the horse with his heels. The animal sprinted in a herky jerky gait. He hunched over. His right arm yanked constantly on the rope tethered to the mule. Off in the distance, the coyote yelped and yapped. He hurried faster. And faster. A spasm roiled around in the pit of his stomach.

When Gray Cloud rode beneath the *Freiheit* arch, he saw lamplight ablaze in the house. The fragile tints shining through the gloom of the storm had little effect on reducing the angst spiraling through him. He went straight to the plank-walled shack that was situated halfway between the house and barn. He scooted to the ground. The horse and mule needed to be attended to, but his instincts compelled him to take care of other matters first.

Inside the twelve-by-twelve living quarters, he removed the mittens and chaffed his hands together. He lit a candle and placed the holder on the potbelly stove, which was cold. He knelt and kindled a fire in it. When the flames grew strong enough he added several split logs from the wood-box. Satisfied that it was banked, he went to the shelf that extended along one wall.

His breathing was tenuous and haggard. He instantly found what he wanted. Several necklaces fashioned from the purple-black seed cones of junipers dangled on pegs; the berries had been gathered along the rim of the barren canyons on all sides of Angel Peak, then dried into hard nuggets that resembled precious gems. He fingered the ghost beads and in a guttural cadence, uttered a lengthy invocation that appealed to all he identified as sacred.

The phrases came in short spurts to become a hallowed litany. Inborn pride rose up in him. He was Gray Cloud, of the Turning Mountain People, born for the Sage Brush Hill Clan. His maternal grandfather's clan was the Mountain Cove Clan; the Badlands People were his paternal grandfather's clan. His forebears were survivors. He had endured the enforced march to Fort Sumner on the Pecos River and overcame all the deprivations that ensued.

His prayers ended in a rush of emotion. The candlelight flickered and cast shadows that pranced frantically on the wall. His deep-set eyes gleamed and a cranky smile chased across the circle of his face. He loosened the collars of his coat and shirt. He bowed his head and carefully put all the ghost bead charms around his neck to protect against unclean spirits skulking to and fro on the prowl for fissures to exploit.

He pinched out the candle. He adjusted his clothing and put the mittens on, then went outside. The wind smacked him. He leaned into it and led the animals to the barn. A dull glow was showing through a few cracks. The sight stirred encouragement. It meant his employer and landlord would be busy working at one task or another. He hoped Hans Weitzel had time and was in a mood for chatter because there was much that needed to be unloaded and interpreted.

Gray Cloud took a nervous glance over a shoulder before entering the barn.

Near Glorieta Pass, Ben Slaton was sinking fast in a quagmire of calamity. The twisting quirks of fate had conspired against him. It was a sorry state of affairs to be sure. There were clumpy clots of blood in his fuzzy beard. His pistol was in his hand. Thoughts of suicide were tripping through his head. He reluctantly entertained that bleak destiny.

The mad siren of the wind was relentless, soaring and caterwauling like a lunatic seeking to break out of an asylum. Slaton was hunkered down on a flat area in a natural hollow of rocks. A few cedar branches had been woven into a flimsy roof. The gathering of the boughs had almost done him in. He was in extreme discomfort, sweating and shivering beside a tiny fire.

When the storm erupted, the itinerant bounty hunter and gambler had been collecting fuel in preparation because of the ominous skies. In a scramble back to the campsite with a third armful of brushwood, he had a fluke accident that would have been comical except for the dire consequences. He started slipping down a slope and his boots became skis.

The contents in his arms went airborne, but not before a jagged log slit a gash out of his chin. His feet skipped and scuttled for balance as his whiskers matted with blood. He floundered helplessly. He was fighting to achieve a semblance of control when his right foot entered a narrow crevice. He careened witlessly. The dreadful snap of bones made him nauseous. His loud and strident squeal was lost and silenced by the raging whiteout.

His lower leg was fractured. It was useless, hinged and held together by skin and fleshy muscle. He summoned all the gutsiness and brass balls he could marshal. It took hour after pain-racked hour for him to secure the scanty overhead shield. He had hopped and humped about whilst wincing and cursing continuously. It then required teeth-clenched willpower to coax sparks to take hold of enough sticks to build sustainable flames.

Now, huddled close to the campfire and leaning against a boulder, he contemplated his predicament. It was critical and getting worse by the minute. If frostbite and the weather didn't kill him, then the injury would leech his life away. The leg needed to be immobilized, but he lacked the wherewithal to do the job. Besides, it was horribly swollen; the inflammation would have to reduce significantly before a makeshift splint could be applied.

In an intuitive piece of improvisation, he had the broken leg propped up by a pile of rocks under the knee. Perspiration seeped from his pores, creating tiny wisps of steam that rose off his clothes and quickly blended into nothingness. Twinges of acute pain flared intermittently, but mostly it was a steady throb that was slowly becoming numb.

His eyes were glassy and unfocused, staring blankly at the six-shooter. The Remington was the only firearm available to him. His rifle, along with foodstuffs and all his gear, was still secured on his horse. The white-socked bay stallion, an intelligent enough animal that regularly refused to heed his voice, had not been hitched. It was nearby and would have to fend for itself.

Ben Slaton had no wish to die, but if it came down to a choice between a feverishly slow death or a single well-placed slug, he was wholly prepared to pull the trigger. He had never shied away from taking action to dominate and rule all that was within his power to regulate. He began to occupy his mind by dipping into philosophical meanderings.

He thought about the principle of getting what he deserved. Good or bad, he had a fatalistic outlook that figured whatever came to him was the result of some past action or behavior. He had little perception of karma. To him it was nebulous and had religious overtones, but not knowing about a topic seldom ever prevented him from wading into it.

He had heard a preacher one time waxing fearfully about reaping what one sows. The sermon was a fuming exposition seared by brimstone and sealed with condemnation. It hadn't nudged him toward salvation, but rather, gave him a platform on which to negotiate on his terms. He constructed a mental ledger and always sought to keep the inventory up to date.

Just now he was wondering if there was enough goodness on the plus side to justify anticipating a crop of fine luck. He accepted that there was more than plenty of wickedness to weigh down the minus scale, but he hoped against the hard facts. There weren't many noble dealings in his background to buoy up his spirits, but one came to mind.

He recollected that just last summer he had been heroic on the streets of Dodge City. It was a hot and dusty afternoon, with the sun ablaze in a clear sky and a stiff breeze peppering the air with gritty grime. He was flush because of fruitful pickings at an all-night poker game, but impatiently hung around town to get a mite richer; he was waiting for a hard-assed judge to release reward funds for a two-bit desperado he had brought in.

The thoroughfare was buzzing with activity. Commerce had no constraints. Pedestrians had to step sprightly to avoid wagon and horse traffic. Slaton was smoking a cigar and minding his own business lounging lazily against the railing outside of the Long Branch Saloon. He marked time by vaguely watching a towhead lad playing marbles near the railroad tracks across the way. The boy was alone and no more than six years old.

There were surly shouts followed by gunshots. Slaton came alert and looked in the direction of the ruckus. People were jostling and rushing out of the way. A pair of snorting steers came stampeding over the rails onto Front Street. The teamster was running behind, red-faced and wild-eyed. Several cowboys on foot raced to dissuade the animals, to no avail.

The child squatting in the dirt shooting agates was in danger. He was engrossed in his amusement, his back to the rampage trampling unswervingly at him. Slaton didn't think; he simply reacted in an explosion of energy. He spat out his stogy and sprinted across the avenue, yelling warnings at the top of his lungs. The berserk beasts were gaining speed and fury.

It was topsy-turvy. Swearwords scorched the air. Dogs were barking. Time solidified. A woman wailed hysterically. Slaton zoned in. His legs were pumping. He was sure that he was about to be at the center of a catastrophe. He dove and tackled the boy, rolling out of the way in a poorly executed somersault just as the hoofbeats obliterated the circle of glass balls.

Then, a crowd clustered around him and Slaton was being clapped on the back. He accepted the congratulations, though his concentration was pinned on the lad's mother. She clung to her son, crying tears of relief. A slim and pretty brunette, she was exceedingly demonstrative in her thankfulness. He received it all with a self-effacing aw-shucks grin.

She was smallish up top but had jutting hips and a nicely rounded derriere that Slaton would have joyfully followed anywhere. And so he did. He took complete advantage of her gratitude. As chance would have it, being an abandoned California widow, she had been willing and lively, and taught him a few tricks and new gambits of carnal pleasure.

Perhaps, in the cosmic scheme of settling the books, that was the only payback for the impressive rescue in which he risked his own safety. If so, bedding her every night for a week would be an adequate final musing, though in all candor, he couldn't even dredge up her name. She had been an accessible vessel to be used and tossed aside.

Slaton came back to the present. The harrowing flurries hadn't decreased at all. His grossly injured leg pulsed with contractions. He was eyeballing the handgun, envisioning the grisly possibilities. If it became a necessity, he had to select where to put the bullet; in the mouth, under the chin or should the muzzle be pressed against the temple?

His jaw clamped so tautly that a blade of pain hacked through his skull. He crunched forward and exhaled noisily. The grimace relaxed. He groaned as he adjusted his backside and put the revolver in its holster. He doggedly decided that he would do much more than survive; he would triumph over the foolish conspiracy aligned against him.

After all, he had five thousand motives to live. Wealth awaited him. For years he had monitored the career of an old acquaintance. Evidence that the splashy punk had achieved the big-time was folded in an inside pocket of his vest—it was a dead or alive proposition.

Ben Slaton intended to cash in and ride the fame of that gravy train.

Whitey Fitzgerald was lost. The will to find his way back was fragmentary bits and pieces floating in a bottle. He had taken a crushing wallop that sent him headlong into an endless flow of whiskey. His eyes were red-rimmed and bleary. Days and nights were all the same, foggy and dissolving in a blur. He fell asleep drunk and woke up in a similar condition.

His head ached and his brain was muddled as he sat on the floor, his knees scrunched up to his chest. He was swaddled in a crusty patchwork quilt. The clapboard shed on the property of the livery was being vigorously pounded and shook by the wind. The planks creaked and wobbled as though the building might get blown down as flat as a flapjack. His lodging was piddling, but he had much proficiency at adapting, adjusting and making do.

Pale light glittered around his cubbyhole from the kerosene lantern mounted on the wall near the doorway. A cylinder stove provided warmth; the pipe vented through the roof was corroded and needed to be repaired or replaced for it glowed brightly in spots, and leaked fumes. He snuggled down a little deeper into the nest he had cobbled together.

Six months ago his life lurched sideways in a tailspin from which recovery seemed improbable. He despised being adrift, but was incapable of getting anchored. A sort of madness had gotten into his bloodstream that chiseled away and finally obliterated what slavery had been powerless to harm. His pride had nosedived to oblivion and been replaced by shame.

He poked a hand inside his tattered frock coat and rummaged around a shirt pocket until he got hold of a half-gone cigar. The stub was three inches long, which would serve him nicely. He muttered as he put a match to it and took several gentle pulls. The smoke curled around his head and for a brief moment became a crown. He made a number of sad-sounding click-clicks between his cheek and gum, and brooded over his disastrous descent.

The plunge had shattered his confidence and drained him of the vinegar that fueled him. He had been bred and molded on a plantation in Alabama. To him, emancipation meant freedom to be and do without regard to prejudice. It used to be that he would have no part of being influenced by intolerance and small-mindedness.

Not so long ago he had the wits and personality to make his way around the animosity and contempt without shucking or kowtowing. Until emotional upheaval devastated him, the likelihood of his perspective to be altered or mood affected by ignorance was nil and none; the poised and buoyant Whitey Fitzgerald would never be scapegoated by Jim Crowism.

It wasn't that way anymore. He was now a defeated man and he knew who was responsible for the whupping. There was nowhere to place blame except on the face he saw whenever he shaved. He had been trounced by his choices. The downfall skewed his bearings and reduced him to a wreckage of humiliation. He was embarrassed and ashamed, and notwithstanding an eagerness to do so, he couldn't help or forgive himself.

"Ain't this a dandy set of woebegones?" he asked, flinching as the headache shot off a cannon blast of pain. Guilt reverberated through him. His self-reliance, along with any vestiges of self-respect, had been forfeited and replaced by depths of self-pity. He dropped the shabby blanket off his shoulders. "I could study on these matters until the man from Galilee walks in here from across the sky and still not know what the holy hell is happening to me."

He stood and chuckled grimly. He moseyed back and forth. "I can't do no ciphering between the lines inside my head, so what to do?" He still possessed an unflagging panache and habitually carried on conversations with the walls and ceiling.

He kept moving at a snail's tempo. "Ain't no nevermore about it," he said sullenly. "I be one helluva fortunate nigger to have a high quality lady care about me." He picked a fleck of tobacco off his tongue and released a jaunty rumble of laughter. He slumped down and parked his butt in his niche. "I has to find a way to kill my rats."

The cheroot was wedged between his teeth. He pulled his carpetbag onto his lap and opened it. He reshuffled the few clothes and gaped at the leather tote that contained the tools of his trades. A lump scratched its way up his throat. The barber and dental instruments were essential to his identity, but he was afraid that he would never use them again.

He sat back and took one final puff on the cigar, then squished it out. He hastily set aside the calico satchel and managed an almost chirpy click-click. Despite the gripes of his hangover, he got up and hurried around in a flash of his former perpetual motion routine. If his befuddled mind had it correct and this morning was no different than the past twenty, he could soon expect company to visit. Therefore, he briskly engaged in a persnickety cleanup of his residence.

Nothing could ever deter Whitey Fitzgerald from his fixation for cleanliness.

When Silas Dawson was eighteen years old he killed a man in Buffalo. He was a drinker and brawler back then, but had already acquired the mulish sense of justice that had him holed up in Chaco Canyon now. The clash occurred in a boisterous barroom. Why the bare knuckles fight was in his mind while he struggled to stave off the freezing cold had him flummoxed, but he pondered the bygone autumn evening.

The reliving was vivid: The air stretching in off Lake Erie was cool and sweet, though it couldn't sweep away the smoke and sweat hovering in the tavern. The basement joint was a popular watering hole for stevedores and greasy dock workers stopping in for a bite or a brew after loading, unloading and slugging it out on the barges and boats of the Erie Canal.

Dawson had put in a sixteen hour day and was tending to a tankard of ale at a crowded table. He ignored the noisy conversations going on all around him. His eyes were on a scrappy jostling match between a neighborhood loudmouth and an amiable barmaid who was hustling about, smiling and laughing as she tried to keep all the customers satisfied.

The man known as Mags—shortened from Magolski—was intent on getting more than a meal and liquid refreshment, which often was an agreeable option for Sophia. She was playful and promiscuous; if the mood and price was right, a backroom was available where her plump curves could be properly enjoyed. It was obvious she desired no such doings with Mags.

He persisted clutching at her, which stoked the ire in Silas Dawson. His blood had a low boiling point, especially when it came to members of the fairer sex being harassed or disparaged. According to the way he had been reared, a lady was to always be treated as a lady; being a gentleman was a requirement, regardless of a woman's social standing or occupation.

Mags got hold of her skirts and pulled her against him. Sophia squirmed to escape.

Dawson stood. "Leave her be, Mags," he bellowed to be heard above the hubbub. Built like a tree trunk, he was a thickset stump of corded muscle. He took a few lateral steps until there was an open laneway between them. "The lady wants nothing to do with you, so back off."

"The lady?" Mags spat and grabbed her bosom. Sophia hollered an objection and hit him. He responded in kind, striking her cheek with a closed fist. She sprawled backwards.

Dawson checked out. He charged in a fury. Mags clambered to his feet and took on a grappler's stance, legs set apart and hands joggling up and down. He had fifty-plus pounds on the oncoming fireball. The set-to had all the makings of an audience pleasing brouhaha. Chairs scraped the floorboards and yells of delight blistered from dozens of tongues as patrons scrabbled into a loose-knit ring of flesh.

The combatants came together in a thunderous smashup. Dawson's shoulders were sledgehammers that clobbered him waist high. Magolski gasped and did a funny looking backpedaling maneuver that had him on his heels. His hands were balled up and he threw several clumsy clouts that were deflected or drifted harmlessly. Dawson dodged and weaved, stalking forward like a hulking predator on the ready for an opportunity to attack.

Magolski jabbed. Dawson ducked. Magolski hooked. Dawson bobbed low and uncoiled an uppercut that connected squarely. The sound of his opponent's teeth clapping together was heard above the roars and cheers of the bystanders. Magolski cussed and sneered in disgust. Gooey runners of red coalesced at the corners of his mouth.

The sight or scent of blood did something to Silas Dawson. He went wild. His fists flew in a hurling blur, each belt finding its mark and doing damage. He was unleashed, punching in a piston-like rhythm that alternated between the head and body. Magolski put up a feeble defense of wrapping him in a bear hug, but every lumbering clinch failed to restrain him.

Dawson's fists were remorseless; he was a hitting machine. Magolski was knocked out. He swooned and swayed in a glaze-eyed daze, but still his beaten frame continued to absorb wallop after wallop. In a weird way, the bombardment kept him on his feet, lopsided and faltering. The assembled gawkers were writhing in conniptions of raucous laughter.

The fracas ended when Dawson released a deathly combination; a left hook to his stomach and a shoulder-rolling right that landed in the bull's-eye of his face. Magolski's neck snapped. A spray of blood and snot splattered as his head lolled and flopped around as though it was attached by strands of rubber. He collapsed to the floor in a boneless heap.

Sophia stooped low to examine him. Her hands had a delicate touch. She was shock-eyed. Her complexion became pasty as she glanced up and shakily whispered, "He's dead."

The mob of spectators inhaled a huge collective gulp of breath. Dawson pursed his lips. His eyes were incensed as he said, "He ought not to have hassled the lady." He took a step toward the door and there was a rush of movement as the gaggle of onlookers gave him lots of space. He strolled out of the saloon. The whiff of freshness gave him crystal clarity.

He started jogging. Soon he heard voices and footfalls coming after him. He bolted. He ran and ran, and kept running all through the night of the following day. He never once looked back; his conscience had no scars because of that debacle. Now, caught in a seething snowstorm, he had no inkling as to why he was fretting over a fistfight that occurred four decades ago.

The miles were naked tombstones marking the passage of time. He was in his fifty-eighth year. His hair, once pitch-black, was now grayish; his beard was as white as cotton. The crow's feet around his eyes had deepened into grooves that appeared to have been hacked out with a hatchet. Though there were creaks in his joints, the years hadn't diminished his vitality.

He was dug in and nursing a ghastly wound in his left shoulder. The soreness was tolerable and as best as he could tell, no infection had set in. He was encamped in some ruins of a once thriving civilization of builders. The sandstone block walls were sturdy; the wreckage of the roof was patchy, though the overhang above him provided sufficient protection. He had stabled his horse in an adjoining alcove. His saddle and gear were stationed behind him.

A campfire was jumping against a wall. The rocks he'd built up around it couldn't prevent the wind from incessantly frolicking with the blaze. He sat on his heels and judiciously fed sticks and rubble into the flames. He had already lain in a store of deadwood and there was much more to be scrounged from fallen timbers.

He had his mind set. There would be no rerouting him. He was an ex-Texas Ranger in pursuit of his nemesis, a pariah outlaw with a flair for depravity. Dawson had a fabled reputation across the southwest. There had been more than a few high-profile exploits, some of which had gotten his name and picture plastered on the front page of newspapers.

The press coverage transformed him into a notable celebrity, which went against the grain of his superior's expectations. Dawson hadn't officially ridden with the Rangers for over a year because he had no inclination or aptitude to negotiate agency politics. He was forced into an administrative role, for which he was ill-suited so he retired from active service.

However, he wasn't quite ready to be put out to pasture or take up front porch living. An underpinning of hot coals still prickled and festered in his belly. He had unfinished business with an elusive hooligan; especially now. The fugitive had committed a barbaric murder, slaughtering a woman in San Antonio.

In previous encounters, the blackhearted criminal became an obsession to Dawson. To track him on this occasion, he had buffed up the insignia and accoutrements of the Texas Rangers. He wore his badge proudly. The execution hanging he intended to carry out would be done under the umbrella of law; western vigilante law, but law nonetheless.

He had arrived in Texas in 1840, when it was a no-holds-barred Republic, brash and independent. The devil-may-care recklessness immediately fit him as tightly as a second skin. He was a rowdy and hotheaded daredevil on the lookout for escapades. He found all he ever wanted when he joined the paramilitary organization tasked with an extensive mandate.

He was born to be a Texas Ranger. He harkened back in his mind. A thin-lipped smile climbed upwards and took hold of his eyes so convincingly that they gleamed as he browsed the nostalgia. Shortly after the 1848 Treaty of Guadalupe Hidalgo ended the war with Mexico, his wildness met its rival. He had been on duty not far from Capital Square when it happened.

It was midday and the streets of Austin were bustling. A cap and ball Navy Colt revolver was prominent on his hip. The brim of his hat was skewed low to shade his eyes, which were alert and peeled to spot trouble; it jumped off directly in front of him. A drunken gambler tottered out of a saloon and collided with a woman on the boardwalk. She fell backwards, but kept her feet under her. The perpetrator proceeded to curse her to damnation.

Dawson took instinctive action and leapt into the altercation. He wordlessly grabbed the malcontent by the scruff of the neck and seat of his pantaloons. In an effortless heave, he tossed him through the plate glass of the establishment he had vacated. The window exploded inward. A shattering of shards and splinters became a chaotic shower. The culprit was blubbering and his arms were twirling around in windmill mode as he crash-landed.

Churlish cusses and complaints salted the air. Gaping passersby came running to the commotion. Dawson spun around to speak to the woman, but his tongue became furry and unusable. He was promptly unaware of others clustering around the hellabaloo—he was staring into bottomless pools of blue that shimmered and shone. Their gaze dovetailed and locked. His heartbeat was thumping inside his head; dizziness eddied through him.

"Thank you," she said in a husky voice that was encased in velvet. Her strawberry tresses were a cascade of ringlets spilling from beneath a stylish sunbonnet. "I appreciate your kindness, but it wasn't at all necessary, sir. I'd have handily taken care of that souse."

He moistened his lips. His mouth opened and closed, but no words emerged.

"Lacey," she declared, bobbing her head slightly. "Lacey Coe."

His jaw dropped clumsily. He kept trying to talk, but remained voiceless.

"Are you deaf and dumb, sir?"

"Silas Dawson, ma'am," he managed dryly. "At your service."

Their courtship began there and then. It lasted precisely two weeks. She was a honeyed rose from Appalachia, with thorns that served to tame him, though in all certainty, he could never be fully domesticated. The wedding was a fun affair that had a detachment of spiffed up Texas Rangers in the church to stand in an arc around the bride and groom.

The edges of his eyes were wet when a loud pop and the scent of burning cloth brought him back from the past. A gnarled log had crackled and distributed an array of embers, some of which were singeing the front of his heavy overcoat. He extinguished the smolders with several exuberant pats. His expression tightened against the emotion rising in him.

He rocked on the balls of his feet to arrange the ground tarp from his bedroll. He put his buttocks on it and got comfortable, with his back propped against the saddle. A boiling swell of irritation radiated from his left shoulder. He lifted the dense woolen material of his greatcoat and raised the poultice to have a gander at the grotesque puncture. He had used a red-hot knife blade to cauterize it, but it was still seeping. He readjusted the compress. Defiance bristled in his marrow. He folded his arms over the barrel of his chest and settled in to outlast the storm.

Hans Weitzel closed the door on the outhouse and bent into the wind. The flurries were ferocious and blinding. Darkness was a frenzied maelstrom that made it impossible to see more than a yard or two in any direction. He traced his way through the elements, his stiff-shouldered gait even more pronounced than usual. He stepped onto the front porch.

Once inside, the aroma of beef and spices stimulated his hunger. His stomach growled. The warmth of the room was cozy and reassuring. He automatically wiped his feet on the rug as he shed his coat and scarf. A place setting and an oil lamp were on the table. The flame was turned low. He adjusted it to be a tad brighter.

There was candlelight streaming through the open bedroom door. He peeked in to find his wife already comfy beneath the covers and reading. "We have fresh elk meat hanging and ready to be smoked," he said, leaning a shoulder against the doorframe.

Eliza glanced at him and placed the book on her tummy. Her hair, straw-colored and tinted by specks of silver at the temples, was pooled halo-like on the pillow. "I was at the window when Gray Cloud returned. He was riding far too hard."

"He was spooked."

"By the storm?"

"He had a premonition of evil," he replied, chuckling.

"Evil?" she asked, voice rising keenly.

Weitzel puckered his mouth. "What is it, Eliza? You know Gray Cloud's pessimism. His premonition is just some superstitious nonsense about the storm."

"I pray you're right, Hans."

His brow knitted into a puzzled frown. "Do you have other notions?"

"I think something is wrong," she said evenly. "Sally Twosongs has been on my mind. I had a sense of foreboding earlier. It was succinct and peculiar. I have been unable to shake it."

"It was likely nothing, Eliza."

"I suspect so, but just the same, it bothers me."

"Don't let Gray Cloud's doom and despair influence you."

"What bugbear does he have nibbling at him now?"

He slid the suspenders off his shoulders. "He heard a coyote."

She propped herself up on her elbows. "Coyotes are plentiful around here."

"According to Gray Cloud, a coyote howling during a snowstorm is a bad omen."

"There could be some basis for that belief," she suggested, eyebrows tenting. "Animals have foreknowledge of weather disturbances so as to take refuge. A coyote being on the run and vocal during a blizzard is uncharacteristic, to say the least."

"Uncharacteristic, yes. A bad omen or reason to connect nonexistent dots, no."

"Lord, have mercy!" she exclaimed with a laugh. "To what dots do you refer?"

"Gray Cloud's obsession with newspapers," he answered as he began unbuttoning his corduroy shirt. "He sees a cryptic pattern in every story and it's going to drive him batty. He reads the same articles over and over, imagining the worst possible outcomes."

She gave a knowing nod. "He does have a conspiratorial trend in him."

"I can't keep up with his theories," he said, gruff disdain in his tone. "He was nearly hysterical with panic and yakking crazily. Something in this storm has him all in an uproar over that woman who was murdered in San Antonio near Christmastime."

"What? That's too bizarre, even for Gray Cloud."

"I'm not making it up, Eliza. He claims he smelled tobacco smoke."

Her forehead wrinkled. "Smoky Crowe?"

"Those are the invisible dots he has connected," he answered glibly. "He will explain it all more clearly tomorrow. Supposedly he has complicated secrets to share with us."

She giggled softly. "Don't be too cynical, Hans."

He dismissed her teasing with a backhanded wave, then turned and went to the kitchen. He got a bowl of stew and ate it while staying near the stove. He savored each bite. When he finished, he took a knee and positioned two hefty logs in the cast iron hearth. He strolled over to deadbolt the door and had a cursory look around before extinguishing the oil lamp.

He entered the bedroom and stripped down to his long johns and socks. He put out the candles and in absolute darkness crept to the bedside, totally certain that she would be holding the blankets up for him. He slipped in beside her. A short moment later they were spooned and cuddled snugly. In their quarter-century partnership Hans and Eliza Weitzel had diligently woven affection, security and contentment into the tapestry of their life together.

Liam Greer loomed over the woman and wagged a handgun. She had refused his twisted romantic overtures and received a thorough pistol-whipping for her audacity. He strutted and swaggered in a fanatical frenzy. His eyes were bulging and lips smacking as he slobbered tobacco juice. The brownish goo dribbled down his chin.

She cringed against the headboard. He had terrorized her more than once. His threats were not idle words. Tears and trickles of blood mingled on her cheeks. The need to escape simmered in her. She wanted to jump and run past him; every ounce of yearning was seared to that desire, but she was overwhelmed by paralyzing fear.

He daintily traipsed like a smarmy pretty-boy. He holstered the revolver and unbuckled the gunbelt. He hung it on a bedpost. "You're going to give me what I want, whore."

"Can't you see that you're wrong about me?"

"I ain't wrong, whore." He stomped forward and menaced her with a fist.

She shrank away from him. "Please don't hurt me anymore."

"I paid for you. Now do me like I ain't ever been done, whore."

"Please don't . . ."

Greer rolled the wad of tobacco around on his tongue. "Don't what, whore?"

"Please don't rape me."

Greer hooted laughter. "Rape you? I ain't a-gonna rape you." He rubbed the front of his trousers. "I put my money on the dresser; now you do to me what whores do."

"Why do you keep coming here?"

"Because you're a famous whore."

"You're mistaken," she repeated boldly. "I'm not a whore."

Greer palmed gunk from the corners of his mouth. "Every woman is a whore."

"I'm sorry. I am not a whore. I cannot accommodate you."

Greer leered and licked his lips. "You're nothing but a whore." He lunged and cuffed her across the face. As she recoiled, he grabbed her blouse with both hands and tore it open. Buttons flew and scattered; the material tore away as though it was merely paper. Her undergarments were exposed, but no flesh was bared. The camisole covered her bosom completely.

"Beat me or kill me. I will not submit."

"I ain't a-gonna kill you. At least not until getting diddled."

She openly stared at him. "I am sorry, Liam. I'm ashamed of what I did to you."

Greer huffed and puffed. His shallow chest rose and fell erratically. A muscle in his neck trembled. His breathing became quicker and more fitful. He clutched hold of his crotch and gave it a squeeze. His hand flexed obscenely as he slurred a vulgar blasphemy. He coughed up a gob of phlegm and chewed on it. He spat the chunky slop and told her to die, die, die. The slippery mess splashed over her. She screamed and valiantly fought him.

It was then that Delores Solrizo came awake. She thrashed beneath the quilt and swam up from the depths of sleep. Her arms reflexively warded off the despicable illusion. She had much experience in doing so for the nastiness was a recurring dream which again and again degraded her. She tottered up and swung her legs over the side of the bed.

She was frustrated and scared. "Sweet Jesus," she prayed in a sobbing gasp. "Will it never end? Can I ever be delivered from this cancerous stain of guilt?" She stood and listened to the wind pelting against the windows. It *sounded* frosty. She shivered. Her skin was clammy with perspiration. She pulled a housecoat on and knotted the fabric belt around her waist.

Her brain was flooded by a fluid montage of violent imagery floating up from her subconscious; her father abusing and raping her was at the forefront, but linked in like a jigsaw puzzle was a foul confrontation she'd had with her son on the streets of Abilene. No doubt both episodes from her past warped together to form the basis for the serial nightmare.

Dawn was still far off, but she had no wish to banish the night with lamplight. She paced anxiously. Her mouth was parched. She felt an old need clamoring. There were no fixings stashed in any hidey-hole, but she craved a cigarette the way a starving woman hungered for a dish of tasteless gruel. She had quit the habit years ago while in the midst of a fundamental renovation of her life, but the appetite for it thrived in moments of severe stress.

She bit the inside of her bottom lip and stamped the urge down. She did her utmost to be rational and levelheaded. She had no inclination to re-visit any ugliness that'd transpired previous to her arrival in Santa Fe. People were dependent on her; she had a multitude of responsibilities that could not be readily cancelled or delegated to others.

She sat on a bentwood rocker near the bedside. The soft squeaking of the chair as she used it caused a smile to inch up and spark the emerald in her eyes. She folded her hands in her lap and took several meditative breaths. Her day was off to an early start, but there'd be no grumbling or complaints. Instead, Delores Solrizo put forth the effort to nurture thanks-giving by quietly praying and preparing for whatever the hours ahead would bring.

Ashes to ashes, dust to dust.

Silas Dawson came awake with those words rattling around his skull. His mouth was clamped shut. He glared toward the eastern skyline in hopes of actually seeing the sunrise, but that was not to be. Nighttime was defi-nitely dwindling and being subdued by the first fingerprints of daybreak, but the murkiness of the storm was unabated.

Ashes to ashes, dust to dust. The phrase callously sliced at him. He could not conquer or rise above the soul-ache of its finality. He had walked away from the graveside, stoic and determined, desperate for faith and consumed by melancholy. He had assured family and friends that he would meet them later, but then disappeared in the opposite direction.

Ashes to ashes, dust to dust. He hadn't slept much since the minister performed the committal ritual. Spades scraped and clinked as workmen lobbed dirt on top of the pine-box. He stood at a distance and lied to those who cared for him. The falsehood was intentional, but not hurtful or mean-spirited. Pain was a gnawing rodent tunneling its way through him. He had to be alone—the solitary confinement on the trail tracking a killer appealed to him.

Ashes to ashes, dust to dust. He bit down hard on his tongue to compel the recitation to vacate his mind. It did so, at least for now; only time would tell whether it was a temporary or permanent eviction. He tightened his arms over his chest. His wounded shoulder hurt. He felt feverish. The wind was making the whimpering squeals of an animal caught in a steel trap. He pushed aside the present circumstances and drifted backwards in time.

It was a bright blue summer day; one of the happiest of his life. His daughter, a beautiful young lady dressed in frills and finery, had returned from her sojourn at the women's academy in Philadelphia. She sat on the seat beside him and primly twirled a parasol. A proud grin filled his face as he drove the buggy along a laneway beside the river that led home.

"How was life in the big city?" he asked, gently elbowing her ribs.

She furrowed her brow. "I wrote you a long letter every month, Daddy."

"And I read them all at least a dozen times, Badger," he said firmly. He craned his neck to eyeball her. "But that's not the same as hearing an in person account."

"It was noisy and dirty. I enjoyed the green lawns of the campus, but did enough sightseeing to know I cannot understand why anyone would choose to live in houses stacked on top of each other," she told him. "I am thankful I had the opportunity to see and learn a different perspective, but city living is not for me. It's too crowded and claustrophobic."

"Your mother will be glad to hear that you're thankful."

"She knows, Daddy. We corresponded regularly," she said, narrowing her eyes on him. "She actually replied to every letter I wrote her. Unlike someone else I could mention."

"I ain't one to put pen to paper."

"It would have been nice to receive just one letter from you, Daddy."

He gave her a helpless shrug. His mouth pursed into a rigid line. He averted his eyes and spoke in a voice croaky with emotion. "Know that you're always in my heart, little girl."

She nodded tersely and looked away. Moisture formed in her pretty eyes.

"Whatever happened to that Davey fella?" he asked, nudging her.

"I sent him packing."

"Did he get fresh with you?"

She laughed roughly. "He tried once and I made him walk funny."

"That's my girl. Any other city slickers take a sweet-talking run at you?"

"No, Daddy."

He thought on that for a while. He guided the reins so the mule made a minor turn up a low incline. He gave her knee a tap. "Now that you're home your mother is planning a big fandango for you. She's got her eye on a couple eligible young men. I'm fairly sure she has her mind set on being a grandmother sooner rather than later."

"Mom's going to be disappointed because it will be later instead of sooner," she answered, shaking her head. "I've got too much riding and living to do before I settle in."

"That's just fine with me, Badger," he said, "but you know how inflexible your mother can get. Once that woman has a bee in her bonnet, it's all over and done."

"And you know me, Daddy. After all, you're the one who nicknamed me Badger."

"Well, that's true enough," he said proudly. "From the day you were born you ain't ever backed down from a battle. You'd dig in and get to tussling faster than lightning, but this here's a whole caboodle of difficulty. Your mother has her ways. I won't be fool enough to say who I'd wager on, but I'll tell you this; I ain't going to get betwixt or between that cat fight."

"Mom and I will work it out, Daddy. I promise."

They rode the rest of the way in silence. He pulled the carriage up near the hitching post, scrambled around and helped her down with much drama. He escorted her up the three stairs. She was fidgety, but played along with a genuine smile. He made a huge production of getting her to stand off to the side on the front porch. She obliged without any protest.

He removed his hat. He cleared his throat, opened the door in a grand sweeping gesture and boomed, "Presenting Miss Maxine Dawson." He took her by the hand and did a half-bow as he led her into the house. He spun her around. She dipped her head and did a wee curtsy.

The house smelled like fresh baked apple pie. Lacey was brushing her hands against her apron as she hurried out of the kitchen. Mother and daughter greeted each other with a fierce embrace and whispered words of affection. They leaned back and regarded each other for a long while before the younger one broke away and went down the hallway to her bedroom.

She returned less than five minutes later. She had changed into mid-calf leather boots, brown canvas trousers and a burnt orange work-shirt. Her hair was tied back. Her parents were waiting. The table was set and spread with a feast of steak, potatoes and all the fixings. She took her seat and announced, "Just so there are no further mistakes, I'm Max, not Maxine." She shoved a wooden-lipped smile at them. "And certainly not *Miss Maxine*."

Silas glanced at his wife, clapped his hands and chortled a roll of laughter. "You hear that, Lace? You can send the girl out of Texas, but you can't school Texas out of the girl." The grin encompassing his face became pinched as fiery pain returned him to the present.

He groaned low in his throat and forced himself to breathe deeply, evenly. The stinging jab was centered in his left shoulder and burned down his arm and across his chest. He sat still for a spell and allowed the delightful journey through the past to fade into obscurity. He got to his feet when he heard his horse snort through the sandstone walls.

He moved into the adjacent room that stabled the animal. He spoke some gruff kindness and the zebra dun greeted him by pawing the ground eagerly. He ruffled its mane, led it outside and set it loose to eat its fill of fresh snow. The stallion frolicked and kicked up its heels, undaunted by the blasting weather.

While the horse foraged, he ruminated on the thorny facts. The food-stuffs—both johnnycake biscuits for him and oats for his mount—were down to one insubstantial feed. He winced mightily as he took a careful peek at the wound. It felt like a red-hot fireplace iron spearing him. He gingerly lifted the poultice and muttered through clenched teeth.

The inflammation was spreading and the seepage of sickly yellow pus was increasing. If a low-grade fever wasn't already percolating, he knew that he would soon be suffering sweaty weakness. His choices were nonexistent. He couldn't last alone. Survival meant he had to find help. He would seize the tiniest opening in the weather and be on the move north.

Silas Dawson glared at the whirling tempest, seemingly daring it to defeat him.

Sally Twosongs woke up with severe distress across her lower back and a catch of breath in her throat. A film of perspiration made her skin clammy and cold. Her bladder was full. She sat up, tossed off the covers and swung her feet to the floor. Her husband stirred behind her. She whispered to him to go back to sleep. He turned over and tugged the blankets around him.

A night-vision, in which she had seen a swarthy bald man standing in inky shadows, was vibrant in her mind. This particular psychic break-through from the spiritual realm had been a frequent visitor for years, but she lacked any understanding of it. She had never met the man, but she *knew* him. In an intangible and unexplainable way, he gave her hope.

She stood and left the bedroom. She quietly hurried to the main door-way. An urge to get to the outhouse was increasing. Her socks were bunched around her ankles. She adjusted them properly and put her mukluks on, then pulled outerwear over her flannel nightclothes. She arranged a thick woolen scarf around her head and neck before going outside.

Snow was softly falling in huge fluffy flakes. Dawn was gray and bleak, cold and still as a tomb. Not a stitch of wind eased through the isolated valley—*WT Ranch* was in high country, walled in by ruggedly steep pinnacles of the San Juan Mountains. The stunning beauty of the site never failed to stir feelings in the chambers of her heart.

She moved as swiftly as possible through the knee-deep snow. She inevitably followed the well-worn pathway hidden beneath the white knolls. The discomfort in the small of her back increased and went straight through her abdomen. She felt faint and wobbly. Sour bile mushroomed in her throat as stabbing cramps assailed her.

She heard an owl hoot. Its song echoed eerily in the morning solitude. Despite her rush, she stopped and listened. Her kidneys issued a keen pang in complaint. The forlorn notes came from the barn and were low-pitched and short at first, but then the insistent *who-who* became louder and louder. She speculated about it; was it a warning or a genial greeting?

The hollow of her back suddenly kinked into a knot that tightened so forcefully that she bent over in the middle like a half-open jackknife. She gasped and nearly lost her balance. Her breathing sped up. She stoutheartedly gathered her wits, her watery eyes framed by etched lines of pain. She trod forward, teeth grinding as she waded through the snow

She fumbled with the latch. Her usually nimble fingers failed to function properly. She was trembling—she realized her whole body had an awful case of the shakes. She finally managed to get the door open. She closed it behind her and hunched her shoulders to let the coat fall. She hitched her nightgown up around her hips and dropped her bloomers.

She got sat down just in time. Urine gushed out, accompanied by rolling twitches and a discharge. She moaned under her breath. Her monthlies had always been unpredictable, but these symptoms were more erratic and pronounced than customary. The misery in the small of her back released and the tension across her midsection relaxed.

Her eyes widened. Comprehension settled in her. The oozing outflow was heavy. She clamped down on the inside of her bottom lip. She was thankful that in the box of newsprint paper there were several rags that could be put to good use. She quickly took care of all that needed attention, then arranged her clothing in anticipation of the elements.

When she crept outside, the owl was hooting nonstop. She wanted to communicate with the bird so she made her way toward the barn. A hot flash passed over her. She felt dizzy. The ebbing downturn of her strength seemed to dissipate into thin air. She was afraid she would take a tumble. There was a ringing in her ears and everything began spinning madly around her.

A blackish blur bounded through the snow toward her. She was crying.

The colorful curtains at the kitchen window were tied open. Naomi Axler vaguely watched the wafting snowflakes as she nursed her daughter and perused a letter that had arrived before the storm. The gray daylight was diffused. She had two oil lamps burning brightly on the table. The flames reflected moisture in her brooding brown eyes.

Her upper body swayed ever so slightly. Logs hissed and popped in the hearth of the cook-stove. The room was warm and cozy, the air permeated by the aroma of coffee brewing for she had put it on immediately upon rising. The week-old baby at her breast fed contentedly. She was, as of yet, unnamed—a round-faced chub-chub with a curly swatch of chestnut hair.

Naomi put the three-page letter down. The substance of the text disturbed her, though didn't prevent her from reading it repeatedly. There was nothing she could actually do about any of it, but she wanted to help and be of service. She heard her husband return from outside. A caress of tender emotion bubbled in her. She listened to him dawdling around the other room. His cheeks were rosy when he came through the doorway into the kitchen.

"Good morning, Pete," she said cheerfully. "The Arbuckle's should be ready."

"Morning." He gave her a meek nod and his pale eyes momentarily engaged hers. He got two large stoneware mugs and poured steaming coffee. He cautiously placed a cup within her reach and settled on a chair across from her. "There's an owl going cuckoo in the hayloft. It was tooting like a banshee as I plowed my way through the drifts back to the house."

"The weather's likely got the poor thing off kilter."

"I suppose," he replied, taking a hearty sip. "The stock in the barn is snug, but when this snow clears me and Caleb will have us a time rounding up those horses ranging free."

"And you'll both appreciate every moment."

He grinned in a subdued manner. "True enough." His eyebrows crunched into a frown, which deepened the permanent cast of his face. He made an indirect gesture at the letter. "I thought we decided to put that away and be done with it."

"Yes, we did, Pete," she agreed with a dejected shrug. "I'm sorry for revisiting it. The situation is so shocking I cannot get it out of my mind. I feel so helpless."

"I understand, Naomi," he said compassionately. "It vexes me too, but we can be of no assistance just now. You write Flora . . ." He stopped and gave her an apologetic smile. "You write Delores. Tell her we'll make a trip to Santa Fe come summer so she can hold baby girl." His smile broadened. "I'll get it posted as soon as possible. That's the best we can do."

She regarded him with mock annoyance. "Perhaps we can give baby girl a name by the time I get to that juncture in my correspondence to her."

"I can't go around on that any more, Naomi."

"Are you really putting the onus on me?"

"We've talked circles into the ground on it," he answered bluntly. "The list of options is longer than a giraffe's neck. I told you baby girl looks like an Abbey to me."

She sighed. "I respectfully disagree, Pete." She lifted her mug and took a large swallow of coffee. She cuddled the infant closer. "You know, I haven't had a letter from Abbey in six months or more, which is unsettling. I hope she and Sam are safe and doing well."

"Nice diversion, dear."

"It wasn't a diversion, Pete. I was just making an observation."

"Sam and Abbey are fine," he told her flatly. "They're probably hobnobbing with Buffalo Bill or other esteemed bigwigs in the wilds of Montana or some such place."

"You're likely correct, but it'd be nice to receive an update from Abbey."

"One will arrive soon enough."

The baby was finished suckling. She burped, as if on cue. Naomi modestly secured her smock. She held the child up in the crook of her arm, beaming at the wide-eyed miracle. "We are doubly blessed, Pete. I pray we never take God's goodness for granted."

"Life has indeed taken a few sweet turns for us."

"I am often in awe of our life together. I offer thanks continually to God."

He tossed off the last mouthful of coffee and swallowed it in a gulp. "I am grateful, truly I am. Your grace and grit has done much to put me in good standing with the Lord, but praying has to be your territory. My understandings of the Almighty's ways are sorely limited."

A single teardrop spilled down her cheek. She fingered it aside and said, "Be patient and receptive to him, Pete. The Lord will *always* be patient with you."

"Why are you crying, dear?"

"Happy tears. I'm so happy I should be sobbing."

He chuckled easily. "Are you happy enough to name baby girl?"

"Yes. My decision is made and it is final."

"Well . . ."

She held a hand up to silence him, motioning to the other room. There was a familiar shuffling sound. He shifted around a bit. An affectionate glance passed between them and in a few seconds, their son padded into the kitchen, dragging a blanket. The sleepy-eyed three-year old was in the middle of an enormous yawn. His sandy hair was askew and tangled.

Naomi coughed to clear her throat. "Good morning, my young gentleman." Her voice had a strict tone of formality in it. "I have an official introduction to make." She angled her arm to support the baby in an upright position. "Jesse Andrew say hello to Amanda Irene."

"Amanda Irene," Pete murmured quietly. "Beautiful. And a perfect fit." He reached out and his son climbed onto his lap. The boy wiggled in to give his father a huge hug.

"Doubly blessed, Pete,"

He eyed her. "Not me. I've got you so I'm triply blessed."

"Aren't you the sly one?"

"Not sly at all. Just being honest."

She tossed her head back and laughed joyfully. Her thick hair, long and loose on her shoulders, fluttered across her daughter like a brunette coverlet. She gently brushed it away. Amanda Irene cooed in response. She squirmed. Her legs and arms pumped actively. Naomi was radiant. The waterworks began in dribbles, which rapidly became a steady flowing stream.

Naomi Axler's heart was full. It couldn't contain her happiness.

Delores Solrizo had a sealed envelope in her hand. It was coarse parchment paper, as was the note inside. The addressee was unknown to her. She had accepted responsibility for delivery, but now was having second thoughts. She questioned whether the person to whom it belonged would ever show up in Santa Fe. She returned it to the mail slot on her desk.

She left her office, which was directly connected to the kitchen of the Suncurl Café. It was still quite early, but she was ready for the day's rewarding labors to begin. She had been wide awake for several hours. Her two-bedroom apartment was upstairs and entirely separate from it were three extra rooms to rent, two of which were currently unoccupied.

She was pleased and mostly at peace, though there were miserable occasions when the recurrent nightmare festered in her mind. There were no qualms or regrets about the choices she had made. She was fully satisfied with how her intentions had been realized. It had taken an investment of dollars along with much sweat and hard toil, but all was worth it.

The Suncurl Café had its impressive opening in the spring of '74 and straightway garnered a sizable reputation for generosity. Her establishment set an exceptional table, but it was more than a restaurant. All across town and along the trails it came to be known if anyone ever had need of anything all they had to do was go to the Suncurl Café and talk to the owner because she would do everything possible to help—food, clothing, housing.

Delores Solrizo was a chronic do-gooder. She entered the *Cantina Room*, which was the grand concourse of the enterprise; all activities and goings-on occurred here. Its dimensions were fifty by thirty feet, with a perfectly arranged series of matching tables and chairs, and a portion sectioned off near the kitchen for an ornate billiard table.

She moved through the elongated room purposefully. The décor was rustic with a touch of feminine elegance in the tablecloths and draperies. A large painting of a waterfall dominated one wall; it appeared as though the splashing mist from the river emerging from the lush green forest could be felt and tasted. She had commissioned a local artist to create the mural. There were a pair of bentwood rockers beneath it—in quiet breaks during the day she could be found sitting and admiring the serene landscape whilst visiting with a customer.

She went to the bay window and opened the pleated drapes to look out onto San Francisco Street, which had the topography of arctic terrain. Snow was drifting and blowing in cyclonic clouds. The hammering wind had lost none of its intensity. She took a seat on a cushion of the built-in bench to watch the awesome splendor of it.

She considered the letters she had written in late autumn, which had been about seeking counsel and processing her way through a sadly tragic development. There had been a sense of despondency in those missives, which lingered in some inner pothole for she still worried on an old friend from Abilene. She had made every effort to provide relief and support. She prayed for him; and wondered if he would ever accept her longstanding invitation.

The room was a bit chilly. She got up, unlocked the front door and went to the ample box stove in the center of the room opposite the picturesque artwork. She checked the fire. The bed of coals was sweltering and awaited an influx of fuel, and though the storage cradle was full of split firewood, she didn't bother restocking the hearth.

A pleasant smirk pursed her lips. She knew that within a half-hour all the necessary chores would be getting done by what she referred to as her breakfast crew; three men who regularly arrived on schedule to exchange brawn and vigor for an abundant meal. She went into the kitchen to do the fulfilling work of prepping food for others to enjoy and be nourished.

Delores Solrizo embodied what it meant to live out her true worth.

Ben Slaton was buried alive. The snow had amassed all around and over him to form a dank cavern; the piecemeal cedar boughs became excellent framework for the roof to be shingled by multiple layers of ice crystals. He convulsed with shivers, frozen from the inside out. His breathing was shallow. He winked in and out of consciousness.

It was dark and bleak. His air supply was diminishing. His campfire was cold, consisting of nothing but charred brushwood and unburned odds and ends. He was perspiring profusely. His lower right leg throbbed with numbness. There was a loud hum twanging in his ears that sporadically pierced through his skull like a barbed darning needle.

His belly hurt. The horrendous pain in his leg had generated ripe bile that churned in his stomach. He gagged involuntarily each time the rancid juices scaled his throat. His brain was agitated and disoriented, yet the elemental impulse to survive kept rising above the tumult. He still had remnants of self-discipline ramming at him.

A rush of agony tore through his head and ripped him apart. He screamed and screamed as the barbed needle twisted and screwed itself into a coiled spring that bounced relentlessly. He cricked into an upright position. The shrieking wail jetting from his throat was escorted by a sluice of regurgitated slime. When the hellish screech became nothing more than a gurgling whimper, he spat out the vile tasting vomit and wiped his mouth.

He was fully awake and aware. An upsurge of sheer clarity galvanized him. He needed an infusion of oxygen or else he would suffocate. His eyes were bugged open and he groped around the darkness. He had to fight against the dastardly destiny of death. If he could not mobilize the resources to do so, then the cave of snow would become his tomb.

His hand came into contact with an ash-covered stick. He attempted to use it like a bayonet to poke holes in the ceiling to provide air, but it broke in half. He uttered a slurred curse and reached for another leftover piece from the burnt out woodpile. He was careful and particular to choose a tool sturdy enough to accomplish his purpose.

Excitement trilled up his spine. He clutched hold of a two-foot stump, which he deemed would be sufficient. It took both hands and the bursting exertion of his muscles to slam it upwards. The first blow was greeted by resistance that sent a jolt of vibration through his upper body. Pain gouged at him. He groaned and clenched his teeth. He persisted and battered the log against the heavily-encrusted rooftop.

Success came in the form of disaster. The cedar branches collapsed on top of him, along with the crushing weight of snow. He thrashed around like a man drowning beneath the towering waves of an angry ocean. He gasped and sputtered. The air filling his lungs revived him; it was frigid and soggy with precipitation. The sky was still hemorrhaging snowflakes.

Hopelessness took dead center aim and struck him between the eyes. Anguish propelled him beyond sanity. His suffering was too much to bear. His body was a shuddering mass of excruciating pain. He clawed and dug himself out enough to get to his Remington. He withdrew the pistol from its holster and did an inspection to verify that the barrel was clear of debris.

Ben Slaton closed his eyes and delicately put a finger on the trigger.

Gilgal stopped without warning. The change was so abrupt that its rider, who was dozing in and out of a catnap, almost fell from the saddle. Deacon Coburn tightened his grip and gathered his senses. Visibility was reduced to a mere ten yards or so in any direction. He wasn't exactly sure of his whereabouts, but figured to be in the middle of Glorieta Pass.

The silver-dappled buckskin neighed and skittishly danced a kind of high-stepping jig. He bent over and spoke soothing words while stroking its mane. A surly noise startled him. He couldn't identify it, but above the riotous wind, he discerned that it seemed to be closeby. He coaxed Gilgal forward. The gelding resisted, then eased along at a tentative pace.

Coburn was on edge. He squinted and stiffened when a horse snorted. Gilgal whinnied in response. A brown form emerged in the whiteness. It was a bay with no rider, evidently lost and alone. Gilgal came alongside it. Coburn gave the animal an assessing once-over. Its nostrils were caked with ice and dripping gobs of mucous; its eyes pleaded with him. It was saddled and provisioned, with a bedroll on its backside and a rifle in its scabbard.

He reached over and took hold of its reins. It was then that a racket erupted from a short distance away; the fury of the wind could not contain or obscure it. A gunshot rang out, followed instantaneously by a bloodcur-dling bewailing that reverberated and was not suppressed by the high-speed roaring of five more shots.

Gilgal lurched in its tracks; as did the bay. Both animals were stressed. Coburn hurried them in the direction of the wail that was now a choked retching. In thirty yards he saw a man half covered in snow and fumbling with a pistol, unmistakably attempting to reload. He dismounted, looped the reins together and ordered Gilgal to stay put.

Coburn trudged as quickly as possible. The trickery of wishful thinking might be fooling him, but he guessed the wind was losing some of its force. He reviewed the scene, taking in all the nuance of details that told the story. It didn't take a great deal of brain power to put the pieces together and surmise the situation. He intended to intervene and prevent any further gunfire.

As he got closer, the man glowered at him, groggy-eyed. "Leave me to it . . ."

"Ain't going to be no more of that," Deacon said, calm and adamant. He lunged and grabbed hold of the pistol. Bullets scattered and disappeared beneath the snow.

"Now what am I going to do?"

"If I got any sway in the matter, you ain't going to be a croaker." Coburn knelt and methodically examined him. His broken leg was bloated wreckage. There was a black powder burn on the right side of his face. The rutted streak was raw and puffed-up.

He spoke in a strained rasp. "There ain't no hope. Shoot me."

"I can't spare the ammo," Deacon said drolly.

"If 'in I was a horse you'd put me out of my misery."

"You ain't no horse," Deacon replied, rising. "I've got jobs to do. You sit tight." He took a couple backward steps to study the area. "I'll strip and care for our horses, get a blaze going to heat us up, slap together some sort of shelter, then have a go at splinting that leg."

"I ain't going nowhere."

Coburn nodded and wagged a finger at him, then spun around and enthusiastically bore into the tasks. When he had the horses properly tended to, he paused for several seconds to take a gander at the blizzard. A smile made his eyes taper into thin slits. The wind *was* dying down.

Kid Greer had the attributes of a rabid weasel. He was slouch-eyed and salivating as he circled the woman. His teeth were bared and the nostrils of his flattened nose were tilted upwards as though he was sniffing the air, which was swamped by a cloying funk of tobacco smoke. A drumming chant emanated from behind him and filled the room. He was slinking around in a semi-crouch, with his arms outstretched and his hands contorted into claws.

The woman was defiant. Bloodied and bruised, she had her focus fixed on her assailants. Her eyes, as dry as desert sand, were gleaming disdain. She resisted and refused to be humiliated by the grievous abominations visiting her. The steel of her backbone would never allow her to surrender. She would fight until her last breath was snatched away.

She was tied on a chair in her kitchen, arms bound behind her by rawhide thongs. Her blouse and chemise had been torn; her flesh exposed. There were crisscrossed lacerations from her neck to her belly button. Her back was mutilated by the same blood-drenched design. The knife-blade artistry had been performed by the white-haired man sitting cross-legged on the floor singing a sinister incantation while smoking a short-stemmed pipe with a skull-like bowl.

Kid Greer swooned, intoxicated by the rhythms rising and falling in the wizened man's distinctive bass voice. His feet began shuffling in a quick two-step shimmy. The mantra spurred him to new heights of violence. He wrapped his hands around the woman's neck and began strangling her. He danced freakishly, squeezing harder and harder as the song hit a rolling crescendo. She writhed and thrashed until the final shudder of her death throes.

An easily recognizable voice shouted, enraged and frightfully unnerved. The panic of it sliced through Max Dawson—she came awake erratically, sweated and gasping. She kicked and punched the air. There was icepick pain thrusting behind her eyes. Her vision was distorted by a deluge of tears. She was disoriented and unfamiliar with her quarters. The reek of horse manure brought realization; she had spent the night bedded down in the livery.

She steadied her breathing and palmed wetness off her brow. Her saddle was on the straw-littered floor behind her. She crawled backwards to perch on it, elbows resting on knees. Her head ached from the persistent dream, which was based on a reconstruction of the crime by the first man to arrive on the scene. The haunting surfaced unbidden and unwanted; a byproduct of her overwrought imagination reenacting the horrific events that had her on the trail.

In her twenty-third year, she was possessed by sorrow. It maliciously bedeviled her. The atrocity of her mother's murder shocked her sensibilities awry. Grief was a boiling cauldron in her soul that had mutated into a craving need for vengeance. The squalling weather had dictated this stop in Santa Fe, but wouldn't redirect or lessen her resolve to avenge the brutality.

Max Dawson stood and readied to go outside in search of a hot meal.

At the Suncurl Café, Avis Lahay had just finished wiping down the tables after the breakfast rush, which due to the windswept streets had been inconsequential. She was alone in the *Cantina Room* at the billiard table racking the balls to get in a few minutes of extra practice. She enjoyed shooting pool and had discovered an innate affinity for angles.

She sank two balls on the break and took a purposeful stroll around the table to evaluate the sequence of options. Just then the door opened and along with blustery currents of cold, a cowboy entered, a bedroll slung over one shoulder and saddlebags balanced on the other. The hat and calf-length duster were heavily sprinkled in snow.

Avis returned her cue to its slot on the wall rack. She hurried over to greet the customer, who had chosen a spot against the wall near the box stove. "What can I get for you?"

"Coffee, for starters. Please and thank you."

Avis halted in mid-step, surprised and wide-eyed. "You're a lady!"

"Max," she replied, peeling off her coat. She set it on the chair where she had already placed the bedroll and saddlebags. "I have a lady's plumbing and have even been to lady school, but you'd be hard pressed to find any man tougher than me." She removed her hat and put it on the table, finger combing her wavy hair as she did so. "Please have the cook fix me a full plate of whatever is tasty and available. I'm hungry, but not at all fussy."

Avis gave her a nod and headed to the kitchen. A few minutes later, she returned with an oversized mug and an earthenware carafe. "Here you go. Enjoy."

Max was seated with her back toward the wall. She was eyeing the waterfall mural. She removed a red-checkered kerchief that had been knotted around her neck. "If you can manage the time to sit a spell, I'd appreciate the company. I've been alone on the trail from San Antonio."

"That's a long ride," Avis said, smiling. She sat and introduced herself.

"Glad to make your acquaintance, Avis." Max poured a coffee and leaned back. She warmed her hands by encircling them around the cup rested on her lap.

"Are you a cowgirl?" Avis asked innocently.

Max laughed. "I doubt I ever thought of myself in that way."

"Why not?"

"I'm not sure, Avis. I'm just me."

"Do you herd cattle?"

"I've spent a fair amount of time around longhorns, especially during spring round up," Max answered, sipping her coffee. "It's not my first choice for work. Mostly I've been involved in chasing bandits or capturing wild mustangs."

Avis was enthralled. "That sounds exciting and dangerous."

"It is."

"Are you ever scared?"

"No, being scared is only for greenhorns or sissies," Max said earnestly. "The trail is no place for those slacker types. One must ride with an expectation of trouble, well provisioned and prepared. Fear comes only when one hasn't been wary and watchful."

"How did you learn? How'd you get started?"

"I was born to it."

Avis frowned. "Really?"

"It's all I have ever known. It's all I ever want to do."

Avis leaned forward to have a closer look at the black Stetson. She was intrigued by the hatband. She tentatively touched it and recoiled. "What is that? Where'd you get it?"

"It's snakeskin."

"Snakeskin? Yuck!"

Max rolled her eyes and grinned. "How old are you, Avis?"

"I just turned fourteen a few days ago."

"I was your age when I killed that rattler," Max said offhandedly. "It was a six-footer. It was then that my parents started talking about sending me east to become ladylike."

Avis stared, sincerely fascinated and somewhat charmed, though the snakeskin made her squeamish. Curiosity was a living thing tiptoeing around the edges of her mind. She started to reply, but then heard her name being called from the other room. She excused herself and scurried into the kitchen, anxious to return and resume the conversation.

Gray Cloud was a nervous Nellie. He kept muttering nonsensical comments that were a collection of disjointed fragments. He was a newshound stuck in a tizzy. There were a dozen newspapers on the floor in the Weitzel's living room. He had them spread out and was on his hands and knees, searching for a specific article, and becoming more and more frustrated.

"Maybe it's not there," Eliza offered softly. She sat beside her husband, on a couch that they had designed and built together. Hans had selected, cut and seasoned the lumber before framing it with tongue and groove joints, reinforced by hardwood pegs at crucial junctures. She had stuffed and quilted the pillows, which were multicolored, practical and comfortable.

Gray Cloud's head and shoulders were shaking robustly. "I will find it. You must be patient and prime your hearts for what is to come from my mouth."

"Just get to it without the histrionics," Hans said, noticeably irritated.

Gray Cloud sat back on his bottom, a newspaper clutched to his chest. "I apologize for the histrionics." His face was almost perfectly round and domineered by plump cheeks, which just now were pushed up by a prodigious smile that nearly shuttered his eyes. "I have found the article as I said I would. I will read the important part and go from there, hunky-dory?"

Eliza restrained a grin at his use of slang. His command of English was impressive, due to his diligence as a student under her tutelage. He demanded perfection and had the capacity to switch from Navajo to English in mid-sentence. "Please proceed, Gray Cloud."

He folded the paper and traced a finger across it until he came to the relevant section. "Listen to this," he said, then cleared his throat with a cough and read in a precise cadence. "*Smoky Crowe was identified leaving the crime scene by the victim's husband. The Indian was in cahoots with the outlaw Kid Greer, a white man. Texas Rangers were dispatched to give chase, but the pair of killers eluded the posse and vanished.*"

"That's not new information to us," Hans said tonelessly. "We read that account."

"It's a horrible story, Gray Cloud." Eliza leaned forward, attempting to be sympathetic and encouraging. "I can't imagine the family's loss, but Hans and I are bewildered by your insistent anxiety over a murder that took place nearly a thousand miles away."

"Smoky Crowe is here," Gray Cloud stated, almost cavalierly.

"Here? Where here? New Mexico?" Hans asked, eyes pulling tight.

Gray Cloud took a deep breath and shivered. The ghost bead necklaces were hanging outside the collar of his homespun shirt. He held them against the palms of his hands. "I know nothing of Kid Greer, but as sure as the sun appears each morning, Smoky Crowe is here. After a kill, he returns to wastelands to worship and make offerings."

Hans balked by throwing his arms up in exasperation. "Why here? It sounds like hogwash to me, Gray Cloud. There are many barren stretches between here and San Antonio."

"Angel Peak is his sacred evil place."

Eliza slid and leaned closer to him. "How do you know, Gray Cloud?"

"I cannot . . ." Gray Cloud's complexion reddened into darker hues, then quickly became pasty pale. His eyes filled with moisture. "I fear Smoky Crowe. I am alive only by chance."

Hans mimicked his wife's posture, plainly intrigued. His hands were clasped together, forearms resting on his thighs. "I must hear more about that butcher, Gray Cloud."

"My words will hurt your ears."

"I suspect I'm durable enough to handle it."

"As am I," Eliza said strongly.

Gray Cloud fidgeted with the ghost beads. "I have never told this to anyone. It is a stain of blackness on my soul that shames me. I do not want to lose your respect."

Eliza sighed in a motherly manner. "You are family, Gray Cloud. There's nothing in your past that'll change our kinship. We value and have much fondness for you."

The Navajo man bowed his head. His black hair, longish and shiny, hid his face. He held that position for several hushed moments, gathering all that he needed to say. As he began to speak, he flipped his hair back and looked straight at her. "Gray Eyes had only kind words about you and Hans. He had tenderness for the Weitzel family. I was not always mindful of my grandfather, but it was his wisdom that brought me here and kept me all these years.

"When I was young, before the unnatural migration to Fort Sumner and the embittered tears shed along the Pecos River, I hated the whites. There was contrariness in me that desired a witch doctor's medicine to do battle against them. Gray Eyes counseled and warned me, but I would not listen. I was inattentive and my foolishness brought me plentiful misery.

"I was alone in the badlands seeking when I met Smoky Crowe. He invited me to partake as he performed a hexing ritual to destroy the white man. He is Ute and there is enmity between our people; I should've departed, but was in rebellion. He proclaimed power and magic, using rattlesnakes as though harmless. He has a bewitching eye that enchanted me."

Gray Cloud's hands were visibly trembling, but his voice remained controlled. "It is told that Smoky Crowe wrestled with the ancient Jester. The eye the Creator gave him was gouged out and replaced with taboo crystals. I fell under his wizardry. Whoever follows him becomes devoted to his mania. I tried to stay on the fringe, but cannot say I succeeded.

"I saw him brutalize and murder an Apache squaw for no reason except the sheer pleasure it gave him. Her screams were ear-splitting, his laughter frenzied. He has a curved knife that he wields as a painter would a brush. When he was finished splaying her skin in strips, he carved her heart out and ate it while smoking bowl after bowl of peyote-laced tobacco.

"It was then that I escaped and have been looking over my shoulder ever since." He exhaled a disgruntled hiss of air. "Many seasons have gone into the past, but still, if he comes upon me, he will kill me as an example for others to understand that Smoky Crowe is the biggest toad in the puddle." His eyes were teary; his countenance full of regrets. "I have seen the face of evil and been forever changed. My life is before and after Smoky Crowe. Formerly I was brave and courageous; afterwards I am a worrywart and fraidy cat."

Eliza shifted sideways, eyes narrowed. "This is not hogwash, Hans."

"No. No, it isn't, Eliza."

"Angel Peak is his sacred evil place. Smoky Crowe is here."

Hans Weitzel locked his arms over his chest. "You have our support and resources, Gray Cloud. No matter what comes, we will make our stand together. Is that clear?"

Gray Cloud bobbed his head. Reflective silence shrouded the room.

Silas Dawson had been after Smoky Crowe for more than a decade. The malignant blood feud between them began when the renegade led painted for glory raiders to slaughter settlers in the hill country of west Texas. Eleven adults were grossly violated, dismembered into bits; four children were kidnapped, which for Captain Dawson, immediately made it personal.

He recruited a crew of six Texas Rangers to go in pursuit; seven hardened and capable men whose goal was to rescue the children and in the process, administer swift and righteous justice. They followed the northerly trail for a month, driven by bloody mile-markers. One by one, they came upon a mangled child; then Smoky Crowe's war party disappeared.

The Rangers went above and beyond in endeavoring to find even a hint of sign, but it was as though the wind had swallowed the Indians. It was on the ride back to San Antonio that Silas Dawson swore a vow. He would retool and regroup; neither hellfire nor any affliction or hazard would prevent him from putting a noose around Smoky Crowe's neck.

In the years that followed, there had been epic chases, but in all their history he had only ever gotten close enough to see the Ute witch twice—and those occurrences, only recently. The first time came about under soul-sickening circumstances that demanded that he remain behind. His heart galloped in his chest and a scream of disbelief scorched his throat.

It was an afternoon a week before Christmas. The air had crispness in it, but wasn't particularly cold. Twilight colors were stretching across a still and spectacularly blue sky. He was relaxed in the saddle as he came up from the river, returning from a three-day campout with his daughter. She lagged miles behind, tracking a mule deer and having solitary fun.

When Silas Dawson crested the rise, the log home came into view and he was startled to see a pair of horses picketed near the porch. He momentarily paused and studied the animals, but perceived no familiarity. He walked his mount closer, eyes tightening. The follicles of downy hair on the nape of his neck were goosed. He heard chanting and smelt tobacco smoke.

Perception came as a pick-axe that pulverized him from the inside out. He sprang off the zebra dun and sprinted into action. The front door swung open. Dawson had his pistol drawn and at the ready when he stutter-stepped to a stop. Air gushed from his lungs as a hatchet-faced warrior emerged, barking uproarious laughter. The man was tall and rangy, with a skeletal frame and wrinkly skin. Beside him was a flat-nosed runt.

Silas Dawson was face to face with Smoky Crowe. Twenty yards separated them. He fired pointblank, but the bullet apparently missed. Disbelief creased his face. He exercised deliberate patience, aimed and pulled the trigger twice more. Both slugs had no visible effect. He squeezed off another shot, which was as harmless as a cotton batten ball.

Their gaze connected. Dawson's insides froze. His bones were suddenly weighted. He couldn't move. It was as though his legs were buried knee-deep in sludge. Smoky Crowe slowly waved a hand back and forth, head tilted oddly to the right. Dawson was almost hypnotized by the milky left eye fixated on him—there was no pupil, only a menacing grayish bulb.

Smoky Crowe was giggling and muttering mumbo-jumbo. His voice was sonorous and full-toned; there was magnetic power in the rasping phrases. The hand he kept seesawing in a slow and rhythmic manner had long clumps of hair clutched in it, which dangled lifelessly. He and his partner scampered to their horses, mounted and rode off.

Dawson came out of his trance and raced into the house. It was then that a bawling shriek ripped out of him. He skidded and crumpled in front of the brutalized remains of Lacey Coe Dawson. She was trussed by rawhide on a kitchen chair. Her strawberry-blonde loveliness had been hacked off at the scalp. He wrapped his arms around her bleeding torso and clung to her with a shuddering fierceness. He wept in her lap, defenseless and vulnerable.

A wrathful rage roiled in him. He fortified it; he wallowed in it.

The second time Silas Dawson laid eyes on Smoky Crowe was two days before the storm started. It was a showdown, in which Smoky Crowe had been lying in wait to ambush him. The midday sky had an ominous look, with the sun encased in densely oppressive graveyard clouds. Dawson had been saddle-bound since the first glow of daylight. He dismounted and led the stallion along, stretching the cramps out and loosening the tension in him.

He surveyed the rolling contours of the high desert. It was lonesome beauty graced by the charm of boulders arising from a sea of sagebrush. He was reaching for his canteen when Smoky Crowe crept into view, seemingly materializing from behind a colossal standing stone. His wispy white hair fluttered in the breeze. He had his bow in hand, arrow aimed.

Dawson held steady in his footsteps. His right hand didn't hesitate. He pulled and fired twice, and was positive that both shots struck flesh. "You *will* die, you bastard."

"No luck, Ranger," Smoky Crowe said, wincing slightly. "Your bullets cannot hurt me."

"I've got a short rope. The noose is already knotted."

Smoky Crowe grinned and angled his head at that peculiar sideward angle. "My death song will be sung at a time of my choosing," he said, as his disfigured left eye widened and seemed to pulse. "I have no time to toy with you as I did your woman, but I will kill you." In a fluid movement, he released the arrow. It hummed straight and true, striking the muscles of Dawson's shoulder. The impact spun him partially around and dropped him to his knees.

His assailant was gone. The fiery pain was horrendous.

Ashes to ashes, dust to dust. Silas Dawson came out of his feverish stupor. The remembrances galled him. He was sweating and shaking. He got up and moved stiffly. He had a peek at the wound from the arrow Smoky Crowe had put in him—it was leaking a continuous ooze of yellowish goop. He desperately required assistance.

He stepped outside his shelter. It was nighttime. The wind had withdrawn and there was stillness in the frosty air. It was the opportunity he had been seeking. He joggled his arms and legs in an effort to eliminate some kinks. The sky was a cloudless black canvas sparkling with stars from horizon to horizon. He took it all in and came to a decision.

A grim smile puckered his mouth. "Only quitters and losers stay down," he said, sucking in a deep breath. With that, he broke camp and packed up. In less than ten minutes, Silas Dawson was on horseback taking a northeasterly route that would carry him out of Chaco Canyon.

Sally Twosongs was missing. Caleb Weitzel had a sense of urgency in him and was on the lookout for her. The fact that Hank was also nowhere to be found gave Weitzel a scintilla of comfort, but not enough. His wife had been gone when he arose in the morning, which didn't alarm him because it was not at all out of the ordinary for her—she was Sally Twosongs and often disappeared at dawn to go on mystic wanderings.

There'd been no contact with her all day. He hadn't been markedly concerned until nightfall because he expected her to be safe and warm at her usual hideaway; a storage shed nestled in an aspen grove. He rode to it at dusk and discovered that there had been a fire in the potbelly stove, but that was hours ago because the coals were cold.

Now, beneath a starlit sky, he was atop Shadrach following tracks that led homeward. The steeldust trotted effortlessly. It automatically slowed and came to a halt in front of the entrance to the barn. He shimmied off, opened the doors and walked the stallion inside. He allowed it to wander to its stall as he lit a lantern. He fully intended to strip off its gear and give it a thorough rubdown, but then a tricolor collie came running to him.

He knelt and grabbed its collar of shaggy hair. "Hank, where's Sally Twosongs?"

The dog barked twice and ran over to the ladder that led to the hayloft. It stood on its hind legs and put its front paws on the third rung, yapping insistently. With the kerosene lamp in hand, Caleb climbed to the loft to find her sitting slumped over on a bale of hay.

"I've been looking for you, Sally Twosongs."

"I'm sorry, Caleb."

An emotional hitch in her voice startled him. "What's wrong?"

"Our baby died."

He took a knee in front of her. A puzzled frown darkened his brow. "Our baby?"

"I was seven, perhaps eight weeks along," she replied dully. "I wanted to surprise you. I was waiting for a special time, but it doesn't matter anymore. I lost our baby this morning."

He removed his hat and set it beside the lantern. He put his arms around her and pulled her close. She was limp in his embrace. He rubbed her back and stroked her long hair. "I didn't know . . . I had no idea, *lucero*. I must be as dumb as a stump."

"I'm sorry, Caleb."

"I should've been with you today."

"I needed to be alone, Caleb. You know how I am."

"I love how you are, Sally Twosongs."

She laid her head on his shoulder. "I was here for a while, but spent most of the day snuggled in the shed amongst the aspens. Hank kept me company and listened to me cry."

"I am so sorry, *lucero*."

"There's nothing you could have done, Caleb." She pressed in tighter to him. "There was an owl here early this morning. It was noisy and acting agitated. I expected some help or wisdom from it, but that was not to be. It mocked me—its jeering frightened me."

He was incredulous. "An owl frightened you?" A hoarse chuckle rumbled low in his throat. He locked his hands against the small of her back. "Sally Twosongs you have more strength and pluck than anyone I've ever known. I've seen you running with wolves and treating them as pets. How could you possibly be frightened by an owl?"

"It was not the owl that frightened me."

"What then?"

"It's ridicule and contempt. A bad omen."

"Put those ideas out of your mind."

"It was laughing at me, Caleb."

He was speechless for a time, which was often the case when communicating with her. She had a heightened sensitivity to otherworldly dealings that often discombobulated him. "I cannot fathom that at all, Sally Twosongs. What does it mean?"

"I may remain barren."

"Don't speak such words, *lucero*." He squeezed her even closer. "You're upset and out of sorts. Your outlook is being filtered through grief."

She heaved a sigh. "It's more than that, Caleb."

"What?"

Her whole body shook. "I cannot . . ."

He clung to her until the trembles passed. He relaxed his hold and leaned back to peer into her dark eyes. "I love you, Sally Twosongs. And you love me. Nature will take its course. In the proper time our bedroom carrying-on will result in us growing a family."

"Our love, as passionate as it is, may not bear fruit. I'm sorry, Caleb."

He gently kissed her lips, then planted one on each cheek. "We are together in this, so I will not hear another apology from you, Sally Twosongs. You are my best friend and my *lucero*, my little bright star. Whatever comes our way, we will walk through it hand in hand."

She managed a feeble smile. "I'm hungry."

"Let's care for Shadrach, then I'll cook your favorite supper."

She nodded agreeably. He scooped up his hat and the lantern, and went down the ladder first. He took hold of her hips and backside to lift her to the floor. He turned her to face him and their arms entwined in an intense hug that melted pretense and all walls of resolve. The silence became loud as their tears of sadness and remorse mingled to be fashioned into hope.

Hank watched them, wagging its tail and whining softly.

≈ ≈ ≈

Delores Solrizo sat in her office turning the sealed envelope over and over. Anxiety was doing nasty things to her digestive tract. The addressee was in the *Cantina Room* and had been since mid-morning, but she had avoided delivery. She waited and waited. She wanted there to be no one present when she handed it over—no witnesses because she suspected a conversation would arise which had the potential for several distasteful turns.

It was late and past her bedtime. She moistened her fingers and pinched the candles out on her desk. She stood and slipped the letter into a pocket of the apron she had been wearing most of the day. She strolled through the kitchen and into the *Cantina Room*. The lamps on the walls were turned low. She went to the occupied table near the box stove.

"I'm Delores Solrizo. I run this place."

"It's quite a joint. Max Dawson. Happy to meet you."

"I should've greeted you much earlier."

"Avis told me you'd come see me before she went upstairs."

Delores sat down across from her. "Is your father Silas Dawson?"

Max smiled and nodded. "I sometimes forget he has a bit of fame."

"I only recently met him," Delores said warmly. "A kindhearted gentleman, if there ever was one. He stopped in here two weeks before this storm started and left a note for you." She retrieved the envelope and handed it to her. "He was adamant about you receiving it."

"Two weeks? He's *that* far ahead of me." Max let out a rushing grumble of breath. She gave a smirky grin and fingered her name written in bold strokes. She wasted no time in breaking the seal and sliding the paper out. It was a small single sheet, folded once. She sat back and held it close to read the message twice. She could hear her father's voice in her head.

> *Leave it alone, Badger. Sometimes the price to purchase pieces of justice is too damn high. Find your own trail and live a life that makes a difference. Daddy.*

The tiniest glint of dampness showed in her eyes. She stared off in the middle distance. Her mouth compressed into a straight line of determination as she stuffed the directive into the envelope. She reached over to pull a large leather wallet from an inside pocket of her duster and placed it in it. The jotting was destined to remain with her until the day she died.

"Can I help?"

"Only if you can make time go backwards."

Delores tentatively broached the topic that would be displeasing on so many levels. "I read the newspaper reports about your mother's murder.

There is no language strong enough to express my sorrow. I am truly sorry for your loss."

"I do thank you for that, though at this point, words are meaningless," Max replied, a dull hardness in her voice. She opened the portfolio on the table, touched the letter from her father, then removed a trifold flier. She smoothed the creases and lifted it up. "These two brutes are responsible. I will not rest until Smoky Crowe and Kid Greer are fodder for buzzards."

Delores bit the inside of her bottom lip. She stared at the crude black lines drawn as a portrait of her son and fought to keep her composure. She had heard all the stories of his violence and crimes, and was sickened by it. Her guilt for abandoning him could slither out from under the forgiveness and grace she had embraced; it would rear up and hurl depraved accusations. Her hands were shaky as she took hold of the wanted poster to study it.

Max lowered her eyebrows, ostensibly confused by the woman's reaction. "That's the first ever picture sketched of Smoky Crowe," she said coolly. "It's taken from my father's description, the only white man to ever see the cunning savage and live to tell about it."

Delores never even glanced at Smoky Crowe. Her attention was riveted on the likeness of the man who had been planted in her womb as a consequence of incest. She had a bellyache that abruptly expelled a geyser of sourness; it clotted at the back of her throat. She covered her mouth and closed her eyes, forcing a swallow and stifling the gag reflex.

"Are you alright?" Max asked, leaning toward her.

Delores flinched and gave her head a slight nod. "Just over tired and indigestion." She got to her feet and dropped the leaflet on the table. Her breathing was erratic and it took several moments for her to steady it. Her cheeks were blushed and blotchy. "There are two vacant rooms upstairs. You are welcome to bunk in either of them."

"If it's all the same to you, the floor here will be adequate for me," Max answered, offering an easygoing shrug. "I'll be at it before any customers show up in the morning."

"That'll be fine. Goodnight." Delores smiled convincingly. She departed in a rush. Her emotions were reeling, her heart aching. Tears flowed profusely. She tried to squash them, but the surge could not be quelled. The wretchedness of bygone years mortified her. She thought of the collateral ripples of her life—residual payments from the past that never stopped doling out cruel dividends. She climbed the stairs to her apartment. She prayed. Then prayed some more.

An hour later, she was whimpering as she fell asleep.

~ ~ ~

Charley Jondreau had done a prodigious amount of traveling. He was worn out to the bones, as was his pony. Beneath a canopy of stars he had made camp in a rocky grotto near a bank of the Rio Grande. The accommodations had obviously been well-used by others; the previous occupants left behind a generous supply of firewood against the back wall.

He had set a fire in a charred pit near the mouth of the low-roofed chamber, which caused the smoke to draft outside in thin bands. The pinto was behind him, its feedbag in place. He had given it the end of its mixture of oats and molasses. He squatted on his haunches close to the campfire, munching on a slice of beef jerky while ruminating.

The night was conducive to clear thinking but Jondreau's head was jumbled. He had no appreciation for chaos. He much preferred to be orderly and precise, but his gray matter was a mushy morass. He couldn't get the bronze-skinned maiden out of his mind. He had never met her, but she often captured a place in his clairvoyant flashes—she returned to him again and again. There was something extraordinary about her that enraptured him.

It wasn't solely her beauty, though from what he had *seen* of her, she was wholesome and strikingly attractive. The marvel of her dark eyes contained deposits of untold wealth. An inner shine radiated from her core; there was curious wonder in it. He had contemplated her on many occasions and came to consider her a princess from some ancient royal line.

In the six years since initially *seeing* her, he had concluded that somehow their lives were inextricably connected as kindred spirits gifted by the Great Spirit; what awaited them was to be brought together to accomplish his purposes. His knowledge as to her location or situation was null and void, yet he had confidence that in the fullness of time all would be unveiled. It was quite difficult to comprehend, but Charley Jondreau had ascertained long ago that the Great Spirit's means and methods were steeped in mysterious riddles.

The Creator's ways were far beyond the plans and contrivances of humans. It was not at all feasible to expect an explanation or understanding to come in a neat little box. He merely accepted the mindboggling perplexity of the unseen world and kept his senses alert for any communiqué delivered along the vibrantly alive grapevine of creation.

He finished his meal. He was grateful for the roomy vault that provided shelter. He put another log on the fire and moved the coffee pot to a level spot. He removed his hat and ran a hand over the bristly stubble from below his chin to the top of his head. In the morning, he intended to boil some snow, lather up and be entirely clean shaven before riding off.

He sat back and settled on the bedroll. A punch-drunk tiredness teetered along the corridors of his brain. He did his utmost to subdue and bring order to the disarray, but then the smell of the skunk came over him like a loathsome blanket.

Ramrod stiffness gripped him and he couldn't elude it. His body straightened out like a felled tree. The veins in his neck bulged and his head shook as though he had palsy. His eyelids fluttered spasmodically for more than a minute, then gaped open with only the whites showing. His hands were fisted. He began boxing the air.

Inside the phenomenon it was blank and uninhabited; he couldn't *see* or *hear* anything. There was vast emptiness. He searched the ill-defined spaces for any clues, but there were none. Frustration arose within him. He strained his ears to pick up any swish of movement that would indicate what was happening, only to be denied.

His body quaked violently when the quirky episode released him. He hastily found his bearings and reached for discernment—he inherently realized that the problematic vision had complex layers of substance. There was significance to be unearthed, extracted and refined. His nostrils flared as he flushed out a blast of air and pinpointed his concentration.

He stretched out on his back, with his fingers interlocked behind his head. Not for the first or last time the conundrum troubled him to the point of annoyance, which was directed inward, but not for long; he soon set it free because anger was useless. He replayed the incident over and over, linking it to whatever insightful grains could be gleaned from experience.

He listened attentively to the night, which kept him company until fitful sleep came over him. He tossed and turned. The travails of conflict and confusion had hold of him, and would not allow any peace. In a dream that was on an unending loop, he saw the dark-eyed woman. She was crying. And Charley Jondreau suffered through the paralysis of helplessness.

chapter two

The Arrival

"Who is wise, and he shall understand these things? prudent, and he shall know them? for the ways of the Lord are right, and the just shall walk in them: but the transgressors shall fall therein."

~Hosea~

At dawn, Deacon Coburn had the fire stoked and the coffee on. He stood with his back to the flames, studying the sky. The wind had diminished to occasional gusts and the snow was negligible mist, but deeply marbled clouds were mobilizing for another assault. He measured the choices and chances ahead, then went and crouched beside his patient.

Slaton eyed him blearily. "What's the verdict?"

"You fancy hanging around here?"

"Hell, no. I've had enough of this scenery."

Coburn thumbed aside his bushy moustache. "It'll be hard slogging, but if you can stay in the saddle, we could make it to the warmth and hospitality of the Suncurl Café."

Slaton raised an eyebrow and grinned. "I ain't ever been there, though I've heard that a good-looking redhead runs it. I'd crawl out of my casket to poke a redhead."

Coburn's face hardened into a wrinkled mask that was easily readable.

"Is she your woman?" Ben asked, giving a lame shrug.

"A longtime friend who is family. She deserves respect," Deacon replied bluntly. "You'd be wise to keep that in mind *if* you're still alive when we get to Santa Fe."

"I didn't mean nothing, mister. I'll be on my best behavior."

Coburn assessed the jerry-rigged splint. It consisted of four reasonably straight branches chopped off a scrub pine tree. He had manipulated the leg and lashed the wood in place with strands of leather. He fingered the knots and was satisfied. "How's the leg feeling?"

"I mean to tell you," Ben said, voice rising excitedly, "while you were doing the job on it I thought you were gonna kill me. I ain't ever had such a hurting put on me."

"The bones needed to be set proper. You passed out."

"Did I really?"

"How's the pain now?"

"Fair to middling. I'll be ready to ride."

Coburn got up and went to the coffee pot. Two tin mugs waited to be filled. "Our horses had a solid feed, which finished off the grain I had packed," he said as he delivered a cup to his new companion. "Both animals will need extra care at the livery."

Slaton grunted. "That stallion of mine likely survived by sheer orneriness."

Coburn took a seat on the edge of his saddle. "I wouldn't argue on that because it does have a stubborn streak. It was in bad shape, but appears to be coming back fine."

"You showed up in the nick of time. I'm damn lucky."

"Luck's got nothing to do with it."

Slaton frowned half-heartedly. "The cards turned up aces for me."

"Did I see you hanging around Dodge City last summer?"

"I had an interlude there," Ben answered, giving him a searching look. "I took advantage of the gambling and the ladies. Made some money and did lots of whoring around."

"You were celebrated for a while, weren't you?"

"What?"

"Did you or did you not save a child from being trampled by a pair of runaway steers?"

Slaton chuckled thinly. "Yeah, that was me."

"I was in the Alhambra Saloon when the hollering ruckus started," Deacon said, and took a gulp of coffee. "I got to the boardwalk just in time to see you snatch the boy and tumble."

Slaton cocked an eyebrow in a self-confident manner. "I'm depending on that act of kindness to buy me some goodwill from the powers that be. You coming by when you did is proof positive that I've got the stars lined up on my side."

"Me arriving here and now is Providential."

Slaton let out a low-pitched whistle. His face lit up as though he had just encountered a secret treasure. "Deacon Coburn. That's what you told me, right?" He raised a hand as if he was ordering a halt to the conversation. "Now I recall the name and why there's familiarity. You got your own game, don't you? You're the whiskey drinking preacher who presided over happenings from a back corner table at the Alhambra."

"Coffee and whiskey," Deacon corrected, eyes glinting. "But I ain't no preacher. I'm just a student of the Bible and an observer of humanity. Sometimes those interests overlap and I get a glimpse of the mystery. And it ain't no game, friend; it's thinking on eternity."

"To each his own, is what I say."

Coburn narrowed his eyes on him and quoted shrewd insights from Solomon. "*Happy is the man that findeth wisdom, and the man that getteth understanding. For the merchandise of it is better than the merchandise of silver, and the gain thereof than fine gold.*"

"Sounds like poetry."

"An ancient Proverb. Weigh the words, my friend."

Slaton drank his coffee in one long pull. "What's got you riding in this storm?"

"A brother of mine went through a tough time," Deacon answered candidly. "He bought himself troubles and is fighting it from what I hear. I want to see if I can help."

"That's awful noble of you, considering the deathtrap of the weather."

"You got any family, Ben?"

"I got a sassy gal in Las Vegas who *never* turns me away." He tried to adjust the position of his broken leg, but winced fiercely and quit. "Does that count as family?"

"Do you have affection and caring for her?"

"When I'm there she *always* has my full attention."

"What's her name?"

"Brenda," Ben replied wistfully. "Brenda Hawkins. She's a bubbly hellcat. We just had us a couple months of bliss. That girl can curl my toes and plain wear me out."

"You plan on marrying her?"

Slaton guffawed and puffed out his chest. "So far I've been fortunate and that topic has never come up. With us it's all about making the bedsprings squeak and sing."

Coburn dismissed that with a throwaway smile. "As jolly as that may be, you're missing what's really special between a man and woman." He finished his coffee and jabbed a finger at him. "If you were smart and looking to the future, you'd marry that girl and make an honest woman of her. She surely deserves that much and likely more."

Slaton eyeballed him intently, then burst into rowdy laughter and spoke around it. "Is that the end of the sermonette from the man who claims he ain't a preacher?"

Coburn stood. "I reckon." He sidled toward where the horses were picketed. "Get yourself together as best you can. We're done lollygagging the day away. I figure we got twenty miles or so. I'll rope you in the saddle if need be." Then, in a hurried yet methodical approach, he packed and prepared for the trail, while keeping an eye on the gloomy clouds. It didn't take much calculating for him to conclude that the forecast for more snow was unchanged.

The grayness of morning had a wedge of brightness glowing in it. Avis Lahay sat in the swivel chair smiling at the glimmering beauty of her handiwork. She had lit a dozen candles and arranged them in a semi-circle on the roll-top desk. Still in her nightclothes, she was fiddling with a pen and thinking. The leather bound notebook was open and awaiting her entry. She sighed, made ready the pen with ink and started writing.

> *February 17, 1878*
>
> *Dear Diary: There's some funny business going on with Miss Delores. She is upset about something and it's not the usual issue. She was troubled for most of yesterday. It began when I gave her an order from a lady customer named Max. She stopped what she was doing and got a miffed look on her face and said, "That's it then, isn't it?"*
>
> *I had no idea what she meant or what I should do, so I just went about the business of getting a carafe of coffee. Miss Delores stayed in the kitchen or in the office for the rest of the day, as though she was afraid or hiding. When I told her goodnight and went to bed she still had not gone into the Cantina Room though there were plenty of opportunities for her to relax in one of the rockers. I have never seen her so reclusive or closemouthed. I am concerned and hope whatever was going on is now over and done.*
>
> *Max is a hoot. I spent a lot of time with her, especially in the afternoon. She's really interesting, like no one else I've ever met. She's a cowgirl, or at least that's what I decided to call her. We talked about horses, which I appreciated because Miss Delores is going to help me buy my very own come springtime. Max told me*

all about her mare and offered to take me to the livery to groom it today. I am so impatient I can hardly wait.

It's going to be fun getting to know her better. She's a pretty woman, but she dresses and acts like a man. I surely have the impression that she doesn't take guff from anyone. I would like to become bold like her. There's something daring or dodgy about her that is exciting. She has at least one gun on her, maybe more.

I have no clue about her story, but I suspect she will have to stay in Santa Fe until the windy weather ends. That's good news for me, particularly if I can convince her to remain here at the Suncurl Café. There's no reason for her not to, but also, no guarantee she'll see it that way. She strikes me as a person who mostly goes and does whatever she wants, wherever she wants. I doubt I will ever have that kind of brass, but I suppose it's a worthy goal and maybe I can get some ideas from her example of courage and daring.

That's enough for now. I have to pitter-patter.

She closed the engraved cover and put the book away in its pigeonhole. She went to the bed and made it, fluffing the pillows before putting them in place. She then laid out her clothes, shed her flannel nightgown and dressed as rapidly as possible. She pulled a pair of socks on and sat on the chair to tuck the trousers into her boots.

She stood in front of the mirror and brushed the waves of her auburn hair thoroughly. Her eyes squeezed almost shut as she vigorously finished the job. She carefully blew out the candles one at a time—each whiff was accompanied by a tinny giggle. She picked up her hooded coat, slung it over a shoulder and was happily smiling when she left her room to go downstairs.

Max Dawson would never be caught unawares or unprepared. She was equipped with an arsenal of protection. She had taken the liberty of setting alight several of the wall-mounted lamps in the *Cantina Room*, and was proceeding to do an everyday routine. With a precision that drew close to tenderness, she checked and positioned her weapons.

On her right hip in an unadorned holster was a bone-handled Colt Peacemaker, which had been her twenty-first birthday gift from her father. In a shoulder-sling under her left arm, beneath a dull-colored jacket she seldom removed, was an over-under double-barreled derringer; its identical twin had a home in a customized sheath inside her right boot. An Arkansas toothpick was housed in the other boot, giving her balance and an extra measure of defense.

When satisfied that each weapon was secure and ready to be used if necessity demanded it, she went to the pool table. She moved with the nimble agility of a dancer and the conviction of a lawman. Her gait exuded cool and graceful fearlessness. She was a straight-line go-getter, who retained not an ounce of tomfoolery.

She arranged the pyramid formation and broke with an authoritative whipsaw stroke. The balls scattered to the four corners. There was no hesitancy in her choices. She alternated between stripes and solids, sinking six in a row before hanging the nine-ball on the edge of a side pocket; it was as though an invisible barrier had arisen. She stepped back and tapped the butt of the stick against the floor, then heard footfalls and turned toward the sound.

The door to the kitchen swung open and Avis Lahay entered. "Hey, Max. I was going to sneak out because I didn't want to wake you, but then I heard the crack of the balls."

"Wake me?" Max let out an airy laugh and shook her head. "You'd have to disturb me long before sunup to wake me, girl. I've made a trip to the outhouse for my morning constitutional, got some fresh air and came in to do some reading."

Avis sat on a tall stool against the wall near the cue rack. She folded her coat over an arm and rested it on her lap. "What are you reading?"

"The only book I have in my saddlebags just now. Homer's Odyssey."

"I haven't read that one yet," Avis replied, sounding rather sophisticated. "Miss Delores has me reading The Merchant of Venice by Shakespeare. And when I have it completed there's a copy of John Bunyan's The Pilgrim's Progress waiting for me."

"Sounds like you enjoy reading."

"Books are my refuge," Avis answered quickly. "I've been all around the world in books and had some wild adventures." She put her feet up on the bottom rung of the stool. "I like to be curious and discover new things. For example, I was interested yesterday when you mentioned going east to become ladylike. Where and for how long?"

Max leaned her backside against the edge of the table. "Are you kidding?"

"No, I'm not. I was just wondering, is all."

"It was three years in Philadelphia," Max said firmly. "I studied many of the classics, which was certainly worth it, but the genteel upper crust protocols were crappola."

Avis giggled. "I thought maybe I could use some of that tutoring."

"Perhaps I ought to zip my lip," Max replied, hunching her shoulders. "It's not my call to make, but I'd encourage you to explore different options,

Avis. I don't want to spoil it for you, but with your reading regimen you're already getting an excellent education. The wisdom of those writers will filter down into your thinker and develop your character."

"You sound like Miss Delores."

"She must be a smart lady."

"Do you know her?"

"I just met her last night."

"Your paths never crossed somewhere else?"

"No. Why do you ask?"

Avis averted her eyes. "No reason."

Max took a step close to her. "You're not a good fibber, Avis."

"Pardon?"

"You just engaged in mendacity, girl."

Avis bit her lip, shamefaced. "Well, sort of, I guess."

"It matters not one way or the other, but you had an objective when you asked if I knew Miss Delores," Max said in a level tone. "You don't want to tell me, which is fine because it's none of my business, but be truthful about it. Honesty is prime with me."

"How could you tell I was fibbing?" Avis asked sheepishly.

"It was your body language and the inflection of your voice."

"Sorry."

"Don't sweat it, girl."

"I didn't mean to be deceitful, Max." Avis slid off the stool. "I'm just trying to figure out Miss Delores better. She was upset yesterday." She tugged her coat on and began fastening the large wooden buttons. "It's been nice chatting, but I have to get going."

"Where are you off to at this hour?"

"My daily mission of mercy," Avis answered, slipping the hood up. "It's kind of a complicated story and I don't know all the details, but I'll tell you what I can later." She spun around and was jiggling her mittens on as she sallied forth through the kitchen.

Max Dawson grinned and returned attention to the billiards table.

Charley Jondreau had his horse moving at an energetic clip through the snow. The pinto responded to the rousing tempo with enthusiasm. It was eager and smiling, its zest and stamina seemingly renewed by the morning crispness of the high altitude. The sky was a close-knit overhang of slate-gray clouds, but no precipitation was falling.

From the information given him, he guessed that he was close and expected to reach his destination by sundown. He picked his way along a trail of least resistance beside the Rio Grande. The freshly shaved skin of his neck, cheeks and top of his head felt tight and prickly in the cold. He had his droopy-brimmed hat pulled low on his brow.

Through years of strict discipline, his eyes were alert to the features of nature—even as his mind processed and replayed the dream that had disturbed his slumber. The meaning of it had him in a quandary. He stewed on the possibilities from every angle, but no matter how forceful his problem-solving skills, he remained confounded.

The bronze-skinned woman had taken up residence in a dusty backroom closet in his subconscious. She emerged at odd times, driving him to depths of bewilderment because regardless of his efforts, he could ascertain no rhyme or reason to her visitations.

He reevaluated all that he had *seen* and continued mulling it over. He sat back in the saddle and beheld the miles and miles of aspens. The pony halted and snorted. He was caught by surprise and had to quickly shift his weight. He felt a shimmy of tension course through the horse's hindquarters, but it was only momentary, then it relaxed and stood still.

There was a snarling growl off to the right. Jondreau looked and saw a mountain lion skulking between the trees. It eased from under cover and approached. The animal was magnificent. It stopped twenty yards away and stretched, its tail swaying back and forth. The piebald pinto wagged its head up and down, neighing calmly. The big cat padded closer, noble and powerful. The horse held its position, unafraid and unwavering.

Jondreau scowled, puzzled by his mount's unperturbed bearing. He leaned forward to gently stroke its neck. "Our wild friend has something to tell us, eh?"

The tawny cougar roared; the spine-tingling outcry echoed off the looming walls of the surrounding mountains. Jondreau beamed a large smile, hearing in its voice boundless courage and resourcefulness, which he sought to assimilate as his own. He prayed in patois and extended his hands high to receive the blessing and guidance offered by the cat's presence.

The clutter in Charley Jondreau's mind cleared; he had clarity.

Six months ago, Whitey Fitzgerald met a sad-eyed woman who almost instantly stole his heart. She was a mulatto with knock-out curves and a perky personality that was all chatter and giggles, which belied her soulful expression and hid devious motives. She breezed into Dodge City on the stagecoach, a nattily-dressed lady with a tragic story to tell.

Fitzgerald made her acquaintance within an hour of her arrival. He was sitting on a bench in front of Rath General Store, taking a midafternoon break from barbering at the Tonsorial Parlor. He watched her sashay across Front Street and come along the boardwalk toward him. He was taken in by her prettiness. He puffed on a cigar and made no effort to disguise his frank admiration. She glided to a stop in front of him.

"Eloise Smith."

"Whitey Fitzgerald."

"May I sit and visit?"

"Please do."

She flirtatiously brushed up against him as she took a seat. "Forgive me, kind sir. I must tell you that I was attracted to you from afar the moment I spotted you. Self, I said, you must hurry on over and meet that fine looking gentleman or else you'll be one sorry girl. So here I am to converse and be sociable. I do hope you be in a receiving mood."

The August sun was hot, but that was not what had beads of sweat forming on his upper lip. His senses were spinning. Her scent, as fresh as springtime lilacs, got inside his head. Her sultry smile and the promise peeking from behind it had him agog. Fitzgerald was speechless, which was the rarest of occurrences. His habitual click-click was even silenced.

"Why, Mr. Fitzgerald, you scamp. Has the cat got your tongue?"

He swallowed hard. He stared vacantly at her, his mouth open.

"Have I embarrassed you with my brazen ways? Perhaps it would be best for me to leave you to be about your business." She ruffled her skirt and shifted slightly. "I was hoping to be friendly a while. I don't know anyone in town and will only be here for a short stay."

He crossed his legs and stubbed out the cigar on his boot heel.

She lightly tapped his knee. "Shall I go elsewhere?"

"Please don't," he said, dry and raspy.

"Since you are polite, I will remain." Her lips parted in an inviting smile as she slowly peeled off white gloves and tucked them in a small drawstring purse. She folded her hands on her lap and leaned close to him. "Perchance you would be good enough to say a few words?"

"I'm not sure I should tell what's on my mind."

"Why not?"

"It could get me into trouble."

"Not with me, Mr. Fitzgerald."

"How can I be sure?"

"My mama never raised a liar," she replied, poking a finger against his chest. "I want to hear what's on your mind and not some flaky gibberish."

"Alright, then," he said, looking directly at her. "You're a vision of beauty." He punctuated that with an emphatic click-click, eyes widened and posture rigid. "My heart is a thumpity mess that is all a-flutter. You've definitely put a sloppy grin on my face."

"You are indeed brash, Mr. Fitzgerald." She batted her eyes and placed a hand on his knee. "It must be kismet for you have taken my breath away. I just wish I had more time to explore what could develop between us, but I must be off to Santa Fe. My baby sister is sick and dying." Her fingers tightened and released, then she laughed and tilted back from him.

Though short and somewhat scrawny in stature, Whitey Fitzgerald possessed an oversized heart—combined with a libido that had now been set loose put common sense judgment into some black hole of no return. All his choices that followed were the result of an eruption of adolescent foolhardiness; he had the hots for a woman who was a stranger.

"We have the day to spend together, Whitey."

"Maybe more?" He raised his eyebrows, optimistically suggestive.

Eloise moistened her lips. "The night? Why you sly fox. My mama would flip-flop in her grave if I were to do such a thing. I know I'm much too flirty for my own good, but I assure you that I'll never engage in any hanky-panky until a preacher says it's right and proper."

"Then I'll court you while we travel to Santa Fe."

"I beg your pardon, sir!"

"You heard me, Eloise."

Less than twenty-four hours later, against the counsel of friends, including an adamant protest from Deacon Coburn, he emptied his bank account, which consisted of almost three thousand dollars, and got out of Dodge City with Eloise Smith at his side. He was utterly undone; a mature man in his middle years being governed by surging male hormones.

Unbeknownst to him, cataclysmic heartbreak had him in its crosshairs.

Silas Dawson was mentally and physically disoriented. Cold gripped him. Energy was draining away in a ceaseless ebb and flow. The bitter dangers of frostbite and exposure were collapsing into the void his strength was rapidly vacating. A frozen landscape stretched out in all directions populated by nothing except ice-covered sagebrush. The emptiness was vast and lonely; the slopes of the rolling, white-blanketed terrain deceptive.

None of what was happening made any sense. His brain was convoluted and dazed. Above him the covering was forbidding; cheerless gray speckled by an endless flurry of swirling flakes. The wind was a vehement maniac, loud and buffeting. Frustration was in him, creeping close to fear. The only marker to help him was the sunrise; an obscure yellow in the eastern sky. He stalked that horizon, blindly riding across a windswept wasteland.

The zebra dun slugged along. No other option was available. All the animal could do was to keep putting one hoof in front of the other through drifts of sand-streaked snow. Dawson's toes were numb, his stony tenacity flagging. Hope, fragile and almost dying inside him, spurred him onward. His senses were razor thin and on high-alert. He had to find or manufacture some type of shelter. The collar of his coat was turned up, his hat wrenched low. He strained forward in the saddle, his face raw from exposure. His skin was burning, tingling, constricting.

Sudden-like something appeared in his range of vision—light! It was pale and faint. His eyes were slits, nearly frozen shut. He labored to open them, which sent a drumbeat of jagged pain through his skull. Light; ahead was the outline of a structure that had a glow in a window. The sight produced excitement in him; a new determination swelled in his veins.

He gave the horse an urgent nudge. It sensed its master's desperation. The stallion kicked into a loping trot and maintained it for a few strides. A sliver of daybreak cut its way through a gap in the murk. Dawson listed to one side of the saddle. Feverish and crazed, he clung to the reins, yanking the animal to a tottering stop. It whinnied angrily.

Dawson straightened. What struck his eyes couldn't be real. He induced the horse to take a few more steps, then pulled up and marveled at beams of blackened lumber that had been affixed into a tall cross next to an iron and wooden arch. The charred symbol from Golgotha excited the last vestiges of consciousness. He reached for it as he toppled to the ground. He spun downwards; drifting, floating, flailing into a dungeon of frightful darkness.

Gray Cloud puttered around the plank-walled shack. The fire was hot and crackling. He kept close to the potbelly stove because he was always cold, especially early mornings. A crock of Navajo tea was brewing and its bittersweet aroma filled the room; he sat on a stool and waited for it to be ready as he listened alertly to every rustle.

The wind song whistled and whispered, and came in occasional gushes that rattled the walls. Dread and dismay dominated him. Nightmares and horrid scenarios romped around his mind all through the night, and now, he couldn't find the necessary means to escape them. Strings of ghost beads were in place around his neck and also, bracelets on both wrists.

The sound of an animal in distress reached him. He stiffened. His head swiveled back and forth, eyes bulging and twitchy. The awful noise came again. He got to his feet and went to the door. He waited and waited until he heard a whickering snort, then cautiously turned the knob. He poked his head out and saw a riderless horse standing near the archway.

He bent forward a bit farther and strained his eyes toward the house. He was somewhat relieved by the telltale indicator that the Weitzels were immersed in the new day. Oil lamps were ablaze and shining from the windows. A tingle slinked up his spine. He sniffed the air. He got his coat and was pulling it on as he ran to see to the needs of the horse.

He staggered and stumbled, almost falling down because his knees buckled when he spotted a body in a sand-encrusted snow bank beside the stallion. His teeth chattered; his stomach cramped. He spun around and screamed for help, unleashing panic in wails that soared above the wind. His voice tore from the bottom of his lungs as his arms flapped hysterically.

Hans Weitzel came onto the porch and was immediately running toward him. It was only then that Gray Cloud clamped his mouth shut and knelt beside the man. He gasped as recognition smacked him; he had seen the face in newspaper accounts. He felt sick; rancid fear molested his senses. It was the Texas Ranger whose wife had been tortured and killed by Smoky Crowe.

Dizziness hit Gray Cloud like a lightning bolt. He passed out.

In southern Colorado near Wagon Wheel Gap, the sky was becoming a fluctuating hodgepodge of colors; multi-hued grays and blues swapped places and shapes as the clouds broke apart and scattered. Sally Twosongs stood in the open doorway enjoying the brisk cold while watching her husband walk away in his stiff-shouldered gait. There was logbook work to be done at the Axler house, which was a half-mile down the valley. The men would be debating and deciding which horses to roundup to fulfill an order for the army come springtime.

Hank sat dutifully obedient at her side. Caleb had given the dog strict orders to care for Sally Twosongs. She got down on one knee to pet the collie just as sunlight crested over the steep summit of the mountain that formed the eastern boundary of *WT Ranch*—W for Weitzel, T for Twosongs. Her eyes flinched, wet and glistening. The name and brand had been entirely his idea; she had in fact refused it, but he persisted and won out.

She stood. "Let's go inside, Hank."

The dog thumped its tail and started turning circles in a squirmy wiggle of a dance. She took a backward step to allow it to scoot past her. She pushed the door closed and went directly to the kitchen for there were breakfast dishes soaking. All she wanted was chores and routine so she could put the letdown of the miscarriage behind her.

Last night, she had cried and cried. And slept restlessly, dreaming and calling out irrational words as her arms and legs jounced and quivered. Caleb held her and stayed snuggled close beneath the covers. The tender attentiveness of his love provided much comfort, but an achy emptiness remained. Questions and worry had her mind messed up.

She finished cleaning the washtub and counter. She wrung the dishrag out, hung it on its hook, then almost tripped over the dog. She caught her balance on edge of the table. "We must have us a talk, Hank. Caring for me doesn't mean you need to be underfoot."

The dog wagged its tail freely, which caused its body to shimmy and shake.

She grinned, thin and tense. She went to a tall-backed oak rocker near the fireplace and sat. The chair had been handcrafted by her father-in-law as a wedding present. She cherished it. She found a soothing rhythm, leaned her head back and closed her eyes. Soon she was humming softly and it wasn't long before droplets were trickling down her cheeks.

Hank came and placed its head on her lap.

She backhanded the tears aside and stroked the dog's neck. "My feelings disgust me, but I can't make them go away, Hank," she said, voice quiet and sad. "A sense of failure is stuck in my heart. I'm afraid I have failed as a woman, I've failed Caleb. It hurts so badly and I know I should pray, but I don't want to because I'm angry at God for abandoning me."

Hank whined and nuzzled against her. Its eyes were expressive and watchful.

She gave its neck a squeeze. "I always have you, don't I, Hank?"

The tricolor collie barked twice and wiggled happily.

"Caleb is upset, but he'll never say so." She sighed and folded her arms over her midsection. "I wonder where our baby is now. Heaven or in some nowhere place? Is our child an angel? Was it a boy or a girl? When I die will I know our baby? What do you think, Hank?"

The dog gave her a quizzical look and started yapping insistently.

Sally Twosongs forced a tremulous laugh. "Of course you're right, Hank. There are questions that have no satisfying answers and sitting around doing nothing only exacerbates all the crummy feelings." She fairly leapt to her feet and rushed to the kitchen. She pulled the flour canister and mixing bowl from the cupboard—it was bread baking day and she got to it.

Her deliberate busyness was unable to ward off watery eyes.

Five months ago, Whitey Fitzgerald woke up with a monstrous pulsation in his head. His breathing was shallow, his heartbeat racing. Sporadic squawking reached his ears. Awareness of his circumstances came sluggishly. He was in a ditch, sweaty and shaky. His right hand was clenched around the loop-handle of his carpetbag.

The sun was blazing straight above him in a blue sky that had no end. He sat up slowly, then wilted and fell flat on his back. He lay still. The spinning throbs in his head unfurled down his spine to make his extremities tingle. He gulped a lungful of oxygen and exhaled it with intentional ease; he repeated that process several times and steadily gathered bits and pieces of understanding. He squeezed his eyes shut and remembered.

Eloise Smith had gotten into his bloodstream. For most of their stagecoach journey over the southern route of the Santa Fe Trail they had been the only passengers. They talked and laughed while making plans for the future; they kissed, caressed and played around some. Each session of necking went farther, but she dogmatically pushed him away at the brink of no return. When they were alone in the carriage, his blood was nearly continually on the rise.

Eloise led him along with sweet promises of a marriage ceremony upon their arrival in Santa Fe. She would need to attend to the care of her sick sister, but that wouldn't prevent her from making all the necessary arrangements for them to begin their life together as man and wife. At inns and way stations she demonstrated her anxiousness to set up housekeeping by being exceptionally attentive to his nourishment and comfort.

At an overnight stopover in Las Vegas, Eloise met an old acquaintance—a sparkly-eyed white man in Sunday go-to-meeting threads, who was introduced as a family friend named Huey Butters. He talked in run-on sentences that never seemed to end; flowery expressions that jumped from one topic to another without warning. It was obvious to Fitzgerald that Butters had a streak of rascal in him, so he was instantly wary and protective.

At Huey's insistence, they went to his hotel room for drinks and socializing. Eloise acted the role of hostess and fixed cocktails from a variety of liquor bottles on the dresser. She did so with aplomb, prattling merrily. She delivered a tall tumbler to Whitey, eyes coquettish and lips parted invitingly. She then planted a warm wet kiss flush on his mouth.

Fitzgerald was nonplussed. His caramel complexion darkened in embarrassment. His jawline tightened and his brow crinkled as lovesickness raced through his veins. He swayed in his footsteps and appeared to be ready to lose his balance. He took a large swallow of whiskey, which burned down his gullet; without hesitation, he drank another mouthful.

Butters laughed brashly. "You lovebirds are delightful. It warms the cockles of my heart to see such a display. I've never been fortunate or lucky in the love department." He sat on a wing back chair and crossed his legs. "Eloise, where did you find Mr. Fitzgerald?"

She demurely lifted a hand in protest. "The good Lord brought us together on a boardwalk in Dodge City. My heart was all a-flutter the moment I saw him."

"I hope I receive an invite to the nuptials."

"Oh, Huey," she said, batting her eyes at him. "Of course you will, though I must tell you that it'll be soon after our arrival in Santa Fe."

Butters scowled in surprise. "That's rather quick, isn't it?"

"Indeed it is, but what else can we do?" she replied, placing a hand over her heart. "My dear cuddly-wuddly would like it to be much quicker. Isn't that right, Whitey?"

Fitzgerald muttered words that were slurred and sloppy. His eyes gaped open. He tilted his glass back and emptied it. He felt tetchy and queerly ill. His vision was blurring; a droning buzz filled his ears. He took a wobbly step that caused him to bump into Eloise.

"What's wrong, darling?" she asked, backing away from him.

Fitzgerald focused on her. He saw pleased smugness glimmering in her eyes. He gasped and abruptly realized that her affection had all been fakery. He had been duped and drugged. The room started circling around him; faster and faster until his equilibrium was no more. He hit the floorboards with a crash and twitched as though he was in the grips of an epileptic seizure. He resisted and struggled in a helpless haze, and clearly heard their conversation.

"Here's his money," Eloise said, giggling. "It's almost three thousand dollars. The poor chump had it wrapped in a handkerchief at the bottom of his satchel."

"That'll spend just fine. You learned your lessons well, pumpkin."

"It was easy breezy. What do we do with him now?"

"He'll be senseless in dreamland until tomorrow," Huey answered, scoffing. "We'll put him on my buckboard in the morning and dump him somewhere south of town."

"When will you see to my needs, Huey Luey?"

"No time like the present, my little mink."

Fitzgerald whimpered and tried to move, to crawl, to gain his feet, but there was no chance of that happening. A paralysis spread from his spine to make his limbs unresponsive. His head felt like a swollen balloon ready to pop at any instant. Blackness blanketed him. Then, just before unconsciousness smothered him, he heard the unmistakable sounds of impassioned lovemaking—Eloise Smith and Huey Butters were doing a raunchy horizontal waltz.

Whitey Fitzgerald choked off the repulsive memory. He opened his eyes. Spikes of sunlight drove through to his brain. He twined his fingers together over the top of his head as though he feared the bones were going to shatter. He blasphemed with a shame-faced vehemence. The roof of his mouth was puckered, his tongue swollen and limp.

In those moments, his folly and stupidity crushed him. There was no place for him to hide, no one to blame for the wreckage and humiliation; he alone was responsible. It was reasonable to presume that Eloise Smith and Huey Butters were flimflam partners. He had been robbed and disgraced. All that remained were a few items of clothing, the instruments of his livelihood and a hundred dollars of emergency funds squirreled away inside his sock.

His dignity was gone. He closed his eyes again, but then, a shrill squawk inflamed the pain in his head and made his eyelids flicker. He had an uneasy look around. Two vultures were perched on a branch of a nearby tree eyeballing him. He scooped up a good-sized stone, hastened to his feet and chucked it at the red-skulled scavengers.

The birds flew off and he whooped at the top of his lungs. He felt woozy. Bent over, with his hands on his knees, Whitey Fitzgerald gathered his sensibilities while reconnoitering his location. He began the long walk to Santa Fe. Each step was misery and contempt because rats were loose in his soul—guilt and self-reproach devoured the fiber of his character.

Avis Lahay had no intention of taking no for an answer on this trip. Her mind was set and she kept on task. She hurried along the shoveled pathway leading to the clapboard shed behind the livery. Fluffy snowflakes were falling. She stopped, steeled her resolve, and then, as she had every morning for the past three weeks, she rapped a rat-tat-tat on the door.

"I be here, sweetie."

She entered the toasty warm room and removed her mittens. "How are you today?"

Broom in hand, Whitey Fitzgerald gave a faltering shrug. "I be a recovering drunkard is what I be. I ain't hit a bottle in over twenty-four hours."

"Good for you, Mr. Whitey."

"Yeah, that's what you say, but I got the shakes."

"All the more reason to come along with me," Avis replied, flashing him a bright-eyed smile. "It's crisp and pretty outside, a brand new beautiful day."

"You be starting mighty early, ain't you?"

"Whatever do you mean?"

He click-clicked and stuck the broom in a corner. "No chitchat like usual. No beating the devil around the stump. You just jumped right in and delivered the invitation."

The wall-mounted kerosene lamp hissed and flickered. Avis adjusted the wick until the flame stabilized. She bounced and shifted weight from one foot to the other and chose to challenge him. "Why do you think I come here every morning, Mr. Whitey?"

"That be a question I ponder."

"I'll be more than happy to tell you." She slouched against the door. "At first I was just following instructions. Miss Delores asked me to visit you and try to be an encouragement. She told me about a Bible man named Barnabas."

"She does like that Barnabas fella. I heard his story from her."

"Miss Delores also told me that being an encourager is good for my health and happiness." She purposefully held her gaze on him. "Then, it wasn't too long before I realized that when you're not a grumpy gus, you got a way that *encourages me*. And I decided that I want you to come to the Suncurl Café, for no other reason than to be my friend."

"I ain't worthy of your friendship, sweetie."

"That's silly talk."

"You don't understand."

"Explain it to me, Mr. Whitey."

Fitzgerald sagged and slumped down to the floor. He sat with his legs stretched flat and his arms clutched into a hug over his chest. "I be shamed. I lost everything about me. I got nothing left of who I used to be." He looked up at her, tears pooling in his rheumy eyes.

"It doesn't have to stay that way, Mr. Whitey. You can be found."

He hung his head. "I was drunk, wandering the streets and passed out in gutters for I don't know how long before Miss Delores almost stumbled over me. She nursed me and set me up in these fine digs, but I swore and said nasty things to her."

"She forgives you, Mr. Whitey."

"I ain't got no way to apologize or fix it."

"Yes, you do."

He balked. "I ain't ever going to find myself."

"Yes, you will. You have to take a first step to a new beginning."

"Ain't no new beginnings for someone who threw his life away, sweetie."

"Miss Delores says otherwise."

He stared at her. He jerked slightly when a log crackled in the cylinder stove. "She be a high quality lady who's walked a rough road, but there ain't no hope for me."

"Miss Delores just wants to help, Mr. Whitey."

"You go away now, sweetie. Leave me be."

"I won't go away today," she said, lowering her voice.

"You just get along or else."

"Or else what, Mr. Whitey? Are you going to swear and say bad words to me?"

His posture sank deeper, his self-embrace tightened. "Go chase yourself."

"Something is wrong with Miss Delores."

The words seemed to strike him physically. "What?" His voice broke and his shoulders straightened rigidly. "What do you mean there's something wrong with her?"

"I can't say for sure."

"Why not? Is she sick?"

"Scared, I think."

"Scared? Scared of what, sweetie?"

"A lady from Texas."

"What?" He sat up stiffly. "You be joshing me."

"Nope," she answered, firm and adamant. "A lady dressed like a cowboy showed up yesterday and ever since Miss Delores is sick or scared or something."

"Sick? Now you be getting me all in a dither. Is she sick or is she scared?"

"I can't be sure one way or the other," she said, taking a couple steps toward him. "Come have a hot meal and see for yourself what's wrong with her."

He chewed it over. "If I do will you quit pestering me?"

She puckered her mouth and furrowed her brow. "Maybe, maybe not."

He got to his feet. "A man ought not to be dragged into the cold like an old dog," he said, shaking his head. He draped a dirty blanket over his ragged frock coat. "Let's go."

"May I carry your carpetbag for you, Mr. Whitey?"

"Don't you dare, sweetie. I won't be needing it," he replied, click-clicking rapidly. "I'm just coming along to eat and check in on Miss Delores. I be back here soon enough."

Avis Lahay stifled a smile. They walked through the weather side by side.

The clouds were wispy brushstrokes of gray on a blue canvas when Naomi Axler parked the homemade sled a few yards from the porch. She had pulled the sleigh from home and was pleased that the runners slid efficiently on the snow. She unstrapped the basket basinet in which her daughter was swaddled, then quickly climbed the three steps. She knocked twice on the door and did not wait at all; she simply opened and entered.

Sally Twosongs came out of the kitchen. "Naomi, I didn't expect you to come today. You should still be resting. I've started without you. The first batch is already rising."

"I've rested plenty. Pete sees to that, hovering over me," Naomi answered as she shucked her coat. "I woke up with cabin fever this morning. I knew I needed fresh air and exercise. Give me a moment to get Amanda Irene settled in your arms and I'll prepare the second batch."

"Amanda Irene. That's a lovely name."

Naomi was an unbundled bustle of energy. "Well, it was quite a chore trying to keep Pete involved in the choosing. It was more difficult than pulling teeth." She stopped still and burst out laughing. "Have I ever told you about the first time I met Pete?"

"No, I don't think so."

"You'd remember it, if I had," Naomi said, smiling rosily. "The next time we're all together I will do so. He was getting a tooth extracted. You have to watch Pete's expression as the story unfolds." She placed her daughter into the younger woman's care. "Jesse isn't feeling well. He's got a bit of the croup and was upset because he couldn't come see you. I medicated him and told Pete to make him take it easy." She turned and went to work in the kitchen.

Sally Twosongs took a seat in the tall-backed oak rocker and cuddled the infant close to her bosom. She removed the frilled lace bonnet that framed Amanda's chubby face and fussed over her. Shivery fears jeered at her as she fingered the baby's curls. She had to be deliberate and toughen herself to hold back the tears. She rested and meditated.

A half-hour or so later, Naomi joined her in front of the fireplace. The baby was sound asleep, as was Sally Twosongs, rocking ever so gently. Her eyelids fluttered open and she hitched in a deep breath. Her cheeks were damp, her eyes red and puffy.

"What's the matter?" Naomi asked, alarm in her tone.

Sally Twosongs stared vacantly past her. Her countenance became stoic. "I had a miscarriage yesterday morning. I was about seven weeks along."

"I'm so sorry. Does Caleb know?"

"Yes."

"He didn't say anything to me when I saw him earlier."

"It wouldn't be Caleb's way," Sally Twosongs told her, pinching a shrewd smile. "He's a Weitzel. He's as closemouthed as they come with everyone except me."

"I've noticed," Naomi said dryly. "You need to see a doctor."

"I suppose I will come springtime. Or possibly not."

Naomi was insistent. "You must see a doctor, honey."

"I really don't want to, Naomi."

"Why on earth not?"

Sally Twosongs kept her gazed fixed on the child in her arms. "I'm afraid I'll never be able to carry a baby full-term and I'd rather not hear a doctor say that aloud to me."

Naomi reached over and rubbed her shoulder. "What makes you think that?"

"Has Deacon ever told you about me?"

"Just that you're special to him."

"I used to call him Mr. Deke," Sally Twosongs said, eyes glassy with moisture. Her chin trembled and her upper body took on rigidity. "He rescued me from a bad man who kidnapped me. I was only eleven years old and vile things were done to me."

"Oh, honey. I am so terribly sorry for you. I cannot imagine your pain." Naomi's eyes swelled with compassion as she knelt in front of her. "I had no idea. You are so strong,"

Sally Twosongs convulsed. Her mouth dropped open as if it were unhinged. Her eyes were blank and disengaged as she spoke in a little girl's voice, tinny and high-pitched. "The monster-man tried to kill Mr. Deke with bullets, but he missed twice. Then Mr. Deke shot once. The bad man died." Her eyes became even more unclear. "Mr. Deke took me to Daniel and Consuelo Twosongs. From then until now and forever, I am their daughter."

A heave shook her. She gasped breathlessly. She blinked again and again. Her eyes focused.

Naomi was baffled and flustered by the transcendental episode. She remained motionless, her hands clasped together. "What just happened, honey? Did you relive that nastiness?"

"Sort of, I guess. I *saw* it." Sally Twosongs inhaled deeply and exhaled between gritted teeth. "It's not something to be remembered. Jesus healed me because he is good medicine."

"Please tell me about the healing."

Sally Twosongs gave a slump-shouldered shrug. "After a few months with Daniel and Consuelo, Jesus came to me in a dream. It was Christmas Eve. He held my hand and touched my heart, and promised to walk my path with me. I've never forgotten and have nurtured the gift, but just now, he seems so distant and aloof. I don't sense his presence or feel his peace. I am afraid."

Naomi crept closer and laid hands on Sally Twosongs; one on her head, the other on her shoulder. "Our Father who art in heaven, hallowed be thy name," she prayed fervently. "I hold before thee thy servant Sally Twosongs. She is grieving a sorrowful loss. She needs thy help and mercy. Let the cries of her heart be heard. Send her grace, grant her peace. Wrap thy strong arms of loving-kindness around her and bless her. Amen."

"Thank you."

"You're welcome, Sally Twosongs. I'm enriched by your friendship," Naomi said, shifting backwards. She unfolded her knees and settled on her bottom. "Yet I would've never met you if God hadn't made a way through the wilderness of my heartaches."

"Whatever do you mean?"

"My first husband and I loved each other for over twelve years in Lancaster County, Pennsylvania. Despite our desires we had no children. Then one autumn afternoon I watched him fall off the roof of a barn." She squinted at the memory. "I can still see him and hear the awful thud. I was alone at his bedside when he passed seven days later. My life could have been over too, for I was utterly defeated, but I resolved to seize the future. God has been faithful."

"I am grateful for you sharing, Naomi. It helps me."

"We nourish hope when we partake in each other's stories."

"I must do better at counting my blessings."

"And go forward embracing hope, honey."

Sally Twosongs smiled amiably. "Father taught me much about hope; it is always good for it fixes us." She swayed side to side and cradled the baby closer. "Amanda Irene will be my harbinger of hope. She is a precious reminder that life itself is indeed miraculous. As long as the sun arises on every tomorrow we have assurance because hope resides in the sunbeams."

The women exchanged affirmative nods and savored the sentiment.

Delores Solrizo was about to be startled; shocked, even. At her desk, she had a slew of numbers on her mind; she was engrossed in the latest reports from her banker and stock broker. Her asset base remained solid, while her silent investment in a mining and timber consortium was doing marginally better than had been projected.

She shuffled the documents into a folder and filed it. She had no reason to make any changes because her finances were in tip-top shape, which freed her to continue her largesse of charitable giving. She heard the kitchen door squeak open. She glanced up and instantly recoiled as though a ghost was standing in the doorframe of her office.

"What's wrong, Miss Delores?"

"My Lord, Whitey!" She gawked at him. He looked frail and worn down to a nub. She had not had any contact with him since he had blown up at her in a cuss-ridden, alcohol-induced tantrum—that occurred over two months ago, after she had written letters to Deacon Coburn and Naomi Axler about finding him addled and sleeping in an alley.

Always diminutive in stature, he was now rail thin. His clothes were tattered and shabby, hanging loose and baggy. There was no spark or joy in his eyes, as though the wiring to his brain was frayed or disconnected. She got past the initial shock, came from behind her desk and rushed to him. She locked her arms around his waist and squeezed for all she was worth.

"You gonna break me, Miss Delores."

"You're a sight for sore eyes, Whitey."

"You be as pretty as a picture, like always."

"And you're still an incorrigible man."

"I be awful sorry . . ."

"It's all done and over," she cut in tersely. "Put away and forgotten, Whitey."

"I be an old fool who has rats to kill and fences to mend. I's hungry too." He gave a peppy click-click and pushed her away. "That Avis gal is a sweetie and she's got spunk. She tells me you're scared of that cowboy lady from Texas out there shooting pool."

"What? Avis said that?"

"You be playing me, Miss Delores?" he asked, eyeing her closely. "Did you collude with that Avis girl? Did you put your heads together to spin me a story?"

"Collude?" she replied, laughing. "That's a rather loaded word, Whitey." She slipped past him. "I am well acquainted with Avis, but there was no spinning of a story. I only asked her to be faithful visiting you. Now, you sit on that stool there while I fix you a tasty meal."

The kitchen was spacious and laid out with efficiency in mind. A variety of dry goods were situated in hanging baskets in one corner. There was a woodblock workstation running almost the length of a wall, along with an island bar in the center of the room that had cupboards above and below it. Shades of pinks and blues created a pleasurable ambiance.

She went to the icebox and removed a shank of smoked ham. She cut several slices and diced them into tiny squares, which were tossed in a cast iron frying pan. "You should be happy to know Deacon is on his way from Dodge City. I expect him within the week."

"There's a storm, Miss Delores. He may not make it until spring."

"Deacon will be here. He sent a telegram and gave me his word."

"I ain't sure I want to see him. Or he me."

"What happened to you, Whitey?"

He disregarded the question. "What ain't you telling me, Miss Delores?"

"I'm not the one being evasive, Whitey. I'll spill the beans first, then you." She narrowed her eyes on him. "Avis is obviously astute and picked up on my mood yesterday. I was certainly in a foul humor and standoffish, but scared isn't the right word."

"Sick?"

She mulled that over a moment, then said, "Heartsick, yes."

"I be here to listen. Maybe I can help."

"Her name is Max Dawson. She is suffering sorrow because of my failures."

"How so?"

"Her mother was murdered in San Antonio."

"You ain't ever been to San Antonio, have you?"

"No," she said dully. She had cracked a couple eggs into a bowl and was now whisking them. "My son was involved in the killing, along with Smoky Crowe. What Avis detected in me wasn't fear, but remorse. The lady cowboy is a living reminder of sin and shame."

"You ain't responsible for your son's crimes."

She began frying the omelet. "Aren't I? I gave him life, then discarded him."

"He made bad choices, Miss Delores. Those choices put him on the outlaw road."

"All the reasoning in the world doesn't remove my guilt and regrets."

"You couldn't put that behind you when you left Abilene?"

"I've tried and keep trying to live in forgiveness, but the ugliness in my past creeps free to torment me," she replied, dribbling crumbs of cheddar on the eggs. "Some consequences are persistent and perpetual. You aren't the only one who has rats to kill, Whitey."

"I suppose not."

"So welcome to the human race."

He chuckled in an old familiar way. "That be true enough."

Compassion pooled in her eyes. "What happened to you, Whitey?"

"I ain't sure, Miss Delores. And I ain't got no hankering to talk about it."

"That's fine for now, I guess." She served the cheesy ham omelet. He moved his stool closer to the island bar and dug in with an exuberance that caused her to smile. She poured two cups of coffee and sat across from him. "There's a room upstairs for you, Whitey."

"Nope!" he blurted angrily. Hardness came over him, glazing his eyes and twisting his mouth into an intimidating grimace. He held his fork up and tipped it at her. "Don't be coddling me, Miss Delores. I ain't gonna have it. I came here to eat, and see to your situation. You be doing dandy, so when I finish up here I'll be on my way."

"I'm not coddling you, Whitey. And I'm not even close to dandy."

He glared at her. "What be your problem?"

"I miss my friend," she answered, tears rising in her eyes. "You have always been there for me from the moment we met. I need you more than you can know." Her lips formed a fragile smile as she regarded him with gracious affection. "As of late, the weather has put a kibosh on business, but this place is often hot and hopping. Here's my offer; room and board in exchange for being my assistant. We can be a cooking and cleaning tandem."

His jaw tightened. "You don't know where I been or what I done."

"It matters not to me, Whitey."

"I ain't safe to be around. My judgment is gone."

"It may be hiding, but you'll find it," she said confidently. "I was a whore when we met and you accepted me, no questions asked. I trust you with my life, Whitey." She lifted her cup and took a sip. "Stay the day. Take advantage of the billiard table. See how it goes."

He determinedly balled up a fist. "I be at my shack before nightfall."

She feigned acceptance, whilst praying for a different outcome.

≈ ≈ ≈

In the dream, Captain Dawson was alone and far removed from his jurisdiction. A compulsive obsession ruled his vigilance and comportment. There'd be no let up or slackening in him until he could attain a full measure of justice, which in his mind, would require the tying of a hangman's knot. He had been in pursuit of Smoky Crowe for over a month; the murdering bandit had committed atrocity on a woman and child in the vicinity of Amarillo.

Dawson was now in the Ute witch's stomping grounds on the high plains desert of New Mexico. The heat was scorching, the humidity as drenching as a saturated sponge. Black cotton thunderheads created a fortress above that was impenetrable for an indiscernible vastness. The fragrance of rain was conspicuous and heavy in the air.

The Texas Ranger was cognizant of his need to find cover but refused to do so because his adversary was within striking distance. Smoky Crowe was lurking in a ravine less than fifty yards ahead. Puffs of smoke gave his position away; it was as if Smoky Crowe had taken a break to indulge his addiction and he didn't care that his location was known. His nefarious ability to escape was remarkable, which substantiated the lore that made him mythic.

Dawson knew he was being taunted; he had gotten this close twice before, only to have Smoky Crowe slip from his reach. He dismounted and picketed his horse on a short tether. He retrieved the Winchester from its scabbard and jacked a cartridge into the chamber. He gave the lay of the land a serious going-over, concentrating on its dips and gullies.

There was no groundcover except sagebrush. He chose an angled approach and crouched low. He crawled on his belly between the shrubberies. He moved in rapid silence on his elbows and knees, occasionally coming eyeball to eyeball with a salamander or beetle; the lizards would scurry away, but the bugs got squashed or flicked aside.

There was sputtering and sparkling activity inside the ever-darkening fortification of the sky. He bent his head heavenward; lightning flashed, thunder rumbled. He cussed mildly. The wind was increasing and just now, a hot eddy of it graced him with a furious whiplash of sand that struck his face like a shotgun blast of rock-salt.

He scowled and winced, teeth grinding and eyes burning. He rolled onto a shoulder and took several minutes to pick grains of grit out of the corners of his watery eyes. He resumed his belly-first position and hunched up to see that a mere three body lengths separated him from the rim of the ravine. He wriggled to the precipice and had a gander along the narrow valley.

A smokeless fire was a stone's throw away. He searched the campsite for signs of his quarry, but saw none. There was no horse anywhere that he could see; no visible evidence that Smoky Crowe was present, but there could be no denying the distinct odor of tobacco smoke in the air. He inched sideways, maneuvering closer and closer.

A crow cawed, but was unseen. Goosebumps ridged along his spine. The solitary bird repeated its clamorous cry, as though it was a sentinel sounding an alarm. A loud crack of lightning flared, striking the ground close to him—the explosion of thunder was instant and bone-jarring. His will to be covert betrayed him; his body crunched into a kneeling posture.

In the exquisite moment of stillness that followed the boom, he heard a bellow of mockery. A low-pitched voice was laughing. Dawson cringed. A rage of defeat slugged him in the pit of his stomach and he was painfully aware that Smoky Crowe was gone; the bloodthirsty guttersnipe had sleazed through some invisible window or vanished on a wisp of the wind.

He murmured a crude utterance that was sacrilegious. It was then that the stronghold citadel launched its assault; the skies opened up in a flogging downpour that pounded with the stinging force of steel pellets. He was immediately soaked by the deluge. He gained his feet, yanked his hat down tightly, and started walking by leaning into the torrent.

He wobbled, straining to see his mount. The rainstorm was blinding. He held steady to his course until he spotted the zebra dun, then made a slight correction and slanted toward it. As he made his way back to the horse, his footsteps got heavy; and heavier. The desert sand became a boggy muddle of muck. His boots were clogged with clay-like mud up past his ankles.

He tried lifting his legs higher, but the morass wouldn't allow it. He humped and pitched forward, but could make no headway. It was as though a swamp of quicksand was sucking him down—he wallowed in it. The wind came up in a burst and slapped him so hard he had to fight to maintain his balance. His breathing was ragged and restless.

Blood rushed to his head; his heartbeat slammed frantically against his eardrums. He grunted and griped, sinking deeper and deeper into the mire. He was weak and feckless. His arms flailed as he clutched at the rain to find some handhold to grasp. He felt the bottom give way and was in a demented free-fall as slippery slime filled his lungs.

He came awake in a stammering lurch. His head and shoulders jerked upwards into a half-sitting position. Perspiration dripped off his hair and beard. He flopped onto his back, delirious and at a complete loss to understand what was happening. His eyes were bulging. He was in an unfamiliar dwelling buried beneath layers of blankets.

A gasp of breath wheezed into his lungs. The noise of it shocked him. He turned his head on the pillow. He blinked uncontrollably, as though his eyelids were shutters being shaken loose in a windstorm. When the spasm passed, his sightline rested on candlelight emanating from a tall dresser. He was soothed by the tiny flames and felt his lips form a smile.

A voice was murmuring to him. He found its source and his mouth opened and closed as he tried to speak to a woman with straw-colored hair sitting at his bedside. Over and over Silas Dawson attempted to converse with her, but his vocal cords were unresponsive. His throat was swollen. He strained harder and harder, but then, unconsciousness came over him.

It was mid-afternoon before the cougar gave a departing snarl and scampered up an uneven incline of the mountainside. Charley Jondreau had a sense of reverence because the big cat had led him. He paused once more to say a prayer that was fueled by thanksgiving. He had a panoramic view of *WT Ranch* nestled in a tapered valley boxed in by craggy peaks.

The layout was arranged intelligently. A pair of corrals was connected by a twenty-yard chute; a dozen horses were milling around the enclosure farthest from the barn, which was the top point of a crude triangle, situated roughly halfway between the two homes. Smoke chugged from the stone chimneys of both log houses, but no one was out and about. He chose to head to the barn, taking note of the large *WT* burned boldly into the wood above the main door.

He stepped out of the saddle and walked the final thirty yards. He released the reins, leaving them to hang loosely. The piebald pinto followed, as though it was a well-trained dog heeling. He cracked the door open just wide enough to usher the horse inside. There were lanterns burning in the backside of the roomy building. The sweetness of alfalfa hay, along with an underneath bouquet of manure, permeated the air.

Jondreau squinted in the grayish light. He heard low voices and took a few steps toward them, then spoke up loudly. "I'm looking for buddy-boy lawman, eh."

"What?" Pete Axler emerged from a stall at the far end. "Is that Charley Jondreau? What the dickens?" He hurried along the wide corridor, a smile cresting on his lips. Caleb Weitzel came along behind him, tucking leather gloves into his belt.

"I was just riding by."

Axler shook Jondreau's hand. Tangible respect passed between them. "I kind of doubt you just happened along to this out of the way place." He made introductions, then asked, "Are you finally in a mood to sell me that piebald?"

"No chance, but we may talk business, eh?" Charley replied, pushing his hat up his forehead. "Last spring I was a wrangler. I came north from Texas with a crew driving a herd of longhorns to the railhead."

Weitzel moved over to inspect the pinto. "That's dusty, dirty work."

Jondreau agreed by puckering his lips tightly. "Two good things about the job; payday was worthwhile and I had a good visit with preacher-man in Dodge City."

Axler had his hands in his back pockets. "How was Deacon?"

"He was well," Charley answered flatly. "I admired his horse. He told me that I had to see its steeldust sire. I spent some time in Santa Fe and took a roundabout route to get here."

"That buckskin of his is equal to Shadrach," Caleb said, ruffling the pinto's mane. "It could have easily sired its own line of splendid horses, but that was not to be." He exhaled wistfully. "It broke my heart to cut it, but that was Deacon's request. He has a fondness for geldings. He claims a higher degree of loyalty and intelligence develops when it's castrated as a colt. I can't say for sure, but wouldn't think of arguing with Deacon. He's too good a friend."

Jondreau was grinning. "One never wants to be on the wrong side of a preacher-man."

"Nope." Caleb laughed heartily. "Especially Deacon. Like my wife, his prayers are powerful. I think they both have a private pipeline to the Almighty." He was absently rubbing the pony's neck. "I like the lines and temperament of this fine animal."

"The stallion has served me well, but it's getting some age," Charley said curtly. "I'm on the lookout for a colt to school for a couple years to be ready to take its place."

Axler nodded. "We've got a yearling you might be interested in."

"Which one you have in mind, Pete?" Caleb asked, head tilting slightly.

"The dapple gray."

"That's an excellent horse, Charley. Another of Shadrach's offspring, strong and savvy," Caleb said, a bit of pride climbing into his tone. "It'll be my pleasure seeing to your mount's care and feeding, while Pete handles the showing. I'll settle on whatever deal he makes with you."

"I may be a hard sell, eh."

Weitzel put his gloves on. "That yearling won't disappoint, I promise."

The men made their way past the stables, with Weitzel leading the piebald pinto. There was interest expressed from inside several of the cubicles; many snorts and neighs as various horses found it necessary to greet the newcomer amongst them. Jondreau poked along, making an effort to take a peek in each enclosure and doing what he could to feed his curiosity.

Sally Twosongs was exhausted, but that had no impact on slowing her down. The desire to put the miscarriage and all the thorny sentiments and questions behind her was pushing her endurance to its limit and beyond. She moved through the twilight shadows at jackrabbit pace, while Hank scampered through the snow in circles around her.

She entered the barn, leaving the collie outside to continue frolicking. Her eyes were tardy in adjusting to the dusky interior. A rolling tide of anxiety came from nowhere and covered her. She felt lightheaded and nauseous; a film of perspiration bathed her skin. She slumped against the door, gulping breath in rapid pants and puffs.

"Caleb," she called, her voice sounding frail in the cavernous structure. "Caleb, venison stew and fresh bread is for supper whenever you're ready." The person she saw was not her husband. Her eyes spread wide in unbelief. She started taking rickety steps toward a solidly built man, who until now, had only inhabited her dreams. There was a vague nagging in the back of her mind that told her she was stressed and hallucinating.

Charley Jondreau gawked at her. The currents of some strange urgency vibrated between them. His mouth was twitching and contorting, as though words meant to be spoken were being snatched off his tongue. He removed his floppy-brimmed hat as he agilely padded forward on the balls of his feet, almost tiptoeing.

Caleb Weitzel and Pete Axler were frozen in their footsteps, their focus fixated on the surreal scene. There was an unfathomable presence that had both men gape-eyed in puzzled amazement. The air had abruptly become heavy and tingling; as if a prevailing supernatural energy was drawing Charley Jondreau and Sally Twosongs together.

Jondreau genuflected and knelt in front of the Navajo woman. He bowed his head in submission, then regarded her respectfully. "I am Charley Jondreau. I have *seen* you."

"I am Sally Twosongs. I *know* you."

He flinched, eyes narrowing. "*Know* me?"

"You were there when the peg-legged monster died."

He smiled grimly. "Jackson Scully was a bad man. He got what he gave."

"He killed Rainy, Gray Eyes, and many others."

"He got what he gave," Charley repeated vehemently. He rose to his feet and took hold of her hands. It was an intensely intimate and sacred crease in time—a holy moment. Veins in his neck bulged and for an extreme instant his body quaked. His eyes went dead and empty of emotion, then freakishly swam back in his head so that only the whites showed.

Her pulse-rate quickened; she was fascinated, though equally wary of the phenomenon.

He refocused, calm and composed. He pressed close and whispered directly in her ear. "You will be with child again. There will be pain and tears, grief and turmoil, but all will be redeemed, eh. Unto you a daughter will be born and it will be well with your soul."

She shrank backwards. "How? When?"

"The Great Spirit has a purpose for us. For you, eh." He stared deep into the dark coal of her eyes, which were full of awe. "You are a princess and I am at your command."

Her head throbbed. A wave of heat hit her smack-dab in the face; she staggered and her complexion became the pastiest shade of pale. The room was getting smaller and smaller, closing in and intimidating her. She clawed at his chest, wailing hugely. Her heartbeat filled her throat; she began breathing abnormally. She lunged forward and fainted into his arms.

Perfect silence cocooned Sally Twosongs.

The western horizon was reddish streaks of orange bleeding through a saw-toothed slash in the hedgerow of clouds. A constant surplus of puffy snowflakes had been falling for two hours when Deacon Coburn tied the horses to the hitching rail. He hoisted Ben Slaton out of the saddle, and after he got balanced on his good leg, stagger-stepped him up the two stairs onto the boardwalk veranda of the Suncurl Café.

Slaton muttered cusswords. He had been tough on the ride, but was now waning and surly. He was red-faced and soaked with sweat, grunting with each hop-step. "I'm hurting and I ain't going to make it. You should've used a slug on me."

"You ain't dying. And I told you, I didn't have a bullet to spare." Coburn shouldered the door open. "I could use some help here," he hollered, straining to twist through the entranceway. He was surprised by a strawberry-blonde in a dull-colored jacket, who hurried over and got on the other side of Slaton to carry his weight.

"Lean on me, mister," Max ordered plainly. "I won't fall over."

Slaton ogled her and slurred the obvious. "You're a woman."

"That I am, but forget about it. Otherwise I'll bust your other leg."

"Deacon!" Delores exclaimed, rushing out of the kitchen. "Oh, my!" She ran across the room. "Put him here in one of these rockers for now. We'll fix him up with a pallet under the mural. Avis, go upstairs and get some blankets and a few pillows."

"Yes, ma'am." She took off like a shot and raced past Whitey, who lingered beside the pool table, shoulders slumped and eyes fixed on the floor. He shuffled over to the wall rack to put away his cue stick, then crept toward the kitchen door but was stopped by a familiar voice.

"Whitey," Deacon said excitedly. "I need your steadiness here."

"I be of no use to you . . . or anyone, for that matter."

"Nonsense," Deacon replied, blasting him with a wrinkly-eyed smile. "Come check out my handiwork on this splint. See if I got the bones set tight and true." He and Max lowered Slaton into the rocker and propped his lame leg up on a chair that Delores slid into place.

"I need whiskey," Ben said, weak and raspy.

"You'll get water for starters," Delores replied sternly.

Slaton slumped back and gritted his teeth. "I *want* whiskey."

Coburn jabbed his shoulder. "You'll have what the lady says."

Slaton sneered. "I may pass out." His eyelids drooped shut.

Fitzgerald was easing closer. He moved as tentatively as a whipped puppy approaching the one who had doled out the mistreatment. His eyes were downcast, his hands in his pockets.

Coburn knelt to size up the situation. He checked and thoroughly felt the leg. "I'm fairly sure I got the broken bones in alignment, but I'd appreciate your input, Whitey."

Fitzgerald gave a lackadaisical and feeble click-click between his cheek and gum. He crouched on his haunches. "I be a barber and dentist, not a doctor."

"I value and trust your skills, my friend."

It was then that Ben Slaton opened his eyes. He sat up straight and rigid, startled and showing bug-eyed anger. "What the hell? I ain't going to let some nigger poke around my leg, especially a greasy rubby-dub who stinks of stale liquor."

Coburn reacted spontaneously. His right hand lashed out and locked around Slaton's throat. "Understand that you're a guest in this establishment. I will not tolerate rudeness or ill manners. Everyone here deserves to be treated with the utmost respect." His vise-like squeeze intensified. "Anything less and I will personally take you to some remote hinterland and strand you in a snow bank to fend for yourself. Do I make myself clear?"

Slaton blanched and choked on slobbery words. "Yeah, loud and clear."

Coburn released his hold. "Now that we got that straight there will be peace between us," he said in a tone that was amazingly cool and unruffled. He inched back. "Have a gander here, Whitey. Is there anything else we can do to help this gentleman's leg to heal?"

Fitzgerald began his examination. His hands flittered with erratic tremors and his eyes kept darting nervously. He filled his lungs and made his habitual noise as he settled into a somber probing, while ignoring the croaky moans emanating from the patient.

Avis Lahay was open-mouthed and wide-eyed. She had witnessed the whole exchange from the instant the injured man spoke critically of who he'd allow to assess his damaged leg. She was on the far side of the pool table, her arms loaded with blankets and pillows. As Whitey bore down, she coughed to make her presence known and started over to the mural.

Max flashed an encouraging smile. "All's well here, Avis. I'll give you a hand."

Fitzgerald stood and stepped back. "From what I can feel and tell, you did a satisfactory job, Deacon. There are no protrusions and the bones are in position to be on the mend. The bruising will be ugly, but as long as the swelling is minimal like it is, that splint should stay on for a couple weeks before it's removed for a look at the progress, then replaced."

"I'm grateful for the consult and confirmation, Whitey," Deacon said, grinning and nudging him good-naturedly. He then shifted and cast a hard-eyed glower on Slaton.

"Yeah, okay. Thanks, mister," Ben said meekly.

Whitey responded with an almost detached shrug. "I just did what I was asked."

Delores put a hand on his shoulder. "Glad to have you here, Whitey."

"The bed is ready," Max announced, and went to Slaton's right side. "Let's get this man down." She slung an arm under his, and Coburn did the same from the left. Slaton hissed a cuss as he stood. The move was accomplished with a smidgeon of grunts. When Slaton was stretched out in relative comfort, introductions were made all around.

Coburn exhaled a loud sigh. "It's been a burdensome day and it still has work to be done. There's a pair of horses outside I need to take to the livery."

"I can handle that," Max said easily. "I need to check on my own mount."

Avis brightened. "I'll come along, if that's alright, Max."

"Happy for the company, girl."

Her smile enlarged. "I'll stop at the shack to get your carpetbag, Mr. Whitey."

Fitzgerald's expression hardened. "No need to do that, sweetie."

Coburn squinted. "Why not?" He blinked and shed his sheepskin parka; he tossed it onto a nearby table. His head pivoted from the girl to Whitey to Delores, then back to the girl. He repeated that pattern twice more. A perceptive gleam became merriment in his eyes as awareness came over him and he surmised the situation. His mouth puckered, causing the corners of his bushy moustache to twitch. "Avis, do what your heart tells you to do."

"Yes, sir."

"Bring that carpetbag back here, young lady," Deacon said in an authoritative tone. "If Mr. Whitey doesn't like that, you tell him to grouse at me. We can talk it all out because we got lots of catching up and hashing over to do."

Avis was beaming when she ran off to get her outerwear.

Delores enfolded her arms around Deacon's waist in a sideways hug. She sighed and her hold on him tightened. "You just made that girl's day. Mine, too."

Fitzgerald sagged, head hanging. "I be outnumbered and hogtied here."

Delores burst into laughter. "You've been done in by people who love you, Whitey." She released her broad-shouldered friend. "I'll get our patient water and a dose of laudanum."

"You got laudanum? Thank God," Ben said, letting loose a relieved murmur.

"I will be the only one who administers it."

"Yes, ma'am."

"I must get to it," Delores said chirpily. "A pot of chicken and dumplings is on the simmer for supper." She strolled to the kitchen, a happy bounce in her steps.

Coburn took a seat in one of the rockers. "Join me, Whitey. It ain't a stoop in Abilene or Dodge City, but this pretty picture makes it a fine spot for us to visit and jaw."

Fitzgerald click-clicked and sat in the other bentwood rocker, obviously angst-ridden. "If it be all the same to you, I be inclined to sit aside you in silence for a spell."

Coburn was agreeable to that proposition. He reached out and patted his forearm; Whitey drew back. He tried on a smile and tears glistened, then trickled from his raw eyes. He turned away and began rocking. Coburn joined him in the metrical motion. While the old friends made the chairs squeak in perfect harmony, Ben Slaton watched until slumber took hold of him.

≈ ≈ ≈

Eliza Weitzel felt as though the past was encroaching on the present. Her hands were swift and busy as she tenderly labored as a nurse. She had far too much experience treating wounded men. At the battle of Gettysburg, their farm had been commandeered into a hospital outpost. She had devotedly provided service as a surgical assistant in the midst of savagery and misery. Those terrible days were a form of purgatory that left its imprint on her character.

Then, in the autumn of 1868, a corpselike scarecrow of a man walked out of the badlands and dropped in his footsteps to be found by her son. The raggedy man had been held captive and beaten by a ruthless band of Utes, who staked him in the New Mexico sun to die. His chest and back were slashed in furrows, as though the knife blade had been a plow. She had prayed and tended to him for weeks before he snuck away from the threshold of death.

Eliza had passion and fortitude thriving inside her. Life was precious; sanctified, even. In her core, she believed that each breath was a gift of God to be treasured. No matter how severe or disheartening the circumstances, she fundamentally believed that where there was life, there was hope— where there was a will, there was a way.

Therefore, she would *always* resist the grim reaper with every scrap of knowledge and skill she had acquired; fight the bastard tooth and nail, until there was nothing else to do but yield to the wisdom and judgment of the One who held the life and times ordained for each person in the omniscience of his sovereign hands.

Silas Dawson was now under her care. She was vigilant, dozing and catching forty winks at opportune interludes, often while sitting at his bedside. Night and day, Eliza kept an array of candles burning on a high dresser in what was once Caleb's room. Hans and Gray Cloud relieved her now and again, but mostly, she took responsibility for the suffering Texas Ranger.

She was well acquainted with the legend of the man. Newspapers and clippings were strewn on the floor at the foot of the bed. She had meticulously studied each one that Gray Cloud provided, reading between the lines, and heeding every detail. The accounts painted the portrait of a singularly hard-boiled lawman with a black and white sense of justice that duked it out with crooks and desperados on his terms; no quarter given, no prisoners taken.

Silas Dawson was a hero in the Lone Star state; his notoriety eked its way across the southwestern frontier. She wanted to know him better; she yearned to hear his version of the reports and tales. To that end, she worked as diligently as possible to nurture recovery. All she needed was arranged on a small table she had moved close to the bed.

Dawson was benumbed and burning up with fever. Since his arrival he had only gained consciousness for a brief moment, but then was wholly unresponsive again. The blankets were folded below the barrel of his chest to have clearance to scrutinize the wound and change the dressing. A curly mat of silvery-black body hair swathed his torso. She had carefully cut and shaved much in the area surrounding the pus-filled puncture in his left shoulder.

At regular intervals she removed the gauze from the festering hole to wash it with vinegary brine infused with crushed medicinal herbs. She was doing so now. The skin encircling the seepage was like nothing she had ever seen; shriveled and discolored to a blackened blotch that was emitting a sickly stench. Veins of angry inflammation were raised in ridges and spreading as a network of spider-webs down the arm and up the neck.

Eliza was fearful. She had familiarity with gangrene's putrid blood odor. The funk wafting from the rotting flesh was different; a bitterly pungent aroma that stung her nostrils. She finished by slathering a gluey salve, loaded with dried osha root and red willow bark, into the foul opening. Gray Cloud assured her that the mix would draw out infection. She secured a clean piece of cottony cloth over the lesion, then tucked the covers under his chin.

Tiredness made itself known to her. There was pressure creeping ever so slowly between her ears. She wiped her hands on a small towel and slowly lowered herself onto the hard-backed chair. She sat stone-faced, gathering her faith into focus. Her lips began moving as she silently called upon God to bathe Silas Dawson in an outpouring of healing mercy.

≈ ≈ ≈

Midway through the next morning, tense vibrations were in the air. Deacon Coburn and Whitey Fitzgerald sat across from each other at the island bar in the center of the kitchen. They were drinking coffee and conversing circles around heart matters, while Delores Solrizo sliced vegetables and prepped supper at the woodblock work station. She listened and occasionally tossed an encouraging glance in their direction.

Fitzgerald was fidgety. "I ain't got much to say."

"I ain't looking for much," Deacon said emphatically. "I'm getting shaggy, so maybe later today or tomorrow you could give me a shave and a haircut."

"It might be choppy since I still got the shakes."

"On your worse day you're still the best barber I know," Deacon told him, smiling. "After all, I rode here from Dodge City and got trapped in a bear claw of a snowstorm, which ought to tell you something about my feelings concerning your expertise."

"Make him pretty, Whitey." Delores turned toward them. "But, please do so in one of the rooms upstairs. I don't want clippings fluttering around my kitchen."

Fitzgerald thought on that for a moment and a sly grin sparked his bloodshot eyes. "I be good with scissors and razor, but he's getting some age. See the smattering of white in his chin-whiskers. He may be past the point of getting to look pretty."

Delores took a step closer to them, tilted her head and raised her eyebrows as she gave Coburn a frank and comprehensive appraisal. "Oh, I don't know, Whitey. It appears there's still some reasonably sufficient raw material with which to work."

"I do my best, Miss Delores, but I ain't promising no miracles."

Coburn held his hands up and waved. "Are you both aware I'm sitting here?"

"Of course," Delores said smartly. Her eyes were alive with whimsy and mischief. She shifted her attention back to her task. "Why else would we have been so honest?"

Coburn cupped his chin in his hand. "I suppose I should be grateful then."

Fitzgerald chuckled; it was muted and sad-sounding. He took a swallow of coffee, followed by a click-click sigh. "You two be good people. I ain't worthy of your friendship."

"None of us are good, Whitey," Deacon said, serious and straight-faced. "Ain't a shred of righteousness or decency in the whole human race. Left to our chicaneries we have all the nobility of slimy snails. It's only by grace that anyone has a chance to walk uprightly."

"In my head I want to grab onto that, but my heart be shamed and fearful," Whitey replied, eyes full of moisture. "I be getting to the place where I need to talk, but I ain't rightly sure I got anything to say. Maybe I just start and see where it goes. How'd that be?"

Coburn nudged him with a pleasant smile. "That's a first-rate idea."

Fitzgerald palmed tears off his cheeks and took a gulp of breath, exhaling it tiredly. "Miss Eloise Smith, if that was even her name, played me for a fool," he began, staring vacantly. "I got no explanation or excuse. I thought we was to be married and living here in Santa Fe. I'd set up shop or take a job in an established parlor, and have at least one meal a week at the Suncurl Café with Miss Delores. Eloise and me dreamed about all of that and more, whilst she kept my blood on the boil the way only a sassy woman can do.

"In Las Vegas she hooked up with her cohort, a supposed family friend, an oily white man known as Huey Butters, which was certainly an alias. I was drugged and fleeced and discarded. At the first opportunity I dove into a bottle and stayed drunk or half-drunk for I don't know how long. I also . . ." He abruptly stopped and shook his head fast. "Nope. I be done. I ain't telling no more. I be ashamed enough without going further. I got rats to kill."

"So kill them, Whitey. Suffocate them with perseverance."

Fitzgerald scoffed derisively. "I ain't got no hope of that happening."

"You ain't the first to flounder in despair," Deacon replied, absently toying with his moustache. "I was lost and had no hope for a long while after Gettysburg. I didn't even know who I was, but one step at a time I persevered forward, not having any assurance that I was going anywhere. Little by little my feet were directed onto the straight path. Plodding perseverance forged and shaped my character, which in the fullness of time gave birth to hope."

"I's scared."

"That's only natural, my friend."

"No, you don't understand," Whitey said angrily. His click-click was out of control; it punctuated each sentence like berserk castanets. "I be scared of me; I be scared I can't change or go back because of what's inside me. The liquor robbed me of my pride and who I was once. Used to be I'd drink a wee-bit on blue moons and such, but no more, yet I thirst for it. I desperately want a bottle now and I's awfully scared what I might do to get one."

"You got a long haul back, Whitey. I will walk alongside you."

Delores came over and embraced him. "As will I."

"Why are you folks so good to me?" Whitey asked, sniffing back tears.

"We're family, Whitey," Delores answered, gently rubbing his back. "You are not alone. I have ample experiential evidence that there's plenty of life after upheaval and heartache. In the best possible usage of the words, I love you, so please don't push me away. You and I are a couple castoff waifs brought together by destiny. And Deacon is our wise older brother."

"Not destiny, Delores," Deacon said, low-key and solemn. "We ride upon the rippling currents set in motion for us by the Almighty. We merely lean into eddies we choose."

Delores was wet-eyed. "I'm grateful we are presently together."

Fitzgerald broke down in an eruption of emotion. His body shook as sobs wrenched out. Delores clung to him and he clutched at her the way a drowning man would thrash and cling to a buoyant life preserver. Coburn's mouth was drawn as tight as tight could be; misty-eyed, he stood and surrounded them in a strong-armed hug. The tense circle constricted, then in a few short minutes, a screaming obscenity from the other room shattered the prayerful huddle.

Ben Slaton came awake dry-mouthed and randy, which given the discomfort of his pained circumstances put him in a coarse and irritable mood. In dreamland, he had been in bed with Brenda Hawkins, his on-again off-again whore girlfriend in Las Vegas. He was aroused and immediately wanted two things; water and female companionship.

He propped himself up on his elbows, glanced at the mural above him and shifted his buttocks. He bundled a handful of blanket over the bulge in his trousers, then had a look around. Max Dawson was shooting pool with the girl. He briefly eyed the youngster, but despite her innocent prettiness and the budding promise beneath her loose-fitting clothes, he chose to put all his attention and effort on impressing the strawberry-blonde.

Her back was to him, stretching across the table making a shot. His consideration hustled to the location it went to whenever the opportunity presented itself; her heart-shaped posterior was straining against the dungarees and he scrupulously relished the sight. She sank the ball in a corner, then strolled to the other side and turned to face his direction. His eyes leapt to her topside. Her jacket couldn't obscure the rounded swell inside the chamois shirt.

"Slaton, eyes up!" Max demanded in a terse tone.

He jerked back, startled. He faked ignorance. "What?"

"I do not accept or permit crappola, Slaton. I *ever* catch you looking at me like that again and I'll happily finish what you obviously failed to do," Max said, level and measured.

"What?"

"Please put away the big-eyed virtuous act," Max replied, grinning snidely. "A greenhorn moron could figure how you got that black streak burned on the side of your face."

"Shut up, you bed-fagot."

"I beg your pardon?"

"You heard me."

Max chuckled throatily. "A real man would *never* attempt what you botched."

"What are you talking about, Max?" Avis asked naively.

"That's muzzle burn on his cheek, Avis," Max answered in a deadpan manner. "He's a quitter with no staying power, a bumpkin and a saddle tramp. He likely put the barrel of a gun under his jaw intending to do himself in, but chickened out as he pulled the trigger."

Slaton fell back, eyes on the ceiling. "You weren't there, missy. You know nothing."

"You tell yourself whatever you need to, Slaton," Max said cheerily. "You can't fool me." She leaned forward and snapped off a pocket-cracking shot; then another.

"I could use some Adam's ale here."

"You better get it for him, Avis. I might drown the bugger."

There was a glass and a silver pitcher of water on a table near him. Avis went to it and poured a drink. When she handed it to him, he held up a finger to indicate he wanted her to wait a moment. He slurped it down all at once, dragged a back hand over his mouth, then crudely ordered her to get him a refill. He grabbed hold of her wrist and tried to pull her onto him. She yanked free and tipped over one of the bentwood rockers before crashing to the floor.

Max dealt with Slaton devoid of pity or hesitation. She was all over him like a bobcat on a field mouse. She kicked him in the head for starters, then in a furious flurry of motion she had a derringer against his ear and a boot firmly planted on his crotch; she was grinding the heel harder and harder. That was when his voice ripped out in a high-pitched screech of profanity.

"Squeal like a sissy," Max said, laughing. "Give me a reason to finish the job on you."

Deacon Coburn was the first to come racing out of the kitchen into the *Cantina Room*. Whitey Fitzgerald and Delores Solrizo almost tripped over each other in their haste to get through the doorway. Delores rushed straight to Avis and put an arm around her, while Whitey dawdled off to the side, hands in his pockets as he click-clicked neurotically.

Coburn sought to defuse the situation. "Let him up easy, Max."

"I don't think so, Deacon. He hasn't learned his lesson yet."

"How do you intend to make it stick, Max?"

"Pull the trigger or crush his gonads and make him a eunuch," she replied, applying weighted pressure to the foot stuck in his groin. "He apologizes to Avis or else."

Slaton squirmed, pop-eyed and scarlet-faced. "I'm sorry, Avis."

"That wasn't too difficult, was it?" Max relaxed as she quickly pulled away from him.

Coburn forcibly prodded her. "You best make yourself scarce for a bit."

Max balked at the suggestion. She returned the double-barreled pocket pistol to its shoulder holster and glared at Coburn. There was ice prickling between them. She kept eyes on him, then retreated by taking a giant backward step; she glimpsed steely strength in him she had no desire to buck against. "I'll be back, but I got horses at the livery to care for just now."

"Do you want me to come along, Max?"

"Not this time, Avis."

Delores spoke up. "You're with me, Avis. Leave this for the men to sort out."

When the room was clear of women folk, Coburn got on his haunches beside Slaton. He did an in-depth checkup on the splint and determined that it was intact. "For a man who told me he would be on his best behavior, I must say that you fall a mite short."

"That wench needs to get knocked down a peg or two."

"Are you daft, Ben?"

Slaton's upper lip curled into a snarl. "I'd straighten her out if I wasn't laid up here."

"If you believe that, you got nothing but empty space between your ears," Deacon said, direct and dead-eyed serious. "A woman who chooses to live in a man's world could hold her own or outdo most every smart-alecky roughneck. I wouldn't cross Max Dawson."

"Well, you ain't me, are you, Coburn?"

"I reckon not."

"You ain't so tough."

"I ain't the one hobbled and needing assistance, am I?"

Slaton grimaced. "An accident can happen to anyone."

Coburn gave him an expressive open-armed shrug. "True enough as far as it goes, but it seems to me that a sign of toughness from someone dependent on the mercy of others would be a liberal demonstration of humility. You ought to give that a try sometime."

"Screw you, Coburn."

"If you're going to talk guff, flap your gums to yourself," Deacon said, standing.

Slaton smirked. "Where's this brother you came to help?"

Coburn gestured toward his friend. "It's Whitey."

"The nigger is your brother?"

"Son, you ain't ever going to get it, are you?" Deacon said, rolling his eyes as he turned sideward. "Whatever are we to do with this foul-mouthed loafer, Whitey?"

"My mammy would've recommended lye soap."

"Lather up his tongue?"

"And make him swallow some."

Coburn wagged his head, lips pursed in disgust. "That ain't nasty enough medicine for a boorish malcontent." He knelt and tapped a finger against Slaton's chest as he spoke. "You have used up my patience and tried my charity, Ben. Violate respect or common decency once more and I will deposit you in a remote wasteland. Don't test or force my hand."

Ben Slaton slumped back in contrite resignation.

~ ~ ~

"Am I in trouble, Miss Delores?"

"Trouble? Heavens, no."

They were behind closed doors in the office off the kitchen. Avis was perched on the edge of a chair, hands folded on her lap. "I'm sorry for that big hullabaloo."

"What happened, honey?"

Avis related the details straightforwardly, as though she was making a clinical assessment as she did so. When she came to the end, she added a flourish of commentary in the form of hero worship. "Max isn't scared of nothing or nobody. You should have seen how fast she moved."

"I'm thankful that she's here," Delores said, resting her forearms on the desk. "You must understand that you have no reason to feel bad or apologize to anybody, Avis. The world is full of men like Ben Slaton who think women everywhere are at their beck and call. They're rogues and ruffians who want only one thing from women, then discard them afterwards."

Avis pouted, unnerved and skeptical. "Ben wanted to do sex on me?"

"It was surely in his mind, honey," Delores replied candidly. "You are everything a bully like Slaton seeks out; a beautiful young lady flowering and filling out quite nicely."

"Me? Beautiful? Really?"

"Yes, really," Delores said, sorrow developing in her eyes. "I hope I can teach you how to deal with men and not be persuaded by sweet talk or taken advantage of by power. I don't want you to get hurt or have something precious stolen from you the way it was taken . . ." A quiver came into her voice and she cut it off by pressing her lips into a taut reddish line.

Avis bent forward, frowning. "What is it, Miss Delores?"

"I'm just worried about you, Avis. Are you injured at all?"

"My bum's going to get a bruise. I hit the floor hard."

Delores smiled slightly. "It could have been significantly worse."

Avis hemmed and hawed for a moment, then asked, "Miss Delores, can we talk?"

"We are talking, Avis."

"I mean, it's been a long while since we discussed the topic of how I came to be here and why," Avis said tentatively. "I'm getting older and wondering about all of it."

"It's no big secret," Delores answered, leaning back in the swivel chair. "I've told you from the beginning. I wanted to help someone and provide a brighter future."

"Why? And why me?"

Delores gave a vague sigh. "It's not complicated, Avis. When I was a little girl in St. Louis I used to walk past an orphanage with my mother. My heart would break for those children. I grew up wanting to rescue them all, to encourage each and every one."

"But why me?"

"That's simple," Delores replied hastily. "I prayed for you. You're the one God guided my agents to locate. I simply told the detectives to find a smart girl who wasn't afraid of hard work so I could train her in the restaurant business. That's what I've been doing, isn't it?"

"Yes, and so much more."

"Are you happy?"

"Of course. I'm happier than ever."

"So quit digging through the ashes," Delores said, pushing to her feet. "Bring the embers forward to kindle a new fire and leave the ashes behind."

"That fire is burning pretty good, don't you think, Miss Delores?"

"Indeed, it is, honey. Does this finally solve the mystery for you?"

Avis tented her eyebrows. "I guess so."

Tender optimism and affection passed between them.

Naomi Axler was distraught. She had done everything she knew to do, but nothing reduced the fever in her son or gave any relief to his congestion. In fact, Jesse seemed to be getting hotter and sicker as each hour passed; the croup had mutated into something far worse, filling his lungs with fluid and phlegm. Just now she was rubbing a plaster of mustard and goose grease on his chest. She covered the balm with a towel and swaddled him.

The boy's eyes were foggy and glazed over, pleading and full of help-lessness. He was still and silent; not a squeak or a whimper passed over his cracked lips. She sat on his bed, bathing his heated brow with a cool cloth. She regularly rinsed and wrung it out in a basin of melting snow on the floor near her feet. Bad thoughts kept trying to influence her. She pushed them away with prayer and Scripture, but could sense anxiety creeping in all around her.

The back door opened and closed. "Naomi."

She felt an inkling of relief. "In here, Pete."

"Can you come to the kitchen? We have a visitor."

The idea upset her. "Jesse's sick, Pete. I haven't got time to entertain."

"It will only take a moment, Naomi."

She was perturbed. "Land sakes!" She dropped the cloth in the icy water and stood. She patted and adjusted her skirt, and was finger combing her hair as she departed the bedroom.

Pete was leaning in the doorframe of the kitchen. A fleeting smile chased over his lips. He took hold of her hand and led her into the room. "This is Charley Jondreau."

"I'm happy to meet you, Mr. Jondreau, but this is not a good time."

He dipped his head and tipped the brim of his hat. "I am Charley." He was beside the table. "It is good for me to be here in this hour. You are the sister of preacher-man, eh?"

She frowned at her husband. "Does he mean Deacon?"

Axler chuckled. "He and Deacon have some history."

"Bring the sick boy to me," Charley said gently.

"For what reason, Mr. Jondreau?" There was a sharp undercurrent of anger in her voice. "You may know my husband and brother, but I'm not at all familiar with you."

"Bring the sick boy to me and he will be well, eh."

Naomi's resistance was evident in the straight line set of her mouth.

Axler put his hands on her shoulders. "I understand, but Charley and Sally Twosongs have some kind of connection. Kindred spirits or something, I don't know."

She studied Jondreau. "Are you Navajo?"

"Iroquois, Scotch-Irish, French. My blood knows much, eh."

Her hands were fidgety, which was uncharacteristic. Her heart gave her clearance to trust him. She hurried to the bedroom. When she returned with Jesse, Jondreau was sitting at the head of the table. His coat and floppy-brimmed hat hung on the back of his chair. In her mind, he had the appearance of a chieftain. She placed the bundled child in the cradle of his arms.

He removed the blanket and handed it to her. His smile was ordinary, but his eyes were faraway and furtive. He pressed a hand on the boy's chest. His eyelids fluttered, then dropped shut. He began rocking side to side, singing a chant low in his throat. The somber notes rose and fell in a rhythmic melody that matched the swaying of his body.

Naomi held her husband's hand, squeezing hard. Pete eyed her, the ever-present sad-sack lines deeper and more pronounced than usual. Her heartbeat raced, but then, as the ardent ritual continued, she realized that the thumping inside her ribcage had become a drumbeat in sync with his song. She watched, amazed and frightened all at once.

Jondreau's voice broke. An ambiguous grin appeared. Beads of sweat glistened on his shaved head. The droplets shimmied down his face. He was sweating profusely, as though he was trapped in a summer swelter. "Your son will sleep and be well when he awakes," he said, handing him to her. "Bring me your daughter so that I might also give her my blessing."

Naomi was open-mouthed, marveling. "How? What happened?" She examined her firstborn, touching him tenderly. He hadn't made a peep the whole while, but now, clear-eyed and smiling, a gurgling bubble of laughter burst forth and he squirmed in her arms.

"The fever is gone, eh. I took it inside me and killed it."

Naomi had awe in her eyes. "I'll return with Amanda, and we can talk."

Jondreau brushed a hand over his slick scalp, then put his hat on. "It will be sensible for us to talk of many important matters, or we can talk of nothing."

Naomi rushed out. Less than five minutes later she bustled back to the kitchen with her baby. "I am at a loss to explain this, but Jesse is sound asleep. There isn't a rattle or wheeze or anything in his chest," she said, immediately putting the infant girl in Jondreau's care. She took a seat across the table from him. "Pete, will you please brew a fresh pot of Arbuckle's?"

"I can do that, dear."

Naomi gazed at Jondreau pensively. "You performed a miracle."

"No," Charley replied, flat and adamant. "The Great Spirit healed your son. He gave me a gift at my birth. I am responsible to be available and faithful when it is needed."

"Available and faithful? You were so here, for which I am grateful, Charley."

Jondreau gave her a lackadaisical shrug. His attention was on the child in his arms. He was toying with her curls as she cooed to him. "You are preacher-man's sister. I am a seeker and wanderer. I came here as a wayfarer to serve and learn what the Great Spirit has for me."

"That's a wise way to live, Charley."

"You are a kind and gentle soul."

Naomi pooh-poohed the comment. "How do you know Sally Twosongs?"

"The Great Spirit led me to her, eh."

"I am concerned and worried about her."

Axler sidled away from the cook-stove. "As of an hour ago, she was doing much better. After she fainted yesterday, Caleb put her to bed and is now waiting on her hand and foot. He will not let her out of his sight," he reported analytically. "Charley is going to pitch in around here for a few days while Sally Twosongs recuperates under Caleb's due diligence."

"Good. I'll fix a crock pot of stew for them."

Jondreau nodded his approval. "Be assured that Sally Twosongs will grow strong and be fine. She is blessed by the Creator. She will outlive all us adults, but not this little one." He made a rumbling noise and riveted his eyes on the baby. He placed a thumb on her chin and released a potent sounding utterance in a choppy cadence, then spoke in plain language. "You are worthy of love, Amanda. You shall live long as a helpmate to many and keeper of the altar fires."

"What are the altar fires?" Pete asked in a mystified voice.

"A blessing that is already aflame in her heart, eh."

Naomi Axler stifled tears and treasured those words.

Gray Cloud had his fervency braced and fortified. His medicine bag—a mix of corn pollen, dried sweet-grass and a handful of pebbles special to him—hung around his neck, along with several strings of ghost beads. He had anointed Silas Dawson's forehead and upper torso with cedar oil, and was now, squatted on the floor at the foot of the bed, burning a smudge; coiled ribbons of sage and cedar smoke rose from an abalone shell.

He used a fan made of four hawk feathers to stir the smoke prayers over him and heavenward. Eliza had just finished cleaning and dressing the wound, and now, she stepped back to give Gray Cloud full access. He stood and slid along the side of the bed, fluttering the fan inches above the patient to cover him completely in wisps of smoke.

In the doorway, Hans Weitzel took in all the activity with a skeptic's eye. He was as stiff and erect as a veteran soldier on guard duty. His wife eased close to give an encouraging and hopeful look. He tried to respond in kind, but hedged and his mouth flexed into a facial expression that conveyed a multitude of doubts against a good outcome.

When Gray Cloud completed the intercessory protocols, he returned to a cross-legged position on the floor in front of the abalone shell. He buffeted a fresh offering of smoke over him, intoning an appeal that had hard-edged syllables. The phrases rose and fell as though being churned on whitecap breakers, then abruptly stopped. He bowed his head in reverence.

"Lord, hear our prayers," Eliza said firmly.

"He better," Hans muttered, gruff and thin-lipped.

Gray Cloud nodded. "The Creator must. Otherwise there is no hope."

"Where there's life there's hope, but God numbers the days for each of us." Eliza swiftly glanced from one man to the other, weariness on her face. "Our Father in heaven always hears our prayers. He alone determines the answer, which we must receive in faith, believing that he does all things well. His purposes are far beyond our understanding."

"The whys and wherefores of God is your territory, Eliza," Hans said, managing to hew the rough edges off his tone. "My concern is this; what else can we do for this good man, who according to all the newspaper reports I've read, is a fighter who refuses defeat." He angled toward Gray Cloud. "Are there any other ceremonies or medicine to give him a chance?"

"Chaparral," the Navajo man answered, eyebrows crooking up. "Maybe."

"I'm not familiar with it," Eliza said, taking a seat at the bedside.

"I have some, but it could be awkward to dole out," Gray Cloud told her, flecks of uncertainty swirling in his dark eyes. "The leaves of the creosote bush are ground into a flaky powder that must be eaten and digested. His condition would make that difficult." He stretched up to look at the unconscious man on the bed, who was breathing shallowly.

"We must try, Gray Cloud."

"Yes, by all means," Hans agreed, stepping behind his wife to rest his hands on her shoulders. "Eliza will find a technique to nurse it down his gullet."

Gray Cloud sighed and raked a hand through his lengthy hair. "I could boil a tea and cool it," he said, hunching his shoulders. "Or I suppose there's a way to concoct a poultice to put on the wound, but I never heard of chaparral being used as such, though we are desperate."

"Do both," Eliza ordered, strained urgency in her voice.

Gray Cloud pursed his lips into a fish-like pucker. Worry and fear emerged in his eyes. "I will do as you ask and leave the results to the Creator. He will do as he pleases."

Weitzel eyed him suspiciously. "What are you not telling us?"

Gray Cloud grunted. "I am afraid; very afraid for Silas Dawson. The puncture was put there by an arrow shot from Smoky Crowe's bow. If it had come from any other bow he would recover, but the stone arrowhead which inflicted the damage was surely dipped in a vile poison created by Smokey Crowe using witch magic. I know of no antidote for it."

Eliza quickened her resolve. "I'll not give up."

Hans squeezed her upper arms. "Neither will we."

Hope coursed between the three of them, encompassing the room.

≈ ≈ ≈

In the evening, the *Cantina Room* was bright and cheery. All the wall-mounted lamps were aglow, casting yellow hues from wall to wall. Laughter popped and wisecracks flew at the far end, where Whitey Fitzgerald and Avis Lahay were shooting pool, joking with each other and developing a bond. Max Dawson sat on a stool waiting to play the winner, alternating between watching and interacting with them, and keeping her nose stuck in a book.

Ben Slaton was asleep beneath the mural snoring in erratic snuffles. After the mid-morning altercation, he had remained subdued and affable, dozing in and out of slumber. There were even a few moments when his attitude came close to gallant chivalry. His pacified mood and drowsy lethargy came as the result of being regularly medicated with laudanum.

Meanwhile, across the room, Deacon Coburn and Delores Solrizo were sitting on the cushions in the bay window, enjoying each other's company while monitoring the scene around the billiard table. Gusts of wind occasionally made the thick pane of glass at their backs squeak. Their conversation was easy and comfortable, running the gamut from the past through the present and into plans for the future. Her pleased smile was large and beaming.

"You are unquestionably in your element," Deacon said, tapping her knee. "Seeing you here is akin to watching a bald eagle soar across a blue sky above mountain peaks."

"Why are you so kind?"

"You mistake kindness for sincerity."

She gave his foot a tiny kick. "Whatever you call it, having you as a big brother is a jewel in my life." She nudged him with an elbow. "Do you ever wonder about the possibilities between us if we would've met at a church social instead of in a whorehouse?"

"I ain't one to conjecture on hypotheticals."

"No, you *ain't*," she said, mimicking him.

Coburn grinned self-effacingly. "Making sense of the trajectory of my time on earth is complex enough without throwing a bunch of what ifs and if onlys into the hopper."

"I relate to the truth of those words," she said sternly. "You helped me plenty." She made a gesture toward the pool table, where Whitey was now on a stool and Max on her feet with cue stick in hand. "You need to be deliberate and have a sit-down with Max. I have no doubt that she would benefit from the counsel and guidance of your friendship."

"She's predisposed to be tenacious, isn't she?"

"Perhaps you could channel it toward a positive objective, Deacon."

"I'll have a chat with her."

Slaton panted a loud snort. Delores glanced at him. "In a day or so I'll begin to wean him off the painkiller, but for now, having him still and sleeping is likely best for his healing. Not to mention what that will do to keep it peaceful around here."

"Sorry about his penchant to beak off and make trouble."

"He's done, I think." Delores stood for a moment and repositioned the cushion, then sat again. "I expect him to set a new standard for gentlemanly behavior whilst he remains here."

"That'd be refreshing."

"Don't underestimate your influence on him."

"Influence? I resorted to threats."

"Whatever transpired after we left the room seems to have taken hold. I noted a stark difference in his comportment this afternoon." She angled her upper body to face him. "When we talked in the kitchen, did you have a sense that Whitey wasn't telling the whole story?"

"Yes, it was clear to me that something else is stuck in his craw."

"What could it be?"

"Does it matter?" he queried with a shrug. "He's still hurting, shamed and unsure of what comes next for him. We must grant him all the time and grace he needs to overcome whatever those rats may be." He shifted to meet her eyes. "What about you, Delores?"

Her forehead wrinkled. "I'm not sure what you're asking?"

"What part of your story are you not telling?"

"Are you being purposefully fuzzy, Deacon?"

"Does Avis know you're her mother?"

Her complexion paled. "What?" She averted her gaze. "Why would you say that?"

"A dimwitted blind man could see it, Delores."

"That's not true," she said inflexibly. "It *can't* be true."

"The girl has got your eyes, and eyes that pretty don't lie," he replied, leaning in closer to her. "If Whitey wasn't muddled and hangdog he'd have seen it straight off."

She slouched back against the glass. Her hands were clasped on her lap. She stared at them for several minutes before speaking in a hushed tone. "I should have known that your watchful ways would ferret this out, but it's a private matter, Deacon. It's better for her that she never knows. She can be her own person with none of my ugly history and baggage."

"Living a lie has dire consequences, Delores."

"Do you remember what I was, Deacon?"

"The past is the past. If you build the present on lies, it'll crash."

Confusion and apprehension amassed in her eyes, along with a film of moisture. She saw that the pool players were entirely engaged, guffawing and carrying on, unconcerned with doings elsewhere. She took a hefty breath and exhaled in a resigned sigh. "Jackson Scully was her father. I got pregnant early in the relationship, when love was blooming between us."

"Love, not money gave birth to this girl?"

"Yes. Jackson and I were complicated," she said forthrightly. "He was stationed at Fort Smith and visited my business. We had an attraction that I still can't explain. He got westward orders the day I was to tell him about our baby. Scully never knew, then he was gone."

Coburn urged her to continue with persistent fluttering fingers.

"I could have used pennyroyal to lose the baby, but the idea of bleeding to death scared me. I went into seclusion and waited out the pregnancy." She kept her voice discreet and level. "I hardened my heart and nurtured denial. When the birth pangs ran their course, I placed her in an orphanage without even holding her. In the paperwork I plucked her name out of the blue. Then I traded Fort Smith for East Texas and went into partnership with Big Bull Wallace."

"It was in that establishment we first met."

"Ah-huh."

"How did Avis come to be here?"

"You won't be satisfied until you hear it all, huh?"

"My satisfaction is not at issue, Delores. I want to assist, if at all possible."

"I know, Deacon." She laid a hand on his forearm and gave it a gentle squeeze. "After Naomi prayed me through a spiritual breakthrough in Abilene, I recalled everything about my baby. It pained me to know that I had buried the memory beneath all the other garbage."

"Our minds have a remarkable capacity to deceive us."

"I sought to rectify matters as soon as I remembered," she said, eyes shiny and wet. "On the morning of that day a tornado struck south of Abilene, I sent off telegrams to contacts in the Pinkertons and set the investigation in motion to find her."

"That twister did a pile of damage."

"Indeed, but it has an incomparable significance for me."

"How so?"

"I identify it as the day I decisively planted my feet on a turnaround path," she answered, dabbing dampness off her cheeks. "Much later, when Jackson's body was found washed up on a bank of Mud Creek, word came to me that he had probably been killed in that storm. By then I was here in Santa Fe setting my course, and so far, I'm still taking steps forward."

"You've done well keeping the faith, Delores."

"Thank you for saying so. I've got a long way to go."

"As do we all," he said, unmistakably down-to-earth. "It was proper and courageous of you to search for your daughter. I assume the Pinkertons earned their wages."

"In the beginning I received only discouraging reports," she replied, solemn and sorrowful. "It turns out that the orphanage I put her in closed its doors within a year of her arrival. She got shuffled from place to place until she ended up in a workhouse school in Little Rock, which is where the detectives found her. She's been with me for two years now."

"When will you share the truth with her?"

"Not now, not ever, Deacon."

"You're wrong, Delores. The girl deserves to know you're her mother."

"There are too many disgraceful elements of the story. How do I sugarcoat my being a whore? And what would I tell her about her father?" she asked, imploring and insistent.

"Lies *always* find a way to surface."

"Maybe this one can be the exception to the rule."

Coburn chuckled; it rumbled sarcastically. "Why do you hide from your story, Delores? You truly want to be a blessing to people? Proclaim the truth head-on. You have risen above and triumphed over sin and heartaches. Your past has been and continues to be redeemed. Everyone ought to hear your testimony of forgiveness and victory, especially your daughter."

"And what do I say about Jackson?"

"That he was a soldier and you loved him," Deacon said, frank and precise. "Whatever he became afterwards is of no significance. Tell her only the good things about him."

"I'll pray on it, but I'm making no promises, Deacon."

"I have full confidence that you'll do the right thing."

"On that note I'm going upstairs." She stood and took a few steps, then paused and turned to him. "Before you hit the sack please lock up and snuff out the lights."

He gave affirmation with a nod, then bent forward with elbows on knees. His eyes drifted to the make-do pool tournament, where Avis was now an observer while Whitey and Max jousted. The blarney and one-liners were still flying along with snippets of laughter. He measured the bronc buster lady from Texas, gauging the mettle of her temperament.

～ ～ ～

Late that night, Deacon Coburn and Max Dawson were situated at a table beside the box stove, beneath the only lamp burning in the *Cantina Room*. The fire was newly stoked, the logs crackling and hissing. Outside, it was as though the wind was in full attack mode, making the building creak against the incessant barrage. The only other sound, aside from their voices, was the uninterrupted nasal growl of the sleeping patient on the floor across from them.

"Vengeance isn't the same as justice, Max."

"I won't debate the finer points or split hairs on the matter," she said genially. "It's settled. If my father has not yet carried out the execution by the time I join him, then together we'll hunt the lowlife maggot down and hang him. I intend to see Mr. Crowe dead."

"You'll have to wait for some thaw in the air."

"The storm will die soon enough."

"Which direction will you be riding?"

"I expect to find Daddy northwest of Santa Fe," she replied, tilting the chair back on two legs. "In or around the badlands surrounding a place called Angel Peak."

Coburn's curiosity was obvious. "Why Angel Peak?"

"I've never been there," she answered, "but I've heard many stories, some of which can make my skin crawl. Since the lights are low, do you want me to tell some spook tales?"

"That seems appropriate."

"My father is undoubtedly the country's expert on Smoky Crowe. He has devoted better than ten years to bringing him to justice," Max said, pride in her tone and admiration glinting in her eyes. "Whenever Daddy speaks about the Ute witch's origins, he starts the dialog by saying: What you have to understand is that Smoky Crowe is an occultist."

Coburn thumbed back the sides of his walrus-like moustache. "That would explain much. From rumors and bits of information picked up on trails and in barrooms, I've had longtime suspicions that he was a conjurer or sorcerer. In every newspaper article I've ever read about him, sooner or later, the writer is amazed or praises Crowe's prowess at escaping."

"Daddy has some theories, but mostly keeps his counsel to himself so as to not get tossed into the booby hatch," Max said, smiling wryly. "He never reveals his conjecture to superiors or speculates to ink slingers, but he's convinced that Smoky Crowe summons doorways or portals in the air that transport him elsewhere. Crowe disappears because he's in league with evil."

"Nothing your father has seen or investigated would surprise me, though spoken for public consumption might get him locked up in a madhouse," Deacon told her wittily. "The enemy of our souls is wily and commands legions. Satan seduces those who bend a knee to power or riches. Smoky Crowe could have made a soul pact to become a necromancer."

Max marveled, eyes spreading wide. She rocked the chair forward to set it securely on all four legs. "Daddy concluded that years ago, but swore Mom and me to silence."

"My yes is yes, my no is no, Max. Your father's deductions are safe with me."

She ran a finger alongside her jawline as she weighed him in the balance of her judgment, then articulated in a confidential tone. "As a young man Smoky Crowe went on a spiritual vision quest in the Angel Peak badlands. He struggled with the trickster coyote in a knockdown drag-out grappling match. It was vicious and bloody. An eye was clawed from its socket, but he refused to release the beast until he was blessed by evil."

Coburn whistled, soft and reedy. "He lost an eye?"

"The left one," she replied casually. "Daddy saw him immediately after he killed my mother. He says the eye has a sick and milky appearance, glazed and unfocused."

Coburn stiffened. He covered his mouth and held his chin tight. "It can't be."

"What?"

"Nothing," he muttered, shaking his head. "What jumped into my mind cannot possibly be, so go on. If there are any more insights from your father I want to hear all."

A confused frown darkened her brow. "Crowe deems Angel Peak as sacred. The place rejuvenates him." She regarded him carefully and continued with an assertive inflection in her voice. "It was there that he acquired a special affinity with crows and coyotes, even though he practices and perfects his torture methods on them. Daddy told me of the many times he came upon carcasses or the bleached bones of crows and coyotes in open-air burial grounds."

Coburn displayed a distracted irritation. "Anything else?"

"He treats rattlesnakes as pets," she answered hastily. "He gathers them to leech the venom and cooks it with the dried flowers and roots of several toxic plants to make a lethal poison, which he dips his arrowheads in."

Coburn's hands were active and jittery, his legs jumpy. He had a preoccupied sheen in his eyes, as though he was not listening to her. "You said your father saw Smoky Crowe."

"Yes."

"Close enough to give a useful description?"

"Of course," she said, getting to her feet. She went to her belongings, which were neatly piled against a wall. She rummaged around and withdrew a trifold flier. "Here's a wanted poster based on details he gave the artist." She returned to her seat and handed it over.

Coburn flicked it open and took a peek. He instantly stooped forward and his mouth clenched as if an iron-fisted haymaker had struck his mid-section. He sat back and shrank into himself, seemingly incapacitated. Air emptied from his lungs in a shivery rush. All the emotion drained from his face. His skin became deathlike; ashen and bloodless.

"What is it, Deacon?"

"Yesteryear has come back to haunt me," he replied, croaky and tense. "Here's proof that what I believed to be impossibility is unadulterated reality." He scratched his whiskers and steadied his breathing. "Almost ten years ago I was seized by warring Utes and held captive to be made sport of and punished. I nearly died. All that ever came back to me was that the leader had a milky left eye and until now, I'd only ever seen him in joyless nightmares."

"Did he cut you?"

"Yes, ma'am. He sliced me as though he was going to skin me alive."

"My God! Can I see the scars?"

Coburn's eyes narrowed. "That ain't necessary, is it?"

"I *need* to see them. Please, Deacon."

He exhaled, loud and heartily. He eyed her as he stood and untucked his corduroy shirt. He unbuttoned and shed it, then peeled his thermal woolens down to his waist and sidled closer to the light. "My daughter has never even seen these," he said, grumbling.

Max Dawson gasped. She leapt up and crowded close to examine him, front and back. She squinted hard and fingered the crosscut lumps of white scar tissue that intersected in a distinct pattern. "That's the exact design the deranged mongrel carved into my mother." She took a staggering backward step and collapsed onto her chair. "You survived Smoky Crowe."

"I never heard the name until years later," he said, putting his shirt on. "And I never made the connection until this very day when you mentioned the sick and milky eye. That prompted a burst of recollection, and the sketch is dead-on accurate as I remember him."

"You survived Smoky Crowe," she repeated, almost awestruck.

Coburn gave her a crinkly-eyed smile. "It was not yet my appointed time to die, so I was delivered from the killer's snare. I was the recipient of the awful grace of God; a highpoint in my life that has been counted and marked. As the Psalmist put it: *Let God arise, let his enemies be scattered: let them also that hate him flee before him. As smoke is driven away, so drive them away: as wax melteth before the fire, so let the wicked perish at the presence of God.*"

"I've done some Bible reading."

"That's good to know, Max," he said, taking his seat. "Perhaps we can talk theological philosophy on the trail. We'll leave for Angel Peak as soon as the weather allows."

"No. I ride alone."

"I won't be persuaded by such foolishness," he countered earnestly. "I know the territory, and the gaps and gulches between here and there. It was in those badlands that Smoky Crowe staked me out to die. I also have a link to Liam Greer." He tapped the wanted poster. "Plus there are stalwart friends who own a farmstead not many miles from Angel Peak."

"Apparently I've partnered up."

He tipped her a wink. She responded with a terse pucker of her lips. Her severity relaxed a trace, then they both sat back to think and listen to the grunting snores and gale-force wind. The night was turning into the wee hours of the morning, but neither of them made a move or gave any indication that bedding down to get some shut-eye was on the agenda.

Inside a deerskin wikiup, Kid Greer was smoking peyote and drinking mescal with his comrade and mentor, Smoky Crowe. The lodge was warm and substantial, pitched near a rock wall of a remote canyon ravine in the shadow of Angel Peak. Thin streamers of smoke wafted from the smallish hole in the center of the roof, venting a well-tended fire.

Greer was slobbery drunk, crunched forward in a near fetal position and trapped within a vaporous dream. The dense air had a visible quality; the haze of smoldering tobacco twisted and pirouetted, seemingly having a will of its own. His eyes were distended and bleary, sending garbled images to his brain. Everything was elongated and shape shifting.

The fantasia frightened him and made his skin crawl, yet he kept swilling mouthfuls of the fermented beverage from a small-necked gourd flask. His squashed nose was running like a broken pump; a constant drip of mucous drained from its upturned nostrils. He only occasionally thumbed the seepage aside; mostly he allowed it to dribble through the fluff of his peach-fuzz moustache and over the crest of his upper lip.

"Aaaaaaarg . . ." Smoky Crowe growled as he puffed mightily on the stubby stem of a pipe with an oversized bowl, which was carved to resemble the skull of a vulture. He inhaled deeply and held it in for more than a minute before releasing it; tendrils of smoke spiraled in a wreath and he sifted wisps through his stringy white hair. "Watch me," he said, standing.

Greer took a swig and dragged a backhand across his mouth. "I'll try."

"Try is never good enough. Do as I command," Smoky Crowe ordered heatedly. The uncommon bass notes of his voice ruptured into a sizzling fury. "I am the great prophet; I am the messenger of death; I am the herald of the dark one. My every word is to be obeyed."

Even in his inebriated state, Greer snapped to a rigid upright posture. His slouchy shoulders stiffened. He slammed a cork into the container of mescal and set it behind him. He adjusted his backside on the blanket and gave his undivided attention to the gaunt and lanky old wizard. He swallowed audibly and bowed his head in reverence.

Smoky Crowe's lips kinked upward in a threatening grin, revealing grossly yellowed teeth stippled by streaky blackish stains. His freakishly pale left eye enlarged and pulsed. With pipe in hand he began chanting a chorus low in his throat; his feet dance-shuffled to its enticing refrain. He was naked except for a chiffon-like loincloth. His blotchy skin was a mass of creased folds that gathered in bunches over the knobby protrusions of his elbows and knees.

Greer concentrated on him. The man capered and gyrated like a whirligig in a fluid hop and skip that was a pitch-perfect accompaniment to the whooping peaks and muted depths of his song. Round and round the fire he lightly stepped, legs lifting high and head swaying. As he did, a creepy metamorphosis engulfed him. He became a white-boned skeleton that was screaming, then in an effortless instant, he was a gigantic black-winged bird shrieking hatefully.

Terror seized Liam Greer. Unseen hands clutched at him. His mouth was warped open, but not even a whimper emerged. He wanted to untether his voice; he wanted to yell at the top of his lungs; he wanted to unleash a wail that would set free the panic scratching at his soul; he wanted to whine and cry like a baby. Yet, despite his strenuous exertions, none of his longings were to be. He hyperventilated and shrank backwards in horrified silence.

Smoky Crowe never missed a beat. He stomped and whirled, his nimble feet keeping pace as the vocalizing built in momentum. The booming from his throat was deafening in the enclosed cloister of the shelter. His transfiguration from one form to another was seamless; he was the white-boned skeleton, then in a tick, he was the giant black-winged bird.

When the crazed melody reached its full-toned crescendo Crowe was the screeching skeleton looming over Greer. The gringo outlaw threw his arms up to ward off the hollow-eyed mutation, but the yellowy smile spread wide and pressed close enough for him to smell its fetid breath; the stench was that of human flesh being set aflame. An ear-piercing blare wrenched out of him; the boy inside the man was a wretched heap of paralyzed emotions.

Greer momentarily blinked into unconsciousness. He gulped and grasped at the air as he came to, slump-shouldered and quivering. His eyes were watery. His eyelids flickered. He gobbled a breath; and another, stronger and fuller. It took several repetitions, but then, his lungs began functioning in an even and steady progression. He had a wary look around. All seemed to be safe and fine. The hallucination or whatever it had been was gone.

Smoky Crowe sat across the campfire from him. "You have returned," he said, smiling placidly. "What did my paleface friend see that took him into blackness?"

"I saw nothing."

"You are a liar, Kid Greer."

"It was an illusion to frighten me."

Smoky Crowe grumbled laughter. "I am the herald of the dark one, not a carnival peddler of tricks." He calmly toyed with six slugs cupped in his palm. "A crusading Texas Ranger put these bullets in my body. He hunted and chased me like an animal for many years." He picked up a piece of lead between thumb and forefinger of his left hand. "Look upon his handiwork."

Greer got on his knees and crept closer to him. "You are the great prophet."

"I am." Smoky Crowe held the slug up high and spoke a rush of words, then with religious precision he placed it on a disfigured bump in the center of his abdomen. "I am the messenger of death; I am indestructible." He slid the bullet across five other tumorous pockmarks of clumpy tissue on his belly and chest. "Six shots, six scars. No blood. No harm. I live. I breathe. I have prevailed for I am consecrated to serve the dark one."

Greer remained on his knees, head lowered. "I'm in your debt and service."

"Dawson's woman gave me a gift," Crowe said, croaking a chuckle. He lifted the straggly remnants of her scalp, which was tangled and crusty with dried blood. He wrapped the bullets in the hair and clasped the bundle in his hands, then pressed it over his heart. "I curse Dawson to burn inside out and make a lingering journey to the place of the dead."

Greer shivered. "So shall it be."

The yap-yap-yapping of a nearby coyote came out of the night as a benediction. Smoky Crowe bared his teeth; more grimace than smile. He put the hair and bullet souvenirs in his lap, then picked up his pipe to scrape the tar and ash from its bowl. He packed in a fresh offering of tobacco and peyote, lit it and relaxed into a peaceful ecstasy of contentment.

Kid Greer settled onto his bedroll and nodded off to sleep.

Charley Jondreau sat in darkness on the floor in the storage shed listening to the wind rustle through the aspens. He was a loner who had a new pal; he did not mind the company. His hands were occupied patting the flowing mane around Hank's neck. The collie had developed a peculiar attachment to him, and was now curled up with its head resting on his thigh.

He was plenty warm. The potbelly stove filled the compact structure with cozy heat. He had removed his boots and outerwear; the shirttail of his homespun shirt was hanging loose. He was comfortable and at ease because the identity of the bronze-skinned maiden who had engaged his psyche for years was finally known. There was still much in the realm of mystery, but meeting Sally Twosongs one-on-one provided a degree of satisfaction.

He reflected on her and the kin-connection that tied them together. There was much that made no sense and did not track in conscious thought, but there could be no denying the inner reality they both experienced. The meaning and purpose was concealed within an indistinct web woven into the future by the Great Spirit; that comprehension gratified him. He would not doubt or question it; neither would he struggle against it. He simply accepted it as truth to be lived.

The dog whined and shifted around, evidently seeking his attention. He gave it a solid nudge and ordered it to sit. The animal swiftly complied and pawed at him. He pressed his forehead against the collie's brow and spoke in a dominating whisper. "You have an essential task and calling. You must *always* protect Sally Twosongs, eh. You got it?"

Hank licked his cheeks, stopped abruptly to sniff him, then backed up and snarled.

Jondreau had an instant of bewilderment at the dog's strange reaction, but understanding came in a lightning-like jolt as the smell of the skunk draped over him; it was heavy and obsessively all-consuming. Rigidity encased him and he succumbed to it, flattening out on his back. His fingers began twitching as though a viral palsy had infected them. His eyes slammed shut and a groaning noise rolled in his throat.

His eyelids had a violent spasm; when it ran its course, frustration bushwhacked his senses. His teeth and hands clenched because there was nothing to see. A funereal veil hid the scene in gloomy blackness, which he clutched at with the fierce desperation of a madman. He combed through all the bleak corners of the shroud only to be denied the discernment of any images, but then, a cacophony of chaotic sounds assaulted his ears.

He heard a gunshot, rapidly tagged by a second blast. A woman screamed so shrilly that its echo reverberated endlessly. A man cussed and cried out for help. There were running footsteps. A horse neighed in distress, squealing as though it was being jabbed with spurs while having its bridle viciously yanked. Then a whoop and the pounding hoofbeats of a getaway. The woman's scream became frazzled sobbing while panicked voices shouted warnings.

He yearned to escape from the clairvoyant episode, but his lurching efforts were futile. The entire occurrence replayed from the beginning. He forced himself to hear every subtle shade in the clamoring racket. On the second go-around, it ended differently—as the woman wept and pandemonium flourished, a dog barked insistently; angry or frightened, or possibly both. He convulsed air into his lungs and sat halfway up, eyes open and normal.

He instantly recognized that the barking was not part of the otherworldly incident. The tricolor collie stood over him woofing and prancing, skittish and persistent. He exhaled in a burst through his nostrils to clear the lingering symptomatic scent. He shushed the dog and reached out to take hold of it. Hank resisted at first, aloof and reserved, head cocked at a curious angle.

"No anger, no fear, eh," Charley said, hugging it close. His newfound friend's sandpaper tongue went to work cleansing the gloss of perspiration that had arisen on his face. Jondreau had a ringing hum lancing back and forth between his ears. He gently shoved the dog and stretched out, twining his fingers around the back of his head.

The collie sniffed thoroughly and took a circuitous route before settling down to snuggle beside him. The night was quiet except for the wind murmuring in the trees. It wasn't long until Hank was sleeping and snuffling softly, but for Charley Jondreau, there was too much strident confusion inside his head. He did his utmost to sort through it all with a composed resolve.

Daylight arrived. He remained awake and downright perplexed.

chapter three

The Journey

"There is a vanity which is done upon the earth; that there be just men, unto whom it happeneth according to the work of the wicked; again, there be wicked men, to whom it happeneth according to the work of the righteous: I said that this also is vanity."

~Solomon~

Two weeks passed. February huffed its final gasp of bitterness many days before the calendar actually turned a page. A warming thaw distributed its sunshine across the southwest as March came in like the proverbial lamb that had waited patiently for temperate weather. The skies were powder blue, the air fresh and vibrant.

Deacon Coburn sat on a deadfall log near the smoldering remnants of a fire alongside of Coyote Creek, which was high and swift with winter run-off. Breakfast and coffee had been at dawn, then camp broke shortly thereafter. He had his Bible in hand, reading while he waited for his traveling partner to return with their mounts.

He was knee-deep in Ezekiel, invigorated anew by a declaration of God's provision and care in the thirty-fourth chapter. He placed a finger on the central passage that stirred his emotions and read aloud. *"For thus saith the Lord God; Behold, I, even I, will both search my sheep, and seek them out. As a shepherd seeketh out his flock in the day that he is among his sheep that are scattered; so will I seek out my sheep, and will deliver them out of all places where they have been scattered in the cloudy and dark day."*

"Amen." He closed the Good Book, rose and waggled his arms.

Max Dawson emerged from a copse of cottonwoods with the horses alongside her. "Fed, watered, saddled and ready for the trail. I see that you've been up to your usual."

"I try to never miss a morning, Max."

"Why read the Bible every day?"

Coburn gave her a sly smile. "I suppose I could ask, why not?"

"Have you read it cover to cover?"

"Many times."

"What's the point?"

"Life and death is the point, Max." He sidled close to Gilgal and petted its neck. "The writer of Hebrews put it this way: *For the word of God is quick, and powerful, and sharper than any two-edged sword, piercing even to the dividing asunder of soul and spirit, and of the joints and marrow, and is a discerner of the thoughts and intents of the heart.*"

"I don't understand, Deacon."

"Reading the Bible gives me a chance to be a better man."

Her brow crinkled. "It's just a bunch of stories, isn't it?"

"Not quite," he replied, eyes squinting. "The Bible is God's story of his interaction with humanity. It has some of the most dramatic tales of struggle ever put down on parchment. It's all about hope and redemption in the midst of good and evil."

She stepped into the stirrup and swung up. She settled comfortably in the saddle as the soot-gray mare took a couple side-steps. "Sounds to me to be at cross purposes."

"Why?" He packed his Bible in the saddlebags. "Mucking our way through evil whilst attempting to be and do good is exactly where we live our lives."

"Good and evil, certainly. But hope and redemption? Really?" She removed her Stetson and adjusted the snakeskin hatband. Her face was as unbreakable as a granite wall when she gathered her hair up under her hat. "Where was hope and redemption for my mother?"

"That's a thorny question, Max." He hopped onto Gilgal and took hold of the reins. They rode along side by side. "I wouldn't presume to soft soap you with impressive words, many of which would be meaningless in the face of the brutality your mother suffered."

"I won't be persuaded, Deacon. Ever."

"Any hope and redemption that comes will be for you."

"For me?"

"Or for your father."

"My father is a widower. My mother was tortured and murdered." Her expression continued to be stoic and severe, but her voice was level and calm; there was no indication of animosity in it. "The killers are likely still on the loose, so do yourself a favor and save your breath; don't bother talking to me about hope and redemption any time soon."

"Fair enough."

The horses were compatible and trail-wise, easing through or around clumpy tufts of grass and thickets on the eastern bank of Coyote Creek. She kept silent for fifty yards or so, then asked, "How much farther to your friend's farmstead?"

"There's a shallow point a few miles ahead, almost a land-bridge," Deacon replied, making a drawn-out gesture to the north. "We'll get across and if there are no difficulties we have another two days of solid riding. Maybe two and a half."

"Let's do it in two," she said, adamancy in her tone. Her eyes shone as she flashed him a challenge of a smile. "Even if we have to travel into the night both days."

"I'm game and up for it." He swiveled to take an extensive look at from whence they had come. He shaded his eyes against the brightness by lowering the brim of his hat. The sun was slightly behind them to their right, rising above the ridge of a rocky escarpment.

"I've got another question for you, Deacon."

"I'm game for that too."

"It might be personal."

"I can't guarantee you'll like my answer."

She laughed, gravelly and full-throated. "I've had the pleasure of taking care of your gelding several times and something about your gear has peaked my curiosity."

His eyes lit up. "The stones."

"Yes. The stones. How'd you know?"

"Sooner or later, the topic arises."

She watched him closely. She waited for more than a minute, but when no additional explanation was forthcoming, she became demanding. "Are you going to tell me? What's the reason for sewing those stones into the bridle? Serves no purpose that I can see."

"I ain't sure you're ready to hear that story, Max."

"Story?"

"Every aspect of my life has its story."

"Tell me about the stones, Deacon."

"Mayhap I will someday."

"Why not now? No time like the present."

"Your heart ain't ready for it, Max."

"What's that supposed to mean?"

He tilted his head to shoot her a wrinkly-eyed grin that conveyed sincerity. "A day may come when you *need* to hear it. Then perhaps your heart will be soft and open to take heed of the lessons," he said, eyebrows dipping low. "I'll know when the time has ripened."

"Why be intentionally cryptic?"

He made eye contact with her. "It's a story of hope and redemption."

Her shoulders flinched. Her complexion darkened. She glanced away. He regarded her for a few moments, but had nothing else to say. Instead, he launched a prayer without words heavenward and gave the silver-dappled buckskin a prod. Gilgal cantered forward until it had some space, then resumed the proficient walking strides. The mare followed close behind.

A reflective silence thickened between the riders.

The dragon came out of the desert to feed its hunger. Sally Twosongs stood and watched it. Horror clogged up her throat and snatched her voice away. She had an eagle feather in each hand. The great serpent cast a baleful eye at her and snarled in disgust, then proceeded to stalk a long line of innocent travelers. She was close enough to smell its brimstone breath.

Dwindling flames burned in the sky, which was the dingy color of dirty dishwater. The dragon hunted with a sadistic cunning. It slinked closer and closer to its prey, undetected as it slithered around boulders and through sagebrush. When it pounced, it separated a family from the herd of sojourners—father, mother and baby were held captive in a dead-end arroyo.

The monster terrorized its prisoners. Screams pierced the air. Using a single curved talon, it sliced them with scalpel-like precision. The bloodletting produced begging shrieks, which were ignored by the ruthless dragon. Its fangs sank into the father's chest, who died first, writhing and twitching as his last breath gasped from his body.

A bellow of triumphant laughter roared and it smacked its bloody lips. The beast turned its attention on the mother. She clutched her baby to her breast and cringed against the sandstone wall. It bent close to sniff and taste her, its forked tongue darting over the gashes. Her eyes were bulgy, her clarion voice pleading for mercy.

The dragon loomed over her. There was no place for her to flee, nowhere to hide. She held on fiercely, but the infant was torn from her arms and tossed aside like a sack of trash. She was spared from being an eyewitness to the fiendish cruelty which would be visited upon her child, for with swift efficiency it slashed her jugular and suckled, slurping noisily.

Then the grotesque serpent crept over and sat on its haunches to cuddle the baby in its forearms. A growling murmur in its gullet had a spine-chilling tenderness; it toyed with its prize. The toddler was crying and wiggling to escape, but that would not happen. A ravenous appetite for evil, as ancient as the garden, had to be satiated. The baby wailed and thrashed, and was still alive when the dragon took its first bite, chomping in gleeful enjoyment.

Sally Twosongs jumped in her footsteps. She wanted to intervene, but her helplessness was complete. It was as though she was shackled inside an invisible bubble. She screeched and shouted; again and again and again, but no sounds were discharged into the air. She fought uselessly against the restraints. Her fists were pounding against her thighs and then, in a shocking suddenness, her vocal cords were freed to vibrate in a braying falsetto.

The blare reverberated from horizon to horizon, interrupting the beast as it finished its meal. Smoke and fire spewed from its mouth and nostrils as the dragon approached and menaced the bronze-skinned woman. Bits of flesh were clinging to its blood-speckled teeth. It crooked its massive head to an unusual slant. Sally Twosongs took a wobbly backward step when she saw that the left eye was a repulsive cavity of pulsating whiteness.

"Watch me," the dragon said in a voice that burst forth from some musty tomb. It sang a mournful tune as it spun and pranced on all fours, kicking and strutting in remarkable rhythm. Its tree-trunk tail slapped the ground like a drumbeat. Faster and faster; tighter and tighter the circle dance contracted as the beast rose up on its hind legs.

Sally Twosongs was wide-eyed. Her arms were clasped around her lower abdomen, as though she was sick to the stomach. Fear crawled all over her; it felt like a swarm of ants were scurrying from head to toe making her skin squirm. An urge to be elsewhere surged in her veins, but she refused it. She held steady and remained staunchly faithful.

The whirling blur of the dance mesmerized her. She noted every detail. The reptilian creature became wilder and looser, thrusting and heaving up whirlwinds of dust. Its song conjured images of bones rattling around in its belly, jangling and clattering to the thumping cadence of its tail. It jeered loudly, then a terrifying transformation took place; the dragon changed into a skeleton with an astounding and worrisome ease.

Her eyes stretched even wider. Her heartbeat was so rapid that dizziness climbed up her spine and thrashed through her brain. She nearly keeled over as her knees buckled, but found balance when tenacity overpowered the wooziness. Sally Twosongs locked her legs and a new strength energized her. The skeletal specter kept spinning and spinning, and as it did, it turned into a gigantic crow with a human face and crowned by a straggle of white feathers.

Just then, the landscape of the nightmare was radically altered. A barren wasteland, marked by steep slopes and minimal vegetation, surrounded her. The crow-man stood across from her, and in the middle of the inhospitable terrain, Charley Jondreau was walking at a stealthy pace, with two horses trailing along behind him.

Sally Twosongs yelled a warning, but it was unheard because her voice was gone. She saw that the black-winged bird's focus was on Jondreau, salivating as it made threatening advances on him. The hellion stayed hidden, but she was certain that it had targeted Jondreau. A tentacle of panic wrapped around her midsection and squeezed. Her ears hummed. She pressed the eagle feathers over her bosom and strenuously prayed in silence.

A demonic yowl lacerated the sky. The evil was palpable. She blinked. The crow-man was now the fire breathing serpent; it skulked forward in a flash of smoke and confronted her, blood dripping from its mouth like streamers of ghoulish honey. She gagged on its disgusting odor. "This does not concern you, Sally Twosongs," the dragon said, grizzled and fierce. "I am the messenger of death. I will ascend to lofty heights. I will kill Charley Jondreau."

The droning in her ears exploded. She came awake in a lather of perspiration. Her breathing was rapid and out of control, but it only took a handful of seconds for calmness to take hold. All fear and panic dissolved in the golden rays of daylight slipping through the bedroom window. Faith found its foothold; it dug in and would not be displaced. The enormity of the evil disturbed her, but she knew what must be done.

She pushed back the blankets and sat up, placing her feet on the hardwood floor, which was chilly. Her eyes were puffy. She rubbed them as she went directly to a shelf that had several flutes neatly arranged. Each one had its own significance. She paused to reflect before making her selection, wanting the most power. After prudent consideration, she chose an instrument that had been crafted with Caleb at her side throughout the process.

She went to the hearth in the living room and sat on the floor, her back to the fireplace. She moistened her lips and bowed her head. She heard the notes in the chambers of her heart, then in reverence, she began playing prayers for Charley Jondreau. She pinched her eyes shut and became so engrossed in the presence of the Creator that she did not hear her husband come in from outside; nor did she see him standing in the doorway watching and wondering.

$\approx \approx \approx$

It was an epic rainstorm. A hard downpour of pelting pellets flooded from the sky. Silas Dawson stared unbelievingly at the deluge. The heavens were shuddering and weeping as though a multitude of angels were in the throes of grief. His brain, seemingly soaked by the torrential monsoon, was fogged up and unable to function properly.

Nevertheless, he comprehended that everything was out of whack. The happenings were all wrong—even in his addled state Dawson perceived that the dream was skewed sideways. He had been chasing Smoky Crowe, but no more. Now the tables had been turned; Smoky Crowe was coming after him, shrewdly circling through the darkness.

Dawson was drenched. His clothes were clinging to him. He was stuck up to his knees. Mud, as thick and gummy as pine tar, had hold of him. He heaved against it, but the more effort he put forth, the deeper he sank. He floundered in desperation. His thigh muscles were aching and burning from the strain, though not enough to halt him. There was nothing in his makeup that would ever allow him to consider the possibility of defeat.

An array of lightning played across the pitch-black clouds. The momentary flashes gave him opportunity to scout the area and secure his bearings. He was alone in the Ute witch's territory, outside the precincts of his command. There would be no miraculous extrication from the messy predicament; no posse of Texas Rangers were coming to his rescue.

The rain increased in velocity. It struck with the stinging force of buckshot. He cringed against it. He tried to make his legs thrust forward, but it was a losing proposition. He sank to his waist in the mucky impasse. His arms flailed as thunder bounced around the sky, then a stunning sheet of lightning illuminated the high desert for a terror-stricken moment. Time froze.

Smoky Crowe stood twenty feet from him, bowstring drawn taut, arrow aimed. The laughter tumbling off his tongue was louder than the strafing barrage of the storm. His left eye swelled and protruded. A coyote grin filled his face. He released the arrow at the immobilized man and it flew straight and struck hard. The arrowhead buried itself in his heart.

Dawson hollered, but in his delirium, he never woke up.

Charley Jondreau was at peace, enjoying the brightness of the morning. There were blue skies in every direction for as far as he could see. He intended to be in Durango by nightfall, which presented no problems because the westerly trail was clear and the horses were behaving. The piebald pinto had taken charge of the dapple gray yearling tethered behind. Jondreau rode easy, his eyes roaming the countryside as he reminisced about a farewell scene.

Three days ago, he was in the barn at *WT Ranch* saddling his mount. With the onset of warm weather, the door and shutters were open to give the building a thorough airing out. He was ready to be on his way when Sally Twosongs came hurrying across the yard. He removed his hat and observed her approach, smiling at the collie trotting beside her.

"I was going to stop at the house, Sally Twosongs."

"No need, Charley." She halted an arm's length away from him. "I have words to say that are only for your ears. Caleb and Pete are still at the table working on plans."

"There is much for us to know of each other."

"We share a secret riddle, Charley. The why of which we cannot understand."

"A brainteaser, eh?"

"Yes, one that demands our faithfulness."

"We stand together in agreement, Sally Twosongs."

"That is what is on my mind." She motioned for him to follow, then went to a stack of hay and took a seat on one of the bales. Her glossy black hair was braided in a thick pigtail that swung to the small of her back. "My head is full, as is my heart."

Jondreau squatted on his heels in front of her, hat in hand. His scalp was shiny as he had shaved at sunup. "You tell me whatever you wish, I will help as I can." A horse neighed in one of the stalls. Hank came over, turned several slow circles and lay down between them. "I am not as wise as you may think, eh. There are puzzles that have no answers on this side."

"Do you know what's on the other side, Charley?"

"The unseen world?"

"The place beyond death."

"Beauteous, marvelous."

"Yes, but can you *see* it?"

"Peace. Paradise. No tears, no sorrow, no pain," Charley answered, keeping his hands occupied fiddling with the brim of his hat. "What does peace and paradise look like? What does it mean for there to be no tears, sorrow or pain? It is the mystery of mysteries."

Sally Twosongs had tremendous sadness on her face. "Our baby died, Charley."

"And your soul cries," he said sympathetically. "Though you will be with child again for I have *seen* it, you wonder where your baby is now. Is it at peace in paradise or in limbo?"

"Can we ever know?"

"In the faith passed to us by giants across the ages; tested and tried and practiced by us, we can know," he replied plainly. "Your child is in the presence of the Great Spirit."

"You bring me much comfort."

"Hold it in the cradle of your heart, Sally Twosongs."

"I thank the Creator for drawing us to one another."

"In this swamp of time we live, we are blessed, eh." He slipped his hat on, shifted his weight and began to absently twiddle his thumbs. "Is this what was only for my ears?"

"No. There is something wrong. I am afraid."

"Of what?"

"I don't know. I just have a sense of fear. It's a bad feeling."

"Feelings can often lie."

"Not mine," she said, severe and unsmiling. "I have learned to read and trust the slightest change in my feelings. I cannot ignore them. I don't have to agree or placate them, but I must be sensitive." She leaned forward. "An aura of danger surrounds you, Charley."

Jondreau pursed his lips to stifle a grin. "Danger and I are old friends. I avoid it when possible, but sometimes one must walk through danger for there is no other choice."

"There's *always* a choice."

"Not always. Not for the likes of us, Sally Twosongs," he countered, taking hold of her hands. "You are blinded by this special intuition and bond between us. You want no harm to ever befall me, which is tender and meaningful." He stared hard into her dark eyes. "You read and trust your feelings, eh? I combine that with an abiding reliance on the four strong winds. The Great Spirit always provides a hawk to guide me onto the chosen path."

"Your wisdom is older than mine."

"The blood flow of your heart is more receptive," he said, giving her hands a firm squeeze. "We are warriors, you and I. There is an anointing upon us. Our lack of understanding matters not. Plague and pestilence will stalk us, but we cannot fear for the Most High is our refuge. We must stand together against the evil that pursues the destruction of good."

"Father taught me that patient endurance conquers all obstacles."

"Therein lies the truth of the ancients."

"Indeed." Her eyes twinkled. "You are going to *Freiheit* first, then Taos?" She reached into a side pocket of her billowy skirt. "Here are two letters. One for Hans and Eliza, one for Father and Mother. Ask anyone in Taos and they'll tell you where Daniel and Consuelo live."

"These will be safely delivered."

"The Creator has been good to us, Charley."

"I must be gone, eh."

They stood together. She embraced him fiercely. "I'll pray for you always."

"I will see you when I *see* you. In this world or in the one which is to come." He broke her hold, touched a finger to her cheek and said, "Live courageously and be free." His eyes were damp and tight when he spun around and went to the piebald pinto. He placed the envelopes in his saddlebags and mounted, then gathered the reins and gave her a nod as he rode away.

Hank yakked excitedly. Each bark was punctuated by a drawn out whine. It pranced and jumped, spinning around in a dizzying tizzy. Sally Twosongs didn't bother discouraging or hushing it. When Charley Jondreau became obscured by the woods surrounding *WT Ranch*, the dog gave her a mournful look, then took off after him. It ran full tilt across the open spaces and entered the forest of aspens without slowing.

Several miles later, Charley Jondreau pulled up on a bald rise and stepped to the ground. He knelt and waited for the collie to run to him, bounding past the horses. Its whole body was wagging as it panted, pawing at him and licking his face. He grabbed hold of the scruff of its neck and ordered it to return. "You must *always* protect Sally Twosongs, eh."

The dog cocked its head askance and exhaled a deep-throated growl. He gave it a persuasive shake and repeated the command to go home. Hank turned around and snapped its jaws twice in protest, then reluctantly obeyed. Jondreau kept focused on the tri-color collie until it could no longer be seen, all the while mulling over his relationship with Sally Twosongs.

Three sunny days later, he remained astounded by their uncanny soul-tie.

It was midmorning. Ben Slaton waited in a rocker on the veranda of the Suncurl Café, viewing the hustle and bustle on San Francisco Street. Folks were socializing or doing business in the growing warmth of the sun, but he didn't give a damn about any of it. He was in a surly mood, scanning the far reaches of the thoroughfare for a glimpse of his horse. It was nowhere to be seen, and he wanted nothing more than to put Santa Fe behind him.

The hold-up galled him. His patience had become as thin as onionskin paper. The delay dragged on and on, infuriating him. Hostility was clamoring for an outlet to be released and the longer he had to idly kill time the more ill will fanned the fire in his belly. The newness of springtime in the air could not appease him.

He had Brenda Hawkins on his mind, which meant his blood was pre-disposed to be stirred up and on the rise. A riptide of lust coursed through his veins. He intended to ride to Las Vegas and get some tender loving care from the ginger-haired vixen; she would do him good and make him feel fine for a long while. His leg had a painful twinge now and then, but mostly the discomfort was bearable. He had seen an actual doctor, who declared it to be on the mend and skillfully wrapped it in plaster of Paris bandages to form a proper cast.

A crutch lay across his lap. He had become somewhat proficient at hobbling around on it, though he would be thrilled to toss the staff aside. He shifted around some, leaning to the edge of the seat, his eyes ever-alert and fixed on the distance. He sat up straight when he spotted his white-socked bay. A profanity formed on his tongue; he spat it out and jerked as though it had cut him. His fists were flexed in white-knuckled anger.

Avis Lahay was perched atop the steed. She had it moving at an easy gait, nodding at passersby. The auburn waves of her hair were loose and bouncy on her shoulders. The sunshine illuminated a face-consuming smile; she was the picture of contentment, which incensed Ben Slaton. She pulled up, dismounted and looped the reins over the hitching rail.

"What took you so long?" he asked, hot and argumentative.

Avis raised an eyebrow, obviously surprised by his animosity. "I was doing the job you paid me to do, mister," she said curtly. "I gave it a rubdown and checked its hoofs . . ."

"Did I say you could ride it?" he cut in, standing to take a hop toward her.

A frown knitted her brow into tight creases as she considered the question for a long moment. She eyed him and answered firmly, "You didn't tell me I couldn't."

"Ain't you a smartass?"

"Not at all, mister. Just being truthful."

"Be truthful elsewhere. I ain't got time for shit."

She grinned as a snicker squeaked out. She skipped up onto the board-walk and sidled close to him. "Thank you for allowing me to care for your horse these last number of days." She reached into the pocket of her flannel shirt to retrieve its contents. "I appreciate the opportunity, especially since it's such a gentle and friendly stallion."

"It's an ornery cuss."

"Never to me. Maybe gentle is as gentle receives."

"Shut your clap-trap, Avis. You're a know-nothing girl."

She ignored his words, smiling. "Here's your change and a receipt for the livery bill." She jiggled the coins and paper into his hands. She retreated in small steps, careful to keep her eyes on him. "Thanks again. I had fun." She turned and skedaddled inside.

Slaton went after her, an insane gleam spinning in his eyes. He moved with a shockingly smooth swiftness; he agilely maneuvered the support under his right arm so that the tip barely even rapped against the floor. The door slammed noisily behind him as he grabbed hold of her shoulder. She threw a fist at him and twisted away, reeling to her knees.

Whitey Fitzgerald sprinted toward the fracas. "Get away from him, sweetie."

"Sweetie?" Slaton slurred the term of endearment, screwing his face into a butt-ugly sneer. "Where does an oily-skinned nigger get off talking like that to a white girl?"

Fitzgerald planted his feet between Avis and her assailant. He puffed out his chest and thrust his hands forward in preparation for a fistfight. "Where does a troublemaker and ne'er do well come up with the nerve to hurt my friend?" he asked, click-clicking rapidly.

Slaton erupted in snide laughter. "Back off, you scrawny weasel."

Fitzgerald appeared to comply. His clenched hands lowered as he took a tiny side-step, then in a blur of speed he darted forward and popped Slaton on the chin with a solid right cross that made an awful smacking sound. He backtracked out of reach, but remained still for only a split-second. His footwork was catlike. He feinted; his head inclined in one direction, while he struck from the other side, clubbing him with a left that sank into his midsection.

Slaton gasped and sputtered swearwords, cheeks mottled and eyes flared. His opponent was quick and wiry, but he was unconcerned and confident. After the initial surprise, he was certain that the brawl would end with the much smaller man sprawled out and bleeding on the floor. To that end, he limped forward, wielding the crutch as a weapon.

He twirled it like a cudgel, then swung mightily. Fitzgerald ducked underneath the arc of the intended blow and slammed a shoulder into Slaton, which sent him loping sideward and entirely off balance. His teeth were grinding as he flailed and fought not to crash like a felled tree. He banged into a table and grabbed hold of its edge to gain steadiness.

While he did so, Fitzgerald readily disarmed him. "Here's how this goes," he said, low and understated. He held the staff as though it was a pool stick. "You leave the Suncurl Café now and *never* return." He immediately put the crutch to good use to emphasize the directive. With unexpected muscle, he gave him a hefty poke in the gut that doubled him over. "Do we have an understanding?" he asked, a nifty grin on his lips complemented by sporadic click-clicks.

"I'll kill you, nigger."

"You better heed Whitey's instructions, Mr. Slaton." The metallic crack of a firearm having a shell jacked into its chamber filled the *Cantina Room*. Slaton whirled around to see Delores Solrizo with a short-barreled shotgun leveled on him. Beside her, Avis Lahay had a heavy chair hoisted to her side, held ready to swing like a bat.

Slaton grimaced, eyes fuming. "I'll kill you all."

"I think not," Delores said heatedly. "I'm not much of a shot, which is why I use this scattergun. From ten yards I can't miss and I've been told the load is lethal."

"You bitch!"

"Not another word," she said, "or I will pull the trigger." Her shoulders were straight and stiff, her countenance darkly crimson. She prodded the gun at him. "I don't tolerate tardiness, sir. Your backside best be moving or else there'll be a bloody mess for us to clean up."

Slaton muttered the Lord's name in vain under his breath. Tension spiked in the air; the sense that he was a package of dynamite with its fuse sizzling was blatant and tangible. His face contorted. He hung his head and his body sank as though it was weighed down. When he raised his eyes, he offered a listless shrug, hands held up and apart in an admission of surrender. Less than five minutes later, Ben Slaton was on his horse and riding deliberately.

Naomi Axler had been busy all morning. Between the regular chores of laundry day and seeing to it that her children had opportunity to revel in the warmth of the sun, she was ready for a break. Jesse had run wild in the freshness, whilst Amanda was cushioned in a swing on the porch. The children were now in bed for their afternoon nap. Both were asleep, but for how long, she could only guess. Tiredness was nipping at her.

Sunbeams slanted through the window above the sink, making the kitchen bright and cheery. She was pacing near the stove waiting for a pot of coffee to brew. The robust aroma put a smile on her face. Her stomach made a small noise, reminding her that she hadn't eaten since breakfast. She cut a thick slice of bread and smeared apple butter on it.

Anticipation kept her feet shuffling restlessly. Her husband had made a two-day trip to the Summitville mining camp for supplies and to post mail. He had returned late last evening with two letters for her, which were resting on her Bible. She glanced anxiously at the table. She poured a cup of coffee and sat down, prepared to savor the correspondence.

She took a bite of bread, then chose the top envelope. She recognized the flowing scroll of her mother's artistic penmanship. She unsealed it and felt a twinge of homesickness for friends and family in Pennsylvania. She unfolded the two sheets of grainy paper and flattened out the pleats. Her heart swelled happily as she sipped coffee and read each word.

November, 1877

Dear Naomi: May the peace that surpasses all understanding continue to be your inner strength. I was pleased to receive your August letter yesterday. I rejoice with you. My cheeks were wet with tears when I learned of your blessed news. I praised the Lord in song. You and your growing family are in my prayers daily.

Seasons come and seasons go. The rhythm of life is unchanged. I have been well. My health has not yet betrayed my spirit, thank the Lord. My hands bother me some after long periods of sewing, but not enough to slow me or for me to complain.

Our quilting prayer circle remains busy, which is a delight. The fellowship enriches my faith walk and our heartfelt sharing keeps me ever vigilant before the throne of grace. There is so much that requires us to faithfully present our requests to God in jubilant thanksgiving.

Your sister Martha conveys her greetings. I have given her your address numerous times and exhorted her to write, but she likely will never get around to the task. Her life is littered with disarray. She is always harried by this or that issue. I am concerned for her. She takes responsibility for too many projects and her family relationships suffer.

Martha had a whirlwind of activity in late September. Anna, her oldest daughter, was wedded to one of the Mueller boys. The ceremony was sweet and simple, but came somewhat as a surprise to me. I had understood that Anna was keeping company with Abraham, but was unaware that a betrothal had been arranged.

When I asked about it, Martha hushed me and was quite flustered. Her manner caused me to suspect that Anna and Abraham were caught in a transgression. Just this past Sunday those suspicions were confirmed. Anna and Abraham have been disciplined. They stood before the assembly and confessed to succumbing to the desires of the flesh. It was tearful, tender and tense. She is expecting a child in April. Martha is distraught. I am not.

The Elders have placed restrictions on Anna and Abraham regarding interaction with the community. It is for a fixed period of time, which matters not to me. I will not participate in the mandate, but rather, do exactly as I did when your brother Deacon was disfellowshipped. I have embraced the young couple and extended love, grace and a full measure of forgiveness.

There is much news and excitement about Kansas that is enlivening the River Brethren. All reports about the land and potential for the area have been presented and thoroughly prayed over. The possibilities for expansion of the Kingdom of God awakens me. Plans and preparations are in the works. A large contingent from Dauphin County and Perry County will be joining together to relocate in or around Abilene in the spring.

The Eisenhower family, our dear friends, are among those who will be part of the resettlement. I am torn. Across the years I have made many deep connections with them. I have a multitude of tear-soaked memories at Love Feasts, where through prayer and supplication, the weeping became triumphant laughter. If I wasn't so old I might be in inclined to throw in with them on this adventure, but sadly, I do not possess your courage.

I must seek the Lord on this notion, but it is in my heart to encourage Anna and Abraham to pursue the prospect of joining the migration. Despite a flighty lapse in judgment that resulted in being overwhelmed by a few moments of weakness they have a strong and vibrant faith. A new beginning in a land rich in favorable circumstances could be a healing balm for them.

It has been more than a year since I have heard from Deacon. The last communication was from Dodge City. He was busy working as an agent for Big Bull Wallace, that cattleman from Texas. He sounded centered, but I still worry on him in fits and starts, which vexes me. Please uphold me in prayer that I may be free of disquiet and unease, and full of faith.

Naomi, my dear, you are a treasure to me. I appreciate the gift your husband carved for me. I was much impressed by the intricate craftsmanship. He is a talented man. Please tell Peter that the decorative plaque has become the centerpiece on the fireplace mantel, where it will be a prompting reminder to pray for him, which I endeavor to regularly do. May the protection and presence of God encircle you and your loved ones. Write soon.

Blessings Always,
Your Loving Mother

Naomi closed her eyes; the lids squeezed out a dribble of moisture. She backhanded it away, then read the pages again. When she finished she bowed her head and prayed. Her voice was soft, her words stouthearted and plainspoken. She thanked God for her mother; she lifted Anna and Abraham up, advocating for heaven-sent favor to be wrapped around them.

A bawling cry from her daughter became an urgent sounding amen, followed by a happy shout from her son. She sighed as she refolded the note and slipped it inside the cover of her Bible. She stood and took a hasty look at the other envelope, which according to the return address was from her niece. She sighed again. That letter would have to wait until later.

Smoky Crowe was born in a remote village near the *Rio de Las Animas*, the River of Souls. A pack of coyotes sang a yapping refrain as his mother gritted her teeth and gave the final push that brought him into the world. She swaddled him in a blanket, then took care of her needs and gathered her strength. Her lanky husband, a capable shaman of renown, entered and stood in the doorway of the lodge, waiting. Pride glinted in the dark hollows of his eyes.

She pressed a black cloth bundle against her heart and smiled thinly at him. All was ready. Their spirit guides, hidden within the forces and principalities of darkness, had prepared them for the evil fullness which was to come. She got up and draped a bearskin robe around her. Together, with their firstborn snuggled to her bosom, the parents went outside.

It was the time of the big wind moon, when water begins to freeze and the curtains separating the physical and spiritual realms are the thinnest. Streaks of crimson bled across the countryside, basking it in an orange-red glow. They moved as silent as shadows through the woods to the riverbank, where an obelisk of rocks awaited them; the four-sided shrine had a pyramidal apex with the skull of a goat attached at its highpoint.

He murmured a sacramental chant. She swayed circularly and trembled, eyes closed. The air was still and chilly. Ringlets of white formed laurels around their heads. He took hold of her elbow and they knelt shoulder to shoulder at the hallowed place. In a solemn ritual of formality, she opened the black cloth of offering and presented it to brother and sister spirits in the brilliant clarity of the blood moon; stones of obsidian and amethyst, plus tobacco and mint.

A crow cawed, strident and demanding. He grinned and while satisfied laughter rattled around his windpipe he uttered a rapturous incantation. Reddish moonbeams sparkled on the placid water. The crow shrieked, leapt off its branch and swooped over them twice. A lone coyote yipped and yelped, then its cries morphed into a long rising and falling howl.

"It is finished," he said tonelessly. "Our son will be brother to the crow and coyote, a prophet and priest of wickedness; the messenger of the dark one. I am well-pleased."

Some four decades later, Smoky Crowe shed tears as he remembered. His mother had repeatedly told him the story from the time of his earliest memories. She'd always recounted the consecration ceremony in a slow and methodical manner, her voice saturated with respect and admiration. He accepted the expectations put on him as a venerable calling to be fostered and pursued; there was never a question of having a choice. As a youngster he had demonstrated an affinity with crows and coyotes, and an innate proclivity for bloodshed.

Now, encamped in a rugged canyon guarded by the monumental sentinel of Angel Peak, he sat on a boulder sunning himself as he made reckonings regarding his life and times. Naked from the waist up, he had a whetstone in hand and was sharpening his favorite knife. The handle appeared grainy, but was sanded smooth; it had been lovingly sculpted from petrified wood. Its curved blade was a stubby six-inches and double-edged.

A flock of a dozen or more crows were entertaining him, flitting around a nearby cluster of scrub cedars. He observed the birds, enthralled by the erratic flight pattern. He sat up straight and as he did so, his right eye became glassy and his head tilted to its oddly awkward angle. A grayish discharge seeped from the milky whiteness of his left eye.

He put the whetstone down and slipped the knife into its sheaf on his hip. There was a hunger escalating in him. He slid off his seat and hissed a blaring whistle between his teeth. The flapping of wings increased to a thunderous tumult. A devious smile peeled his lips back. He held out his right arm and let loose another trilling screech.

A single crow broke away from its mates and flew in a high arc. It was a large-bodied bird with an imposing wingspan. Smoky Crowe shuffled his feet and followed its path as it climbed higher and higher. He made a series of calls. The crow responded by speedily dropping out of the sky. It fluttered and slowed its approach, then landed on his outstretched arm.

Crowe petted it tenderly. He purred in a hoarse tone that resembled the dying croaks of a wounded animal. He fingered its beak. His left eye pulsed. It stepped lively on his forearm, squawking and cawing in a spitting urgency. He listened. His posture went rigid, his breathing became rapid and rickety. A pattern of raised goosepimples formed on his torso.

Anger flooded his bloodstream. The bird kept at it, delivering its insistent bulletin over and over; the inflection of its assertions never changed or fluctuated. He received and internalized its meaning. He exhaled a bitter chuckle, nodding knowingly. He unwound and relaxed in stages, then quieted and calmed the bird, clasping it close to his heart.

"Thank you, my friend," he said, soothing and gentle. The crow squirmed against his hold, which gradually constricted. His yellow-stained teeth clamped tight as he wrung the bird's neck. It squealed and flopped valiantly, but in vain. The instant its death throes subsided, Smoky Crowe withdrew his knife, slit its throat and drank its blood to feed a primeval appetite.

He sucked thirstily. The crows amongst the scrub cedars were all at once roosted serene and soundless, as though honoring the sacrifice. When he was appeased, he gave the feathered corpse a delicate kiss on the side of its head, then discarded it. He licked his lips and wiped his mouth clean. He heard the flap of the wikiup ruffle and get tossed open. He pivoted to see his flat-nosed ally exiting, looking bleary-eye and miserable.

Greer dragged his feet in a lazy shamble away from the dwelling. He unhitched his suspenders off his shoulders and undid the front of his trousers. He urinated a strong stream against a porous rock, unconcerned or unaware that his boots were being splashed. He tucked in and adjusted his clothing, squinting at the white-haired man. "Ain't you cold?"

"You know nothing of the fire in me."

"No, I guess not," Liam muttered, scratching his head. "I'm going to care for our horses, then go ranging and do some hunting so we can have fresh meat for supper."

Smoky Crowe grunted approval. "First you must hear my words," he said, a gravelly resonance throbbing in the boom of his voice. "Trouble for us this way comes."

"What kind of trouble?"

"Powers of light have aligned against me."

Greer scoffed. "I ain't scared."

"You will be tested."

"Me? How? When?"

"Not today."

Greer stretched and yawned. "I ain't getting the wet willies over it."

"We will watch and wait," Smoky Crowe said, shrugging. "You hunt. For now I will smoke." He went and crawled into the deerskin shelter. He came out soon. His pipe was already smoldering and secured at a corner of his mouth. He squatted and alighted on his rump, so that an outcropping of the craggy landscape served as a backrest. He remained in that contented position, bare-chested and scheming, as the sun eased its way across the infinite blueness.

March 4, 1878

Dear Diary: The night is peaceful, but I am anxious. I have candles burning all around me. The flames are pretty. It has been over a week since my last entry. So much has happened. I have been upset and chose not to make time for this daily exercise. I can see now that in being stubborn about it I have deprived myself of the opportunity to make sense of stuff.

The morning after Deacon and Max left, Miss Delores sat me down in her office and told me that I was her daughter. She didn't hesitate or prepare me at all. She just blurted the news out. I was shocked and did not believe her. She started crying as she tried to explain.

I listened as best I could, which didn't amount to hardly nothing because I had my defenses up immediately. I was angry and scared and a whole bunch of other yucky feelings that I cannot even describe. My stomach hurt as she went on and on. All I could think of was why; why had she abandoned me to a hardscrabble life of being bullied and mistreated?

I wanted to yell at her. I wanted to scream. I wanted to run away and be gone. I wanted her to stop, but she just kept talking. She never paused to take a breath or gather her thoughts. The story gushed out of her as though it had been clogged up inside a castle, then the walls came crashing down. She sobbed and asked for my forgiveness. She apologized over and over.

It was terrible. I remained silent. I couldn't find any words to say. I wanted to respond, but my brain wouldn't work and my mouth was dried out and cottony. We stared at each other for what must have been ten minutes or longer. She broke through the strain by telling me she loved me and understood that it would take time for me to process the information. She also said she prayed that I would get to the place where I could forgive her.

Since that day, Miss Delores hasn't treated me any different. We go through our daily routine and assignments cheerfully. I'm probably not as chatty as I used to be with her, but that's because I'm sorting through junk and attempting to deal with a sense of confusion that seems to be continually overwhelming my perspective.

I don't know how to feel. That's what's in me, but it looks weird put into words. I should be grateful. I should forgive Miss Delores. I should give her a big hug and thank her for rescuing me and being brave enough to finally tell me the truth. All of that and more is in my head, but no matter how hard I try I cannot get there in my heart. I hope Miss Delores is praying for me.

One thing she told me about my father has got me thinking lots. He was a soldier, a cavalryman named Jackson Scully. I wonder if I have any of his horse sense in me. Maybe my longtime appreciation of horses comes from him. He fought for the Union in the War Between the States. He was wounded on the battlefield and was probably a decorated hero.

He never knew about me. He and Miss Delores were in love in Fort Smith, but duty took him to the western frontier before she had a chance to tell him she was expecting a baby. Would my life have been different if he had known the truth? Would he have resigned from the army and married Miss Delores? Would we have been a happy family?

I can't know the answer to any of those questions, but it sure is fine to dream about all the possibilities. What if my father wanted to raise horses? Would he have taught me everything there is to know about horses? Imagine what it would have been like growing up on a ranch. It would've been hard work, but I've never been afraid of dirt and sweat.

I really am at a loss. My head is pell-mell and upside-down. I don't like being this way. After Miss Delores told me, I didn't mean to, but I must have been moping around because Mr. Whitey noticed right off that something was wrong. We sat outside one afternoon and talked lots. He was pleased about the news, which surprised me.

He clapped his hands and laughed aloud so much. He informed me that I was one lucky young lady. I had to give him a good-natured poke in the ribs more than once. He kept touching my chin or cheek and making that click-click noise and saying over and over, "I must be going blind. I should've seen it straight-up. Your smile be a perfect picture of your mother."

Mr. Whitey said that there was no reason for me to be mad. In fact, he told me that I was being silly because there's no explaining mistakes people make. He was adamant about it; we all take missteps time and again, and its best to go easy on others, learn a lesson or two, forgive and go forward. He is such an encouragement to me. I don't want him to ever leave Santa Fe.

I am thankful for him. Mr. Whitey is the best friend I've ever had. I am going to miss him. I wish I could talk him into staying with us here, but the plans are all set. I'm not sure exactly when Mr. Deacon will return, but whenever he does, Mr. Whitey will be traveling with him back to Dodge City. Their friendship is obviously special. They both regaled me with tall tales about the last time they were on the trail together when they moved from Abilene to Dodge City.

Mr. Whitey says that there's nothing like traveling cross country on horseback. Max would certainly agree with him. I wonder if I'll ever have a chance to experience life in the saddle and be tested by the trail. It would be an exciting adventure, but first I have to get my own horse. Now that springtime has arrived, I suppose I could start seriously looking at some prospects. Maybe when Mr. Deacon comes back he can help me select the best one.
I am exhausted so I'm going to scoot to the sack.

Avis Lahay perused all that she had written. She closed the leather notebook and put it away. Her heart was full. She stood and stretched, shedding a fleecy housecoat. She hung it on one of the bedposts, then was careful to extinguish all the candles. The drapes were drawn shut so she was in total darkness. She waited for her eyes to adjust and listened to the solitude.

She bunched up her nightgown and slipped beneath the covers. She squished the pillow around and burrowed deep into the bed. Her mind took off running and jumping from one idea to another. She drifted with the scattered imagery until locking on one that soothed her to sleep, where dreams about horses and cavalry charges kept her lips pressed into a tiny smile.

Silas Dawson was young and strong, wandering around a dense forest too lush and green to be real. His eyes were as round as silver dollar coins. Copious sheets of soupy mist rose from a slow moving river. The whiteness clung to the trees and hung from branches like banners. His steps were tentative; every muscle in the thickset stump of his body was in tension.

Sublime stillness blanketed the unfamiliar terrain. The sinister intensity of the quietness was formidable. He crept through the gloom of fog, straining to ascertain any clue that would help him discover his whereabouts. He was lost, which was a newfangled phenomenon for him. He had never been in a place that bamboozled his instinctive knack for finding his way.

He had no inkling as to how long he'd been in these woods. Time, as he understood it had no meaning or frame of reference. His brain was a potpourri of frustrated confusion. He was beginning to think that this backcountry, with its lofty trees adorned in veils of steamy haze, was a labyrinth. A swish of sound snuck into his consciousness. He stopped and waited on it. His head turned ever so slowly as he tried to determine its location or source.

The rustle came again. He eased in its direction. His hackles raised. He put one foot in front of the other, paused and pricked his ears up. There was no telling what it was, but he was convinced he had its origins in his sights. He took a careful step. And another. The noise was suddenly behind him. He spun around and rushed toward it, but then, it was nowhere.

The confounding aggravation swirling inside his head increased. He fisted his hands and forced himself to remain stockstill. Expectancy raced through his veins. The flickering ripple popped up in a different place. His breathing became nonexistent as he moved with sly precision, getting closer and closer. He could hear it clearly behind a hedge of shrubbery. He parted the leafy undergrowth and reached out, but it was spectral and disappeared.

His mouth wrenched into a grimace. Whatever was in this woodland had provoked him into second guessing mode. For a crazed instant the forest was alive and writhing as it closed in all around him. He reacted by hooking his hands up as a shield, but the peculiarity passed as fleetingly as it had started. His shoulders momentarily sagged, then resolve stiffened him.

The whispery riffle came once more. It began as it had been; a soft swoosh of satiny material ruffling the air, but unpredictably, the sound became loud and persistent handclaps, as though it was taunting or defying him. He zeroed his attention on it and took off running. His heart hammered in his ears as his legs and arms churned.

He was a blur in the mist; a coil of speed darting around trees as though he was on an obstacle course. Faster and faster his knees pumped. Desperation roiled through him; he would not be denied. The clatter was a mere few yards ahead. He lunged for it, reaching and grasping, but came away with handfuls of nothing for the noise had dissolved into oblivion.

Silas Dawson staggered off-balance. He skittered into a low hanging limb and got tossed onto his keister. His chest heaved as he sat for a moment and collected his senses. He scooped up some moss and rubbed it together between his palms until it disintegrated into crumbs. He was utterly disoriented and stymied, which caused his teeth to grind.

He scrambled to his feet and cussed out the bewildering outlandishness. He wagged his head, mystified and uncertain. A flutter of movement appeared at the farthest range of his field of vision. His eyes stretched even wider. He was straightaway fascinated. Something or someone was gliding free and easy from tree to tree.

A hardened lump materialized in his throat. He choked it down and did his utmost to study what he saw. A gaping fissure appeared in the fog as he took hurried strides toward the motion. He climbed over a fallen tree without ever losing his focus. He was fixated on a form that flittered about and looked to be enshrouded in sheer layers of whiter than white silk.

He approached, wary and watchful. He steadily skulked along, as though he was a thief drawing near to an elusive payday. The distance was getting shorter and shorter, but he still couldn't distinguish what he was stalking. He kept his bearings in check as much as possible, ever vigilant and aware that the river was being put farther behind him.

The wetness of humidity persisted, but the mist was thinning out. Blades of pale sunlight came in low from the east and cut swatches between the trees. He persevered onward. A flurry of fluttering fabric spurred him. He took a hitch-hop step and began jogging. The silken creature murmured merriment and floated effortlessly deeper into the timberland.

The vibration of its voice lingered. His stomach did a queasy rollover. His ears burned and got all tingly. He sped up. His footfalls struck the softness of the forest floor and sank in the mossy velvet, which meant he had to work his muscles harder and harder. He had an intuitive flash that he was chasing a ghost through a dark and murky borderland.

That insight drove him to dig deeper for more strength and stamina. He was closing the gap. Vibrant hope put extra zip in him. His insides were aflame with energy. He accelerated and in doing so, was abruptly within a yard or so. Its gossamer garments billowed up. He leaned and strained, and his fingers almost skimmed against the hem. He sprang and pounced, fully extended in a do-or-die chance, but his objective vanished in the underbrush.

He careened and tumbled. His plunge came to a halt and entangled him in the thorns of a wild rose thicket. He stared at the barbed creepers and was amazed that he was unharmed. He disengaged from his predicament and gained his feet. Somewhere an orchestra was playing an evocative dirge. His brain revolted, sending urgent warnings to get away.

He evaluated his circumstances. The hinges of his jaw cramped. He refused to quit. His head swiveled, eyes alert and gutsy daring undeterred. A sliver of light shimmied, then the wraithlike entity reappeared way over yonder on the other side of a vine strewn gauntlet. He never hesitated. He slashed and fought his way through the nearly impenetrable brambles.

The music was soaring violins rising and falling in a layered whirlwind. Juiced up and inspired by the harmonious strings, he pressed past any and all limitations. He smashed and leapt over a corkscrew wall of thistles and briers to arrive at a grassy clearing. The breakthrough revealed that the satiny apparition was waving to him, seemingly beckoning him.

He willed his legs to run faster than ever. In the open spaces he high-stepped and pursued with ferocity. He was awestruck by the beauty surrounding him; a flowery meadow that was at least a thousand shades of green highlighted by a multitude of purple violets and bunches of yellow daffodils. The scent in the air was sweetly seductive, a musty mix of honey and heather. He dashed toward his quarry, but the scenery instantaneously changed.

In the dream he woke up. The foul odor of gone-to-rot flesh scratched at the lining of his nostrils. He coughed and gagged as he expelled a gush from his lungs. The orchestral song was somber; the violas and cellos were in a duel, exchanging solemn and melancholy notes that rhymed. His eyes were slits, his head disordered and baffled.

The melody descended to woeful depths to become the thump-thump crawl of a weak and thready heartbeat. He took a wobbly step and mused over the new setting. Denial swept through him and a cry got trapped in his voice box. He was alone, but not really. Silas Dawson was standing over the bed where he lay dying. His eyes bulged, then blackness entombed him.

Naomi Axler was awake in the middle of the night. There was eagerness chasing through her mind. Rather than analyze the darkness or toss about and disturb her husband, she stole from beneath the covers to get to it. She put knitted slippers on and was tying the belt of a colorful patchwork housecoat as she departed the bedroom. She closed the door behind her.

Her body was tired, but her imagination was roused and animated. She had a plan and intended to carry it out while the house was tranquil. A comforting diversion awaited; one that would take her on a pleasant and likely informative journey. She went directly to the kitchen table and picked up the unread mail from her vagabond gypsy niece.

The envelope was bulky, which overjoyed her because it meant that the letter would be lengthy. She unsealed it to find four pages. She so enjoyed correspondence from Abbey Langton because every post was well-written and full of details. She walked into the living room, where she stooped over and arranged two good-sized logs on the fire, jabbing at them a bit.

When she was satisfied that the smoldering coals were being rekindled into flames, she hung the iron poker on its hook and took hold of the matches. She meandered around the room, lighting enough candles and oil lamps to provide suitable brightness. She sat on an overstuffed chair in front of the fireplace and put her feet up on the hearthstone. She relaxed and settled in to be enthusiastically immersed in the excitement of news and updates.

December 1, 1877

Dakota Territory

Dear Aunt Naomi: Greetings and warm wishes. I suspect by the time you receive this your blessed event will have taken place. Jesse will have a brother or sister. I pray that all is well with you and the baby. I also pray that soon the road for us will turn so that I can meet my cousins. I'll revisit that topic before concluding this missive.

In the past you have broached the matter of Sam and I starting a family, so you may be wondering whether or not there's any gossip or rumors from that department. Let me assure you that no such responsibilities are in the works for us. I'm not sure why, since our love for each other is vigorous, and we are often quite demonstrative in our affectionate doings.

The why or why not of it has never been a factor in our relationship. We don't even talk about children being an option, and to be perfectly honest, that is fine with me because we are always on the move, which is how we want it to be. Raising a child in some of the wild places we've lived would be an extremely difficult challenge. If the Lord chooses to grace us with a little one, we'll be happy, but drastic changes would be in the offing.

I have some sadness to report that, even as I write this, causes my vision to get blurry with tears. Old Blue up and died near the end of October. I was surprised by the shock of grief that permeated my emotions. I know something about loss and sorrow. I should have taken the death of my tail-wagging shepherd and protector in stride, but instead I was inconsolable.

I cried and cried while we buried our faithful companion. The digging was therapeutic for me. We spent the next day gathering rocks to build a marker monument for a dearly loved friend. The grave is outside of Deadwood on a sloping hillside overlooking Mount Moriah Cemetery, Wild Bill Hickok's final resting place. I thought the spot was fitting and somewhat poetic considering that their paths unquestionably crossed in Abilene.

I'll not soon forget Old Blue. We had a remarkable kinship that I never expected, but will now miss forever. I cannot number the times my safety and well-being was dependent on that dog's vigilance. My journals are full of stories about Old Blue's exploits. With some edits and rewrites there are surely several that could be the basis for a book.

Just last April that rascal stood its ground against a mama grizzly that had no intention of letting us pass. Old Blue convinced it otherwise by snapping and herding it. The bear turned tail and ran. There's not much chance I'll ever choose to give my heart to another dog because it would be too unfair; no canine could ever get out from under Old Blue's shadow.

I cherish my memories of Old Blue and press on. Life continues with all its highpoints and upsets, triumphs and failures. We are both hale and hearty, with no complaints. Mostly our Conestoga wagon is still our base, as it has been for the last few years. When we are not exploring new country, we set up near a town or mining camp.

We have taken a room at a boarding house in Spearfish for the winter, which will be a nice respite from the trail. I look forward to getting involved in the community, while Sam sorts through a collection of artifacts and souvenirs gathered at the Little Big Horn battlefield, where we spent June and most of July. Military personnel and politicians were plentiful. There's already lots of scuttlebutt about the site being preserved as a national cemetery.

In August and September, we camped at Fort Robinson in the Pine Ridge region of Nebraska. It's a barren and windswept area. The outpost continues to be a pivotal garrison in the U.S. Army's efforts to subdue the Sioux. Battalions of soldiers come and go. Scouting forays are routine, along with other activity to make a show of force. There's an Indian village nearby, though I would call it a settlement for refugees because the inhabitants are dispossessed.

The conditions at the encampment are disgraceful. These people have been stripped of their way of life and are losing their identity to become completely dependent on handouts from the government. What is being systematically done to the Indians cannot be properly expressed because the policy is beyond words. Despicable, offensive, contemptible—a strong enough adjective has yet to be invented to describe the ugliness of the full picture.

We did what we could to help those accepting of us, though our efforts were feeble and largely scorned by officials of the Red Cloud Agency. I was infuriated by the attitude, but managed to hold my tongue. I've discovered that once nameless bureaucrats set a course there's no argument to be made to persuade underlings to do otherwise, so I ignored them. I proceeded to befriend a few widows of Sioux warriors. I was honored by their welcome and openness.

The Lakota Oglala leader Crazy Horse surrendered at Fort Robinson in May. I saw him close-up once and was struck by his courage and nobility in spite of the abuse and forfeiture he had suffered. He walked proudly and held his head high. He resided peacefully amongst his people until early September when tensions arose because of fear that he harbored resistance to the white ways and when an opportunity came he would return to the fight.

Even though Crazy Horse proclaimed that he had maintained the peace and would continue to do so, he was arrested under the cover of nighttime and escorted to the guardhouse, where there was confusion or a scuffle and a zealous private bayoneted him in the back, supposedly because he was resisting imprisonment. He died shortly thereafter.

Sam says that no one will ever know for sure what actually happened in the close quarter confines of the darkness. He was on the fringes of the investigation and interviewed as many of the principles as were made available to him by the authorities. He's usually not a cynic, but he's convinced that the specifics of the tragic incident will be whitewashed. He wrote an article that dissected the particulars and inconsistencies, which was printed in some eastern papers.

All of which brings me to big news that might be life-changing. Sam has told me for years that I have a way with words, which should be developed. I usually sloughed it off because he regularly has an inflated opinion about me, but he kept encouraging me to put pen and paper to good use. I've learned from him and have quietly taken his advice to heart, and am now pleased to report that I will soon have my own byline in Harper's Magazine.

The composition is a first-person account of my observations and experiences at Fort Robinson. It is based on my involvement and friendship with Indian women in the village, many of whom are husbandless mothers whose future is destitute and bleaker than bleak. Their story is narrated through my eyes. Sam and I bounced ideas around. He was helpful and supportive, but his only editorial assistance was to correct a careless spelling error.

We have been doing much planning about our travel itinerary for the foreseeable future. The truth is that we are always discussing possibilities. Neither of us ever stops looking toward the next horizon. We both want to see what's at the end of every valley or on the other side of the next mountain. God's hand was undoubtedly involved in drawing us together.

I need to make you aware of our current conversations. If this is agreeable, we intend to arrive at Wagon Wheel Gap in midsummer and stay at WT Ranch until the spring of '79. Then, depending on which way the wind is blowing, I expect we'll be heading back to Dodge City for a prolonged spell. Sam has a hankering for life in a cowtown again, but before that he wants to reconnect with Pete and learn the horse ranching business.

So, Aunt Naomi, if the Lord is willing and I earnestly pray that he will be, sometime next July I will be making a fuss over my cousins. It will be so wonderful to be together. The days will pass quick enough, then contentment will take hold of us as we sit and visit for many, many long hours. Until we meet again, take care and let nothing disturb or affright you.

Much Love,
Abbey

P.S. It just occurred to me that there is one more piece that I had forgotten. I will finally meet Caleb Weitzel and Sally Twosongs, folks who are such an integral part of Deacon's life.

Naomi Axler wanted to leap and shout for joy. A hilarious image passed through her mind; she had a cowbell in hand and was walking around the house announcing the good tidings like a town crier. The notion faded fast, but not before causing her to laugh aloud. She closed her eyes and slouched deeper into the chair. She was grinning when sleep overtook her.

On the road north of Santa Fe, the sun was rising on a new day, all pink and golden. Ben Slaton was in the saddle and coping with the discomfort and difficulties of his injury. A snarly grimace had become stamped on his face. Edgy and restless, he intermittently shifted his weight, as though pins and needles were implanted in his backside. The white-socked bay had a mind and will to run, but he mastered the reins and was making unfaltering progress.

There were no illusions in him. He realized he was in a bad box, but had no intention of giving up on what had first taken him away from the softness of a featherbed and the attentions of Brenda Hawkins. The wanted dead or alive poster in an inside pocket of his vest reminded him that he had big nuts to crack; five thousand big nuts to be exact.

His girlfriend would nurse him back to health. Her charms and talents would have him fit and fine in nothing flat, then he would track down Liam Greer and Smoky Crowe, though he didn't give a damn for the redskin. He would drop his boyhood sidekick with one shot and cash in; for the price of a bullet and the sweat of hard traveling, he'd be rich and famous.

He was no chucklehead. He realized that there were hindrances ahead; the undertaking would not be a picnic. Instead it'd be like trying to catch a weasel asleep, but he was certain that once healed and whole, he would be up to the task. The interval of convalesce would be a short setback equipped with the tenderness and warmth of a good woman.

Everything about Brenda Hawkins was enjoyable to him. He appreciated her bubbly and vivacious personality, but it was the promise of pleasure found in the roundness of her curves that kept him focused and riding just now. "We'll have us a hog-killing time of it," he said tiredly. His mouth twitched into a brief smile, then returned to the drawn scowl.

His leg was aching, but the soreness couldn't prevent him from think-ing about all the antics that awaited him. He purposefully daydreamed. Her lusty giggle rang in his ears. He had been with uncounted whores and shady ladies who were all forgotten soon after he finished using them, but for rea-sons unfathomable, he was unable to get her out of his system.

He *always* returned to her; he always *wanted* to return to her. She had a contagious enthusiasm that attacked life, which he admired. Her attitude had a positive influence on his character and outlook. He winced as some words recently spoken to him by a Good Samaritan tripped through his head: *If you were smart and looking to the future, you'd marry that girl and make an honest woman of her. She surely deserves that much and likely more.*

He cussed aloud and looked backwards. He adjusted his position in the saddle and took a gander all around him, as though he expected to see the whiskey drinking sermonizer in the vicinity. A shiver, slippery and cold, skated down his spine. He was alone in the broad valley, except for a large herd of pronghorn antelope feeding a mile or so to his west.

"Hellfire," he exclaimed in a rasping wheeze. "How'd that preacher get inside my head?" He swiveled sideways to have another look at his back trail. "Ain't no reason to be marrying her. You hear me?" He struggled to do so, but was able to push himself up. "You hear me, Coburn?" he shouted, ruddy-faced and blister-voiced. "I ain't going to do it!"

The horse nickered. He slapped its neck and gave it a kick. The stallion reared up on its hind legs, which caught the rider by surprise and almost tossed him. He secured his hold and leaned forward to mutter derisive ob-scenities that slandered the animal's parentage. The bay snorted and scar-pered forward in loping strides. He gave it freedom to gallop for a furlong, then exerted control and it gradually slowed to its previous laidback pace.

The dreadful jostling had unkind consequences; the throb in his lower right leg was now full-blown pain circulating through him. His teeth were clenched. He altered his weight and balance until attaining a modest relax-ing of the distress. Determined and hurting, Ben Slaton rode onward, eyes angled over a shoulder, worried or paranoid about what was behind him.

Eliza Weitzel woke up with an abruptness that caused her to gasp. Exhaus-tion had her completely stupefied. It took several seconds for her senses to begin functioning normally. The slivery shard of a sunbeam struck her groggy eyes and she double-quick jerked an arm up as a shield. She floun-dered and nearly fell off the hard-backed chair.

"It's just me," her husband said softly. He stood near the bedroom window, curtains in hand; he finished what he'd started and tied them open. "I snuffed the candles and oil lamps because this room needs some warm daylight. How long have you been at his bedside?"

"I'm not sure," she answered, slowly rising. She pushed her hands through her hair. "It was full dark so I would guess several hours. I was asleep on the couch when I heard a terrible groan. I came in here to find him agitated and thrashing as if he were trying to run."

"What? He hasn't flinched a muscle in two weeks."

"I know."

"Maybe you imagined it?"

"No chance, Hans."

"A nightmare perhaps?"

She gawped in blank-eyed uncertainty. "Me or him?"

He suppressed a chuckle. "Dawson, of course."

"Always possible, I suppose," she said, hands on her hips. "I lit all the candles and lamps that you just doused, which took a few moments. The blankets were thrown off. His legs and arms kept moving. I watched until he collapsed into stillness, then I waited. When it seemed timely, I washed and dressed the wound. He moaned and stirred some as I tucked him in."

"Are you certain, Eliza?"

"Yes," she replied, exasperated. She gently touched Dawson's cheeks, then placed a palm on his forehead. "All along I've been sponging or spoon-feeding him trickles of beef broth and it appears to me he's gaining strength and recuperating. I think our prayers and various remedies are working. Check for yourself, Hans. He's no longer feverish."

Weitzel did as she requested. Deep furls dug across his brow as his mouth tightened into a tentative smile. He went to the doorway. "Gray Cloud, come quick."

The Navajo man entered from the kitchen, brushing flour off his hands. "I'm fixing biscuits to go with a pot of cornmeal mush," he said, his roundish face cracked in a grin.

"Never mind that right now." Hans pointed at the Texas Ranger. "There's been a breakthrough." He hastily repeated all that his wife had witnessed and ended by saying, "If I was not so pragmatic I might be inclined to suggest we have reason to rally hope."

"It can't be." Gray Cloud gave his head a robust shake. His deep-set eyes were so full of doubt that pessimism seemed to spill out to flood the room. "I know nothing about nothing, but I know this: No one survives the poison of Smoky Crowe's arrowheads."

"We ought to be optimistic," Hans said, forceful and blunt.

"No. It is false hope. Silas Dawson will die. And we will suffer."

Weitzel eyeballed him skeptically. "We? What the devil are you saying?"

"Lord, have mercy! Stop it!" Eliza snapped, heat in her voice. "A man is fighting for his life here. I am going to pray and you two *will be* in agreement with me." Her face was blotchy with tension, eyes sad and reddened. She stretched her arms out, inviting them to join her.

The men glanced awkwardly at each other, then shuffled over to link hands together and form a circle with her. She spoke to God in succinct terms, pouring out her faith and passion for healing. When she said amen, her breathing was labored as she tried to hold back the tears.

One month after Whitey Fitzgerald woke up in a ditch south of Las Vegas, he came out of his drunkenness in a violent burst of energy; it was as if the rats gnawing on him had chomped down on a vital organ. His bloodshot eyes blinked and he leapt into a crouch. He was in an alley off Sandoval Street in Santa Fe, and had spotted Eloise Smith across the way. In his inebriated condition, his first thought was that he couldn't trust what was registering in his brain.

He shed the raggedy quilt around his shoulders and slinked against the wall to get closer. His stomach cramped. The bleariness in his vision cleared as he studied her, then a hot rush of rage erupted through him like a geyser; it was the sad-eyed woman who had played him for a fool, slashed his dignity to shreds and robbed him of his life savings.

There was no mistake about it. His chest began heaving fast and frantic. The steaming fury rising in him became a high-speed whirl of hornets buzzing inside his head. He pressed his hands over his ears and watched her. She was alone, carrying bags and parcels. He slouched forward onto the boardwalk for a better look and stayed hidden behind a parked wagon.

Her presence did something to his composure; five minutes earlier he had been sloshed, but now he was stone-cold sober. Instead of disturbing or distracting him, the droning noise zipping around his skull crystallized and pinpointed his concentration. His brain cleared of all the residual fog of alcohol and was fully functional as he serenely evaluated a course of action. He knew what he had to do; the step by step plan came together in an instant.

He kept her under surveillance as his eyes darted upward. It was late in the afternoon, an autumn day with a chill in the air. Tendrils of grayish clouds decorated the twilight sky. She was engaged in casual window shopping on the other side of the street. She conversed with a retailer in the doorway of his dry goods store, then sauntered off. He assessed the activity on the block and chose a route that gave him the best chance of remaining secreted from her.

She moved quickly in her sashaying style. He followed, discreet and cautious. His clothes were filthy; his body, too. He had not laundered or bathed since being drugged and dumped by Eloise Smith and Huey Butters. Now, rather than being a dapper gentleman, he had the appearance of a deadbeat beggar. He hadn't been reduced to mooching because he was not yet penniless, but the stash in his sock had been drank down to the last few dollars.

When she turned a corner, he carefully paused, then went to the intersection and arrived just in time to see her enter a tenement house. He scampered through the lengthening shadows of dusk and took up a position from which he could keep a lookout on the three-story building. His diligence was soon rewarded. A newly-lit lamp flickered in a top floor apartment and a moment later, he saw Eloise Smith at the window drawing the drapes shut.

He tapped a finger against his forehead as though he was using Morse code to file away her location in his brain. His mouth warped into a grin that had a tinge of madness in it. He returned to the alley where he had discarded his ratty bedding and scrunched down in what had become his usual nighttime spot. The relaxation of revenge accompanied him to sleep.

Bright and early the next morning, Whitey Fitzgerald was on task. He possessed a clarity of intention that was freakishly cocksure; all qualms had been consumed by the buzz of hornets in his head. He was on alert for Eloise Smith or any sightings of Huey Butters. He figured that it was reasonable to presume that where one crook was the other could be closeby.

He went to a ramshackle tavern he frequented, but instead of procuring liquor, he had a two-bit meal and made inquiries about handguns. He listened more than he talked. The bartender and several patrons recommended a gunsmith specializing in low-priced firearms. When his belly had the edge taken off its hunger, he headed crosstown to cut a deal.

After exuberant bartering with the proprietor, who was a top-notch skinflint, the best his remaining funds could purchase was a second-rate revolver, an old Smith & Wesson Model 1 from the mid-fifties that was beat-up, for it had been sorely used. The cylinder had a slight wobble, but he was assured that the gun fired straight and true. It took all of Fitzgerald's persuasive skills to get six cartridges included in the transaction.

Fed and armed, there were no worries or reservations to slow or moderate his purpose. He kept his eyes strained and observant as he hurried to his destination. He was bent on carrying out the final step of his plan.

The seething anger in him was an aroused monster; its formidable and all-consuming impulse illuminated his brain and goaded him onward.

The sun wasn't yet at high noon when he stopped near the frame structure that housed Eloise Smith. He immediately noted that the curtains she had closed the previous evening were open, which caused him to sprint across the street. He entered the building and navigated the staircase to the third level. The corridor was vacant. He withdrew the pistol from his waistband and walked directly to what he determined to be her apartment. He knocked twice.

The door opened. The mulatto woman gasped and tried to slam it, but he blocked her effort and shouldered his way inside. "Good day, Eloise," he said, click-clicking.

Her soulful eyes flashed and her lips parted in a moist smile. "You're not a ghost?"

"No, but you soon will be."

"Oh my goodness gracious. The sight of you scared me half to death." She clasped her hands over her bosom. "You're alive, thank God. Huey told me that he killed you."

"And where is Huey Butters?"

"He beat and raped me, Whitey."

"No more lies. I despise a liar."

"My momma never raised no falsifier, so hush your mouth."

"Get on your knees, Eloise, if that's even your name,"

"Of course it is, Whitey." She sidled away from him. "I'm so pleased to see you. My heart is overflowing. Now you put that silly old gun away so we can talk sensibly."

He lashed out and used the butt of the six-shooter to strike her upside the head. She took the blow and returned a defensive punch that he evaded by bobbing low. He swung a closed fist that smashed her chin and sent her sprawling on her fanny. Her lips were bloodied; her eyes frightened and seeping disbelief. He loomed over her, glaring.

"Sweet mother of Jesus . . ."

"Get on your knees," he cut in, ramming the weapon at her.

"Please . . . please . . . please don't do this, Whitey." She scrabbled backwards, looking like a crippled crab. "I'm sorry . . . I'm sorry. It was all Huey Butters, I swear."

"Where's my money?"

"He took it and left me. He's scheming another swindle."

He was unmoved. She wore a plain maroon housedress, but the straight-line cut of it couldn't obscure the sweet curves of feminine beauty.

His eyes, full of disdain and hate, roamed over her body, then he click-clicked dismissively. "Get on your knees. Say your prayers."

Fear spilled from her eyes as she obeyed by kneeling and clinching her hands together. She pleaded to the Almighty in murmurs. Her fervent words of supplication were thickened with emotion and interspersed by wrenching sobs. He completely ignored her. A gusher of rage incited him to finish the job. He slipped behind her and pressed the barrel against the base of her neck. She was begging and apologizing. He could only hear the irresistible clamor of hornets.

Whitey Fitzgerald squeezed the trigger, crazy-eyed and smirking insanely.

It was mid-morning. Delores Solrizo stood propping the kitchen door open, her heart heavy and determined. "Do you have a few spare minutes for me, Avis?"

"Sure, Miss Delores. What's up?"

"I could use some company, is all."

"Mr. Whitey's not back yet?"

"He's likely doing more socializing than grocery shopping," Delores answered, pinching a smile. She watched as the teenager returned the pool cue to the rack, amazed at their striking similarities, as though she was recognizing them for the first time. Her nose was wider and her reddish hair had dark brown in it, but she had the same oval face and mischievous eyes.

"Mr. Whitey likes to chatter, doesn't he?"

"That, my dear, is one of his truest charms."

Avis slipped past her. Delores followed. They sat on stools across from each other at the island bar. Delores picked up a paring knife to continue the preparation begun twenty minutes earlier before she had gotten distracted by memories and sneaky feelings. She was peeling potatoes and carrots, and cutting them into bite-size chunks for an elk meat stew.

"I could get a knife and help."

"That's not necessary, honey," Delores said, a hitch in her voice.

Avis frowned and gave her a cursory look that lingered to become a concentrated stare. She saw dampness accumulating in her eyes. "What's wrong, Miss Delores?"

"My mother died when I was ten years old. I've been remembering her lately," Delores replied, shrugging. "Kind of silly, I guess. It was all so long ago and faraway."

"What was she like?" Avis asked, leaning forward on her elbows. She supported her chin in her hands. "It would be good for me to know something about her, wouldn't it?"

Delores perked up some. "I used to visit with her in the kitchen when she did things like what I'm doing here. I suppose that's where I learned to appreciate the secrets of putting ingredients together. Fixing meals has always been satisfying to me."

"Did your father enjoy her cooking?"

Delores glanced away from her busy hands, lifting an eyebrow in surprise. "I think so. If he didn't then there was something wrong with him, though that's not news to me."

"What do you mean?"

"Your grandfather was not a nice man," Delores said severely. "Suffice it to say that my father was a drinker with emotional problems which he often took out on others. With much prayer I've done my best to forgive him, but the scars he put on my soul still remain."

Avis appeared thoughtful and reflective. She intertwined her fingers under her chin. "Mr. Whitey told me that people make mistakes and we should go easy when those missteps affect us because down the road when we mess up we'll need someone to go easy on us."

"That's wisdom, but it's not what comes natural."

"I know. It can be awful hard."

"My mother explained lessons about forgiveness, but I was so young, I never took hold of them," Delores said, shaking her head sadly. She put the knife down. "One time when I was struggling, a woman named Naomi, who just happens to be Deacon's sister, pointed me to the Lord's Prayer. She taught me that the principle is clear. If we want to live in God's forgiveness then we cannot refuse to forgive those who wrong or hurt us."

Avis furrowed her brow. "Miss Delores, why did you lie to me for so long?"

"I don't know, honey. I was scared and worried. I was wrong."

"Were you ashamed of me?"

"Put that out of your head," Delores answered, peering into her eyes. "It was an extreme blunder and my only excuse is that I wanted to protect you. I am proud to call you my daughter. You are a joy and the moment I found you I should've told you so."

"Protect me from what, Miss Delores?"

"Conversations like this, for starters."

"I don't understand."

"Sometimes neither do I," Delores said, attempting to be facetious. She filled her lungs, exhaled a sigh and forced a smile. "In my teen years bad things happened and my response made matters worse. I built my days on mistake after mistake; I piled them on top of each other. My life was ugly when you were born and it got much uglier. I was not a good woman, Avis. Then God's grace reached down and empowered me to begin the process of healing and hope."

Avis was teary-eyed. "Thank you, Miss Delores."

"For what?"

"For telling me the truth. For sharing all this."

"I would like us to develop a closeness."

"We're heading in the right direction," Avis said, "but I likely need more time and space to get to where this is all aligned in my head and more importantly, my heart."

"I pray you'll get there, Avis."

"I do, too."

Delores leaned closer to her. "I don't wish to overburden you, but there is something else for your consideration. If you so desire, when you give the say so, I can contact my lawyer and have the necessary paperwork done to legally change your surname to Solrizo or Scully."

"Huh." Avis pushed back and sat up straight. "I hadn't thought about that possibility, though I have wondered how I got my name and whether it had any significance."

"I picked it," Delores said frankly. "It sounded pretty. To my knowledge it has no family tree connections. Even with my thinker in disarray, I wanted you to be your own person."

"That's helpful information, Miss Delores. Thank you."

Delores nodded and smiled cordially. She considered the mood of the conversation and had an urge to go deeper, but then there was a rapping on the backdoor. "That'll be Whitey with a cart of groceries. We've got some toting and lifting to do, young lady."

They stood and in harmony went to work.

Charley Jondreau had his eyes peeled to enjoy the stark beauty of the scenery. He was surrounded by thousands of acres of roughhewn landscape, picking his way through a network of canyons and ravines. The midafternoon sunshine reflected off the weather-beaten hillsides and bluffs, transforming the dry terrain into ever-changing displays of variegated color ranging from bright red to rust to grayish shades of blue and black.

The highest peak in the badlands was crowned by a thickish column of rock that had been windswept and eroded to have large curved wings; a hoodoo of sorts. He spotted it hours ago and was using it as a signpost to guide him. Distances in the high desert were deceptive; the angel shaped standing stone continued to be many miles ahead and just now, he squinted because a lone dot appeared in the sky above it.

The bird circled lazily once, then made a beeline for him. He strained to identify it, but the piebald pinto distracted him with an abrupt stop and snort for attention. He leaned forward, spoke into its ear and gave it a nudge. The animal pawed the ground and whinnied. He gently coaxed it, but the pony refused to move. He turned in the saddle to check on the dapple gray in tow. The yearling was acting skittish too.

He dismounted and returned his concentration to the visitor soaring across the vastness of blue. There was no ambiguity in its flight path; it was approaching him in sweeping spirals. He watched in wonder as it flew at full tilt, gobbling up space at an incredible speed. It soon became clear that it was a hawk. He grinned and waited on it as though it was an old friend.

The white-breasted bird flew directly to him. When it closed the gap, it descended in a swoop and rapidly decelerated to a hovering position less than twenty yards above him. He was in awe. It arched its widespread wings and screeched a screaming cry that was disconcerting; not once, but rather, three times the bird of prey enunciated its shrieky omen.

He stretched out his arms and closed his eyes for a moment of supplication to gain understanding. When he opened them the hawk was gone. He spun around and craned his neck, startled and increasingly disturbed; no bird could ever disappear that fast—there weren't any nearby nooks for it to be in hiding. He searched for the red-tailed raptor but it was nowhere to be seen. Undeterred, he thoroughly scanned the heavens again with the same result.

The horses were noticeably worried and uneasy. Jondreau soothed them with whispered reassurance, then had a swig from one of the canteens. A shiver passed through him. He plodded along at a sluggish pace, leading the animals. He mulled over the meaning of the visitation and his mouth puckered into the downward expression of a bulldog. Evil was afoot; he *knew* it.

In Colorado, Naomi Axler had an oak medallion in her hand. Her smile was radiant and on the verge of bubbling into laugher. She kept the merriment contained in her throat, but its insistence to escape had her squeezing her sides in a bear hug. She stood with her backside tight against the wall as she peeked around the doorframe into the living room to watch tenderness expressed in boisterous horseplay and clownish tomfoolery.

Her husband was on the floor flopping around with their son. Their shenanigans were rough and rib-tickling. She was straining to maintain composure, but finally a burst of giggles squeaked out and she decided to join them. She slipped the wooden keepsake into her apron pocket, then hoisted her skirt and got on all fours to crawl toward them.

"Mommy!" Jesse hurled himself at her, almost tipping her over.

She wrestled and jostled with him. He squealed excitedly. She kneaded his belly, then gave him a hefty shove "Is this a private party or do you two have room for me?"

Pete caught him. "Join at your own peril, dear."

"Well, supper is cooking, so if I get done in, you won't go hungry," she said, folding her knees under her. "Amanda is still napping so we ought to keep this to a dull roar."

Jesse was squirming and scrapping to get free. His father put him on the floor and knocked him onto his backside. The boy's cheeks were crimson. Breathless gasps came between squeaky hollers of laughter. His mother took hold of his wrists.

"Let's get his gizzard, dear," Pete said, holding his legs down.

"Yes, let's do."

Jesse cried out in glee. They grappled with him to uncover his bellybutton, then poked around and goosed it by gently squeezing. The operation was repeated and all the while he tried kicking and thrashing, but couldn't get loose. He was sweated. Pleas of surrender signaled that he was ready for the rowdiness to end. They let him up easy. He scampered to the play corner where he squatted, dumped a basket of colorful blocks and began building something.

"He's a fine boy, Naomi."

"And you're a great father, Pete."

"I don't know."

"Well, I do," she said, without hesitation. "That boy idolizes you and for good reason. I am often overwhelmed by the kindness and integrity in you. I have been richly blessed by your love and friendship. You are a good man, Pete Axler." She was amused by the reddening of embarrassment filling in the wrinkly lines of his face. "You have tenderness that sweetens me. I am proud and thrilled to be your wife and the mother of your children."

He stuttered and stammered. He rubbed his bristly whiskers, eyes averted.

"You don't have to say anything, Pete."

His hands flexed nervously. "You don't understand."

"I do."

"I want to say something."

"I know, but it's not necessary," she said, taking hold of his hands. "Every day you tell me what's in your heart. Your affection is expressed by your actions. When I came west after Adam died I never dreamt of this life. God has given us something special."

He hung his head, seemingly shamed or timid. When he lifted it there were dribbles of moisture showing in his squinty eyes. "I am a lucky man. You are a remarkable woman."

She kissed him hard and long on the lips, then pushed back and beamed an amorous smile. She retrieved the oak medallion from her apron pocket. "Do you remember this?"

He was flushed and flustered. "Of course."

"What is it?"

"It's the first gift I gave you," he replied, wiping away the evidence of tears. "You usually have it propped in front of the mirror on your dresser."

"Yes. Do you remember what you told me about it once?"

"When?" He scowled. He took it from her and turned it over in his hands. It was about the size of a pocket watch, smooth on one side and a perfect replica of a horse's head on the other, with an impressive mane and deep-set eyes. "I need more help, Naomi."

"You need more help, or are you stalling?"

"Why would I stall?"

Her brown eyes were flirtatious. "Perhaps you're dodging?"

"Dodging? Dodging what?"

"A job that needs doing."

"Naomi, I'm no slacker."

She placed a hand on his knee and began caressing it. "On the morning I was certain I was with child, you promised to whittle a matching one for our firstborn."

"Did I?"

"Yes, and now we have two children, so you better get to carving."

"I apologize for not getting it done. It slipped my mind," he said candidly. "I am sorry. A promise ain't to be taken lightly. I ought to be better at carrying through on my word."

"I was mostly teasing, Pete."

His lips formed a sly grin. "Maybe so, but I best get busy if I ever again expect to find any tender treasures hiding behind the warmth of your smile."

She shooed him by giving him a frisky push and slapping his shoulder. He fell back and sprawled as though he'd been stricken by a powerful blow. She sat astride his midsection and pinned him down. He made a doddering protest. Jesse raced to join in and was soon airborne. Entangled together, they tumbled around while an uproar of hilarity filled the house.

Charley Jondreau figured he had been walking for at least five miles. It was slow going because the piebald pinto and dapple gray were being cantankerous. He did not disregard the apprehension exhibited by the animals, but instead, he had sensitivity to it. He too was edgy, yet he trudged onward and led the animals with a firm hand.

The scorching eye of God that was the sun had less than an hour until its lid closed on another day. Its rays were fading into a blend of purplish hues; the colors flittering on the ridges and cliffs were disappearing into deepening shadows of gray. His eyes were wary, his nostrils flared. There was a peculiar and prickly foreboding in the air, which he took seriously for he trusted his senses; it was the unmistakable miasma of evil.

A faint noise reached his ears; it was akin to the scratchy nick of a match. Ahead and to the left was an opening to a canyon. He stiffened and stopped to listen, but the gorges and gullies made it difficult to determine from which direction the sound had come. He walked on and in a moment, the odor of burning tobacco caused him to halt once more. Then, he clearly heard two distinct voices conversing. He recognized the second one to speak.

"The hour of your testing has come."

"Bring it on. I ain't scared."

"The powers of light are strong in the man."

"Light ain't going to stop no bullet."

"We wait. We see."

Jondreau withdrew his pistol and checked its loads, making no effort to do so silently. He had no fear. He snapped the cylinder shut and spun it before returning the gun to its holster worn high on his right hip. His mackinaw was already stored with gear tied down on the yearling. He now measured the movement required to shift the elk-hide poncho aside. Satisfied, he rapidly picketed the horses near a scraggly bunch of juniper trees, then strolled forward.

Pinkish shimmers of twilight glimmered on his pathway. He inclined to the left and entered the ravine from whence the smoke and talk originated. At the far end, fifty or so yards away, two men stood side by side in front of a domed wikiup. The older one was tall and skinny, naked from the waist up and puffing on a pipe; the other was a stoop-shouldered youngster who miles and years ago, Charley Jondreau had declared to be unredeemable.

The half-breed, a descendent of Iroquois warriors and Hudson Bay Company trappers, didn't hesitate for an instant. He strode toward them boldly, moving on the agile feet of a cougar. His belly was fixing for a fight. He pulled up spitting distance from them, feet set the width of his shoulders and hands hanging casually at his sides.

Greer eyeballed him, recklessness in his stare. "Been awhile, Charley."

"Not long enough," Charley answered, cool and restrained. "I see you got your six-gun strapped on. You awaiting a chance to shoot me in the back, eh?"

"I'll face you down and kill you dead, Charley."

"I suspect you'll require clearance from your counselor."

"I am Smoky Crowe," the white-haired man said, taking a short step toward him. "I will ascend the mountains and walk upon the clouds. You have no power to stop me."

"I am Charley Jondreau," he replied curtly. "I heard the eagle scream on the day of my birth. I have been to the mountaintop and beyond, and came away strengthened."

"Are you here to die, Charley Jondreau?"

"No. To kill if necessary, but not to die."

"You are trouble?"

"I'm passing through, eh."

"Yet you confront me."

Jondreau thrust his chin upward. "I stand where I am."

"I will bring you down to the depths."

"Not likely, for the hawk is my brother."

Crowe's teeth tightened on the stem of the pipe. "I will be exalted. Bow down in worship and receive my mercy. Otherwise as the earth trembles and quakes you will be eaten by maggots set loose at my command. Until the waters run no more my kingdom will be high and lofty."

Jondreau gave him an ambivalent shrug. "I am a mere clay vessel, but hear this: Your kingdom as you call it, is nothing more than sand being sifted by the Great Spirit. As dust is tossed into the wind and disappears, so shall it be with your empire of blood."

"You dare to defy me?" Smoky Crowe tilted his head to an odd rightward angle so that his milky left eye was unfettered and focused on him, bulging and pulsing. He spoke fluently in an unknown language and conjured a malicious spell, which he cast on the man ridiculing him, but it became ever more evident that his nefarious powers were anemic and ineffective.

"Your medicine cannot harm me," Charley said, smiling.

"Your death will come soon."

Jondreau's face wrinkled into mockery. "You are the author of death, eh?"

Smoky Crowe recoiled, then lurched forward. His feet shuffled in a dance and he leaned back as a yap-yap-yap yowl tore from his throat. The bloodcurdling blare bounced off the rock walls and echoed across the badlands. He crooked a finger at Greer and sneered. "Won't someone deliver me from the contempt of a fool? The time to feed violence is now."

Jondreau rolled his eyes. Dusk was a gray branch drooping into darkness. He studiously appraised the two men and the dynamics coursing between them. He caught an inner glimpse of Liam Greer as a dog being let off its leash by its master. He linked his fingers together and began twiddling his thumbs. "Is today a good day for Kid Greer to die?"

"It won't be my blood spilt, Charley."

"You want to die quick or bleed out? It matters not to me, eh."

Kid Greer sidestepped a few paces. His slouchy eyes were cold and dead, and riveted on him. "I could ask the same of you, Charley. I ain't no simpleton tenderfoot this time."

Jondreau waited, patient and calm as he fiddled with his thumbs.

"Are you ready?" Liam asked anxiously.

"I was born ready. Make your play, hoss."

"Stop twitching your damn hands!"

Jondreau ignored him, grinning nonchalantly. Greer took a huge breath and exhaled it through clenched teeth. His right hand flinched. He went for his gun, but gasped and jerked to a stop before it cleared leather. His face contorted into an unbelieving grimace and he blasphemed indignantly. Jondreau had his pistol in hand and leveled at his chest.

"You still got a lot to learn, punk," Charley drawled, backing up.

"Go," Smokey Crowe said, "but know that I will taste your death."

"Bullspit." Jondreau kept moving steadily. He never allowed his focus to budge from them as he backpedaled, covering the distance even quicker than when he had arrived. His skin was clammy and tickly. He hurried to the grove of juniper trees and released the horses. He glanced at the stars beginning to twinkle, then mounted and rode away chuckling.

A few miles later he halted for the night and set up a secure camp.

Caleb Weitzel did a skip and hop onto the front porch. He had been hard at it from sunup to sundown, and now, as the smudgy grays of evening turned to full dark, his muscles ached in a good and familiar way. There was contentment for jobs well done in his weariness. He did some sideway stretches, then went inside and shed his jacket.

The house smelled of beef, beans and fresh baked bread. His stomach growled and an expansive smile cracked his squarish face. He tossed his hat onto a twelve-point mule deer rack mounted on a plaque centered above the pegs for sweaters and outerwear. There was an impish gleam swimming in the murky blue of his eyes as he crept toward the kitchen. He eased along the wall, but the wind was snatched from his sails when his wife popped into the doorway.

"Gotcha!" she exclaimed, giggling.

"Unfair." He grabbed her shoulders and pulled her into his embrace. He locked his hands against the small of her back. "It was my intention to sneak up on you, Sally Twosongs."

She bussed his cheek. "A cowboy cannot surprise a maiden watching him through a window. Especially if that cowboy gave a dog orders to care for the maiden. You had barely closed the barn door and my protector was barking to let me know of your approach."

"Thanks a lot, Hank," he said, frowning at the collie. The dog whined and wagged its tail aggressively, then it turned and padded to its favorite spot to curl up near the fireplace.

"The table's set and ready. Are you hungry?"

"Famished." He gave her bottom an affectionate pat as she slipped away. He went to the basin to wash his hands and face. "That roan mare should foal in the next day or two."

"Are you worried?"

"A little, yes. Pete is going to check in on it later."

"Good." They sat down together in candlelight and while holding hands she spoke words of thanksgiving; amen was said in unison. She served him, then put a dainty portion on her plate.

"So Hank has been devoted in tending to you?"

"Sometimes too much," she replied openly. "I'm not a hothouse flower. I feel fine. I would be grateful if you would instruct Hank to give me some space."

"I can do that, but . . ."

Her dark eyes narrowed on him. "But what?"

"I'm not the only one who gave Hank orders."

Comprehension flickered over her face. "Charley."

"Yes. He told me so."

She sighed and shook her head. "I suppose I best get used to being waited on and watched over by a dog because God only knows when we'll see Charley again to rescind his directive. Hank won't let up until he hears straight from Charley. Those two shared rapport."

"That'd be my conclusion, Sally Twosongs."

"You better listen to me, Caleb Weitzel. I feel fine," she said with forced emphasis on each syllable. "In another week or so, I guarantee you'll find out just how healthy I am."

He folded a slice of bread around a hunk of beef and took an enthusiastic bite. "Then I'd be wise to get plenty of nourishment to be strong and ready," he said whilst chewing.

"I'll see to it." Her smile was full, her cheeks rosy. He reached for her hand, but she unpredictably wrenched backwards and shuddered; at the same time Hank went batty. The collie was up and spinning in circles, barking and growling as though deranged. It was salivating and snapping its jaws in the grips of frenzied hysteria.

The temperature in the room dropped perceptively; Caleb's blood ran cold. His complexion blanched, but his expression remained impassive and stoic. He was on his feet hushing the dog in a firm and imposing voice, but his demands were unheeded; perhaps even unheard. It whirled and woofed, gyrating and bucking like a wild stallion.

Sally Twosongs was twitchy. Her eyelids fluttered, appearing to be unhinged. Her shoulders heaved as her body trembled in terrible spasms. Her head swayed back and forth. She gulped in air. Her mouth opened and closed, then in a numb tone she said, "The crow-man is a dragon. He wants to kill Charley Jondreau, but cannot. Charley Jondreau is safe."

In that instant, two occurrences transpired simultaneously: Sally Twosongs convulsed and immediately sagged on the chair like a ragdoll; Hank stopped and dropped to its belly as still and soundless as a corpse. She found composure and stiffened her posture. Her eyes widened and fastened on her husband, who was on a knee beside her, a hand on her hip.

"Worry not for me," she said, assured and unruffled.

"The crow-man is a dragon?"

Her eyebrows dipped low in a miserable frown. "The crow-man is evil inside human skin, but that makes no never-mind to Charley Jondreau or me. There is a hallowed call on us. We stand against evil wherever we must and we don't get to choose the battleground."

"I don't possess your faith, but ofttimes it has been proven to me that your gifts are from above. You have my support and allegiance always. I would die for you, Sally Twosongs." He rested his head against her bosom. She pulled him close and let her fingers comb through his sand-colored hair. He closed his eyes and was gladdened by the song of her heartbeat.

~ ~ ~

"The pistol misfired. Twice."

Delores Solrizo was white-faced. She attempted to keep her poise and remain passive, but shock drained her complexion. In a late-night gabfest Whitey Fitzgerald had just confessed. Her skin was frosted by slick goosebumps. It felt like the air in the dimly-lit *Cantina Room* had been frozen into icicles. She was rigid and speechless in the bentwood rocker.

"I had it planned," he said in a muffled monotone. His click-click was muted and erratic, coming in nervous bursts. He rocked in tiny motions. His eyes were wet and preoccupied by an obscure detail in the middle of the mural—he stared vacuously. "She was blubbering and pleading and praying, but whoever I had been before was gone. I had nothing but rage and violence in me. The second time the hammer clacked, I turned the gun on myself."

"My God, Whitey."

He never paused; neither did he change the inflection of his voice. "I pulled the trigger thrice with my mouth wrapped around the barrel. My bladder exploded and a scream jarred me. It seemed to be far-off, but was ripping out of my lungs. The man you knew in Abilene died in that room, with his pants pissed and a woman slobbering on the floor." He turned toward her, helplessness on his face. "The gun malfunctioned or the bullets were defective."

"Thank God."

"Why thank God, Miss Delores?"

"You're alive, Whitey. And you're not a murderer."

"I got murder in my heart."

"That's one of those rats you're working to kill."

"I guess that be true."

She gazed at him, her eyes sensitive and reassuring. "My experience tells me that you can't change what happened and you can't change what you did. What is possible is to suffocate those rats and live refusing to be defined or defeated by them. After all, what are we talking about here? Six months of an emotional nightmare and one day of madness?"

"The nightmare and madness be inside me, Miss Delores."

"Maybe so, but there's plenty of goodness in you, Whitey," she replied sincerely. "I was the beneficiary of it many times in Abilene. I've seen it here growing stronger every day and am grateful for it because you are such a positive influence on my daughter."

"Avis be a sweetie-pie."

"She'll always need you as her friend, Whitey."

"I will try, but I be scared," he said, sad and disheartened. "I ain't me no more. I pretend to be fine and go through the motions, but there's fierce rage in me. When I stalked that woman the violence was alive and buzzing in my head. If the pistol hadn't failed I'd have blown her brains out and then mine. I be terrified that the beast lurking in me is only in hibernation."

"I'm so sorry, Whitey."

"I just want some peace, Miss Delores."

She gave him a sympathetic smile and patted his forearm. "It's seldom easy. I have firsthand knowledge that the road of peace and redemption is often hard slugging."

"You'd be the one to know of such things."

"Then trust me, Whitey. It gets better."

"Your example gives me hope, but I still be scared and full of doubt."

"You have to stop the bleeding and put the misery behind you," she told him. "Time and distance will allow this horrible episode to fade into the background, though in all honesty, in dark and lonesome moments, it'll haunt you. That's all part of the slugging it out."

"I ain't right, Miss Delores. I feel like I ain't ever going to be right."

"Give it time, Whitey."

"Time ain't changing what's inside me."

"The beast you speak of can be caged."

"You don't understand, Miss Delores. I ain't *me*." Pain and bewilderment filled his face and made his eyes watery. "When I was coming of age on that plantation in Alabama, Master Fitzgerald decided I needed to be knocked down a notch because I wasn't jumping high or quick enough for him. He strung me up and had me whipped to teach me my lessons. I got the stripes on my back to prove it, but through it all I kept my pride.

"I never submitted to him, ever. I acted a role that gave him a sense of victory, but not so. He beat me, but he couldn't win. I had murderous thoughts for him, but let them go because I wanted to be my own man, walking upright and in self-respect. If ever I was to lose myself it should've been then, but no; I overcame being stripped naked and flogged, along with all the other inhumanities of slavery with honor and dignity unbroken.

"How is it that Eloise Smith can steal my heart, trash it and by doing so, devastate everything I valued? And what of Huey Butters? I'm consumed with hate and maniacal thoughts about him. I *want* to kill him. My brain fantasizes about finding him and being joyful as I watch him die. I be afraid that one day I will tip over again and there'll be blood on my hands. I be frightened that the nightmare in me will escape and harm you or Avis.

"I still be ashamed for the nastiness I shouted at you."

"I'll not hear any of that, Whitey Fitzgerald. It's forgiven and forgotten," she said tersely. Her eyes were large and dampened by compassion. "I understand your pain and fear. And don't get me started on my intimate acquaintance with shame."

"I know, Miss Delores."

"Then grant me the courtesy of being heard, Whitey."

He cringed and glared at her. "I be listening to you, ma'am."

She smiled, soft and tender. "You may be listening, but you are not hearing me." She engaged his eyes to regard him with profound intentionality. "There is hope and life and new opportunities on the other side of anguish. The badness we do or is done to us can only have power when we allow it. Confession, repentance, forgiveness means going forward choosing to shed the stench of the rubbish and debris we've waded through."

"Please pray for me, Miss Delores. I be a sorry man."

"I pray for you every day, Whitey. I'll gladly pray with you right now."

He nodded. There was no shyness or apprehension; they moved together, turning the rockers so that their knees were touching. She exhorted him to be in agreement with her and took hold of his hands, which were moist and shaking. She assaulted heaven with bold petitions for compelling mercies to fall upon her friend. When she concluded, they were both crying.

Gray Cloud had a ghastly feeling swirling in the pit of his stomach. He was pacing in circles around the table, arms waving expressively. His fitful movements were so swift that the candle flames were flickering erratically. He had been at it for almost ten minutes, alternating between lip-clamped silence and muttering rapid sentences.

Hans Weitzel sat observing him, hands fisted and eyes hot. His jawline was taut and stamped in frustration—that fuming annoyance finally spewed out in a grouchy growl. "Stop this nonsense and quit dithering. Whatever the frig is on your mind sit down and spit it out."

"Hunky-dory, hunky-dory," Gray Cloud said, coming to an abrupt halt. He swung a chair around and straddled it; his fingers interlocked around its back. "I apologize. I am all out of sorts because nasty thoughts in my head keep shouting. I worry on Silas Dawson, but more and more I have much uneasiness for my workmates Hans and Eliza."

"Dawson will recover or die. We've done everything possible," Hans replied stiffly. "He has been having severe bouts of restlessness all afternoon and evening, so we are on watch." He looked askance at the mantle to see the clock; it was advancing on midnight. He took a mouthful of cold coffee, grimacing as he swallowed. "Eliza has enough hope to truly believe Dawson is on the precipice of breaking through to consciousness. You ought to settle down or go off to bed."

"We should pray."

Weitzel grunted. "I am praying. Have been all along."

"A scourge is coming."

"No riddles, Gray Cloud. Declare in plain language."

"My head is full. It hurts. Pestilence will follow Dawson."

Weitzel scowled at him. "Could you be just a bit more specific?"

"We're doomed to suffer Smoky Crowe's wrath."

"Doomed? I think not. Mr. Crowe will get judged by my wrath."

"A curse will be put on *Freiheit*," the Navajo man answered precisely. "Whether Silas Dawson lives or dies makes no difference. There will be no escaping the consequences."

"Consequences?"

"We came to Dawson's aid. We're harboring him."

"The man collapsed unconscious at the foot of that charred cross," Hans said, terseness strangling his tone. "We did the only decent thing and cared for him. I'm no Bible thumper, but it seems to me that good works are supposed to bring rewards."

"In the afterlife, maybe."

"I swear. State your meaning."

"Friends of Smoky Crowe's enemy are his enemies."

"Is that supposed to frighten me?" Hans asked, chuckling derisively. "I will stand against that mongrel mutt on the virtues of right and wrong. Smoky Crowe needs killing."

"That is true, but who will kill him, Hans? He has wizardry."

Weitzel glowered as his hands clenched tighter and the knuckles whitened. Genuine anger detonated in his eyes. "Please! Don't give me any of that claptrap gibberish. Smoky Crowe is a witch, a sorcerer, a necromancer? Who cares? Whatever aura emanates around him, he's a flesh and blood man. If he *ever* makes a move against me or mine *I will* kill him."

"How?" Gray Cloud queried, amazement in his expression. His deep-set eyes glinted darkly and seemed to sink lower into the sockets. "Your Henry rifle will have no effect against the black arts. Smoky Crowe is invulnerable to bullets. He has powerful magic."

"All men die, Gray Cloud," Hans said, relaxing his hands. "I'll not agonize over the how of it, but if push comes to shove, I will put Crowe down as quick as I would a rabid animal."

Gray Cloud winced in fear. His shoulders crumpled downward and he opened his mouth to speak, but a rush of movement and an excited call from Eliza stopped him. His chair got knocked over as he fretfully jumped to follow Hans down the hallway to the bedroom. His legs were frail and rubbery with fright, and almost failed him.

He grabbed hold of the doorframe to gain steadiness. Hans and Eliza were side by side at the foot of the bed, their faces etched in a combination of confusion and compassion. The three of them exchanged distressed glances and stood attentive vigil over the man on the bed. Blankets were strewn and tangled. The Texas Ranger was agitated and thrashing. His elbows and knees were jerking in spasms as a gagging, moaning groan rolled and gurgled in his throat.

Silas Dawson had been in the flowery meadow for hours. He would run until he could run no more, then recoup his stamina to continue the chase. The ghostly creature forever lingered out of reach. His muscles were strained and his lungs shivered in raggedness with each breath, but a refusal to be denied or to give up drove him onward. The catchphrase—*only quitters and losers stay down*—was a mantra burning in his veins to nourish and sustain him.

The silken apparition had become more than an obsession; it was an ever-present reality that loitered on the outskirts. His hands were on his knees. Somewhere violins and violas were spiraling higher and higher to the crystalline sky. He listened and was soothed by the vibrant strings, but then, stood straight and tall as the sweetest voice ever grazed his ears.

He scoured the green pasture. The fragrance of heather and honey was thick and cloying in his nostrils. He inhaled the scented air deeply and was invigorated. His lungs swelled and contentment enveloped his face. He turned round and round, doggedly probing every niche and recess in the four corners of the rolling grassland.

The engaging tones struck him afresh and anew. He searched with an increased intensity, eyes becoming larger and larger. Realization whistled through him, along with a bone-wobbling shudder; the voice was calling him by name. His head tilted and he carefully sought to know its location. Tentative and wary, he crept forward. Within a dozen steps he figured he was going in the wrong direction. A wave of frustration crested inside him.

He made a full turn and in the midst of it, spotted the phantom seemingly fifty or so yards away. The form was still and exquisitely attractive, apparently dressed in layer upon layer of lace embroidered material that was whiter than whiter and purer than pure. A gentle wind came from nowhere to flutter the garments ever so slightly; the wonder of it took his breath away.

A gasp rose up and rippled out of him. He leapt into a sprint as though launched from a catapult. He ran through the knee-deep grass lifting his legs high and staying on a straight-line course. He kept whipping past bunches of violets and clusters of daffodils, but was unable to gain any ground. It was as though he was running on the spot.

Kettle drums were booming a resounding beat in rhythm with the violins and violas. He kept moving faster and faster, focused entirely on his target. He stumbled and reeled out of control when recognition hammered to his brain. He plunged into a vaulting somersault and came to rest flat on his face, arms and legs stretched forth. His mouth, parched and puckered, flapped brokenly as he crawled into a crouch and stared startle-eyed.

His objective was no ghost. His hands locked over the top of his head as though he feared the shock would shatter the bones of his skull. Lacey Coe Dawson beckoned him with a smile that made his heart thump against his ribcage. Her beauty stunned him. There was ringing in his ears and dizziness clouded his senses, yet he clambered to his feet.

Awe-filled silence, as transparent and flawless as perfect diamonds, filled the space between them. She was waiting near a woodland of weeping willows. Her strawberry-blonde loveliness cascaded over her shoulders to lay in the hollow between her breasts. He was set free and racing to her. He caught her up in his arms and swung her around in a mighty arc. They laughed and cried happy tears as their kisses mingled with murmured words of love.

A purple haze of radiant mist fell upon them as a single halo. They clung to each other. A sunbeam blazed a golden passageway before them. They were young and strong; handsome and beautiful walking hand in hand, unclothed and unashamed in a realm of innocence. His lips bent up and his eyes crinkled in blissful serenity.

Silas Dawson was in paradise before he died.

Ashes to ashes, dust to dust.

Charley Jondreau was awake and staring at the moon. He was harassed by a choice made in an instant, which was pristine territory for him to reconnoiter. By force of will, he intuitively collected information and trusted his instincts, but just now, he was buffaloed by his decision not to pull the trigger on Kid Greer. An acute conflict of second guessing roiled through him, an experience so foreign to his understandings that he replayed the moment again and again.

He sat on his saddle in the shadows away from the campfire. He *knew* that Greer would kill again; he *knew* that the young outlaw's heart was twisted beyond all natural law. On more than one occasion Jondreau had *seen* the abominable sickness in Greer's bloodstream that muddied his mind with an unreasoning intoxication.

There were no illusions or sentimentality in Charley Jondreau. He had *known* at the beginning that Liam Greer was a bad seed who coveted evil the way a thirsty man craved cool water. He had *seen* all that and more while observing Greer interact with a charming damsel at the Alamo Saloon in Abilene on a hot evening in the summer of '72.

Even so, Jondreau had been drawn into involvement with Greer at the insistence of a broad-shouldered preacher-man. He always *knew* that it was a longshot, but had faithfully made an effort to lead Liam Greer away from a violent path, but that was not to be. The alliance with Smoky Crowe was coal oil tossed on the flames of Greer's evil; the result was a firestorm of mayhem. So why had he not put a bullet between the eyes of Kid Greer?

The question befuddled him. He adjusted the position of his buttocks and clasped his hands together under the poncho. His thumbs automatically began twiddling. He contemplated the self-doubt, but the pondering was short-lived. The smell of the skunk came over him; the veins in his neck enlarged and his eyes took a rolling spill so that only the whites showed. A contraction cramped its way up his spine and he stiffened into an apparent statue.

Inside his head he saw only varying shades of murkiness but heard plenty. Chaos and pandemonium assailed him. The distinctive blast of a pistol blistered clearly above the noisy clamor, followed instantaneously by a second shot that vibrated like a clanging bell. Bedlam and hysteria ensued; the hue and cry was exacerbated by the unfettered screams of a woman. Her shrillness hit notes that were at the extreme top end of the scale.

Panicky voices shouted and overlapped. A man cussed a loud outcry for help. There were running footsteps accompanied by more shrieks from the woman. A distressed horse let out a wailing bevy of neighs and snorts. The animal's persistent squeals of discomfort were greeted by whooping gaiety, then hoofbeats pounded off into the disappearing distance.

Silence as gluey as tar filled his ears. He was twitching uncontrollably. The veil of gloomy dimness lifted for the briefest of split-seconds. He strained into it and saw a pintsized black man crouched on a boardwalk, mouth yammering in a wild-eyed manner. His hair was the color of cotton and his hands were covered in blood.

Then Jondreau was released and there was nothing except the nighttime surroundings of his desert campsite illuminated by the glow of moonlight. His nostrils burned and itched as the vinegary odor dissipated. He sucked in air. His eyes were watery and stinging, as though irritated by gun smoke from the handgun in the psychic forewarning.

He stood and sidled off into the darkness to where the horses were picketed. He spoke softly to the piebald pinto and stroked its mane. The stallion blew in response. He leaned against its hindquarters and meditatively closed his eyes. He opened them to behold the starlit sky. The immensity of the glimmering mystery stirred both assurance and ambiguity in him.

There would be no sleep for Charley Jondreau on this night.

chapter four

The Aftermath

"And let the beauty of the Lord our God be upon us: and establish thou the work of our hands upon us; yea, the work of our hands establish thou it."

~Moses~

The air had a wintry chill in it. Deacon Coburn rode alongside his partner, eyes narrowed and shoulders rigid. "If I have my bearings correct, we have a couple miles to go."

Max Dawson took a gander at the starry sky. "I figure we've been in the saddle for sixteen or so hours," she said tiredly. She swiveled her torso back and forth. "A hay bale bed in the barn will feel as refined as a high society boudoir because I've got kinks in my kinks."

"I'm a mite done in myself."

"The use of a proper privy will be sheer luxury."

Coburn chuckled low in his throat; it promptly became a robust laugh. "On that front you'll not be disappointed. Hans Weitzel takes great pride in construction, which means every building, including the outhouse, is of topnotch quality."

"You have high regard for these folks."

"The highest, Max." He was rubbing his right temple. A pronounced pain had become established behind his eyes. "They kept me alive after my run-in with Smoky Crowe."

"It's quite probable that Daddy passed this way."

"If so, we'll know soon enough."

She leaned from one side to the other several times. "If not, I'll take tomorrow to rest up and replenish, but at first light the next morning I'll be heading out to track him."

"We best take a couple days, Max," he said sternly. "Our mounts will appreciate that kindness. They need a well-earned breather, and several feeds of oats and molasses."

"Are we allies for the duration?"

"We're friends until death comes a knocking on one of our doors, I can assure you of that much," he replied, squinting at her. "I'll stick with you now until we find your father, if for no other reason than to tell him that he raised a fine daughter with rare character."

"That's as crazy as popcorn on a hot stove," she exclaimed impatiently. "I'm no prima donna needing to be mollycoddled. I never expected mush from you, Deacon."

"It ain't mush to tell the truth, Max."

"Daddy's not one to receive praise or compliments graciously."

"That'd be on him," he said, shrugging. "Life is short and full of blisters. A man ought to hear that he done good in the most important work to which he ever set his heart and hand."

She smiled and rolled her eyes at him. "I swear, Deacon. The next time I'm in a town that's got a catalog store I'm ordering you one of those white dog collars worn by priests."

"Don't waste your money, Max. I'll not wear it."

"Why the blazes not?"

"It'd be pretentious. I ain't no preacher."

"Maybe not, but you exemplify Christian virtue."

"I think not," he answered, gruffness grumbling in his tone. "I con-scientiously put forth the spiritual sweat and muscle, but most days I don't even get a passing grade."

"If that's the case, there's no hope for the rest of us."

"There's always hope and grace, Max. *Always.*"

"So you say."

"The Bible is often misconstrued or misrepresented, but here's where my understanding takes me," he said, nudging Gilgal to sidestep closer to her mare. "Our task is to crawl out from under crud by taking hold of faith and exerting determination to put it to action."

"What exactly is faith?"

He tilted his head to give the moon thoughtful scrutiny. "Faith means taking God at his word. Abraham took God at his word and relied on it, and because of that, according to James the brother of Jesus, it was accounted unto him as righteousness. Abraham was a deeply flawed man, but he put his trust in God, and in doing so, he became God's friend."

"The Bible really says so?"

"In the second chapter of James."

"Why is it that church makes faith so convoluted?"

"The church is people, plain and simple."

"That doesn't shed much light, Deacon."

"Ain't a one of us who ain't susceptible to pride." He pushed his hat up and pressed a palm against his forehead. The soreness poking at the backside of his eyes seemed to be weakening. "Pride constantly tempts us to define righteousness as being better than some poor pilgrim, which results in human garbage getting put in front of the cross of Calvary."

"And the cross is where hope and grace is found?"

"No truer words were ever spoken, Max." He arched his back and covered his mouth to obscure a reflexive yawn. "Our part is to embrace the hope and grace of the cross in faith. God's part is to meet our frail and feeble efforts with hope and grace. Then as we walk in faith, God fills in the gaps of all our stumbling failures with liberal doses of hope and grace."

"Faith is all about hope and grace?"

"You betcha."

"I'm buying you that collar, Deacon."

"It's your money, girl."

"And you ought to cheerfully wear it," she said, shaking a finger at him. "I'd be attentive at your pulpit because you make more sense than any priest or preacher I ever heard."

He demurred with a self-conscious grin. There was a rustling of movement or something in the still night air that summoned his attention, which stitched the grin into a frown. He tossed a bemused look at Max and was readying a response, but then, pursed his lips tensely when he heard a woman speak his name. He gave Gilgal orders to pick up the pace.

Eliza Weitzel sat in her rocker on the front porch. Her eyes were red and blurry with moisture. It had been less than a half-hour since Silas Dawson drew his final earthly breath. She had a shawl over her shoulders and looped around her arms. Shivers skated over her skin, though not because she was particularly cold; she heard voices conversing.

Her ears perked up. The pale darkness, brightened by yellow-tinted moonbeams, was misleading as to from which direction the talking originated. She stood and walked across the yard. Her footfalls were draggy from weariness. She stopped under the *Freiheit* archway to intentionally listen. A smile burst across her face and sparkled her raw eyes.

"Deacon Coburn," she said, clear and strong. Her expression expanded in eagerness as the sound of trotting hoofbeats and smell of dusty sand came in a rush. She filled her lungs with several deep breaths and felt strengthened by a renewal of vitality.

The silver-dappled buckskin whinnied a greeting and halted in front of the blackened timbers of the cross. Its rider dismounted and tipped his hat in gentlemanly conduct. "I certainly didn't anticipate finding you awake and waiting, but it sure is fine to see you, Eliza."

"Deacon Coburn," she said again, as though she needed to so as to know that she wasn't imagining his arrival. She took brisk steps over and hugged him fiercely.

Tension and anxiety seeped from her pores. He grimaced and tried to tilt away from her as puzzlement distorted his face. Her earnest demonstration plainly surprised him and extended for such a length of time that he was visibly uncomfortable. He broke free of her forceful squeeze and gently pushed her back, then introduced the women. He would've had to be blind not to notice the pained flinch that almost slammed Eliza's eyes shut.

"Good to meet you, ma'am."

"Likewise," Eliza said quietly.

He gestured to the cross. "Glad to see Caleb's workmanship still standing."

"Hans keeps it in repair and reinforced."

"Where's Hans?"

"He and Gray Cloud are in the barn measuring and cutting lumber."

"At this hour? What for?" he asked, balking.

Eliza moistened her lips. "Miss Dawson . . ."

"Max, ma'am."

"You need to come inside with me, Max," Eliza said, urgent and tentative all at once. She intensified her grip on the shawl as she hesitatingly backed up. "You, too, Deacon."

"I best take care of the horses."

"The horses can wait, Deacon," Eliza replied sharply. Her eyes bulged and implored him. There was steeliness in her that demanded respectful compliance. She latched onto Max's hand and led her. Max compressed her mouth in wonderment, but didn't resist. As they entered the house, Max removed her Stetson and shook her hair loose. Coburn dutifully followed.

≈ ≈ ≈

Ten minutes later, with candlelight sputtering from atop the dresser, Max Dawson processed grief by tamping it down and stomping on it. She had closed the door and was alone in the bedroom beside the corpse of her father. Her senses were filleted and laid bare; disbelief marred her countenance. She moved around the bed in undiluted shock.

Her jaw was locked, causing her pulse-beat to throb at her temples. Her eyes were dry and hard as she coldly calculated the events that had transpired to bring about this outcome. First her mother was tortured and butchered by Smoky Crowe, and now, her father had died a lingering death as a result of one of the witch's poison arrows.

Boiling rage simmered in her; she shoved the fiery heat into the same pit where grieving had been kicked and put boot heels to it. Her willful pigheadedness was cranked to the highest level. She shed her duster and dropped it on the floor. She turned the wooden chair around and sat astride it so as to rest her arms and chin on its back rail.

"It's a helluva end, Daddy," she said, barely audible. "I presumed finding you camped out in the badlands with that Ute bastard in your sights. You were better than two weeks ahead of me so I guess your years of experience trumps my resolve and grit. I still have much to learn to be as trail-wise as you, but I'll be doing it on my own now.

"You know I won't be putting any roots down until I finish this business with Smoky Crowe once and for all. I'll not allow him to live. You and Mom rest in peace because I will do him in and have an eye for an eye. There'll be no slacking or dillydallying from me. Whatever it takes to see him dead will be done. You can bet your money on me, Daddy.

"I've been riding with a good man. He's a Bible reader and talks about faith in a way that pricks my curiosity. Like you, I cannot abide hypocrisy, but there's no hint of that in Coburn. He attempts to live out what he says he believes, accepting his foibles and failures as challenges to be dealt with straight-up. He's real. He wanted to meet you so he could tell you that you raised a daughter with *rare character*." She exhaled a soft laugh and stooped her shoulders.

"I intend to pick his brain about life and death matters. I'll give him an objective listen, but I doubt he can provide any insights or conclusions." Her lips pressed into a thin line. "What disturbs me is that there's no logic to death; no rationale for you to die whilst seeking to mete out justice to a killer, or for Mom to be bloodied and beaten."

She clamped her teeth together. She put her thumbs at the sides of her head and began to slowly massage in a circular motion. "The unreasonable unfairness in how death deals out its blows burns me up inside. There's no meaning or significance in death. As the final arbiter of life it's random and capricious. The emptiness death leaves is bothersome.

"If I had my druthers I'd merrily slit death's throat and ask; how do you like that, you lily-livered reaper?" Her voice rose above its whisper and cracked as though it was glass. She immediately placed a hand over her lips and got to her feet. Her legs felt prickly and numb. She wiggled them and took a few halting steps. She stared at him. Dampness filled her eyes.

"Daddy," she murmured lovingly. She leaned forward and stroked his face, then abruptly grabbed fistfuls of his whiskers. "I remember using your beard to climb you like a mountain. I remember you throwing me so high in the air that I thought I could fly. I remember you teaching me about guns and hunting. I remember our first horseback ride together. I remember that saying about the mountain lion eating a bull. I remember the time you heard me use what I think of as your word; crappola. You turned red and laughed so hard you cried."

She bent close and planted a kiss on his forehead. "I'll not ever forget you, Daddy." She turned away. "Damn these tears," she said, palming the wetness off her cheeks. She squatted on her haunches and pulled the black duster onto her lap. She rocked on her heels and removed the large leather wallet from an inside pocket.

"You would've liked these folks who nursed you." She stood, swung the chair around and sat on it properly. "They're good people. Right now the husband, who I haven't even met yet, is in the barn cobbling together a coffin for you. He'll be starting a fire to thaw the ground on the spot where your grave will be dug. I suppose you'll be boxed and buried tomorrow."

She propped her right ankle on her left knee and began slapping the wallet against her thigh. "I suspect Coburn will say a prayer and read some Scripture. I'll ask him to make it brief and keep the philosophizing to a minimum." She continued to fidget with the billfold for a spell, then pulled the note from her father out. She unfolded it and read it once more.

> Leave it alone, Badger. Sometimes the price to purchase pieces of justice is too damn high. Find your own trail and live a life that makes a difference. Daddy.

"I appreciate finally getting something in writing from you, Daddy," she said, squashing her lips into a pinched smile. "Short and to the point, though it may be, it's in your hand. I will treasure it, and I swear, I'll get to my own trail, but for my life to make a difference I must see Smoky Crowe dead. Being a Dawson means to not shirk a duty and to never quit. Ever." She joggled the small sheet of paper and it fluttered. That action elicited a muffled chuckle.

There was a delicate rap on the door, a discreet pause, then it opened a foot or so. Eliza poked her head in. "There's coffee and a ham sandwich on the table for you."

"Thank you, ma'am. I'll be there in a moment."

The door clicked shut. Max stuck the letter back in its slot, closed the wallet and returned it to the duster. She kissed her father's brow again and finger combed his hair. A sob strove to escape her throat. She braced herself by purposely drawing deep breaths to attain a portion of emotional sobriety. Her breathing was even when she eased her way to the kitchen.

Pete Axler arose off the stool and lit a second kerosene lantern. He moseyed around in his lackadaisical way and had a look in on the roan mare readying to foal. Then, satisfied that all was making headway safe and quiet for now, hung the light on a peg outside the stall. He sat back down to wait and keep productively busy with a middle of the night whittling project.

He had a block of oak, which he had chosen with great care and consideration. Its grain was superior; there were no knots or protrusions to hinder his craftsmanship. He was currently in the beginning stages, thinning it down and rounding off the corners. He had an unencumbered expectation of what he needed to uncover within the wood, simply because it was to be a duplicate of the original he'd fashioned for Naomi six years ago in Abilene.

His skill and patience would be tested and developed; he knew that no matter how hard he tried to be precise he could never get it exactly as the earlier piece. He was certain it would be the same dimensions, but as to the intricacies of the horse's head, allowances had to be made for the give and take between creativity and the texture of the oak.

Carving relaxed him and was good for his soul. It set his mind free to calibrate solutions to problems or to sift through feelings and sentimental issues. Settling in, he proceeded to slice slivers teenier than the thinnest toothpicks. He kept the blade of his jackknife honed razor-sharp so the shavings came off clean and gathered in a small pile at his feet. His hands were swift and sure, seemingly operating of their own accord.

He began thinking about the zigzag road of life that had taken him from Fort Smith to Abilene to Wagon Wheel Gap. He had learned and worked the horse business in Fort Smith; put on a badge and patrolled the streets of Abilene as a lawman; now he had finances and sweat invested in a horse ranching operation that was gaining an impressive reputation.

Amazement over his good fortune often produced a sly smile that lifted the more or less permanently weathered wrinkles around his eyes and across his forehead. The corners of his mouth turning upward had become a regular occurrence in the years since meeting Naomi Engle in an unrestrained spin of awkwardness that remained laugh-worthy.

She graced and enriched him in ways that he could never take for granted. She did for him much that he could not discover the ability or means to do for himself. Her love and direct example of faith was dismantling barriers in him. He took pride in hard work and a job well done; being a good provider was an expression of devoted affection. He was dependable and stalwart, but she roused tenderness and hauled it up from some deep well within him.

Becoming a father had increased his sense of responsibility, but also, sped the flow of softness from the mostly hidden aquifer. First Jesse and now Amanda were beneficiaries of the changes wrought in his emotional makeup. He was no fool. He credited Naomi for removing the clamp on the lid of his heart. She accepted him as he was, but saw depths and eddies that needed to be tapped, which she accomplished by guilelessly loving him.

He had no illusions. He knew that he was the luckiest man alive; he had married up and on some days still couldn't fathom the wonder of it. Naomi was extraordinary; her strength and independence never wavered. She told the children Bible stories every day and sang Scripture songs and choruses to them. Her faith was a natural extension of who she was; she conquered sorrows and despairs by affirming the timeless promises of God.

She had many favorite verses to be shared at appropriate times, but one was the bedrock foundation that anchored her stance. It came from the book of Romans, and he had burned it on a plank tablet for her; it was prominent above the kitchen sink: "*For I reckon that the sufferings of this present time are not worthy to be compared with the glory which shall be revealed in us.*"

Uncertainty and disbelief were banished from her assessment and practice. Whereas for him, faith and eternity and all things related to God were skeptical add-ons fertilized by doubts. Over the years many seeds had been planted, but he truly wondered about the status of his faith. The spiritual dimension prevailed as an abstract and absolute quandary to him.

It wasn't that he didn't see the results of faith at work, but the immeasurable mysteries confounded him. There were scenarios that were incomprehensible. Most recently, the farseeing bond he had witnessed between Charley Jondreau and Sally Twosongs threw him for a loop. He respected them and viewed both as friends, but their clairvoyant affinity had caused him to test and try all those realities which he had previously reconciled.

Charley Jondreau and Sally Twosongs had unorthodox methodology and interpretation of faith that within church circles would be the weren't biting. I got bored pretty quick and was off climbing trees, catching lizards and such. He stayed put, casting his line out over and over.

"Nothing. Not even nibbles. He switched spots, changed the bait. I ran over and asked when we would be going home. I remember it was the first time I heard what I would learn was his personal code of honor. He took a knee and pulled me close. He cupped my chin in his hand and told me: *A Dawson never shirks a duty and never quits. Ever.* I've spent all my years since then admiring how he lived and modeled those words."

Eliza looked up from her task. "Did he catch a fish that day?"

"Of course. Otherwise we'd still be there," Max replied with an outburst of airy laughter. She raised her eyebrows and gave a half-shrug. "When I was ten we traveled to West Virginia to visit Mom's people in some hollow with a backwoods name. We were there for a week or more, and like always, Daddy never took his hat off until bedtime at the end of the day.

"At a family reunion barbecue that was our big send-off, some buck-toothed cousin made a smart-alecky remark as to why Daddy never removed his headgear. The man was bare-headed and tipsy with moonshine. Ole Silas looked him straight in the eye and said: *An empty shed doesn't need a roof.* There were hoots and guffaws from those in earshot."

Eliza grinned. "So Captain Dawson had a sense of humor."

"Yes, ma'am." Max put both feet on the floor and leaned forward, elbows on knees. "It was often understated, but once in a while he'd pull a memorable stunt. I'll not soon forget my twelfth birthday supper," she said, eyes brightening. "Daddy had been suffering from a toothache and was scheduled to see a dentist the next day. His soreness didn't prevent him from joshing me about putting my tomboy ways behind me because I was getting lady bumps.

"Mom had cooked three big racks of ribs. We dug in and were enjoying them, when all of a sudden Daddy yelps and drops the bone he was gnawing on. His cheeks went crimson and he clutched at his jaw, choking and making gurgling noises. He moaned and groaned. His eyes even watered. He complained that the tooth had broken and he swallowed it.

"Well, he kept at it for a bit, then calmed and recovered. He drank some water and tore off another rib. We chatted about this and that, happenings here and there. Everything was fine and rosy, then Daddy heaved back from the table and almost toppled his chair. He bent double and bear-hugged his midsection, growling and bemoaning in pain.

"Mom and I were alarmed. We asked again and again to help, but he shooed us. His face was screwed into a scarlet grimace. I was getting scared, but then, a grin magically appeared and he exclaimed: *My tooth bit me.* His lips and eyes spread wide as raucous amusement bounced off the walls.

equivalent of bones rattling around pews, but like his wife and brother-in-law, the underpinning of their beliefs were firmly resolved and centered on the truth of one Supreme Deity. Pete understood that, but the linkage of their second-sight was eerie and put him in a place where complicated questions blathered endlessly.

He stopped paring the wood and wagged his head. It seemed that every time he thought he was getting up to speed on faith concerns something or other happened to derail him. He had made honest attempts to grab hold of it; he wanted to acquire the assured confidence to be at peace, but wa seriously inching toward the assumption that it would never be for him.

What remained was to be a blameless husband and father, which h willingly rolled up his sleeves and put a shoulder to at the dawn of each da He snapped his jackknife shut and slipped it into a side-pocket of his cov hide vest. He gave the progress of his handicraft an approving glance, the stood and placed it on the shelf beside a lantern. The roan mare snorted ar blew as if to call for help. He was smiling when he entered the compartme:

"Telling stories is always healthy, Max."

Midway through the morning, with sunrays slanting through the w dow, Eliza was completing the preparations for Silas Dawson to be lai(rest in the pine box manufactured and sanded smooth by her husband. had thoroughly washed his body and was now at the foot of the bed arr: ing his clothes, which she'd laundered shortly after his arrival.

"I know, ma'am," Max said stoically. She sat on the hard-backed cha the doorway of the bedroom. "I'm grateful for your gentle care, but Da would've been embarrassed."

"I'd not worry, Max. I've nursed many men," Eliza replied, unfol his shirt. She had repaired the arrow hole. "I read newspaper accoun your father's exploits as a Texas Ranger, but I'd like to know more abou man. Do you have a favorite memory to share?"

"He was modest and actually quite shy," Max answered, smiling gr "None of those reports in the press were cock and bull exaggeration toiled and did battle to bring peace to the frontier. Until I walked int room last night I thought he was indestructible."

"He fought with ferocity to the end."

"That'd be a given," Max said over top of a chuckle. "To quit o render was anathema to him." She crossed her legs and sat back. "W was six or seven years old we went fishing. It was early in the day, but tl

Mom slapped his shoulder hard, but he cackled on and on. The tooth hadn't really broken off. It was all an elaborate act and he sold it like a bunko roper."

"What a character!"

"Indeed, he was, ma'am."

Eliza was almost finished dressing him. "The newspapers portray a one-dimensional lawman harnessing a streak of violence to pursue agitators and comancheros."

Max brandished a cockeyed smirk. "The scribblers got the harnessing a streak of violence right. I only ever saw him fight once, which was all I ever needed to have confirmation that he was one tough hombre. It was a social event in San Antonio. A big springtime fundraiser. Everyone was dressed in their finery, including me because Mom insisted that I had to act like a lady. I was fifteen years old and filled out a frilly yellow dress nicely.

"A loud, brash talker joined the festivities. He was tall and strapping, and carried himself in a jaunty gunslinger's gait. I gave him no invitation or encouragement, but he strolled directly to me. He had a sloppy leer, which I adequately understood, thank you very much. I was at the punch bowl. Mom and Daddy were across the table from me.

"The man greeted me, then made an off-color comment regarding my figure. In doing so he took the Lord's name in vain and inserted a gross vulgarity in the middle. Daddy warned him in a tone as hot as Hades. The blowhard jeered and sloughed him off. He was head and shoulders taller than Daddy, and gave the impression that he was good with his dukes.

"The beef-headed man ogled me and swore again, then it was all over but the walloping smack-down. Daddy lit into him like a man possessed. He flew over the table as though fired from a cannon. He furiously struck him with three massive blows to the head that jerked him around like a marionette. He dropped to the floor and sprawled spread-eagled. Ole Silas advanced on him and went to coolly kicking his manhood into smithereens.

"There were irate protests and scandal was imminent. Mom was entirely unfazed by any of it. The indignation and threat of disgrace disappeared due to facts discovered during the investigation. Turned out the man was a robber and chuck-line rider with paper on him from Arkansas, so Daddy came off smelling like a rose for capturing a criminal.

"He had no misgivings about the incident. According to Daddy the loudmouth windbag got what was coming to him. He justified his actions by parlaying a piece of western wisdom he doubtless picked up around some barroom or campfire: *After eating an entire bull, a mountain lion felt so good he started roaring. He kept it up until a rancher came along and shot him. The moral: When you're full of bull, keep your mouth shut.*

"Shortly after that I set forth to an academy in Philadelphia."

"Lord, have mercy," Eliza said, an expressive smile curving her lips. Sympathy brimmed in her eyes as she stood with her hands in the pockets of her skirt. "You have varied reasons to take pride because of the blood in your veins. Allow me an indulgence that isn't syrupy sap meant to placate, but rather, words to encourage: Your parents will live on in you."

"Heartfelt thanks, ma'am."

"Eliza. Please call me Eliza." She took a step away from the bed. "Could I enlist your assistance to prepare a hot noontime meal? The men will be hungry from digging."

Max agreed with a nod as she rose to her feet. She moved the chair to a spot near the head of the bed and had a look at her father. His garments were baggy because he had lost so much weight. Her face cracked in a broad smile when she spotted the silver Texas Ranger badge pinned on the left lapel of his vest. She patted it twice, then departed for the kitchen.

Above the Wyanhell Roadhouse, Brenda Hawkins procrastinated in bed while counting dust bunnies gathered in a corner. The morning sunlight gave the wispy gray swirls no place to hide. She rolled over and sat up, tugging the blankets around her. The air was crisp, but kindling a fire would have to wait because her bladder was full.

After squatting on the chamber pot, she repositioned her bloomers and went to the potbelly stove. She knelt and took care of business. In a few minutes split logs were crackling. She closed the iron door and chaffed her hands in front of it for a long while. When she was sufficiently warmed, she stood and pulled a woolen housecoat over her camisole.

She looked out the frosted window. Her cozy and comfortable two-room apartment was at the rear of the two-story frame structure on the outskirts of Las Vegas, the most notorious settlement for desperados in New Mexico. The sun had already risen midway to the top of the sky; its rays were playing prettily on the eastern mountains. She took in the magnificent assortment of colors and felt all giggly inside.

She moved to the other room, which was nothing more than an aggrandized cubbyhole, but served her needs for a kitchen and pantry. She fixed a pot of coffee and took it to the stove. While she waited for it to boil, she did her everyday housekeeping chores. She swept the floor, being sure to get all the dust bunnies she had numbered. She put the broom away, then made the bed and was fluffing pillows when she heard the clip-clop of a horse.

She idled over to have a peek, but from her vantage point saw no one. The coffee was smelling good. She filled a mug and took a seat in the only chair in the place, which she had traded for two years ago. It was a home-made rocker that had been carried west when James Buchanan was president. The wood squeaked like frisky mice, but it was rock-solid.

The black caffeine tasted heavenly. She heard someone on the outside stairway. Her ears perked up. Soon a peg-legged gait shuffled along the hall-way, then an insistent knock on her door. She pursed her lips angrily; it was too early for a customer. She would not be putting on a happy face to fake her way through pretending she enjoyed swapping money for sex.

"Go away. I'm not receiving just yet."

"Open the door, Brenda."

She squealed in delight. She lurched from the chair and tipped the mug over as she tried to place it on the floor. She didn't care. She rushed over and flung the door open. "Benny!" Her arms went around his waist and held tight. "I didn't expect to see you this soon. I'm glad you're here. I've missed you terribly. What's with the crutch? What happened to your leg?"

Slaton had a wince stitched around his eyes. "Take it easy, babe. Get me inside and I'll tell you everything. I have to lie down or I'm going to fall over."

"Come on then," she said, shifting sideways. She took his weight on her shoulders and hop-hobbled with him to the bed. He dropped the crutch, tossed his coat aside and flopped onto the feather mattress. When he stretched out, she labored to remove his left boot. She examined his right leg and foot, which over the plaster cast was wrapped in strips of linen rags.

"I'm sorry I ever left, babe. It was a disaster." He flipped his hat off and propped a pillow under his head. She sat on the edge of the bed. She stroked his unshaven chin and touched a black wound on his right cheek as he filled her in on all the lowlights of the past month. He spent an inordinate amount of time emphasizing that he almost died at Glorieta Pass.

"What's that?" she asked, palming the burnt scar.

"My gun backfired. Forget it. I don't want to be no pain in the ass."

"Benny, you're no trouble," she said flatly. "I care for you deeply."

"Don't get dewy-eyed and gushy on me."

She tossed her hair back and laughed in a vivacious way. "Heavens, why would I take offense? It's not like I sit here thinking about you or plan-ning for when you're around."

His eyes narrowed skeptically. "Bless you for being a charitable hussy."

"Right back at you for being a reprobate gambler."

He grinned boyishly. "You really think about me when I'm gone?"

"Yes, I do."

"Why?"

"I want to be with you, Benny. You make me feel safe."

"Safe?"

"You give me a sense of belonging," she replied, resting a hand on his chest. "I haven't had much of that in my life. Based on where I come from and my track record, even with your catch me if you can shiftiness, you're the most stable relationship I ever had."

"That's some heavy lifting, Brenda."

"Are you saying those strong shoulders and big muscles can't handle me?" she asked, slipping her hand to his beltline. She abruptly jerked to her feet and settled on the rocking chair. "If you got no sweetness for me, then tell me, Benny. I have to take care of myself."

"Whoa, slow down," he said snappily. "You just hold your horses, Brenda. When have you ever heard me say that I didn't have sweetness for you?"

"When have I ever heard you say that you did, Benny?"

He shrugged, aimless and lazy. "I guess I ain't got those type of words in me."

"It'd be agreeable to me if you could find some," she said soberly. She commenced moving back and forth and sighed at the itsy-bitsy mouse sounds. She fixed her eyes on him. "I was cut loose early and had to make my way on my own. Ma died a week after I was born. Pa had big plans to strike it rich in the west. He was a dreamer and they were on their way to someplace better than Missouri. On a stopover here she went into labor.

"Pa didn't stick around for long. He pawned me off on some old couple who were both croakers before I ever knew them. I became the foundling of the community. I grew up quick and clever. In my early teens I got taken on as a barmaid downstairs. Soon enough I was supplementing my measly income turning tricks.

"Three years ago, I sort of inherited this apartment from the previous tenant, a deflowered dove who got old and ugly." She gave him a feckless smile. "That's my sob story, Benny. I'd like to do much better with you, if you're of a mind to make a go of it." She got up and slumped her shoulders to shed the housecoat. "I'm going to get the doc to check on you."

"That ain't necessary."

"I'll be the one deciding what's necessary," she answered, opening an ornate armoire. It was tall and mahogany. She picked a drab dress and pulled it on over her head. She adjusted it, then fastened the buttons from her belly to its high collar. She fetched a large-toothed comb and closed the armoire to use the mirror on its door. She began fussing and fixing her hair.

He watched her, alternating between her posterior and the reflection of her face. She was slim and supple. Her eyes, as blue as a summer sky, were always lively. She had apple-dumpling cheeks and luxurious tresses the color of cinnamon with reddish shades that just now caught some sunrays and seemed to dance. "Have I ever told you that you're a pretty lady?"

She spun around, beaming. "No. Never."

"Well, you are," he said roughly. "And you make my whole body hard looking at you, or even thinking about you." He tossed her a rakish grin. "Does that qualify as sweetness?"

"It's a nice start, Benny."

"It weren't even difficult to say."

She batted her eyes at him. "Sweetness makes me purr."

"I'll think on that whilst you're out and about, so don't idle or be a dawdler," he told her, slouching onto his side. "My horse is at the hitching rail out front. It needs to be taken to the livery because I ain't going to be hastening my leaving."

"I'll handle it, then get the doc."

"Bring me my saddlebags."

"Yep," she said, tying her boots. "You rest." She put on a knee-length coat and headed off in a rush. She hurried to the stairs and skipped down them as buoyantly as a schoolgirl. Her yearning was that the doctor would be available and not be too inquisitive or meddlesome. She scampered contentedly for there was much to keep her occupied on this sunshiny day.

Deacon Coburn heaved a shovelful of dirt up from the bottom of the hole and almost collapsed. Pain soared through his skull and nausea swelled from his stomach to the back of his throat. A grunted moan escaped his mouth as bright spots swirled in front of his eyes. His legs were rubbery. He dropped the spade and caught himself on the edge of the grave.

He blacked out for an instant. His breathing became alarmingly shallow, then as speedily as it had come over him, the affliction and weak-kneed light-headedness passed. He gulped a lungful of air and felt hands on him. His vision cleared to blurriness, and he saw Hans Weitzel and Gray Cloud grappling him up to carry-drag him to the wheelbarrow.

"Let me go," Deacon said, weak and raspy.

"Sit," Hans ordered, tilting the barrow forward onto its handles.

Coburn got seated in the wagon of the pushcart. "Leave me be. I'll be fine."

Weitzel scowled at him. "What was that?"

"I've had a headache since yesterday," Deacon replied, breathing deeply. He had his thumbs at his temples and was massaging vigorously. "It flared into the extreme."

"I have some powders I can fix for you," Gray Cloud said gently.

Coburn forced a crooked smile. "Afterwards, thanks. Let's finish this chore first."

Weitzel poked his chest. "You, my friend, are done. You rest and watch. Gray Cloud and I will level the bottom." He glanced at the hole. The sides were squared off and it was five feet deep. "You think or pray about those words you'll need to be saying here shortly."

The grave-digging was grueling work, which had engaged them for several hours. At the beginning the three men were confident it would not be difficult and were proven correct for the first couple feet because the fire had done its thawing job. Then it became laborious and slow going; picks were required to break the frozen ground into fragmented chunks.

"Alright," Deacon said, pressing the heel of his hand against his forehead. He leaned forward and balanced easily in the improvised chair. He watched his coworkers get back to the task and thought through a few ideas as his head cleared and he recovered from the convulsive physical faintness. He scratched his bushy upper lip and spoke in a hoarse tone. "Choices."

Weitzel stopped excavating. "What?"

"Choices is what I ought to talk about," Deacon answered firmly.

Weitzel bobbed his head. "Such matters are your area of expertise."

Coburn smiled wryly. "How our lives become the accumulation of our choices."

Gray Cloud shouldered his shovel. "I don't like that idea, but it's accurate."

"And unfortunately, there are some choices for which we never stop paying." Deacon twined his fingers together. "I'm realizing some of that and seeing it more directly."

"We live and die with our choices," Hans said, testy and unyielding.

"But it ain't the dying that's the choice, Hans. It's the living," Deacon replied, tipping him a raised eyebrow. He scrunched forward. "While we're living is when we make our choice for or against the only hope the human race has; the hope of the resurrection."

Weitzel shrugged heavily. A shrewd smile cricked the corners of his mouth. "I thought we might delay any God talk until the burial, but like always, I'll give you a fair listen."

Coburn shook his head and chuckled. "I wouldn't expect any less from you, Hans. I'd almost forgotten of your wariness when it comes to Bible matters."

"Not so mistrustful when you're the one articulating, Deacon."

Coburn wagged a finger at him. "I appreciate your friendship and trust. I pray I never violate it, Hans." He locked his hands around his right knee and pressed back a bit. "The hope of the resurrection is the hope of spending eternity in the glorious presence of God; the hope of an incorruptible inheritance. If it ain't truth, we who profess faith in Jesus Christ are to be pitied. If the hope of glory ain't true, if it's all over for us when we take a dirt bath, then life has absolutely no meaning and believers have been duped by a hoax.

"It is, however, an inescapable reality. The evidence is compelling. On a Sunday morning in the first century, a couple Galilean fishermen eyewitnessed the empty tomb. Mary Magdalene arrived in the garden at sunup, but when she saw the stone rolled away from the entrance, she raced to Simon Peter and John to tell them that someone had stolen the body of Jesus.

"Peter and John immediately took off, likely running as fast as possible. John outran Peter because he was younger and quicker. He got there first, but didn't enter the sepulcher. John bent low in the cave's doorway and saw the strips of linen that had been swathed around the grossly desecrated body of Jesus. Then Peter caught up, and in my mind's eye, I can see him rushing past John into that dank chamber, breathing hard and eyes as large as saucers.

"Neither he nor John understood that Jesus had to rise from the dead, but they believed and their lives were forever transformed. In a fit of depression and desperation, Judas Iscariot had committed suicide, so he missed the great good news of that wondrous day. The resurrection of Jesus Christ changed the course of history in ways that are often unfathomable."

Weitzel stepped close to him. "Do you stake your life on the resurrection?"

"Yes," Deacon answered unflinchingly. "The facts cannot be rejected. John survived being boiled in oil. The other apostles suffered horrible deaths. To avoid martyrdom all they had to do was recant, to say that it had been an extravagant conspiracy; that they'd never encountered the risen Christ, but each man stood firm on the bold testimony of their experience."

"How is that proof?" Hans asked, doubtful and hesitant.

"I wouldn't willingly die to preserve a lie, would you, Hans?"

Weitzel puckered his mouth. "No, I suppose not." He turned back to the gravesite and cast a despondent look at the gaping cavity. "Are we done, or what?"

Gray Cloud gave a thumbs up. "Everything's hunky-dory."

"Let's go then," Hans said and took a glance at the blue skies. The sun was almost directly overhead. "By now Eliza and Max are surely waiting for us. Let's go eat, then put Silas Dawson in the coffin and bring him out here to have a service and sing a hymn." He and Gray Cloud walked side by side. Deacon Coburn stood and followed them to the house.

In was noontime in Dodge City. The man Whitey Fitzgerald knew as Huey Butters was visiting the *Queen of the Cow Towns* for the first time, and was enjoying himself immensely. He had been in town for a week, which was long enough for him to substantiate his status as an eastern financier and entrepreneur with deep pockets.

He was clean-cut and elegantly dressed, a tall and slinky whippet of a man strolling along the boardwalk on Front Street with a brass-handled cane in hand. He wore gray pants and a double-breasted black frock coat, topped off by a felt derby hat; he routinely tipped it to every female he passed, sometimes with outlandish showmanship.

There were many cowboys loitering on the street. He surreptitiously sized several of them up, marking them as potential pigeons to be plucked of their funds at faro, poker or some other game of chance which, with a nifty sleight of hand, he could effortlessly rig on a whim. A train whistle blew at the station. He paused and waited to watch it chug away.

Born in a bordello in New Orleans, he had spent his childhood being passed from one prostitute to another, never forming an attachment that lasted more than a few months. He mostly raised himself; a street urchin who ascertained early how to fend and get along in a merciless environment. He honed talents as a thief and bilker, and learned that feigning social niceties could translate into schemes which created conduits to opportunities for financial gain.

His amoral proclivities were perfected by the time he reached puberty. He conned his way to adulthood on the road, absorbing and filing away useful information to be applied when a swindle required it. He was a consummate liar and wearer of many masks; he had an ability to convey complete falsehoods in a silkily effective smoothness that dripped with sincerity.

Now at forty, he never lacked for money or brashness. He made his livelihood off the sweat of others, and had been quite successful at it under a half-dozen aliases across the west. He preferred to work alone, though as a rascally diversion, was not averse to affiliating with a woman for short periods because he was adept at turning them out.

The locomotive had disappeared but he could still see its plumes of smoke dissipating against a cloudless blue background. He gave the walkway a tap with his cane, then turned and bumped into a fossil-eyed cowpoke with an unruly patch of chin-whiskers. He apologized and sidled past to return to his intentions of making his way to the telegraph office.

He arrived and entered the storefront shop with a flourish. "Greetings and felicitations, my good man. It is a fine and fair day here on the prairie. Might I engage your apparatus?"

The operator, a short and bespectacled graybeard whose cheeks were mottled by the welted scars of severe acne, looked up from his desk. "Are you daft, blind, or trying out as a comedian? Does or does not the signage proclaim the purpose of this establishment?" He stood and tottered in a duck-like waddle to the counter. "Don't be busting my balls with stupidity."

"I beg your pardon, my good man. Morgan Fletcher at your service."

"Huh. Butch Mackenzie," he said in an abrasive voice that sounded as though it were grinding gravel. "You got copy for me or shall I await some fresh fanfare of whimsy?"

Fletcher handed over a paper, along with two quarter-eagle coins. "That ought to cover the fee, as well as provide a reasonable gratuity to atone for my initial superciliousness."

"Huh." Mackenzie eyed him suspiciously, then fished around the top pocket of his shirt and came out with a stub of a fat cigar. He stuck it in a corner of his mouth, but didn't put a match to it. He read the note, eyebrows dipping low. "You know Big Bull Wallace?"

Fletcher doffed his hat and balanced it on the cane. "That is to whom the telegram is addressed, so it is an astute assumption on your part to come to that conclusion."

"Huh. I've never met the man," Butch said, dismissive and regretful.

"I've had occasion to do business with Mr. Wallace in the past."

Mackenzie chewed the cigar to the other side of his mouth. "A fella named Deacon Coburn acts as his agent here, so during shipping season there's lots of telegraph traffic back and forth. Coburn ain't around just now, but I expect he'll be back before the first herds arrive."

"What kind of man is this Coburn?"

"Huh. The kind not to be trifled with, I can tell you that much."

"A tough-guy, is he?"

"Tough and tender would be my assessment," Butch replied decisively. "I'd not cross him, but when I get hauled to Boot Hill, I'd like him to say some Bible words over me."

"A religious sort, is he?"

"Huh. Nope, not religious. Different."

"Different? How?"

"Huh. What am I? A pump to be primed?"

"Just making conversation, my good man."

"Huh. I can relay this much," Butch replied, placing the sopping wet cheroot on the edge of the counter. "Coburn is as honorable as any canonized saint without the sanctimonious affectations. It ain't no betrayal to tell you that based on the telegraph correspondence between them, Big Bull Wallace trusts Deacon Coburn with his life and considerable fortune."

"I shall look forward to making acquaintance with Mr. Coburn," Morgan said, sliding his hat around until he had it perched at a dapper incline. "Send that message and please deliver Mr. Wallace's reply as soon as it comes across the wires. I'm staying at the Dodge House Hotel."

"Huh. My clerk will be all over it like a bull humping a cow, Mr. Fletcher."

On the boardwalk, Huey Butters a.k.a. Morgan Fletcher glanced to the left, then to the right. He mulled over the knowledge he had just gleaned and compiled it to be utilized at some future juncture. A smarmy smile filled his narrow face as he set off for the China Doll brothel, where he intended to spend the afternoon in the company of an eager and feisty whore.

Naomi Axler was laughing inwardly as she made her way past the corrals and hurried to keep pace with her fleet-footed son. She had a large hooped basket in her left hand and her daughter snuggled in the crook of her right arm. Jesse was running and skipping ahead, evidently oblivious to the fact that his mother was falling further behind him.

The day was unusually warm, with the mountain peaks surrounding *WT Ranch* tinted purplish and highlighted by streaks of sunshine. She glanced at the beauty and offered a small whisper of gratitude. She saw that Jesse had gotten as far as he could get. He was in front of the barn door trying to make the latch work, but having no luck.

When she caught up, she knelt close to him and said, "You stay hushed when we get inside, Jesse. If we want to surprise Daddy we have to be sneaky and stick together."

His eyes were bright and happy. He nodded rapidly. She unbolted the door and let her son lead the way. He tiptoed in an exaggerated way, lifting his legs high with each step. She had to press her lips tight to keep laughter contained. Horses neighed or blew as they crept along the corridor. She heard her husband before spotting him. He was snoring.

She giggled aloud. Jesse gave her a wide-eyed look and touched a finger to his lips. She almost lost it, and had to nibble on the inside of her bottom lip; she could no longer keep up the pretense because the gaiety in her strained to be released. She tilted her head and used it as a pointer in a gesture to her son, urging him to go forward.

Jesse did a little hop, then continued to creep in a contrived manner. He came to an empty stall at the far end and stopped. The bottom half of the door was closed, but the top was open. She came up behind him and took a peek inside. Her husband was stretched out on his back on a bed of loose straw, snoozing with his hat over his face and hands intertwined on his belly.

"Incoming trouble, Pete," she said in a chuckled warning. She lifted the clasp on the handle, which allowed her son to push inside. He hooted, which was just enough notification to rescue his father from a stomping. Pete threw his forearms up to defend himself against the flying feet of his son. He snatched him up under his armpits and thoroughly shook him.

"Daddy!" Jesse squealed and wiggled spasmodically.

"What's all this now?" Pete asked, and rolled to his feet with the boy hugged under an arm. He scooped up his hat and put it on. "Is that fried chicken I smell in that basket?"

"It is," Naomi replied, leaning in to peck his cheek. "I plucked a hen yesterday. It was to be for supper tonight, but a few hours ago I glimpsed Caleb and Sally Twosongs going off on a buggy ride to bask in the pleasant weather. It inspired me to get busy and fix us a picnic."

Axler rubbed his spiny chin stubble. He gave a half-smile, eyes reflecting shimmers of affection. "Ain't this an ace-high way to wake up from a nap?" He exited the stall and lowered his son off his hip, then draped an arm around his wife's shoulders. They walked to the workshop section of the barn, where there were stools and a heavy-framed table.

"How's the mare?" she asked softly.

"Dandy and full of vinegar. Delivered a healthy colt just before sunrise," he reported, giving her a squeeze. "I was dead tired and fancied grabbing a couple hours of shuteye."

"Half the afternoon's gone, Pete."

"Afternoon? Lord, I must've gotten a dose of lazy."

"No chance of that, Mr. Axler."

His head craned sideward. "What's that mean?"

"You never let up or give any slack," she said, scolding in her tone. She set the basket on the blocky table. "You may be a slow-mover, but you seldom ever take a break from your labors. Even when you're whittling you're thinking about jobs to be done and such."

"How is that trait worthy of a rebuke?"

"It's not a rebuke, Pete. Your work ethic is commendable. I'm just saying that you need to be more careful in proper personal maintenance so as to not get worn down." She handed over the baby. "You were on the go all day yesterday, wrestled Jesse for an hour before supper, then knowing you as I do, I imagine you were up all night with that roan."

"Well . . ."

"Well nothing," she interrupted, thrusting a finger at him. "Take a load off and rest. Have a chat with your daughter and keep an eye on your son while I prepare you a plate."

"Yes, ma'am."

He roosted on a stool and held Amanda close. "How's my baby girl?" He loosened the strings of her bonnet and placed a palm on her chest. "You're as pretty as your mother."

"No need to be a fibber, Pete."

"I stated a fact, Mrs. Axler."

She scoffed at the comment. "You're getting to be much too sly, Mr. Axler."

He began gradually swaying side to side. "It was good to be here. I'm plum tuckered out, but I got carving done and waded through some serious thinking." He toyed with the infant's fingers. "I got to weighing faith, and how yours is so strong and mine is so weak, if it's even there at all. I thought about your verse: *For I reckon that the sufferings of this present time are not worthy to be compared with the glory which shall be revealed in us.*"

"Romans 8:18," she said impulsively, then halted midway through emptying the basket to stare at him in jaw-dropped astonishment. Her eyes misted over. "You memorized it?"

"Of course. It took a long while to brand it into the wood."

"You sly fox." She dabbed moisture off her cheeks and marveled at the profound depths of the currents that flowed through her husband. "I am mightily pleased to be your helpmate."

He squinted so hard that his eyelids jiggled in a spasm. His shoulders shrugged. A horse snorted, followed by a docile whinny. He shifted in the direction from which it came. "That's the roan and colt," he said, somewhat proudly. "We can check in when we finish here."

"Jesse will like that," she told him. She sniffed the air. It was pungent with the aroma of manure and hay. "I wonder if Noah's Ark smelled like this?" she asked, grinning.

"Likely so."

She had the table set. She called her son. When he came running, she hoisted him in her arms and bowed her head. She took a few moments, then said grace in a voice that quavered with emotion. Her words expressed earnest appreciation for her children and especially her husband, then almost as an afterthought, she gave thanks and requested a blessing on the meal.

Charley Jondreau had been following a hawk for more than an hour. He was relaxed in the saddle, riding across rolling countryside awash in dull green waves of sagebrush. The terrain had hollows and depressions that were deceiving, but the piebald pinto traversed the ground easily, along with the dapple gray compliant on the lead line.

The red-tailed raptor circled languidly. Jondreau kept his focus on it as expectancy mobilized in him. He knew he was close to his destination, on a southern course with the sun low to his right. Long feelers of dusk were streaking the blue tableau with dusty shades of charcoal. The hawk veered eastward. He nudged the pony and it made the adjustment.

He came to a steep gully and paused for a moment, then rode down into it. The bottom was soggy from melting snow. He crossed it, then urged the horse up the loose sand of the other side. When he cleared the crest, he stopped to survey the area. Satisfaction showed on his lips. From the rise he saw the farmstead; he could identify it because Sally Twosongs had instructed him to look for a prominent archway with a tall charred timber cross beside it.

The hawk bent a wing and dipped near enough for him to see its eyes. It gave a short shriek, then whirled about to begin a spiraling ascent; it climbed higher and higher. He removed his floppy-brimmed hat to honor the bird of prey guardian. There was a thrill of awe in him as he bid farewell in a slow wave of a salute.

He waited until the hawk became a mere dot and disappeared in the twilight. He glanced over a shoulder. The sun was sinking; a blazing ring that appeared to be bleeding multitude colors across the horizon. He ran a hand over the smoothness of his freshly-shaven scalp, then replaced the hat and returned attention to the end point of his journey. He measured the distance of the downward slope to be a half-mile.

There was comings and goings on the property. He prodded the pony onward and studied the activities. As he made his approach, he noted that three men and two women were clustered together. He sat upright and curiosity gripped him. He recognized the preacher-man he had first met in Abilene. His breathing tensed. About halfway to the arch, he was utterly mindful of the happenings; he had come upon *Freiheit* in the shadow of death. Not a good omen.

Charley Jondreau dismounted to observe the burial from afar.

That evening, after the graveside service for Silas Dawson, the Weitzel home was lit up by candles and oil lamps to be peaceful. There had been a congregating around the table for supper, and now everyone lingered in their chairs. Everyone, that is, except Charley Jondreau; he had moved off by himself to sit on a stool near the doorway.

All eyes were on Deacon Coburn, as though he was holding court. He felt the need to speak hope and comfort, but in all reality, his mind hadn't yet arrived at any possible inroad to take that might do something to assuage grief. There was a mug of coffee and a slug of corn whiskey in front of him. The Arbuckle's was steaming and black; the white lightning hooch from a private jug Hans opened only on rare occasions.

Gray Cloud was wringing his hands in his lap. His eyes were fearful, darting as though the house had rustles in every corner. "We're doomed. Smoky Crowe's wrath will descend on us like fire from the sky. Our time to come has been compromised forever."

Weitzel leaned closer to him, coldly furious. "We're safe and secure, Gray Cloud. Put an end to the apocalyptic Sodom and Gomorrah pronouncements."

Gray Cloud nodded, grim and tight-lipped. "I try . . . I try."

"The stones," Max said, staring at Coburn.

Eliza immediately exchanged a meaningful glance with her husband.

Max read it. Her eyes narrowed. "You know?"

"Yes," Eliza answered, "I sutured them in place."

"Tell me, please."

"Not my story to tell, Max."

Coburn tossed back the whiskey and sipped a mouthful of coffee. He swished it around before swallowing. He tapped the edge of the glass. Hans poured him a second shot.

Max bore in on him. "I need to know about the stones."

Coburn smiled gently. "You must have ears to listen, a heart to hear."

"I could use all the hope and redemption I can get, Deacon."

"The children of Israel were slaves in Egypt for four hundred years," Deacon began, elbows on the table. "God strung together a series of back to back miracles and delivered them out from under Pharaoh's thumb. He led them by a pillar of fire at night and a cloud by day. The end of the sojourning was to be the Promised Land, a place rich with milk and honey. They were free of bondage, but were still shackled by their own desires and inclinations.

"The ancient Israelites were exactly as we are, stiff-necked and rebellious. No guidance or blessing God gave them was ever good enough. Yesterday was always greener for them. At Kadesh Barnea, on the threshold of the Promised Land, an uprising occurred in which the people revolted against God by refusing to trust him and press forward.

"The judgment was consequential; it meant that a whole generation was barred from entering the Promised Land. Two men, Caleb and Joshua, were exempt from the banishment because at Kadesh Barnea their advocacy for the Israelites to put faith in God was tremendous." He took a drink of coffee. "Forty years of wandering in the wilderness ensued, then Moses, the great leader and emancipator who had confronted Pharaoh, died. For thirty days, the Israelites grieved. Weeping and wailing filled the encampment on the plains of Moab."

He made eye contact with every person in the room as he brushed aside his moustache, then continued, "The mantle of leadership fell on Joshua's shoulders, a man who had been born into the lineage of slavery; he had supped its bitterness, but he had also seen the deliverance of God. His faith was robust. He vehemently believed that these ragtag descendants of Abraham could conquer the Promised Land simply on God's say so; a half-million or more sons and daughters of slaves were going to seize what God had for them.

"The Bible tells us that Joshua was *full of the spirit of wisdom for Moses had laid his hands upon him.* God commanded Joshua to be strong and very courageous, and gave him orders on how to take possession of the Promised Land. The priestly class of Levites would be out front to lead the way carrying the Ark of the Covenant, which contained the stone tablets of the Ten Commandments given by God to Moses at Mount Sinai.

"Imagine an army assembled for an invasion with a platoon of priests as the point of the spear. When the people were ready to cross over, the Jordan River was in flood stage, but the instant the Levites touched the water's edge, the headwaters upstream piled up and were held back. The Ark of the Covenant was firm on dry ground in the middle of the Jordan River while the whole nation passed over and set up camp on the border of Jericho.

"Joshua recruited one man from each of the twelve tribes of Israel. He told them to go to where the Ark of the Covenant remained in the dry streambed and pick a stone to serve as a symbol of what had been accomplished by God. The stones—boulders really—were stacked as a memorial so that in the future when children asked about the meaning, parents and grandparents could tell them how God demonstrated the power of redemption by cutting off the flow of the Jordan River." He paused, perceiving the tension in the strawberry-blonde across from him.

Max shifted on the chair, bluntness in the expression darkening her brow. "What's that Bible story got to do with your bridle, Deacon? What mean *those* stones?"

"Ears to listen, a heart to hear, Max," Deacon replied easily. "The place where Joshua set up the twelve stones to commemorate what God had done was called Gilgal." He allowed that to sink in for a moment, then as he resumed, he intentionally kept her in his sight lines. "Shortly after I settled in Dodge City, I came here to visit my friends, Hans and Eliza.

"On the journey I went on pilgrimage to Angel Peak because those badlands were a crucible where I almost died. I had determined that what happened there was a crossroads for me. I didn't know it then, but it was Smoky Crowe who sliced me and staked me out to be cooked by the sun. In the fire and winnowing, I was reborn. My recovery was iffy, but when God's grace was coupled with the persistence of Eliza Weitzel, I recuperated.

"I knew I hadn't changed, but neither was I any longer the same." He made an almost helpless motion with his hands. "I always wanted to do something to esteem what God had done to rescue me from death and in that liberation, to renew hope and redemption in me. I collected twelve smooth stones from as near as I could figure to the spot where I had been tortured and left to die. I went out and bought a new bridle, then had my nurse sew six stones on either side."

"Thank you for allowing me to do that," Eliza said, reaching out to touch his hand. "I felt privileged and humbled by your request. I never told you before, but I regarded my part in your paying tribute to God's faithfulness as an act of devotion and prayer."

Coburn gave her a slight nod as his eyes tightened with emotion. He had his right palm cupped under his chin, with a pair of fingers along his jawline. "I never used the unique bridle until I started riding Gilgal two years ago. It is a constant reminder to me of what God hath wrought in my life, which keeps me connected to a passage from that old weeper Jeremiah: *Thus saith the Lord, Stand ye in the ways, and see, and ask for the old paths, where is the good way, and walk therein, and ye shall find rest for your souls.*"

"That's all well and good, but rest for my soul?" Max was wagging her head slow and methodically. "Interesting pieces of history, even if I can't find what to apply for me. Perhaps someday, but not now. I have unfinished business. Justice may be an elusive commodity, but I'm chasing it down. If I were to walk away from my duty of seeing Smoky Crowe hanging on a short rope from a tall tree, then there's no peace or rest for me."

Coburn snapped the whiskey down and finished off the coffee, which caused his lips to pucker because it was room temperature. "Max, no one can walk or choose the trail for you. The way it works is that we each have to make our own path, but we are wise to learn from and lean on others. None of us gets through the sorrows and sludge of life on our own."

"I'll do alright, Deacon. Thanks for the story about the stones."

"Take it with you, Max."

"I will," she said, offering a lame attempt at a smile. "It's good fodder to chew over and gives some insights, but can't help or answer much when it comes to death."

"Max," Hans interjected, rapping his knuckles on the table. "Nobody wants to extend any brain power considering it, but death has each one of us targeted. Death and tragedy unfold, but somehow we pretend it will never actually happen to us. We act as though we'll cheat death, but no one ever does because death is the great equalizer."

Coburn agreed. "Death ain't no respecter of persons."

"Death is unfair," Max said, terse and bitter.

"As is life, Max," Deacon countered, eyes crinkling narrowly. "At its core, the question becomes about the choices we make. We can choose whatever whims we desire, or we can glean truth from the prophet and look for those old paths where the good way can be found. Whatever eternity might be, I want to get there with my soul as unblemished as possible."

"Me, too. I suppose." Max shrugged, sober and pensive. "The way I see it, that means being strong and standing on my own two feet to do what's right and get justice done."

"That's part of it, no doubt," Eliza said, leaning in to pat her shoulder. "The cleansing of blemishes on our soul, however, only comes from forgiveness and redemption."

Max exhaled a moan as she pushed both hands through her hair, which created a lull in the conversation. Gray Cloud exploited the opportunity. "I listened. I am afraid. You escaped Smoky Crowe long ago, but he will want vengeance. He will know you are here."

Jondreau chuckled rather derisively. "Good story, preacher-man. You and I will talk of it tomorrow, eh," he said, and stepped over to place an envelope on the table. "This is from Sally Twosongs for Hans and Eliza." He grinned and headed for the door. "I fear no man. I will be in the loft of the barn, watching and waiting. Smoky Crowe will not harm this home."

"I must go to my shack, but I won't sleep," Gray Cloud said, and trailed him out.

Max stretched to her feet. "Thank you, Hans and Eliza. I appreciate your hospitality and friendship. My bedroll is in the root cellar. I shall sleep just fine. Goodnight."

Coburn tilted her a nod as she departed. A few moments after the door closed, he made an observation that was far too obvious. "That young lady is a festering powder-keg. She needs to grieve." He stood and put his hat on. "I'm joining Charley in the loft. He can be on guard all night if he so chooses, but I'll be dozing like an old dog." He exhibited a broad smile, then went outside. He looked up; the moon and stars poured forth the glory of God.

Ten minutes later, the Weitzel house was filled with dark shadows that were restrained by a shining bubble of lamplight centered on the table. The candles that had been arranged around the kitchen and living room were now extinguished, which left two oil lamps in front of Hans and Eliza. They were alone, sitting side by side chatting about all that had transpired in the past twenty-four hours, with the flames flickering on their faces.

"It's a godsend having Deacon here," she said, turning the envelope over in her hands. "His gentle wisdom is so refreshing and encouraging. I pray that the retelling of the Joshua story, along with his testimony will have an impact on Max."

"That girl has been through it, but she's tough."

"Underneath that hard-shell exterior, she's hurting, Hans."

"We can only help as much as she will allow, Eliza." He placed a hand over hers and squeezed. "Enough of this. I would like to hear what our daughter-in-law has to say."

"Yes." She peeled back the seal and removed the two-page letter. It took several seconds for her to unfold and straighten the creases. She scuttled the chair closer and adjusted her posture so that she was leaning against her husband's chest as she read aloud.

> *March, 1878*
>
> *Dear Hans and Eliza: All is well in Colorado. This winter has been a hard one, but we have dug out from under and look ahead to the hope that comes with springtime. WT Ranch has a new addition to remind us about the wondrous seasons of life. Naomi had a baby girl in early February, and named her Amanda Irene. Both mother and child are doing fine.*
>
> *I had quite a surprise a few weeks ago, which has been rather encouraging to me. The man who I entrusted with this letter showed up here; as it so happens, he had an acquaintance with Pete and Deacon from their Abilene days. I'd never met him before, but had often dreamt about him. We share a gift that baffles and edifies. My husband truly appreciates him. Charley Jondreau is a good man and a genuine friend.*
>
> *Caleb is Caleb. He works and plans, then plans and works. He tells me, and it is not difficult for me to see, that the partnership with Pete has been extremely beneficial. Naomi and I marvel at*

how much they accomplish, while laughing and trying to figure the ins and outs of their communication. Watching them, it appears that nods and grunts are the norm. We think the men read each other's minds because few words ever pass between them.

By mid-April they will be delivering a dozen horses to the army. The contract was signed and sealed last September. In down times, the men have studied the logbooks to determine which animals to include in the roundup. It is so fun for me to see Caleb succeed. He is excited and vigilant about the possibilities. He says that this could be a huge boost for WT Ranch. If we can develop a good relationship with the army, it could mean a reliable income stream.

I do some work with foals, which I enjoy. I have an empathic bond that rewards and enlightens me. It is difficult to explain, but I get a sense of their nature and temperament. Surely the raising and experiences contribute to how that character is shaped and formed, but it is fascinating to groom a colt and have an understanding of its essence.

In each case, Caleb picks my brain and takes notes. He is always so thorough. There is no stone he will not turn over. He is attentive in recording copious amounts of facts and details regarding everything he can learn or has observed about each horse. It seems that he can never accumulate enough information. He leaves nothing to chance because he is convinced that the bloodlines have to be guarded and built upon.

Shadrach continues to provide the majority of the stud service, but will soon have some competition. Caleb and Pete captured a yearling stallion last September that they agree has great promise. It is a wild and belligerent brindle which, little by little is being charmed by Caleb. He assures me that the horse will come around and be valuable to our herd. So far the brindle has been kept isolated from the steeldust. I do have some curiosity as to how Shadrach will respond to the upstart, but am told, though problematic, these things get resolved.

I hope that the winter has not been too difficult at Freiheit. I pray for you daily. I so look forward to a time when we can visit and be together. Especially now. Caleb and I have had a sadness. I do not want to cause alarm or worry, but I suffered a miscarriage. I was seven or eight weeks along when the discomfort struck and it was over quickly.

Caleb is Caleb, a strong rock that refuses to be chipped or shaken, but I feel his hurt and hear his unspoken questions. We remain much in love. His tender care for me is a blessing that has no end. He convinced Hank to treat me like a fragile china plate, which I playfully complain about, but in reality, am grateful for the collie's devotion.

Please do not be burdened by our difficulty, for our love is constant. Pray for us, but let not your hearts be dragged down by sorrow. We have our plans and as the Creator determines our steps and in his perfect timing, I am confident that I will be with child once again. Until then, life goes on; it has pleasures and pains, and we will go on with it.

With much affection and prayers,
Sally Twosongs

Her voice had thickened with emotion and she was crying; it was discreet and stifled, but tears were dribbling down her cheeks. "I want to move to Colorado."

"Eliza . . ."

"I mean it, Hans. What keeps us here now?"

He eyed her uncertainly. "Think it through, Eliza. Sell and move on?"

"Why don't you add, at our age?" she asked, challenging him.

"That variable never entered my mind, Eliza."

"I was wrong. I apologize." She twisted around to face him. "We set out from Gettysburg to be the first settlers in an area of New Mexico. Well, we've done that and more. We tamed the land. We were burnt down, but not out. We overcame and rebuilt."

"All true, but aren't you making an assumption?"

"What am I assuming?"

"That we'd be welcome at *WT Ranch*."

"Here's what I know, Hans; life is short and life is fragile," she said adamantly. She sat up straight. "I want to be with Sally Twosongs when our grandchild is born."

He put his arms around her and pulled her tight against him. "You pray on it and I'll do some contemplating, then in a week or so if we are both agreeable to the notion, we can make our case in a letter to Caleb and Sally Twosongs. That's as far as my thinking takes me."

"Which is just fine," she whispered, snuggling closer. No more words were spoken, but much was communicated between them. Their breathing came into perfect rhythm. The wicks on the oil lamps needed to be adjusted, but neither made any move to do so. Instead they sat in the pale glow of the erratic shimmers and shared the silence of the night as it crept around them.

$\sim \sim \sim$

It was midmorning. Ben Slaton had a blissful smile on his kisser. He was alone. An hour ago the bedsprings had been singing a song of passion, but his lover was gone. She had lain in his arms for a while, but then, a thin sheen of perspiration produced by her exertions caused her to take a chill. She had gotten up and dressed, and was now downstairs procuring some grub.

He tossed back the covers and sat up. His lower right leg was encased in a new cast that had a curved piece of wood plastered onto its bottom. A mild cuss grunted out as he swung his feet onto the floor and yanked at his one-piece thermal underwear. He pulled the raiment up over his bottom and tied its arms around his waist like a belt.

The sunshine coming through the window was halfway up the wall. He scratched at the thatch of fuzz on his chest and stood. There was a clumsiness in his hobble. He put his left sock on and fought to make one fit over the bulky contraption on his right foot. He finally quit trying, then sorted through his clothes on the rocking chair. When he placed hands on his vest, he groped around until retrieving the wanted poster from its inside pocket.

He flapped it open. It had been the rationale for leaving in the first place, which resulted in a broken leg and a too close encounter with death; it became the five thousand reasons that had kept him alive. He sat on the bed, with his back against the cedar headboard, studying the portraits of Smoky Crowe and Kid Greer. He cursed his bad luck at Glorieta Pass, but swore that he hadn't missed his chance. He would be in peak condition and on the hunt soon enough.

When Brenda Hawkins returned, she had a towel covered tray in hand. She placed it on his lap and said, "I rustled up what I could from the kitchen while shielding off the cook who wanted to play grab-ass. He's an old Mexican who lives in hope of getting between the sheets with me, but there's not enough money in all the world for that to ever happen."

"I guess that might depend on how long it's been since you won a pot, no?" he asked, setting the wanted poster aside. "Being flush means living high and easy, but in lean times it's a helluva different set of choices. I've done some nasty stuff when I was busted." He dug in. The plate was loaded; eggs and potatoes, along with slabs of bacon piled high.

She went to the mirror and brushed her hair. "I may be an angelica with easy virtue, but my ace in the hole is that I do have some standards and boundaries. I can make you a flat-out promise that no crooked-toothed biscuit shooter will ever get done by me."

"Ain't no shame in being a whore, Brenda."

"Easy for you to say." She moved over and perched on the edge of the bed. "If you want to get into the business I'll bring that bean master up to be your first customer."

"Hellfire, you woke up sassy." His eyes were fixed on her, smiling contentedly. He ate slowly and savored each bite. "I'll be ready to drop the hammer again any minute now."

"You won't be dropping it with me, mister."

"My own damned fault. I poked you too good earlier."

She laughed and slapped his chest. "Just never mind those doings, Benny." She filched a hunk of bacon and nibbled on it. "I thought maybe we could do some talking."

His forehead furrowed. "About what?"

She picked up the wanted poster. Her eyes widened as she reviewed it. "Five thousand dollars. That's a tidy sum. Is this what got you all fired up? Is this why you took off?"

"Yeah," he answered, and gave an exaggerated shrug. "I heard tell of that woman getting slaughtered down in San Antonio. I went to the jail and a stack of these fliers had just arrived. I tucked one away and was off shortly thereafter. When I get healed I'll be on the trail again."

She nodded, lips pursing. "That Kid Greer has been here."

"You mean in Las Vegas?"

She hesitated, then replied, "Yep, in Las Vegas."

"Did *you* see him? Where? When?"

"Yep. Here. The last time was in October, I think."

"Here? At the Wyanhell Roadhouse?"

"Yep. Right here," she said, making a vague gesture.

His eyes bulged as comprehension sank in. "This bed?"

"This room at least. We never made it to the bed."

"You did Liam Greer?" he asked, flabbergasted.

"Whores have to pay rent, Benny," she answered sweetly. She giggled and flipped her hair off her shoulders. She traced a finger around one of his nipples and drew an invisible line to his bellybutton. "You're the only one who has ever gotten me free of charge."

He rolled his eyes and laughed in a harsh rumble. "Holy moly. I can't believe that you did Liam Greer. I knew him when he was a milksop sissy. I called him Dogface."

Disbelief discolored her expression. "What?"

"Yeah," he said, curbing the humor growling in his throat. "His old man and mine had a fly by night horse trading operation, mostly out of Fort Smith. They weren't too successful." He slouched back. "I was a couple years older so I showed Greer the ropes and he kind of looked up to me, you know? I haven't seen him since I took off on my own at seventeen."

"You grew up with a coldblooded killer?"

"Ain't you getting high and mighty?"

"I am not! I just asked a question."

"It sounded like you were passing holy-roller judgment on me, and I ain't one to take that," he said, grinning lopsidedly. "He used to be a pussified pisspot squealing and scared of his own shadow." He brooded and his demeanor took on the appearance of a shifty-eyed ferret. "He may be a cutthroat now, but by God, at least I never slept with him."

"Neither did I," she said testily. "There was no *sleeping* involved."

His cheeks flushed. He glanced around the room and pictured her on her knees in front of Greer. He aired out his lungs, expelling foul swearwords. "I hope you got paid cash money."

"Top dollar, and then some," she replied, anger and sorrow glinting at him. She was biting the inside of her bottom lip. She slid off the bed and turned her back to him. "Can we please change the subject? I really want us to have a serious talk."

He groused a cuss under his breath. "I ain't in a mood to do no talking now." He bumpily slammed the tray on the mattress and the empty plate clattered. "I'll have a coffee."

The air seemed to get all hot and prickly. She refused to look at him as she silently prepared a pot and placed it on the stove. While she waited for it to boil she sidled to the window to stare at the mountains. She pressed her face against the glass. Her lips quivered and her vision got blurry, which was unknown to him, because he never saw the flood of her tears.

Morgan Fletcher, a man of many names and faces, sat at a desk in his hotel room rolling cigarettes. He was fastidious about tailoring every quirley to perfection. Upon satisfaction with each one he placed it in a gold-plated case that was boldly monogrammed with the initials, *MF*. The container held twenty-five, which was better than a day's supply for him.

When finished, he slipped the swanky packet in an inside breast pocket of his jacket, then formed another ciggy and lit it. He held the first drag at the bottom of his lungs until his eyes got watery. He released the smoke in a thin rush, lips angling it downward. He tied a loop knot on the drawstring bag that held the paper and tobacco fixings, and put it away.

It was high noon. His room was on the second floor facing the street. He had the curtains open to watch wagon and pedestrian traffic on the thoroughfare. The activity was brisk and constant. He sat smoking and scheming about the proposition that would set him up for the rest of his life. The details were complex and fluid, which excited him. Time had to run long on this deal, so there would be small frauds along the way until the big score, but in those he'd have to be careful to keep up his masquerade as a fine upstanding gentleman.

He took a final pull, then snuffed out the cigarette in a tin ashtray. There was a knock on the door followed by an announcement of a telegram. He sauntered across the room, as though he had no interest whatsoever in the delivery. The clerk was a pubescent juvenile with a pustule of a pimple at a corner of his mouth that appeared ready to erupt at any moment.

Fletcher took the offered dispatch and in a flourish handed over a quarter-eagle coin as a tip. "Thank you kindly, my good man. Do have a scrumptious day." He closed the door. He returned to the desk and sat, anxious but resolved. Positive or negative, the message from Big Bull Wallace would determine the course of his future. He opened it and read slowly.

> Extreme interest. It may take years, but could be worth much. Not yet ready to invest beyond initial discussion. Pursue possibilities. Keep me informed of every development.

"Perfect," he murmured breathily. He knew Big Bull Wallace to be a no-nonsense man who didn't bandy words unnecessarily. They had engaged in only one enterprise together; a land speculation deal in Arkansas, which proved profitable for both men. Fletcher made sure that his partner had earned a large enough pay-off to keep his interest hooked for other endeavors. Morgan Fletcher was convinced that his standing with Bull Wallace was solid.

The current proposal had all the earmarks for success, but recent information had Morgan Fletcher deeply troubled and plotting his way through it. Deacon Coburn concerned him. Since his initial knowledge of the man from Butch Mackenzie at the telegraph office, Fletcher had done some impromptu digging and listening. The magnitude of the man's moral integrity presented a roadblock; Coburn would be a problem requiring intervention to be resolved. The why of which didn't bother him; the how was what had him conniving.

At the first opportunity, Fletcher meant to befriend Coburn and draw him into his circle of influence, which would be done surreptitiously and only be the means to an end. All the while he would be seeking out a vice or weakness to be leveraged against him. He toyed with the idea of using a fresh-faced woman to seduce him and as necessity demanded it, put powerful poison to good use and completely eliminate the obstacle.

It was a delicate matter, but certainly wouldn't be the first time he had made arrangements to have a man killed. The potential for a financial windfall dictated the terms and procedures to be pursued in each double-dealing rip-off; the details were destined to occupy his mind for weeks and months, which would turn into years. There was no rush because much groundwork had to be done before the final bonanza would come to fruition.

He stood, put on his derby hat and picked up the brass-handled cane. For this exploratory trip, he had only a few days remaining to be in Dodge City. He would perambulate around the streets, then stop in at the Alhambra Saloon to pick up more tidbits on a straight-laced paragon of virtue. Morgan Fletcher would be meticulous. He intended to thoroughly mine all possible sources, so as to find a wedge to compromise Deacon Coburn's stellar reputation.

Meanwhile, Deacon Coburn and Charley Jondreau were sitting on stumps across from each other near the woodpile on the far side of the barn at *Freiheit*. The sun was high, the sky a forever blue except off to the south where a lengthened string of gray speckled clouds chugged along like a slow moving freight train.

Jondreau was sharpening a throwing knife, which he carried on his left hip in a fringed leather sheaf hooked on the same belt that holstered his six-shooter on the right side. He frequently switched the shiv and whetstone from the hollow of one hand to the other, never missing a stroke. There was tenderness in the painstaking care he took with the dagger.

"You ever have cause to use that blade?" Deacon asked dryly.

"For real? Only once. A matter of honor, eh," Charley answered, shrugging. "To be proficient with a weapon often means never having to use it." He stood and pointed to a stack of wood that had not yet been split. His left hand blurred. There was a glint of sunlight on steel, then the twang of the knife sinking into the sawn end of a log.

He adjusted his floppy-brimmed hat and covered the twelve or so steps like a cat. He pulled the stiletto free, moistened a thumb with a gob of spittle and pressed it over the sliced mark. As he returned to his previous spot he cupped the handle in his right hand. He pivoted and his right wrist snapped. The blade struck the saliva dampened spot of the first throw.

"You're ambidextrous."

"I got fast hands, eh."

Coburn chuckled at his unassuming attitude; there was no braggadocio in him. "I am reminded of a Psalm attributed to Moses: *And let the beauty of the Lord our God be upon us: and establish thou the work of our hands upon us; yea, the work of our hands establish thou it."*

"Our days are the beauty of the Great Spirit on us."

"That interpretation fits well."

Jondreau wiped the knife on the thigh of his trousers, then put it in its holder. "How we live each day is the work of our hands, for which we will be judged."

"Judgment Day arrives at every sunset."

"A succinct sermon, preacher-man."

"One from which there is no escape."

Jondreau nodded and took a seat on his block of timber. "The story of the stones had meaning for me in that regard. I think on these things in quiet hours. It's vital to have prompts that regularly direct me to pay heed to the Great Spirit's provision."

"We are a forgetful people, are we not?"

"Mercies come and mercies go, my old friend. Unnoticed and un-counted," Charley replied pithily. "We ofttimes have no memory beyond breakfast this morning."

"Sad, but true enough."

"The stones in the bridle, very wise, eh."

"I humbly receive your approval, Charley."

Jondreau hunkered forward, elbows on knees. "You have no need to hear any such thing from me, preacher-man. We are from different places, but have the same chances." He began twiddling his thumbs. "I traded cour-tesies with Smoky Crowe on my travels here."

Coburn raised his eyebrows, disbelieving and startled. He urgently waggled his hands in a demanding gesture. Jondreau told the tale in quick and plain-spoken sentences. He concluded by saying, "I erred, eh. I should have shot Greer and then put an end to Crowe."

"Greer, maybe," Deacon said, "but killing Smoky Crowe would prove to be a much more difficult challenge. I am amazed to see you, Charley. Few men see his face and live."

Jondreau dismissed that with a brusque wave. "Smoky Crowe is evil, but he has no magic over me. He believes he is invincible, but is the bluster-ing threat of thunder. One day, the Maker of all things will require his soul in a triumphant lightning storm. All evil in the universe will be weighed in the balance and found lacking. Then Crowe will discover his insignificance."

Coburn smiled warmly. "It sure is fine to jaw with you, Charley."

Jondreau returned the smile, but it cooled and faded into a shadow. His eyelids flickered and fluttered rapidly. When the tremors passed, he asked, "What's going on with your head?"

"Nothing. A change of weather headache, is all," Deacon answered glibly. "Never mind me. Max should be our concern. It would be good if you could make time for her."

"She's in a dark place. Her heart is not right."

"Which is why she needs friendship," Deacon said, frowning at him. "Grief either comes out, or it grows inward like a lethal weed that strangles all that is true and noble."

"A stinkweed."

Coburn shifted and straightened up some. "Yes. Unresolved grief becomes putrid. Max is in danger and doesn't even realize it. She comprehends the external peril of Smoky Crowe and is prepared to confront him, but is entirely unaware of the internal menace. Grieving must happen. Otherwise it will be a destructive force that distorts and decimates her life."

"She will not listen. She is mulish. I *see* it."

"You must try, Charley. The work of your hands."

"Nice. You seek to push me, eh."

"I prefer to call it iron sharpening iron."

"More Old Testament."

"I can give you New Testament if you like that better," Deacon said, laughter nipping at the edge of his voice. "The book of Hebrews puts the iron sharpening iron principle this way: *And let us consider one another to provoke unto love and to good works.*"

"Provoke? Why not goad or aggravate?"

Coburn grinned shrewdly. "And you such a weak vessel."

Jondreau raised his hands in mock surrender. "I am strong enough to know that I ought not to get into a push pull battle with you, preacher-man."

Coburn shaded his eyes and switched his attention southward. He gazed at the distance for a bit, then motioned in that direction. "The brevity of our days on the planet is breathtaking, for we ain't much different than those clouds, Charley. We drift along on the breezes and tides the Almighty stirs up for us, here today and gone tomorrow. The work of our hands is about seeing and seizing opportunity, and allowing the Lord God to take us where he will."

Jondreau gave tacit agreement; his jaw tensed and his mouth took on its bulldog look as he turned toward the southern horizon. The clouds now appeared to be rolling tumbleweeds, stretched out and misshapen by the currents. The men were engrossed in the silence of their thoughts, watching the wisps of grayish-white move eastward.

"There are men who need killing."

The announcement came from Kid Greer. He sat in the murky haze of the wikiup, restless and jittery. His shoulders were slouchy and he was giving himself a fierce hug as he rocked side to side. His eyes were glazed and curiously wild from peyote. The flap was partially open, but the air in the lodge had no freshness. Bluish smoke, thick and stagnant, hung like curtains.

Smoky Crowe passed the pipe to him. "I'm listening to hear."

Greer took a generous hit. His chest swelled as he inhaled and held it in. His lips peeled back to reveal teeth clenched and grinding. "I seek your release to go and do the killing."

"Tell who and why. Only then will I decide."

"Benny Slaton. Sam Beadle. Charley Jondreau."

"Tell me more." Smoky Crowe took the pipe, tapped the ashes down in the bowl and clamped the stem between his yellowed choppers. "Tell me more." He puffed mightily and swished his hands to bathe his face in waves of smoke.

"Benny Slaton bullied me."

"Bullied? Were you a child?"

Greer slumped back and pulled his knees up. "A punk kid. Benny was a sorry excuse for a friend. He terrorized me and beat me to a bloody pulp on more than one occasion."

"Why?"

"Benny didn't need a reason to put a whupping on me," Kid Greer replied, locking his arms around his shins. "I made a vow to kill him."

"Why say words, why not just do?"

"I wasn't ready then, I am now."

"Ah. You are too loose and not wise."

"I seek your guidance, Smoky Crowe."

"Who else must die and why?"

Greer smirked. "Sam Beadle stole my woman."

"You could not keep her?"

"He *stole* her!" Kid Greer blurted, sounding churlish and petulant. "Abbey Langton was my woman. Beadle came along and grabbed her up right out from under me. He ridiculed me and busted my nose. I'll give him better than what he gave me. I'll do him in."

"Where will you find this Sam Beadle?"

"I cannot yet say, but it won't be difficult to track him."

Smoky Crowe grunted contemptuously. "And what of Charley Jondreau?"

"Jondreau shamed me. More than once."

"Bullied. Stolen from," Smoky Crowe said, "and shamed. You carry much hate in your heart. There may be an ax to chop at the root, but I must hear more about Jondreau."

Greer crouched his knees up into a tighter embrace. "I rode with Charley for a couple years when I was starting out. He gave me protection for a time. I tried to learn from him, but he had funny ways." He used both hands to fan smoke away from him. "His code of behavior had too many rules and such for me to keep in good standing with him."

"Funny ways? Tell me more."

"He talks to his horse," Kid Greer answered blandly. "He goes where the hawk flies and if there is no hawk he waits for it. We would linger and waste time until a hawk appeared."

"That tells me much about the man," Smoky Crowe said, clucking low in his throat. "He is one who understands the mysteries of the hidden world."

"He drove me batty."

"Now you say he needs killing. Along with Slaton and Beadle." Smoky Crowe altered his position to put the milky whiteness of his left eye on him. "Are there any others?"

"A whore named Flora. *Sweet Flora.*"

"A woman?" Smoky Crowe cocked an eyebrow. "Tell me more."

"She gave birth to me, then discarded me."

"You would kill your mother?"

"The woman who bore me is a whore."

"Tell me more."

"She was Delores Greer. She became Sweet Flora. I last seen her in Abilene before I made my first kill," Kid Greer said, sneering indifferently. "I know not where she is, but if you give the word I will find her. It will be my pleasure to make her dead."

"You would kill your mother?" Smoky Crowe queried again. "You are misguided, Kid Greer. I remember the days of long ago when the woman who gave me life nurtured me onto the path of strength and power." He fingered saliva off the mouthpiece of the pipe. "Your hand must never bring harm to the woman you call Sweet Flora. I command you."

Greer's eyes bulged as his complexion took on the color of blood. His mouth twisted into a doglike snarl that made his upturned nostrils flare. He wanted to scream in protest, but instead, meekly submitted; as he did so, the redness drained from his face. "I will obey."

Smoky Crowe held a hand up signifying he had heard enough. "I must take counsel and think on all this. You will have an answer when I give it." He crammed tobacco into the bowl without removing the debris and put a match to it. His cheeks hollowed as he sucked hard and long. The smoke encircled his head like ribbons being tied in some decorative design.

Kid Greer flopped onto his back and sulked.

It was nighttime at the Suncurl Café. The drapes were closed, but the *Cantina Room* was lit up as though it was midday. Every wall-mounted oil lamp burned brightly. Vibrant laughter and boisterous voices came from the only occupied table in the joint. A rummy tournament was in full swing, but the card game was merely a stage for joshing and farfetched stories.

"No, no, no," Delores said, smiling cheerily. "You got it wrong, Whitey."

Fitzgerald click-clicked and wagged his head. "I be right, Miss Delores."

"I did no such thing, Whitey." Delores put her cards down. "I was ladylike. You're going to have Avis thinking that I was crude and ill-mannered. I curtsied. I did not bow."

"My opinion is that I should hear another version," Avis chimed in, giggling as she shuffled her cards and folded them in her lap. "Mr. Whitey can exaggerate."

"Mr. Whitey is a prevaricator."

"Why, Miss Delores, I be scandalized you'd say such a thing." Whitey rolled his eyes at her and grinned hugely. "I ain't no prevaricator. I just be a plain ole teller of tales."

"Maybe so, but you messed up the details of that street dance in Abilene." Delores slid her cards aside and leaned her elbows on the table. "I can see it like it was yesterday, but it was late September in '71. Wild Bill Hickok was the town marshal. At one point during the shindig he was kicking up his heels. The band, Whitey. Do you remember the band?"

"I surely do. Banjos and fiddles."

"Yes, and a concertina," Delores said wistfully. "The evening was dandy. There was decorations and bunting hanging from storefronts. Torches were burning all along Cedar Street, which had been swept spic and span. I was on the boardwalk watching and keeping time to the music when Mr. Whitey Fitzgerald came beside me. We exchanged a fun-loving look and that was that; he didn't ask and I didn't say a word. We just jumped into dancing together."

Fitzgerald chuckled. "We done shocked and appalled the citizenry. *Look at the white lady and the nigger.* Hee haw, we was laughing and caught up in all the excitement."

Delores reached over and gave his hand a gentle squeeze. "It was fantastic, but soon we were the center of attention. Some were hooting encouragement and others shouted catcalls and ugly things; nigger lover, jackamammy, floozy, jungle bunny, tramp."

Avis shook her head angrily. "That's mean and nasty."

Fitzgerald sloughed it off and click-clicked. "People is ignorant, is all."

"Except the rabble-rouser. He was dangerous," Delores said sadly. "He was a drunken fool. A firebrand with a filthy potty mouth. He pulled a revolver and fired six shots in the air. The band stopped and the crowd hushed. He started swaggering toward us and swearing a blue streak as he reloaded his gun. It was frightening, but before Marshal Hickok moved a muscle, Deacon and Old Blue tuned up the hellion and manhandled him off into the darkness. We never saw or heard from the disorderly boozer again that night."

"I figured Mr. Deacon would get into the story. He always does with you two," Avis remarked, eyes wide and full of amusement. "What happened next?"

"The fiddles started a lively reel, then the banjos and concertina joined in," Delores told her, content and reflective. "The makeshift ballroom of the street cleared, leaving Whitey and I alone in the middle of it. The crowd, which was likely every resident in town plus a shebang of stragglers and hangers-on, was cheering us on. We hopped and bopped up a storm. When the song concluded, I did a little curtsy, and a clapping roar burst forth from the onlookers."

"I swear, Miss Delores," Whitey said, eyes gleaming mischievously. "I thought you bowed and the cowboys were applauding in approval of your fine behind."

"Mr. Whitey!" Avis exclaimed in a squeal.

Delores Solrizo turned beet-red and swatted his shoulder. "You are an incorrigible man full of hogwash. The show of appreciation was for our exceptional dancing."

"Alright then. I admit you be saying the truth."

"That was a splendid evening, Whitey," Delores said, leaning back and twining her fingers together. "When I consider it now, I think maybe that was the beginning of the end of our time in Abilene. Shortly after that night Wild Bill shot Phil Coe and Mike Williams outside the Alamo Saloon. He was never the same after those killings. Neither was Abilene."

"You be as right as rain, Miss Delores." Whitey stood. "I be off to bed now."

Avis frowned at him. "I thought we were playing rummy."

"The cards are cold and I be bone tired, sweetie. I'm calling it a night."

"Sleep well, Whitey," Delores said softly.

"I surely do my best." He gave a cursory nod and was click-clicking as he sidled across the room. Delores watched until he was gone, flecks of sorrow spinning in her eyes.

Avis noted her pained look. She moistened her lips and took a deep breath. She cleared her throat and hesitantly shifted forward. "You're going to miss him, aren't you, Mom?"

Delores jerked in her seat as though jabbed by a cattle prod. It took her several moments to fully absorb the ramifications of the handle her daughter had used. "Yes, I am."

"Me, too."

"Avis."

"Yes, Mom."

"Thank you," she said, crying openly. Her bottom lip was quivering. "Hearing you call me Mom makes my heart glad. I never thought it would feel so wonderful."

"It's good for my heart too, Mom," Avis replied in a voice that was struggling to maintain a modicum of composure. "About that name change idea. I have decided not to do it."

"Any special reason?"

"Indeed," Avis answered briskly. "My mother named me Avis Lahay because it sounded pretty and she wanted me to be my own person. That's more than good enough for me."

Mother and daughter embraced. A wellspring of emotion ruptured like a gusher from a hot spring, which could not be restrained or in any way controlled; nor could it be expressed in plain language. Time had no meaning or power over them. The balm of their tears mingled as they fiercely clung to each other. There was much healing in the shared tenderness.

A new day dawned. Avis Lahay was up early, though she had scarcely slept a wink. Her mind was too full of joy and delight. She had tossed and turned in bed, or sat up with her back against the headboard staring at the darkness. Now, with the curtains drawn open and sunlight streaming through the window, she sat at the roll-top desk. She had her leather bound notebook ready for an entry. She thought and dawdled with the pen, then began writing.

March 7, 1878

Dear Diary: Life is both happy and sad. Happy because I've come to terms with and worked through lots of crud about how I came to be here and why. I listened to the wisdom of Mr. Whitey, and thought and prayed so much that I was afraid I was stuck going around in circles. Little by little I broke through and had clarity that warmed me.

Last night, Mom and I cried until there were no more tears to shed. Then we laughed and talked about what the future might hold for me. My heart is overwhelmed. Mom told me that the only limits to what I can do or who I can be are those restraints I put on myself. She will support and encourage me in any positive choice I make to get established.

Being involved in some way with horses is an idea that has always excited me. Or, maybe since I am learning the restaurant business, I could someday have my own café. Mom listened to me, but then, pointed out that university is an option for me to consider. That is something which I had never dreamt of ever being possible. I'll need to think about it, I guess.

Somehow our conversation turned to boys and men. Mom said that I shouldn't be in a big hurry to get into a romantic entanglement or any such thing. I only have one heart, so I ought to be careful with it because there are so many potholes and wrong turns. She talked from her experience and gave me her best advice: Don't be blinded by smooth talkers in fancy clothes; look for character and strength, and let friendship develop first.

It wasn't just roses between us. There were thorns. Mom opened up about her past. It was obviously difficult for her, but she insisted. It turns out that her father—my grandfather—had a mean streak. After her mother died, he did dirty things to her that messed her up. Her honesty made me cringe a time or two. She made mistakes and choices that could have destroyed her. It's almost impossible to believe, but she confessed she spent years working as a prostitute.

When she finished acknowledging the upsetting stuff, we cried some more. I was shaken but now understand why she put me in an orphanage. She really was in a fragile place. I am so grateful that she valued me enough and had the courage to share. All of what transpired between Mom and I will be treasured. I do not regard her any less highly and I am proud to be her daughter. There is, however, a sadness that runs around the edges of everything.

Quite soon—much sooner than I like—Mr. Whitey will be packing to leave Santa Fe and return to Dodge City. He expects Mr. Deacon to be back by the end of the month, then they will spend most of April on the trail. He says that springtime is the best season to be a traveling man because the buds and blooms

*are fresh and new. He went on and on about all the different wild
flowers that are like beautiful speckles and spangles on the prairie.*

*Mom is going to miss Mr. Whitey something terrible. As will
I. He is so kind and wise, and now that he is over whatever it
was that had him drinking like a souse, he is cheerful and has a
confidence that can be contagious. It's easy for me to see why he
and Mom get along so well. They have a compatibility and comprehension of each other that is uncanny.*

*Mr. Whitey has given me a standing invitation to visit him in
Dodge City and stay for as long as I want. Mom says that is an offer to file away because hanging out with Mr. Whitey for a couple
months would be a worthy education. There's too many special
things for Mom and I to do together first, but down the road I'll
want to follow up on that opportunity.*

*I'm tired, but enthusiastic. Today is going to be busy and fun.
Sometime this morning or afternoon Mr. Whitey and I are going
to the livery to see some horses that will be put up for auction in a
few weeks. He tells me that he will be tickled to help me look and
get some ideas, but that it would be best to wait until Mr. Deacon
is here before I actually decide to make a bid. I trust Mr. Whitey's
advice, so I am going to pay attention and learn. All I really know
is that I want my first horse to be gentle, but I'm not sure if it
should be a mare or a stallion.*

The day's getting away, so I must go. Later.

She closed the journal and dropped it in its compartment. She stripped
off her pajamas and went to the washstand. The water in the pink-patterned
pitcher was cold. She poured some into the matching basin, then splashed
her face and hands. She dried off and stood in front of the mirror, where she
spent an exorbitant amount of time brushing her hair.

When the auburn waves were shiny she used a black velvet band to tie
up a loose braid. She turned to the side and jerked her head in a quick bob
to check out the bounce of the ponytail. A smile filled her face as a chirpy
giggle fluttered off her lips. She dressed in denims and a checkered shirt. She
spun around and did a little wiggly jig, then traipsed downstairs.

Charley Jondreau emerged from the barn and strolled across the grounds to
the corral to check on his horses. The sun was high above in a cloudless sky.
He tugged the droopy brim of his hat low over his eyes. As he came close to
the enclosure, he muttered a greeting and gave a nod to Max Dawson who
was sitting comfortably balanced on the top rail.

"You staying around for long?" she asked casually.

He leaned against the slats beside her. "Depends on the hawk, eh."

"Not me. I'll be gone by morning."

"Heading where?"

"For starters, those badlands," she replied, motioning a hand toward Angel Peak. "I figure I can pick up sign of Smoky Crowe somewhere in the vicinity of that column of rock."

"Not so smart to go it alone."

"That's my business, mister."

"It's risky, is all I'm saying. Smoky Crowe is dangerous," he said icily. "I just left Hans and Deacon in the workshop. They're almost finished with the marker for your father's grave."

"I gave them the information. I'll see it soon enough."

He pointed at the soot-gray horse. "How old is your mare?"

"Six."

"Ever foal?"

Her brow creased. "Nope."

"My pinto would be a good stud."

"Not interested."

"The colt would be perceptive and durable."

"Not interested," she repeated, eyes showing some heat. "I will be riding light and fast for the foreseeable future. I won't even be taking Daddy's zebra dun. It'll stay with Gray Cloud and he'll care for it. He tells me it will be here if I ever have need of a rested mount."

"Hurt can be funny, eh."

The crinkle in her forehead deepened. "Hurt?"

"Sorrow."

"I'm already over it."

"No."

"We just met, Charley. Where do you get the gall to tell me no?"

"No gall, Max," he answered, jawline tightening. "I see what I *see*. Sorrow has crawled up inside you and latched onto your heart. You're in a bad way."

"You're treading on a thin wire, friend."

He smiled calmly. "Not my intention, Max. I come in peace, eh."

"Then don't presume."

"I ain't presuming nothing."

She laughed, harsh and vitriolic. "You can't know the inner particulars of my emotions. I'm much better acquainted with my workings than you can possibly be."

"No. The hurt of sorrow is blinding and misleading," he replied unflappably. "You are being deceived or are deceiving yourself, for you haven't begun to go through sorrow."

"There's no time or place for sorrow," she said, shaking her head. "Smoky Crowe must be made to pay for his savage crimes and barbarity. I have to do what needs to be done."

"Maybe so." He pursed his lips and gave a low-pitched two-note whistle. The piebald pinto looked up and twitched its ears, then trotted over to him; the dapple gray followed close behind. Both horses nuzzled him through the gaps in the fencing. His hands ruffled their manes as he spoke to them in a patois mix of Iroquois and French.

He dismissed them with a backhanded command, but before departing, the pinto nosed around Max Dawson. She patted its forehead. The stallion stomped its hoofs and whinnied, then ran across the corral, with the yearling at its side. "Impressive, but I'm still not interested in breeding my mare. I have a trail ahead that must be ridden free and unfettered."

"Smoky Crowe is evil. I'll not argue on the merits."

"Then we're in agreement."

"Death is the only justice for him, eh."

She focused a severe look on him. "That's my life investment, Charley. I will not rest until I see him dead. Hanging from a tree or getting picked apart by vultures. No amount of chatter or urging from you, Eliza or Deacon will dissuade me from my decision."

"I have seen Smoky Crowe."

"You're full of it, Charley."

"No bullspit, eh. I have seen him."

She balked, hands flexing. "Where? When?"

"In those badlands, three days ago."

"Then he ought to be easy to find."

"No. Not alone."

"This is my fight, Charley."

"Are you tougher and trickier than your old man?" he asked slyly. "You deserve much respect, which I freely offer, but given what is known about the immense evil of the adversary, it would be foolish to take on the task alone. We should ride together."

"I want no company."

"I have to go to Taos to deliver a letter," he said, beginning to twiddle his thumbs. "Why not come along to see the country, eh? We might discover we are good partners."

"You're not an easy one to hear the word no, huh?"

"I understand just fine. There is grief in you. And defiance."

She chuckled huskily. "The defiance is in my blood, Charley."

"This is the way it will be," he said, determination in his tone. "You must do what you must do, but I am compelled too, eh. I will entrust you to the Great Spirit and do my errand to Taos, then I will return and find you. No matter where you are, I will find you."

She stared at him, her lips twitching as though she was smothering words. She sighed and glanced toward her father's gravesite. Her eyes were murky. She removed her Stetson and distractedly fingered the rattlesnake skin band. After a tense period of silence, she turned her attention on him. "If that's the way it plays out, then we can ride together for a stretch."

"At the critical moment, you will not be alone, eh."

She started to respond, but bit it off. An unspoken empathy passed between them that took both by surprise. Her complexion darkened; his mouth stiffened downward into a look that invoked images of a bulldog. She averted her eyes to the horses as he squinted at sunspots. The obviously uncomfortable moment passed, but the connected feelings of friendship lingered.

Brenda Hawkins had anchored her decision. She was returning from an hour or so walk about town to clear her head and steel her resolve. There would be no diverting her. She had stopped in at the bar to purchase a bottle of whiskey, which she would use to ease into a conversation. She took the stairs two at a time and scurried down the hallway to her apartment.

"About time," Ben said grumpily. He greeted her from the bed. It was mid-afternoon, but he was still undressed, lounging in his thermals. "I'm feeling raunchy and ready."

"That'll pass or stay on simmer, one or the other," she told him in an unmistakably stern voice. "You can wait. There'll be no more screwing around until we do some talking."

"Let me put a real smile on your face, then we can yak afterwards."

"That's what you promised last night and this morning," she said, hanging her coat on a peg. "Both times I was smiling alright, but a minute and a half after we were done you sounded like a bear snoring." She poured him three-fingers of whiskey and handed him the glass.

"Many thanks," he said, giving her a big-eyed grin. "You wear me out, girl. I do you like a bear, then I have to hibernate to regain my strength for the next round." He downed the drink in one swig and held the glass out for seconds.

"Sip this one." She served another sizable measure. "If you want to hear those bedsprings do any more squeaking, we're going to have us a heart-to-heart chat." She put the cork in the bottle and placed it on the counter in the other room. "Do you ever think about the future, Benny?" she asked, fluffing out her skirt as she settled in the rocking chair.

"Mostly not much farther than next week or so. Why would I?" He shrugged uncaringly. "If I scored that five thousand dollar bounty, maybe I'd do some looking to a far horizon."

"I want us to have more than this."

"What's wrong with what we got, babe?"

"Nothing. Have you ever heard me complain?"

He sat up straighter and leaned against the headboard. "Not yet, but it sounds like you're getting ready to unload a freight wagon of bellyaches that you've been storing up."

"Don't be like that, Benny."

"Like what?" he snapped, eyes flashing.

"Mean and sarcastic. I'm trying to be tender." She disarmed him with a smile that made her apple-dumpling cheeks bright and rosy. "I daydream of a house and a family."

"What?" He choked on laughter. "You want ankle biters?"

"I want children, Benny. Your children."

"Slow down, Brenda. I ain't no father material."

"People change, Benny. We can learn together, can't we?"

"Quit farting around, Brenda. What the frig's gotten into you?"

"Something didn't happen that has me thinking."

"That doesn't make any sense."

She began rocking; slowly at first, but it developed into a frenetic tempo. The chair made its creaky mouse noise, which seemed to be loud in the quietness that had cropped up between them. She released a thin hiss of air and narrowed her eyes on him. "I'm late."

He cocked his head, bewildered. "What?"

"My time of the month. I'm pregnant, Benny."

His eyes tensed, then widened. "Are you sure?"

"Yes. The doc confirmed it the other day."

"What's it got to do with me?"

"It's your baby, silly."

"It could be one of your customer's for all I know."

"It's your baby, Benny."

"How do you know for sure?" he asked, blistering her with a scornful look. "How can any whore know which trick might be the father of a baby? It's a roll of the dice."

Her lips clenched and her face reddened, but she kept her wits on an even keel. "I was with you exclusive from Christmastime until you took off in February." She crossed her arms over her midsection. "Besides, you're the only one I ever let finish down there, you know?"

"It could be Dogface Greer's baby."

A snicker tumbled off her tongue and grew into cutting laughter. "No chance of that, Benny. He's a big talker, but Mr. Greer has shortcomings and difficulties in that area."

"Shortcomings and difficulties?"

"Easiest money I ever made," she replied, grinning crookedly. "He visited me four times and it was always the same. After he put his cash on the dresser, all I had to do was bend low and show him some cleavage or lift my skirt to give him a sniff. He never once got his tiny pecker all the way out of his drawers before he squirted his spurt."

He clapped his hands and hooted like gleeful child. "Ain't that a sweet kick in the ass? And some handy information to dump on him just before I put him out of his misery."

"I don't care about any of that," she said, pushing forward to the edge of the chair. "All I want to hear is what you have to say about us. And what of our baby?"

"Hellfire, Brenda. There ain't no us," he answered snidely. "You're just a whore slut throwing me free humps because I poke you so good and keep you satisfied."

"Really? Is that all I am to you, Benny?"

Slaton took a deep breath and closed his eyes. "Yeah. You're the liveliest woman I've ever had in the sack, but you're nothing more than a whore." His eyelids never once flickered as he spoke. He heard a breath of emotion murmur from her, then in his head Deacon Coburn's admonition rattled free: *If you were smart and looking to the future, you'd marry that girl and make an honest woman of her. She surely deserves that much and likely more.*

His eyes popped open and he cussed as he rolled to his feet. He polished off his whiskey, then besmirched her in an accusatory attack of vulgarity. "Get out of my way!" he ordered, teeth bared at her. He got dressed, muttering cursing grumbles the whole while.

"Is our talk all over?" she asked mildly.

He glared at her. "I'm going downstairs to play cards and do some gambling."

"It's your baby, Benny," she reiterated, passionate exasperation rising in her. "I want to build a life with you, but I'm not going to fight you every step of the way. And I'm not allowing you to label me as nothing but a whore. I'm done compromising."

"What's that mean, Brenda?"

"If you walk away now, don't bother coming back."

"Are you serious?"

"Yes. My door will be closed to you."

"I'll put money on the dresser next time."

She stood, hands on her hips. "No, I'm through with all of it."

"Ain't you the hoity-toity whore?"

"I'm no kind of whore anymore," she replied irately. "Those choices are over. A kindly couple owns the mercantile. I've helped do inventory in the past. I'll get hired on there. It won't be much money, but it'll be honest work." She took a challenging step toward him. "And, make no mistakes, we're done. It's your baby, but boy or girl, the child will *never* carry your name."

Slaton's hands fisted. He threatened her and let loose a litany of swear-words. He grunted and grabbed his crutch and saddlebags. "To hell with you," he said, glowering. He hobbled across the floor and stormed into the corridor, slamming the door with a shuddering thud.

"Goodbye, Benny," she whispered joylessly. Her body was shaking. She rushed over and bolted the door. She leaned a shoulder against it and fought back the hot tears blurring her vision. She returned to the rocker and sat, still and rigid. A sob snuck off her lips. She laid a hand on her flat stomach, and in silent urgency, promised to do right for the child growing inside her.

Brenda Hawkins wished she knew how to pray.

Night had fallen. Sticks smoldered in a pit at the center of the wikiup. Smoky Crowe swayed his upper body in a tiny circle to a rhythm only he could hear. He sat cross-legged, naked except for a loin cloth swaddled at his groin like a diaper. He smoked serenely. The pipe yielded more smoke than the fire; all of which vented through the smallish hole in the roof.

Kid Greer watched him, eyes flitting as skittishly as a cat whose tail had been repetitively stomped. He appeared to be anxiously crouched atop a prickly cactus. The lodge was murky and cheerless; the stale air was musty and stank of grimy body odor. He inched forward, wary and nervous, hands pressed together in supplication. "What's your answer going to be?"

Smoky Crowe bowed his head. "You will have my answer when I give it."

"Forgive me. I mean no disrespect."

"You have no patience."

"I apologize. I am young."

Smoky Crowe grunted disdainfully. "A poor excuse. You are a slow learner. Our alliance is a blood oath that cannot be shattered into shreds. You are a killer. I am what I am. I have been at your side. I teach, but your spirit fails to expand, for you do not grasp my words."

"Forgive me, master."

"Aaaaaaarg . . ." The bass notes of the snarl snapped indignantly off his tongue. "There is no forgiveness to be had from me. You are ignorant or foolish; a pup not a man. I have spoken of soul-twisting riddles and secrets, but your ears are plugged and your heart distracted by childish things. Be a man. Forgiveness is for weaklings. Do not ask for it; do not give it."

Greer blanched and winced. "I wish to be trained by you. I want the fire in your belly."

"Wish and want should be take and have."

"I will take what you give and have what you are," Kid Greer said reasonably. "I will be Smoky Crowe's student. Your fame will sprout large in me. When my name is pronounced you will receive honor and glory. I surrender all to you. Have dominion over me as you will."

"Be a man," Smoky Crowe instructed, removing the pipe from his mouth. He tapped the bowl against the heel of his hand. Burnt tobacco and sparks of ash tumbled forth and landed in the dirt. "Vengeance is to be savored. A man knows not to rush or its taste will be sour."

Greer nodded and chaffed his hands together. "When I put a bullet in those who need killing I want it to be sweet. How do I make that so?"

"Aarg," Smoky Crowe mumbled and grinned menacingly. His right eye squeezed shut as the malignant grayish bulb in the left socket enlarged and pulsed. "I train, you do."

"Tutor me. I will be a good student."

"As you declare." His lips pulled back in a triumphant smile that flaunted the tobacco yellowed boneyard of his teeth. His right eyelid flickered open. "The wheel of time rolls without the aid of the likes of Smoky Crowe or Kid Greer; neither can we hinder its revolutions. It has no beginning and no end. The chances that have been will come around again."

"Patience is a difficult lesson to conquer."

"Aarg. I have defeated it, humiliated it," Smoky Crowe replied proudly. "The rotations of time are of no concern to me; nor should you be like a stallion that needs to have its will broke. I am the destroyer of strongholds, the slayer of bloodlines. I bless you and grant you power."

"I humbly receive your gift."

"The revenge you seek awaits at the turn of some tomorrow, but first you must prepare and be immersed in the fountainhead of evil," Smoky Crowe said as he thumbed tobacco into the pipe and tamped it tight. "You were tested and tried by Charley Jondreau. He bested you. You will stay beside me for a few more seasons so your authority can grow strong."

Greer lowered his eyes and folded his hands on his lap. "I will do as I am told. Teach me to touch the face of evil. I will do your bidding until you set me free to avenge tit for tat."

"As time turns your hour of infamy arises and vengeance will come to you." Smoky Crowe took a burning twig from the fire and lit the pipe. "I will know when the darkness aligns in your favor. Then you will be released to inflict blood and havoc." He inhaled several puffs as he shook a finger confidently at him. "Take an ear from each kill. After all are dead, bring the trophies back to me. I will make you a medicine bag and you will be invincible."

Kid Greer beamed. He braced his backbone as his chest swelled. He held out a hand to accept the pipe. He genuflected reverently and moistened his lips. His eyes were gleaming; tears spilled out and engulfed his cheeks. He took a few drags and held the smoke in his lungs so long that he teetered dizzily. When he exhaled, his shoulders straightened and sickly laughter emerged. The cackle of noise that intermixed with the smoke was akin to death rattles.

Smoky Crowe smiled pompously.

The sunrise was a pinkish-orange line that stretched across the eastern horizon for as far as could be seen. Max Dawson dismounted near the *Freiheit* arch and looped the reins around the pommel of the saddle, telling the soot-gray mare to wait. She strode across the property toward her father's final resting place, determination in every step.

Stars were beginning to disappear from the roof of the sky. She stopped midway to her destination. She looked up at the widespread array of sparkling dots; some of which blinked out even as she watched. Her heart was affected by the majesty and wonder of the language of nature, but the sensation had no opportunity to develop because she strangled it.

There were many undercurrents of emotion swirling in her; none of which could be identified because her brain was overloaded with grief. Loss had dug a gaping hole within where vines of bitterness flourished and choked off whatever was noble, right, pure or lovely. The barren emptiness of her interior tarnished all that she thought and all that she saw.

Her jaw was set in a stony expression. She jammed her hands in the side pockets of her trousers and moved swiftly. The darkness of night was fading into shades of gray, which made her anxious. She wanted to have some private moments and be gone before anyone on the farmstead stirred. She removed her Stetson and took a knee to the right of the marker.

"Daddy," she said in a muted whisper. She placed a hand on one of the rocks that were piled on the grave. She rubbed it lovingly, as though passing affection through it into the corpse of the man beneath the ground. "I swear that I will not rest until I see Smoky Crowe dead." Her eyes watered involuntarily, which caused her mouth to clench more stringently.

She examined the memorial that Hans Weitzel had fabricated and put into place. It was three feet tall and almost as wide as the burial site. There were matching designs carved into the top corners of the plank slab, which was framed in angle iron and had been sturdily driven into the ground. The epitaph was sculpted in a bold script and burnt into the wood. She carefully and with much tenderness fingered the deep groove of every letter of the inscription.

> *Silas Cody Dawson*
> *October 1820—March 1878*
> *Captain Dawson never quit or shirked a duty. Ever.*

She read the revered sentiment again and again. A smile, as tense and taut as a tightrope, formed on her lips and made her eyes sparkle. "You lived that, Daddy. I've recently come to understand, not for the first or likely last time, that I cannot quit or shirk either. I'll not fail or shame the Dawson name. I am proud to have your and Mom's blood in my veins."

A sigh eased out as she gathered her strawberry locks up under her headgear. She patted a rock, then abruptly got to her feet and spun away. Her left leg had a kink, but it vanished as she hurried to her horse. The grayness of dawn was being cut to ribbons by sharp blades of daylight. Out of an abundance of habit, she rechecked the cinches of the saddle and was about to step into the stirrup when the charred cross caught her attention.

The mare snorted. She hushed it and took several sideward steps so that she was standing directly in front of the symbol made famous at Golgotha, a spot so desolate it was known as the place of the skull. It was there that a carpenter from Nazareth suffered an excruciating death, which was divinely ordained for eternal purposes. Her heartbeat quickened as she contemplated its meaning. The blood shed by Jesus was supposed to cleanse sin and bring healing.

Redemption. Hope. Grace. The words jumped to the forefront of her mind. She wanted to grab hold and make them her own, but in some hidden recess, resistance was a living force that warred against any residual desire to embrace those abstract promises. In an infinite way that was somehow ingrained in her, she knew that the cross represented facts that could not be denied, but a sword of merciless sorrow slashed until the truth was cloaked inside her pain.

An inner conflict tugged at her. To believe or not to believe. She reached for belief, but headstrong instincts reared up and took charge. A cringe chased over her face. She remembered the hideously violated body of her mother; she recalled the man buried behind her. The crimes against them needed to be dealt with severely. She had frequently made a pledge to do so.

She turned away from the blackened timbers and hopped on the horse. A sound reached her ears. She glanced and saw lamplight coming on in the house where her father had died. She clamped her teeth on an edge of her bottom lip and nudged the mare. It stepped spryly. The reins were loose in her palms. She rode in coarse single-mindedness, her body rigid and upright.

Max Dawson heard the loud echoes of evil and followed them.

Charley Jondreau jolted into a sitting position and gasped. He wasn't even fully awake, yet the smell of the skunk had its grip on him. It was as though hooks had impaled his pectorals. His lungs constricted and tightness spread across his chest and up his neck. A twitching spasm throbbed in his temples. There was blankness in the glassy pools of his eyes. His hands were grasping handfuls of straw from his rigged bed in the loft of the barn.

The phenomenon of his second sight had him riveted. He was situated above and off to the side of the happenings as though he was on a rooftop across the street from a thriving row of businesses that included a drug store, saloons and a dry goods establishment. A golden haze hung around the fringes of the scene, which were frayed and elongated.

He took notice of a slouchy man meandering in a suspicious pattern from the east. He rode a bag of bones horse that had its head hanging and hoofs dragging. It was a speckled bay that definitely fit the crowbait category. The rider picked his way along the thoroughfare, swiveling his head side to side in an obvious search for someone in particular.

Jondreau gave him a close study. There was something familiar about the way he sat in the saddle, but no matter how hard he strained or from which angle he came at it, he couldn't get a clear glimpse of the cowboy's face. It was obscured by a battered old hat that he had yanked low on his forehead. An untamed patch of stringy whiskers was an identifying feature, but just now, the uncultivated beard served as a mask, as effective as a bandana.

The stranger pulled up in front of the City Drug Store. He called out in a snarky voice. Chaos rapidly erupted, followed by pandemonium. Two gunshots rang out atop each other. The smoking gun was in the hand of the man on the broken down horse. A grin cracked wide and he chortled, but the sound of his mad laughter was drowned out by the liberated screams of a woman in the throes of an endless wail that reverberated along the avenue.

There were cusses and cries for help; a thunder of running footsteps dusted the air as bystanders descended on the uproar. The shooter spurred his mount and twisted the reins, which resulted in the speckled bay bucking wildly as it screeched and snorted. The animal whirled around in the midst of whoops and hollers. It was then, as the rider hunched over to make a galloping getaway, that Charley Jondreau realized who pulled the trigger.

His focus got foggy. His hands flexed powerlessly. The shrieks of the woman had become wretched gurgles and palpitating gulps as she struggled to breathe. She was in extreme distress, surrounded by a knot of panicky and fearful onlookers trying to help. Voices shouted orders that overlapped the action of moving her to a place of safety.

Jondreau lurched. The golden haze at the borders began to fold in and progressively distort the images. Through the enclosing vapor he looked to see two men sprawled and bleeding on the boardwalk. One was unrecognizable; the other was the bronze-skinned maiden's husband. A white-haired black man knelt over him, blood on his hands up to his elbows.

Inside of helplessness, Charley Jondreau understood everything. The extrasensory spell terminated as abruptly as it had started. He collapsed against a bale of hay. His heart swelled in his chest. He pinched his nose and blew to dispel the vinegary stench lingering in his nostrils. His hands unthinkingly came together and he twiddled his thumbs in sheer desperation.

~The End~